Marah Ellis Ryan

The Bondwoman

Marah Ellis Ryan

The Bondwoman

ISBN/EAN: 9783337737610

Printed in Europe, USA, Canada, Australia, Japan

Cover: Foto ©Andreas Hilbeck / pixelio.de

More available books at **www.hansebooks.com**

THE BONDWOMAN

BY

MARAH ELLIS RYAN,

AUTHOR OF

"TOLD IN THE HILLS,"
"A PAGAN OF THE ALLEGHANIES,"
ETC.

CHICAGO AND NEW YORK:

RAND McNALLY & COMPANY, PUBLISHERS.

MDCCCXCIX.

THE BONDWOMAN.

CHAPTER I.

Near Moret, in France, where the Seine is formed and flows northward, there lives an old lady named Madame Blanc, who can tell much of the history written here—though it be a history belonging more to American lives than French. She was of the Caron establishment when Judithe first came into the family, and has charge of a home for aged ladies of education and refinement whose means will not allow of them providing for themselves. It is a memorial founded by her adopted daughter and is known as the Levigne Pension. The property on which it is established is the little Levigne estate—the one forming the only dowery of Judithe Levigne when she married Philip Alain—Marquis de Caron.

There is also a bright-eyed, still handsome woman of mature years, who lives in our South and has charge of another memorial—or had until recently—a private industrial school for girls of her own selection. She calls herself a creole of San Domingo, and she also calls herself Madame Trouvelot—she has been married twice since she was first known by that name, for she was never the woman to live alone—not she; but while the men in themselves suited her, their names were uncompromisingly plain—did not attract her at all. She married them, proved a very good wife, but while one was named Johnson, and another Tuttle, the good wife

persisted in being called Madame Trouvelot, either through
sentiment or a bit of irony towards the owner of that name.
But, despite her vanities, her coquetries, and certain erratic
phases of her life, she was absolutely faithful to the trust
reposed in her by the Marquise; and who so capable as herself of finding the poor girls who stood most in need of training and the shelter of charity? She, also, could add to this
history of the woman belonging both to the old world and
the new. There are also official records in evidence of much
that is told here—deeds of land, bills of sale, with dates of
marriages and deaths interwoven, changed as to names and
places but—

There are social friends—gay, pleasure-loving people on
both sides of the water—who could speak, and some men
who will never forget her.

One of them, Kenneth McVeigh, he was only Lieutenant
McVeigh then!—saw her first in Paris—heard of her first
at a musicale in the salon of Madame Choudey. Madame
Choudey was the dear friend of the Countess Helene
Biron, who still lives and delights in recitals of gossip belonging to the days of the Second Empire. The Countess
Helene and Mrs. McVeigh had been school friends in Paris.
Mrs. McVeigh had been Claire Villanenne, of New Orleans, in those days. At seventeen she had married a Col.
McVeigh, of Carolina. At forty she had been a widow ten
years. Was the mother of a daughter aged twelve, and a
six-foot son of twenty-two, who looked twenty-five, and
had just graduated from West Point.

As he became of special interest to more than one person
in this story, it will be in place to give an idea of him as he
appeared in those early days;—an impetuous boy held in
check, somewhat, by military discipline and his height—
he measured six feet at twenty—and also by the fact that his
mother had persisted in looking on him as the head of the

family at an age when most boys are care-free of such responsibilities.

But the responsibilities had a very good effect in many
ways—giving stability and seriousness to a nature prone,
most of all, to pleasure-loving if left untrammelled. His
blue eyes had a slumberous warmth in them; when he smiled
they half closed and looked down on you caressingly, and
their expression proved no bar to favor with the opposite
sex. The fact that he had a little mother who leaned on him
and whom he petted extravagantly, just as he did his sister,
gave him a manner towards women in general that was both
protecting and deferential—a combination productive of
very decided results. He was intelligent without being intellectual, had a very clear appreciation of the advantages
of being born a McVeigh, proud and jealous where family honor was concerned, a bit of an autocrat through being
master over extensive tracts of land and slaves by the dozen,
many of them the descendents of Africans bought into the
family from New England traders four generations before.

Such was the personality of the young American as he appeared that day at Madame Choudey's; and he looked like
one of the pictured Norse sea kings as he towered, sallow
and bronzed, back of the vivacious Frenchmen and their
neighbors of the Latin races.

The solo of the musicale had just ended. People were
thronged about the artiste, and others were congratulating
Madame Choudey on her absolute success in assembling
talent.

"All celebrities, my lad," remarked Fitzgerald Delaven
as he looked around. The Delavens and the McVeighs had
in time long past some far-out relationship, and on the
strength of it the two young men, meeting thus in a foreign
country, became at once friends and brothers;—"all celebrities and no one so insignificant as ourselves in sight. Well,

now!—when one has to do the gallant to an ugly woman it
is a compensation to know she is wondrous wise."

"That depends on the man who is doing the gallant," returned the young officer, "I have not yet got beyond the
point where I expect them all to be pretty."

"Faith, Lieutenant, that is because your American girls
are all so pretty they spoil you!—and by the same token
your mother is the handsomest woman in the room."

The tall young fellow glanced across the chattering
groups to where the handsomest woman was amusing herself.

She certainly was handsome—a blonde with chestnut hair
and grey eyes—a very youthful looking mother for the
young officer to claim. She met his glance and smiled as he
noticed her very courtier-like attendant of the moment, and
raised his brows quizzically.

"Yes, I feel that I am only a hanger-on to mother since
we reached France," he confessed. "My French is of the
sort to be exploited only among my intimates, and luckily
all my intimates know English."

"Anglo-Saxon," corrected Delaven, and Lieutenant Mc-
Veigh dropped his hand on his friend's shoulder and
laughed.

"You wild Irishman!—why not emphasize your prejudices by unearthing the Celtic and expressing yourself in
that?"

"Sure, if I did I should not call it the Irish language,"
retorted the man from Dublin.

They both used the contested tongue, and were evidently
the only ones in the room who did. All about them were the
softened syllables of France—so provocative, according to
Lord Lytton, of the tender sentiments, if not of the tender
passion.

"There is Dumaresque, now," remarked Delaven. "We

are to see his new picture, you know, at the Marquise de Caron's;—excuse me a moment," and he crossed over to the artist, who had just entered.

Kenneth McVeigh stood alone surveying the strange faces about. He had not been in France long enough to be impervious to the atmosphere of novelty in everything seen and heard.

Back of him the soft voice of Madame Choudey, the hostess, could be heard. She was frankly gossiping and laughing a little. The name of the Marquise de Caron was mentioned. Delaven had told him of her—an aristocrat and an eccentric—a philanthropist who was now aged. For years herself and her son had been the patrons—the good angels of struggling genius, of art in every form. But the infamous 2d of December had ended all that. He was one of the "provisionally exiled;" he had died in Rome. Madame La Marquise, the dowager Marquise now, was receiving again, said the gossips back of him. The fact was commented on with wonder by Madame Choudey;—with wonder, frank queries, and wild surmises, by the little group around her; for the aged Marquise and her son Alain—dead a year since—had been picturesque figures in their own circle where politics and art, literature and religion, met and crossed swords, or played piquet! And now she was coming back, not only to Paris, but to society; had in fact, arrived, and the card Madame Choudey held in her white dimpled hand announced the first reception at the Caron establishment.

"After years of the country and Rome!" and Sidonie Merson raised her infantile brows and smiled.

"Oh, yes, it is quite true—though so strange; we fancied her settled for life in her old vine-covered villa; no one expected to see the Paris house opened after Alain's death."

"It is always the unexpected in which the old Marquise delights," said big Lavergne, the sculptor, who had joined Sidonie in the window.

"Then how she must have reveled in Alain's marriage—a death-bed marriage!"

"Yes; and to an Italian girl without a dot."

"Oh—it is quite possible. The marriage was in Rome. Both the English and Americans go to Rome."

"Italian! I heard it was an English or American!"

"Surely, not so bad as that!"

"But only those who have money;—or, if they have not the money, our sons and our brothers do not marry them."

"Good!" and Lavergne nodded with mock sagacity. "We reach conclusions; the newly made Marquise de Caron is either not Anglo-Saxon or was not without wealth."

"I heard from Dumaresque that she had attended English schools; that no doubt gives her the English suggestion."

"Oh, I know more than that;" said another, eager to add to the knowledge of the group. Between Fontainbleau and Moret is the Levigne chateau. Two years ago the dowager was there with a young beauty, Judithe Levigne, and that is the girl Alain married; the dowager was also a Levigne, and the girl an adopted daughter."

"What is she like now? Has no one seen her?"

"No one more worldly than her confessor—if she possess one, or the nuns of the convent to which she returned to study after her marriage and widowhood."

"Heavens! We must compose our features when we enter the presence!"

"But we will go, for all that! The dowager is too delightful to miss."

"A religieuse and a blue stocking!" and the smile of Levergne was accompanied by a doubtful shrug. "I might devote myself to either, if apart, but never to both in one. Is she then ugly that she dare be so superior?"

"Greek and Latin did not lessen the charm of Heloise for Abelard, Monsieur."

Sidonie glanced consciously out of the window. Even the dust of six centuries refuses to cover the passion of Heloise, and despite the ecclesiastical flavor of the romance —demoiselles were not supposed to be aware—still—!

Lavergne beckoned to a fair slight man near the piano.

"We will ask Loris—Loris Dumaresque. He is god-son of the dowager. He was in Rome also. He will know."

"Certainly;" and Madame Choudey glanced in the mirror opposite and leaned her cheek on her jeweled hand, the lace fell from her pretty wrist and the effect was rather pleasing. "Loris; ah, pardon me, since your last canvas is the talk of Paris we must perhaps say Monsieur Dumaresque, or else—Master."

"The queen calls no man master," replied the new comer as he bent over the pretty coquette's hand. "The humblest of your subjects salutes you."

"My faith! You have not lost in Rome a single charm of the boulevardes. We feared you would come back a devotee, and addicted to rosaries."

"I only needed them when departing from Paris—and you." His eyes alone expressed the final words, but they spoke so eloquently that the woman of the world smiled; attempted to blush, and dropping her own eyes, failed to see the amusement in his.

"Your gallantry argues no lack of practice, Monsieur Loris," she returned; glancing at him over her fan. "Who was she, during those months of absence? Come; confess; was she some worldly soul like the Kora of your latest picture, or was it the religieuse—the new marquise about whom every one is curious?"

"The Marquise? What particular Marquise?"

"One more particular than you were wont to cultivate our first season in Rome," remarked Lavergne.

"Oh! oh! Monsieur Dumaresque!" and the fan became a shield from which Madame peered at him. Sidonie almost smiled, but recovered herself, and gave attention to the primroses.

"You see!—Madame Choudey is shocked that you have turned to saintliness."

"Madame knows me too well to suppose I have ever turned away from it," retorted Dumaresque. "Do not credit the gossip of Lavergne. He has worked so long among clays and marbles that he has grown a cold-blooded cynic. He distrusts all warmth and color in life."

"Then why not introduce him to the Marquise? He might find his ideal there—the atmosphere of the sanctuary! I mean the new Marquise de Caron."

"Oh!" Dumaresque looked from one to the other blankly and then laughed. "It is Madame Alain—the Marquise de Caron you call the devotee? My faith—that is droll!"

"What, then, is so droll?"

"Why should you laugh, Monsieur Loris? What else were we to think of a bride who chooses a convent in preference to society?"

"It was decided she must be very ugly or very devout to make that choice."

"A natural conclusion from your point of view," agreed Dumaresque. "Will you be shocked when I tell you she is no less a radical than Alain himself?—that her favorite prophet is Voltaire, and that her books of devotion are not known in the church?"

"Horror!—an infidel!—and only a girl of twenty!" gasped the demure Sidonie.

"Chut!—she may be a veteran of double that. Alain always had a fancy for the grenadiers—the originals. But of course," he added moodily, "we must go."

"Take cheer," laughed Dumaresque, "for I shall be there; and I promise you safe conduct through the gates when the grenadier feminine grows too oppressive."

"Do you observe," queried Madame, slyly, "that while Monsieur Loris does speak of her religion, he avoids enlightening us as to her personality?"

"What then do you expect?" returned Dumaresque. "She is the widow of my friend; the child, now, of my dear old god-mother. Should I find faults in her you would say I am jealous. Should I proclaim her virtues you would decide I am prejudiced by friendship, and so"—with a smile that was conciliating and a gesture comprehensive he dismissed the subject.

"Clever Dumaresque!" laughed Lavergne—"well, we shall see! Is it true that your picture of the Kora is to be seen at the dowager's tomorrow?"

"Quite true. It is sold, you know; but since the dowager is not equal to art galleries I have given it a rest in her rooms before boxing it for the new owner."

"I envy him," murmured Madame; "the picture is the pretty octoroon glorified. So, Madame, your god-mother has two novelties to present tomorrow. Usually it is so difficult to find even one."

When Delaven returned he found Lieutenant McVeigh still in the same nook by the mantel and still alone.

"Well, you are making a lonesome time of it in the middle of the crowd," he remarked. "How have you been amused?"

"By listening to comments on two pictures, one of a colored beauty, and one of an atheistical grand dame.

"And of the two?"

"Of the two I should fancy the last not the least offen-
sive. And, look here, Delaven, just get me out of that engagement to look at Dumaresque's new picture, won't you?
It really is not worth while for an American to come abroad
for the study of pictured octoroons—we have too many of
the originals at home."

CHAPTER II.

Whatever the dowager's eccentricities or heresies, she
was not afraid of the sunlight, figuratively or literally. From
floor to ceiling three great windows let in softened rays on
the paneled walls, on the fluted columns of white and gold,
and on the famous frescoes of the First Empire. She had no
feeling for petite apartments such as appeal to many women;
there must, for her, be height and space and long vistas.

"I like perspective to every picture," she said. "I enjoy
the groupings of my friends in my own rooms more than
elsewhere. From my couch I have the best point of view,
and the raised dais flatters me with its suggestion of a throne
of state."

She looked so tiny for a chair of state; and with her usual
quaint humor she recognized the fact.

"But my temperament brings me an affinity with things
that are great for all that," she would affirm. "One does not
need to be a physical Colossus in order to see the stars."

The morning after her first reception she was smiling
rather sardonically at a picture at the far end of the
great salon—that of a very handsome young woman who
laughed frankly at the man who leaned towards her and
spoke. The man was Dumaresque.

"No use in that, Loris," commented his god-mother, out

of his hearing. "It will do an artist no harm, but it will end nowhere."

Their attitude and their youth did make them appear sentimental; but they were not really so. He was only telling her what a shock she had been to those Parisians the day before.

"I understand, now, the regard of Madame Choudey and her pretty, prim niece, Sidonie. They will never forgive me."

"You, Madame!"

"Me, Monsieur. Their fondness will preclude resentment towards you, but against myself they will feel a grievance that I am not as they pictured me. Come; you must tell Maman."

The dowager nodded as one who understood it all.

"They will not forget you, that is sure," she said, smiling; but the girl—for she was only a girl, despite the Madame—shrugged her shoulders.

"Myself, I care little for their remembrance," she replied, indifferently; "they were only curious, not interested, I could see."

"You put my picture in the shadow at all events," protested Dumaresque, pointing to a large canvas hung opposite; "my picture over which art lovers raved until you appeared as a rival."

"How extravagant you are, Monsieur Dumaresque, a true Gascon! To think of rivaling that!"

As she faced the canvas the dowager watched her critically, and nodded her approval to Dumaresque, who smiled and acquiesced. Evidently they were both well satisfied with the living picture of the salon.

The new Marquise de Caron had lived, probably, twenty years. She was of medium height, with straight, dark brows, and dark, long-lashed eyes. The eyes had none of the shy-

ness that was deemed a necessity to beauty in that era of
balloon skirts and scuttle bonnets under which beauty of
the conventional order hid.

But that she was not conventional was shown by the turban of grey resting on her waved, dark hair, while the veil
falling from it and mingling with the folds of her dress, suggested the very artistic draperies of the nuns.

Not a particle of color was in her apparel, and but little
in her face; only the lips had that thread of scarlet sung of
by Solomon, and the corners of them curved upwards a trifle
as she surveyed the canvas.

The turban was loosened and held in her hands as she
stood there looking. The picture evidently attracted her,
though it did not please. At last she turned to the artist.

"Why do you paint pictures like that?"

"Like that? Pouf! You mean beautiful?"

"No, it is not beautiful," she said, thoughtfully, as she
seated herself on the dais by the dowager's couch. "To be
truly beautiful a thing must impress one with a sense of fitness to our highest perceptive faculties. A soulless thing is
never beautiful."

"What then, of dogs, horses, lions, the many art works
in metal or on canvas?"

"You must not raise that wall against her words, Loris,
unless you wish to quarrel," said the dowager in friendly
warning. "Judithe is pantheist enough to fancy that animals
have souls."

"But the true artist does not seek to portray the lowest
expression of that soul," persisted Dumaresque's critic.
"Across the Atlantic there are thousands who contend that
a woman such as this Kora whom you paint, has no soul
because of the black blood in her veins. They think of the
dark people as we think of apes. It is all a question of longi-
tude, Monsieur Dumaresque. The crudeness of America is

the jest of France. The wisdom of France is the lightest folly of the Brahims; and so it goes ever around the world. The soul of that girl will weigh as heavily as ours in the judgment that is final; but, in the meantime, why teach it and others to admire all that allurement of evil showing in her eyes as she looks at you?"

"Judithe!" protested the dowager.

"Oh!—I do not doubt in the least, Maman, that the woman Kora looked just so when she sat for the picture," conceded the girl; "but why not endeavor to awaken a higher, stronger expression, and paint *that*, showing the better possibilities within her than mere seductiveness?"

"What fervor and what folly, Marquise!" cried Dumaresque. It is a speech of folly only because it is I whom you ask to be the missionary, and because it is the pretty Kora you would ask me to convert—and to what? Am I so perfect in all ways that I dare preach, even with paint and brush? Heavens! I should have all Paris laughing at me."

"But Judithe would not have you that sort of extremist," said the dowager, laughing at the dismay in his face. "She knows you do well; only she fears you do not exert yourself enough to perceive how you might do better."

"She forgets; I did once; only a few weeks ago," he said briefly; and the girl dropped her hands wearily and leaned her head against the dowager's couch.

"Maman, our good friend is going to talk matrimony again," she said plaintively; "and if he does, I warn you, though it is only mid-day, I shall go asleep;" and her eyes closed tightly as though to make the threat more effective.

"You see," said the old lady, raising one chiding finger, "it is really lamentable, Loris, that your sentimental tendencies have grown into a steady habit."

"I agree," he assented; "but consider. She assails me—

2

she, a saintly little judge in grey! She lectures, preaches at
me! Tells me I lack virtue! But more is the pity for me;
she will not remember that one virtue was most attractive to
me, and she bade me abandon it."

"Tell him," said the girl with her eyes still closed, "to not
miscall things; no one is all virtue."

"Pardon; that is what you seemed to me, and I never
before fancied that the admirable virtues would find me
so responsive, when, pouf! with one word you demolished
all my castle of delight and now condemn me that I am
an outlaw from those elevating fancies."

He spoke with such a comical air of self-pity that the old
lady laughed and the young Marquise opened her eyes.

"A truce, Monsieur Loris; you are amusing, but you like
to pose as one of the rejected and disconsolate when you
have women to listen. It is all because you are just a little
theatrical, is it not? How effective it must be with your
Parisiennes!"

"My faith!" he exclaimed, turning to the dowager in dismay; "and only three months since she emerged from the
convent! What then do they not teach in those sanctu-
aries!"

The girl arose, made him a mocking obeisance, and
swinging the turban in her hand passed into the alcoved
music room; a little later an Italian air, soft, dreamy, drifted
to them from the keys of the piano.

"She will make a sensation," prophesied Dumaresque,
sagely.

"You mean socially? No; if left to herself she would
ignore society; it is not necessary to her; only her affection
for me brings her from her studies now. Should I die tomorrow she would go back to them next week."

"But why, why, why? If she were unattractive one could
understand; but being what she is —"

"Being what she is, she has a fever to know all the facts of earth and all the guesses at heaven."

"And bars out marriage!"

"Not for other people," retorted the dowager.

"But to what use then all these accomplishments, all this pursuit of knowledge? Does she mean to hide it all in some convent at last?"

"I would look for her rather among some savage tribes, doing missionary work."

"Yes, making them acquainted with Voltaire," he said, laughingly. "But you are to be envied, god-mother, in having her all to yourself; she adores you!"

The dark old face flushed slightly, and the keen eyes softened with pleasure.

"It was Alain's choice, and it was a good one," she said, briefly. "What of the English people you asked to bring today?"

"They are not English; one is American and one is Irish."

"True; but their Anglo-Saxon makes them all English to me. I hear there are so many of them in Paris now; Comtesse Biron brings one today; there is her message, what is the name?"

Dumaresque unfolded the pink sheet, glanced at it and smiled.

"My faith; it is the mother of the young lieutenant whom I asked to bring, Madame McVeigh. So, she was a school friend of the Comtesse Helene, eh? That seems strange; still, this Madame McVeigh may be a French woman transplanted."

"I do not know; but it will be a comfort if she speaks French. The foreigners of only one language are trying."

*   *   *   *   *

Mrs. McVeigh offered no linguistic difficulties to the dowager who was charmed with her friend's friend.

"But you are surely not the English-Americans of whom we see so much these days? I cannot think it."

"No, Madame. I am of the French-Americans—the creoles—hence the speech you are pleased to approve. My people were the Villanennes of Louisiana."

"Ah! a creole? The creoles come here from the West Indies also—beautiful women. My daughter has had some as school friends; only this morning she was explaining to an English caller the difference between a creole and that personality;" and the dowager waived her hand towards the much discussed picture of Kora.

The fine face of the American woman took on a trace of haughtiness, and she glanced at the speaker as though alert to some covert insult. The unconsciousness in the old face reassured her, though she could not quite banish coldness from her tones as she replied:

"I should not think such an explanation necessary in en-lightened circles; the creole is so well known as the Ameri-can born of the Latin races, while that," with a gesture towards the oriental face on the canvas, "is the offspring of the African race—our slaves."

"With occasionally a Caucasian father," suggested the dowager wickedly. "I have never seen this new idol of the ballet—Kora; but her prettiness is the talk of the studios, though she does not deny she came from your side of the sea, and has the shadows of Africa in her hair."

"A quadroon or octoroon, no doubt. It appears strange to find the outcasts of the States elected to that sort of notice over here—as though the old world, tired of civilization and culture, turned for distraction to the barbarians."

"Barbarians, indeed!" laughed the Countess Biron—the Countess Helene, as she was called by her friends. She laughed a great deal, knew a great deal, and never forgot a morsel of Parisian gossip. "This barbarian has only to show herself on the boulevards and all good citizens crane their necks for a glimpse of her. The empress herself attracts less attention."

The dowager clicked the lid of her snuff box and shrugged her shoulders.

"That Spanish woman—tah! As *Mademoiselle d'Industrie* I do not see why she should claim precedence. The blonde Spaniard is no more beautiful than the brown American."

"For all that, Louis Napoleon has placed her among the elect," remarked the Countess Helene, with a mischievous glance towards the Marquise, each understanding that the mention of the Second Empire was like a call to war, in that salon.

"Louis!" and the dowager shrugged her shoulder, and made a gesture of contempt. "That accident! What is he that any one should be exalted by his favor? Mademoiselle de Montijo was—for the matter of that—his superior! Her family had place and power; her paternity was undisputed; but this Louis—tah! There was but one Bonaparte; that subaltern from Corsica; that meteor. He was, with all his faults, a worker, a thinker, an original. He would have swept into the sea the envious islanders across the channel to whom this Bonaparte truckled—this man called Bonaparte, who was no Bonaparte at all—a vulture instead of an eagle!"

So exclaimed the dowager, who carried in her memory the picture of the streets of Paris when neither women nor children were spared by the bullets and sabres of his slaughterers—the hyena to whom the clergy so bowed down that not a mass for the dead patriots could be secured in Paris, from either priest or archbishop, and the Republicans piled in the streets by hundreds!

Mrs. McVeigh turned in some dismay to the Countess
Helene. The people of the Western world, the women in
particular, knew little of the bitter spirit permeating the
politics of France. The United States had very knotty
problems of her own to discuss in 1859.

"Tah!" continued the dowager, "I startle you! Well,
well—it profits nothing to recite these ills. Many a man,
and woman, too, has been put to death for saying less;—and
the exile of my son to remember—yes; all that! He was
Republican—I a Legitimist; I of the old, he of the new.
Republics are good in theory; France might have given it a
longer trial but for this trickster politician, who is called
Emperor—by the grace of God!"

"Do they add 'Defender of the Faith' as our cautious English neighbors persist in doing?" asked the girlish Marquise
with a smile. "Your country, Madame McVeigh, has no such
cant in its constitution. You have reason to be proud of
the great men, the wise, far-seeing men, who framed those
laws."

Mrs. McVeigh smiled and sighed in self-pity.

"How frivolous American women will appear to you,
Madame! Few of us ever read the constitution of our
country. I confess I only know the first line:—'*When in the
course of human events it becomes necessary,*' but what they
thought necessary to do is very vague in my mind."

Then, catching the glance of the Marquise bright with
laughter, she laughed also without knowing well at what.

"Well; what is it?"

"Only that you are quoting from the Declaration of Independence, and fancy it the constitution."

"That is characteristic of American women, too," laughed
Mrs. McVeigh; "declarations of independence is one of our
creeds. But I shall certainly be afraid of you, Marquise.
At your age the learning and comparing of musty laws

would have been dull work for me. It is the age for dancing and gay carelessness."

The Marquise smiled assent with her curious, dark eyes,
in which amber lights shown. She had a certain appealing
meekness at times—a sweet deference that was a marked
contrast to the aggressiveness with which she had met Dumaresque in the morning. The Countess Helene, observ-
ing the deprecating manner with which she received the im-
plied praise for erudition, found herself watching with a
keener interest the girl who had seemed to her a mere pretty
book-worm.

"She is more than that," thought the astute worldling.
"Alain's widow has a face for tragedy, the address of an
ingenue, and the *tout en semble* of a coquette."

The dowager smiled at Mrs. McVeigh's remarks.

"She cares too little for dancing, the natural expression of
healthy young animalism; but what can I do?—nothing less
frivolous than a salon a-la-Madame D'Agoult is among her
ambitions."

"Let us persuade her to visit America," suggested Mrs.
McVeigh. "I can, at least, prescribe a change promising
more of joyous festivity—life on a Carolina plantation."

"What delight for her! she loves travel and new scenes.
Indeed, Alain, my son, has purchased a property in your
land, and some day she may go over. But for the brief
remnant of my life I shall be selfish and want her always on
my side of the ocean. What, child? you pale at the mention
of death—tah! it is not so bad. The old die by installments,
and the last one is not the worst."

"May it be many years in the future, Maman," murmured
the young Marquise, whose voice betrayed a certain effort
as she continued: "I thank you for the suggestion, Madame McVeigh; the property Maman refers to is in New

Orleans, and I surely hope to see your country some day; my sympathies are there."

"We have many French people in the South; our own part of the land was settled originally by the cavaliers of France. You would not feel like a stranger there."

"Not in your gracious neighborhood, Madame;"—her face had regained its color, and her eyes their brilliant expression.

"And there you would see living pictures like this," suggested the Countess Helene; "what material for an artist!"

"Oh, no; in the rice fields of South Carolina they do not look like that. We have none of those Oriental effects in dress, you know. Our colored women look very sober in comparison; still they have their attractions, and might be an interesting study for you if you have never known colored folks."

"Oh, but I have," remarked the Marquise, smiling; "an entire year of my life was passed in a school with two from Brazil, and one from your country had run away the same season."

"Judithe; child!"

The dowager fairly gasped the words, and the Marquise moved quickly to her side and sank on the cushion at her feet, looking up with an assuring smile, as she caressed the aged hand.

"Yes, it is quite true," she continued; "but see, I am alive to tell the tale, and really they say the American was a most harmless little thing; the poor, imprisoned soul."

"How strange!" exclaimed Mrs. McVeigh; "do you mean as fellow pupils?—colored girls! It seems awful."

"Really, I never thought of it so; you see, so many planters' daughters come from the West Indies to Paris schools. Many in feature and color suggest the dark continent, but are accepted, nevertheless. However, the girl I mention was not dark. Her mother had seven white ancestors to one of black. Yet she confided her story to a friend of mine, and she was an American slave."

The dowager was plainly distressed at the direction of the conversation, for the shock to Mrs. McVeigh was so very apparent, and as her hostess remembered that slavery was threatening to become an institution of uncompromising discord across the water, all reference to it was likely to be unwelcome. She pressed the fingers of the Marquise warningly, and the Marquise smiled up at her, but evidently did not understand.

"Can such a thing be possible?" asked Mrs. McVeigh, incredulously; "in that case I shall think twice before I send *my* daughter here to school, as I had half intended—and you remained in such an establishment?"

"I had no choice; my guardians decided those questions."

"And the faculty—they allowed it?"

"They did not know it. She was represented as being the daughter of an American planter; which was true. I have reason to believe that my friend was her only confidant."

"And for what purpose was she educated in such an establishment?"

"That she might gain accomplishments enhancing her value as companion to the man who was to own her."

"Madame!"

"Marquise!"

The two exclamations betrayed how intent her listeners were, and how full of horror the suggestion. There was even incredulity in the tones, an initiative protest against such possibilities. But the Marquise looked from one to the other with unruffled earnestness.

"So it was told to me," she continued; "these accomplishments meant extra thousands to the man who sold her, and the man was her father's brother."

"No, no, no!" and Mrs. McVeigh shook her head decidedly to emphasize her conviction. "I cannot believe that at the present day in our country such an arrangement could exist. No one, knowing our men, could credit such a story. In the past century such abuses might have existed, but surely not now—in all my life I have heard of nothing like that."

"Probably the girl was romancing," agreed the Marquise, with a shrug, "for you would no doubt be aware if such a state of affairs had existence."

"Certainly."

"Then your men are not so clever as ours," laughed the Countess; "for they manage many little affairs their own women never suspect."

Mrs. McVeigh looked displeased. To her it was not a matter of cleverness, but of principle and morality; and in her mind there was absolutely no comparison possible without jarring decidedly on the prejudices of her Gallic friends, so she let the remark pass without comment.

"Yes," said the Marquise, rising, "when I heard the story of the girl Rhoda I fancied it one the white mistresses of America seldom heard."

"Rhoda?"

"Yes, that was the name the girl was known by in the school—Rhoda Larue—the Larue was a fiction; slaves, I am told, having no legal right to names."

"Heavens! What horrors you fancy! Pray give us some music child, and drive away the gloomy pictures you have suggested."

"An easy penance;" and the Marquise moved smilingly towards the alcove.

"What!" cried the Countess Helene, in protest, "and the

story unfinished! Why, it might develop into a romance. I dote on romances in real life or fiction, but I like them all spelled out for me to the very end."

"Instead of a romance, I should fancy the girl's life very prosaic wherever it is lived," returned the Marquise. "But before her year at the convent had quite expired she made her escape—took no one into her confidence; and when her guardian, or his agent, came to claim her, there were storms, apologies, but no ward."

"And you do not call that a romance?" said the Countess. "I do; it offers all sorts of possibilities."

"Yes, the possibility of this;" and Mrs. McVeigh pointed to the picture before them. The Marquise halted, looked curiously at the speaker, then regarded the oriental face on the canvas thoughtfully, and passed her hand over her brow with a certain abstraction.

"I never thought of that," she said slowly. "You poor creature!" and she took a step nearer the picture. "I—never—thought of that! Maman, Madame McVeigh has just taught me something—to be careful, careful how we judge the unfortunate. They say this Kora is a light woman in morals; but suppose—suppose somewhere the life that girl told of in the convent really does exist, and suppose this pretty Kora had been one of the victims chosen! Should we dare then to judge her by our standards, Maman? I think not."

Without awaiting an opinion she walked slowly into the alcove, and left the three ladies gazing at each other with a trifle of constraint mingled with their surprise.

"Another sacred cause to fight for," sighed the dowager, with a quaint grimace. "Last week it was the Jews, who seem to me quite able to take care of themselves! Next week it may be Hindoo widows; but just now it is Kora!"

"She should have been born a boy in the age when it was

thought a virtue to don armor and do battle for the weak or incapable; that would have suited Judithe."

"Not if it was the fashion," laughed the Countess Helene; "she would insist on being original."

"The Marquise has a lovely name," remarked Mrs. Mc-Veigh; "one could not imagine a weak or unattractive person called Judithe."

"No; they could not," agreed her friend, "it makes one think of the tragedy of Holofernes. It suggests the strange, the fascinating, the unusual, and—it suits Madame la Marquise."

"Your approval is an unconscious compliment to me," remarked the dowager, indulging herself in a tiny pinch of snuff and tapping the jeweled lid of the box; "I named her."

"Indeed!" and Mrs. McVeigh smiled at the complacent old lady, while the Countess Helene almost stared. Evidently she, also, had heard the opinions concerning the young widow's foreign extraction. Possibly the dowager guessed what was passing in her mind, for she nodded and smiled.

"Truly, the eyes did it. Though she was not so fully developed as now, those slumbrous, oriental eyes of hers suggested someway that beauty of Bethulia; the choice was left to me and so she was christened Judithe."

"She voices such startlingly paganish ideas at times that I can scarcely imagine her at the christening font," remarked the Countess.

"In truth her questions are hard to answer sometimes. But the heart is all right."

"And the lady herself magnetic enough without the added suggestion of the name," remarked Mrs. McVeigh; then she held up her finger as the Countess was about to

speak, for from the music room came the appealing legato
notes of "Suwanee River," played with great tenderness.

"What is it?" asked the dowager.

"One of our American folk songs," and the grey eyes of
the speaker were bright with tears; "in all my life I have
never heard it played so exquisitely."

"For a confirmed blue stocking, the Marquise understands remarkably well how to make her little compliments,"
said the Countess Helene.

Mrs. McVeigh arose, and with a slight bow to the dowager, passed into the alcove. At the last bar of the song a
shadow fell across the keys, and the musician saw their
American visitor beside her.

"I should love to have you see the country whose music
you interpret so well," she said impulsively; "I should like
to be with you when you do see it."

"You are kind, and I trust you may be," replied the Marquise, with a pretty nod that was a bow in miniature. She
was rising from the piano, when Mrs. McVeigh stopped
her.

"Pray don't! It is a treat to hear you. I only wanted to
ask you to take my invitation seriously and come some time
to our South Carolina home; I should like to be one of your
friends."

"It would give me genuine pleasure," was the frank reply. "You know I confessed that my sympathies were there
ahead of me." The smile accompanying the words was so
adorable that Mrs. McVeigh bent to kiss her.

The Marquise offered her cheek with a graciousness that
was a caress in itself, and thus their friendship commenced.

After the dowager and her daughter-in-law were again
alone, and with an assurance that even the privileged Dumaresque would not break in on their evening, the elder

lady asked, abruptly, a question over which she had been puzzling.

"Child, what possessed you to tell to a Southern woman of the States that story reflecting on the most vital of their economic institutions? Had you forgotten their prejudices? I was in dread that you might offend her, and I am sure Helene Biron was quite as nervous."

"I did not offend her, Maman," replied the Marquise, looking up from her embroidery with a smile, "and I had not forgotten their prejudices. I only wanted to judge if she herself had ever heard the story."

"Madame McVeigh!—and why?"

"Because Rhoda Larne was also a native of that particular part of Carolina to which she has invited me, and because of a fact which I have never forgotten, the young planter for whom she was educated—the slave owner who bought her from her father's brother was named McVeigh. My new friend is delightful in herself but—she has a son."

"My child!" gasped the dowager, staring at her. "Such a man the son of that charming, sincere woman! Yes, I had forgotten their name, and bid you forget the story; never speak of it again, child!"

"I should be sorry to learn it is the same family," admitted the Marquise; "still, I shall make a point of avoiding the son until we learn something about him. It is infamous that such men should be received into society."

The dowager relapsed into silence, digesting the troublesome question proposed.

Occasionally she glanced towards the Marquise as though in expectation of a continuation of the subject. But the Marquise was engrossed by her embroideries, and when she did speak again it was of some entirely different matter.

CHAPTER III.

Two mornings later M. Dumaresque stood in the Caron reception room staring with some dissatisfaction across the breadth of green lawn where the dryad and faun statues held vases of vining and blooming things.

He had just been told the dowager was not yet to be seen. That was only what he had expected; but he had also been told that the Marquise, accompanied, as usual, by Madame Blanc, had been out for two hours—and that he had not expected.

"Did she divine I would be in evidence this morning?" Then he glanced in a pier glass and grimaced. "Gone out with that plain Madame Blanc, when she might have had a treat—an hour with me!"

While he stood there both the Marquise and her companion appeared, walking briskly. Madame Blanc, a stout woman of thirty-five, was rather breathless.

"My dear Marquise, you do not walk, you fly," she gasped, halting on the steps.

"You poor dear!" said the Marquise, patting her kindly on the shoulder. "I know you are faint for want of your coffee," and at the same time her strong young arms helped the panting attendant mount the steps more quickly.

Once within the hall Madame Blanc dropped into the chair nearest the door, while the Marquise swept into the reception room and hastily to a window fronting on the street.

"How foolish of me," she breathed aloud. "How my heart beats!"

"Allow me to prescribe," said Dumaresque, stepping from behind the screen of the curtain, and smiling at her.

She retreated, her hands clasped over her breast, her eyes startled; then meeting his eyes she began to laugh a little nervously.

"How you frightened me!"

"And it was evidently not the first, this morning."

She sank into a seat, indicated another to him, away from the window, removed her hat and leaned back looking at him.

"No, you are not," she said at last. "But account for yourself, Monsieur Loris! The sun is not yet half way on its course, yet you are actually awake, and visible to humanity—it looks serious."

"It is," he agreed, smiling at her, yet a trifle nervous in his regard. "I have taken advantage of the only hour out of the twenty when there would be a chance of seeing you alone. So I made an errand—and I am here."

"And—?"

"And I have determined that, after the fashion of the Americans or the English, I shall no longer ask the intervention of a third person. I decided on it last night before I left here. I have no title to offer you—you coldest and most charming of women, but I shall have fame; you will have no reason to be ashamed of the name of Dumaresque. Put me on probation, if you like, a year, two years!—only—"

"No; no!" she said pleadingly, putting out her hands with a slight repellant gesture. "It is not to be thought of, Monsieur Loris, Maman has told you! Twice has the same reply been given. I really cannot allow you to continue this suppliance. I like you too well to be angry with you, but—"

"I shall be content with the liking—"

"But I should not!" she declared, smilingly. "I have my ideals, if you please, Monsieur. Marriage should mean love. It is only matrimony for which liking is the foundation. I do not approve of matrimony."

"Pardon; that is the expression of the romance lover— the school girl. But that I know you have lived the life of a nun I should fear some one had been before me, some one who realized those ideals of yours, and that instead of studying the philosophies of life, you have been a student of the philosophy of love."

He spoke lightly—half laughingly, but the flush of pink suffusing her throat and brow checked his smile. He could only stare.

She arose hastily and walked the length of the room. When she turned the color was all gone, but her eyes were softly shining.

"All philosophy falls dead when the heart speaks," she said, as she resumed her chair; "and now, Monsieur Loris, I mean to make you my father confessor, for I know no better way of ending these periodical proposals of yours, and at the same time confession might—well—it might not be without a certain benefit to myself." He perceived that while she had assumed an air of raillery, there was some substance back of the mocking shadow.

"I shall feel honored by your confidence, Marquise," he was earnest enough in that.

"And when you realize that there is—some one else—will you then resume your former role of friend?"

"I shall try. Who is the man?"

She met his earnest gaze with a demure smile, "I do not know, Monsieur."

8

"What, then?—you are only jesting with me?"

"Truly, I do not know his name."

"Yet you are in love with him?"

"I am not quite certain even of that," and she smiled mockingly; "sometimes I have a fancy it may be witchcraft. I only know I am haunted—have been haunted four long weeks by a face, a voice, and two blue eyes."

"Blue?" Dumaresque glanced in the mirror—his own eyes were blue.

"Yes, Monsieur Loris—blue with a dash of grey—the grey of the sea when clouds are heavy, and the blue of the farthest waves before the storm breaks—don't you see the color?"

"Only the color of your fancy. He is the owner of blue eyes, a haunting voice, and—what else is my rival?"

"A foreigner, and—Monsieur Incognito."

"You have met?"

"Three times;" and she held up as many white fingers. The reply evidently astounded Dumaresque.

"You have met three times a man whose name you do not know?"

"We are even on that score," she said, "for he has spoken to me three times and does not know what I am called."

"But to address you—"

"He called me Mademoiselle Unknown."

"Bravo! This grows piquant; an adventure with all the flavor of the eighteenth instead of the nineteenth century. A real adventure, and you its heroine! Oh, Marquise, Marquise!"

"Ah! since you appreciate the humor of the affair you will no longer be oppressed by sentimental fancies concerning me;" and she nodded her head as though well pleased with the experiment of her confession. "You perceive how wildly improper I have been; still, I deny the eighteenth century flavor, Monsieur. Then, with three meetings the cavalier would have developed into a lover, and having gained entrance to a lady's heart, he would have claimed also the key to her castle."

"Astute pupil of the nuns!—and Monsieur Incognito?"

"He certainly does not fancy me possessed of either castle or keys. I was to him only an unpretentious English companion in attendance on Madame Blanc in the woods of Fontainbleau."

"English! Since when are you fond enough of them to claim kindred?"

"He was English; he supposed me so when I replied to him in that tongue. He had taken the wrong path and—"

"And you walked together on another, also the wrong path."

"No, Monsieur; that first day we only bowed and parted, but the ghost of his voice remained," and she sighed in comical self-pity.

"I see! You have first given me the overture and now the curtain is to rise. Who opens the next scene?"

"Madame Blanc."

"My faith! This grows tragical. Blanc, the circumspect, the dowager's most trusted companion. Has your stranger bewitched her also?"

"She was too near sighted to tell him from the others. I was making a sketch of beeches and to pass the time she fed the carp. A fan by which she set store, fell into the water. She lamented until Monsieur Incognito secured it. Of course I had to be the one to thank him, as she speaks no English."

"Certainly!—and then?"

"Then I found a seat in the shade for Madame Blanc and her crochet, and selected a sunny spot myself, where I could dry the fan."

"Alone?"

"At first, I was alone."

"Delicious! You were never more charming, Marquise; go on."

"When he saw Madame Blanc placidly knitting under the trees, while I spread her fan to dry, he fancied I was in her service; the fancy was given color by the fact that my companion, as usual, was dressed with extreme elegance, whilst I was insignificant in an old school habit."

"Insignificant—um! There was conversation I presume?"

"Not much," she confessed, and again the delicious wave of color swept over her face, "but he had suggested spreading the fan on his handkerchief, and of course then he had to remain until it was dry."

"Clever Englishman; and as he supposed you to be a paid companion, was he, also, some gentleman's gentleman?"

She flashed one mutinous glance at him.

"The jest seemed to me amusing; his presence was an exhilaration; and I did not correct his little mistake as to mistress and maid. When he attempted to tell me who or what he was I stopped him; that would have spoiled the adventure. I know he had just come from England; that he was fascinating without being strictly handsome; that he could say through silence the most eloquent things to one! It was an hour in Arcady—just one hour without past or future. They are the only absolutely joyous ones, are they not?"

"Item: it was the happiest hour in the life of Madame La Marquise," commented Dumaresque, with an attempt at drollery, and an accompaniment of a sigh. "Well—the finale?"

"The hour ended! I said 'good day, Monsieur Incognito.' He said, 'good night, Mademoiselle Unknown.'"

"Good night! Heavens—it was not then an hour, but a day!"

"It was an hour, Monsieur! That was only one way of conveying his belief that all the day was in that hour."

"Blessed be the teachings of the convent! And you would have me believe that an Englishman could make such speeches? However, I am eager for the finale—the next day?"

"The next day I surprised Monsieur and Madame Blanc by declaring the sketch I was doing of the woods there, was hopelessly bad—I would never complete it."

"Ah!" and Dumaresque's exclamation had a note of hope; "he had been a bore after all?"

"The farthest thing possible from it! When I woke in the morning it was an hour earlier than usual. I found myself with my eyes scarcely open, standing before the clock to reckon every instant of time until I should see him again. Well, from that moment my adventure ceased to be merely amusing. I told myself how many kinds of an idiot I was, and I thrust my head among the pillows again. I realized then, Monsieur, what a girl's first romance means to her. I laughed at myself, of course, as I had laughed at others often. But I could not laugh down the certainty that the skies were bluer, the birds' songs sweeter, and all life more lovely than it had ever been before."

"And by what professions, or what mystic rhymes or runes, did he bring about this enchantment?"

"Not by a single sentence of protestation? An avowal would have sent me from him without a regret. If we had not met at all after that first look, that first day, I am convinced I should have been haunted by him just the same! There were long minutes when we did not speak or look at each other; but those minutes were swept with harmonies.

Now, Monsieur Loris, would you call that love, or is it a sort of summer-time madness?"

"Probably both, Marquise; "but there was a third meeting?"

"After three days, Monsieur; days when I forced myself to remain indoors; and the struggle it was, when I could close my eyes and see him waiting there under the trees!"

"Ah! There had been an appointment?"

"Pardon, Monsieur; you are perhaps confounding this with some remembered adventure of your own. There was no appointment. But I felt confident that blue-eyed ogre was walking every morning along the path where I met him first, and that he would compel me to open the door and walk straight to our own clump of bushes so long as I did not send him away."

"And you finally went?"

She nodded. "He was there. His smile was like sunshine. He approached me, but I—I did not wait. I went straight to him. He said, 'At last, Mademoiselle Unknown!'"

"Pardon; but it is your words I have most interest in," reminded her confessor."

"But I said so few. I remember I had some violets, and he asked me what they were called in French. I told him I was going away; I had fed the carp for the last time. He was also leaving. He had gathered some wild forget-me-nots. He was coming into Paris."

"And you parted unknown to each other?"

"How could I do else? When he said, 'I bid you good-bye, Mademoiselle Unknown, but we shall meet again. Then—then I did correct him a little; I said *Madame* Unknown, Monsieur."

"Ah! And to that—?"

"He said not a word, only looked at me; *how* he looked

at me! I felt guilty as a criminal. When I looked up he turned away—turned very politely, with lifted hat and a bow even you could not improve upon, Monsieur Loris, I watched him out of sight in the forest. He never halted; and he never turned his head."

"You might at least have let him go without the thought that you were a flirtatious matron with a husband somewhere in the back-ground."

"Yes; I almost regret that. Still, since I had to send him away, what matter how? It would have been so commonplace had I said: 'We receive on Thursdays; find Loris Dumaresque when you reach Paris; he will present you.' No!"—and she shook her head laughingly, "the three days were quite enough. He is an unknown world; a romance only suggested, and the suggestion is delicious. I would not for the world have him nearer prosaic reality."

"You will forget him in another three weeks," prophesied Dumaresque; "he has been only a shadow of a man; a romantic dream. I shall refuse to accept any but realities as rivals."

"I assure you, no reality has been so appealing as that dream," she persisted. I am telling you all this with the hope that once I have laughed with you over this witchcraft it will be robbed of its potency. I have destroyed the sacred wall of sentiment surrounding this ghost of mine because I rebel at being mastered by it."

"Mastered?—you?"

"Oh, you laugh! You think me, then, too cold or too philosophic, in spite of what I have just told you?"

"Not cold, my dear Marquise. But if you will pardon the liberty of analysis I will venture the opinion that when you are mastered it will be by yourself. Your very well-shaped head will forever defend you from the mastery of others."

"Mastered by myself? I do not think I quite understand you," she said, slowly. "But I must tell you the extreme limit of my folly, the folly of the imagination. Each
morning I go for a walk, as I did this morning. Each time
I leave the door I have with me the fancy that somewhere
I shall meet him. Of course my reason tells me how improb-
able it is, but I put the reason aside and enjoy my walk all
the more because of that fancied tryst. Now, Monsieur
Loris, you have been the victim of my romance long
enough. Come; we will join Madame Blanc and have some
coffee."

"And this is all you have to tell me, Marquise?"

"All but one little thing, Monsieur," and she laughed,
though the laugh was a trifle nervous; "this morning for an
instant I thought the impossible had happened. Only one
street from here my ogre materialized again, or some one
wondrously like him. How startled I was! How I hurried
poor Madame Blanc! But we were evidently not discovered. I realized, however, at that moment, how imprudent
I had been. How shocked Maman would be if she knew.
Yet it was really the most innocent jest, to begin with."

"They often begin that way," remarked Dumaresque,
consolingly.

"Well, I have arrived at one conclusion. It is only because I have met so few men, that *one* dare make such an
overwhelming impression on me. I rebel; and shall amaze
Maman by becoming a social butterfly for a season. So, in
future bring all your most charming friends to see me; but
no tall, athletic, blue-eyed Englishmen."

"So," said Dumaresque, as he followed her to the breakfast room, "I lay awake all night that I may make love to
you early in the morning, and you check-mate me by
thrusting forward a brawny Englishman."

"Pardon; he is not brawny;" she laughed; "I never said

so; nevertheless, Monsieur Loris, I can teach you one
thing: When love has to be *made* it is best not to waste
time with it. The real love makes itself and will neither be
helped or hindered; and the love that can be conquered is
not worth having."

He shrugged his shoulders and rolled his eyes towards
the ceiling.

"In a year and a day I shall return to the discussion. I
give you so long to change your mind and banish your
phantasy; and in the meantime I remain your most devoted visitor."

Madame Blanc was already in evidence with the coffee,
and Dumaresque watched the glowing face of the Marquise,
surprised and puzzled at this new influence she confessed to
and asked analysis for. This book-worm; this reader of law
and philosophy; how charming had been her blushes even
while she spoke in half mockery of the face haunting her.
If only such color would sweep over her cheek at the
thought of him—Dumaresque!

But he had his lesson for the present. He would not play
the sighing Strephon, realizing that this particular Amaryl-
lis was not to be won so. As he received the coffee from
her hand he remarked, mischievously, "Marquise, you did
not quite complete the story. What became of the forget-
me-nots he gathered?"

But the Marquise only laughed.

"We are no longer in the confessional, Monsieur," she
said.

CHAPTER IV.

Mrs. McVeigh found herself thinking of the young Marquise very often. She was not pleased at the story with which she had been entertained there; yet was she conscious of the fact that she would have been very much more displeased had the story been told by any other than the fascinating girl-widow.

"Do you observe," she remarked to the Countess Helene, "that young though she is she seems to have associated only with elderly people, or with books where various questions were discussed? It is a pity. She has been robbed of childhood and girlhood by the friends who are so proud of her, and who would make of her only a lovely thinking-machine."

"You do not then approve of the strong-minded woman, the female philosopher."

"Oh, yes;" replied Mrs. McVeigh, dubiously; "but this delightful creature does not belong to that order yet. She is bubbling over with enthusiasm for the masses because she has not yet been touched by enthusiasm for an individual. I wish she would fall in love with some fine fellow who would marry her and make her life so happy she would forget all the bad laws of nations and the bad morals of the world."

"Hum! I fancy suitors have not been lacking. Her income is no trifle."

"In our country a girl like that would need no income

to insure her desirable suitors. She is the most fascinating creature, and so unconscious of her charms."

Her son, who had been at a writing desk in the corner, laid down his pen and turned around.

"My imperfect following of your rapid French makes me understand at least that this is a serious case," he said, teasingly. "Are you sure, mother, that she has not treated you to enchantment? I heard the same lady described a few days ago, and the picture drawn was that of an atheistical revolutionist, an unlovely and unlovable type."

"Ah!" said the Countess Helene. "You also are opposed to beautiful machines that think."

"I have never been accustomed to those whose thoughts follow such unpleasant lines, Madame," he replied. "I have been taught to revere the woman whose foundation of life is the religion scorned by the lady you are discussing. A woman without that religion would be like a scentless blossom to me."

The Countess smiled and raised her brows slightly. This severe young officer, her friend's son, took himself and his tastes very seriously.

Looking at him she fancied she could detect both the hawk and the dove meeting in those clear, level eyes of his. Though youthful, she could see in him the steadiness of the only son—the head of the house—the protector and the adored of his mother and sister, who were good little women, flattering their men folks by their dependence. And from that picture the lady who was studying him passed on to the picture of the possible bride to whom he would some day fling his favors. She, also, must be adoring and domestic and devout. Her articles of faith must be as orthodox as his affection. He would love her, of course, but must do the thinking for the family.

Because the Lieutenant lacked the buoyant, adaptable

French temperament of his mother, the Countess was inclined to be rather severe in her judgment of him. He was so young; so serious. She did not fancy young men except in the pages of romances; even when they had brains they appeared to her always over-weighted with the responsibility of them.

It is only after a man has left his boyhood in the distance that he can amuse a woman with airy nothings and make her feel that his words are only the froth on the edge of a current that is deep—deep!

Mrs. McVeigh, unconscious of the silent criticism being passed on her son, again poised a lance in defence of the stranger under discussion.

"It is absurd to call her atheistical," she insisted; "would I be influenced by such a person? She is an enthusiast, student of many religions, possibly; but people should know her before they judge, and you, Kenneth, should see her before you credit their gossip. She is a beautiful, sympathetic child, oppressed too early with the seriousness of life."

"At any rate, I see I shall never take you home heart whole," he decided, and laughed as he gathered up letters he had been addressing and left the room.

"One could fancy your son making a tour of the world and coming back without a sentimental scratch," said the Countess, after he had gone. "I have noticed him with women; perfectly gallant, interested and willing to please, but not a flutter of an eyelid out of form; not a tone of the voice that would flatter one. I am not sure but that the women are all the more anxious to claim such a man, the victory seems greater, yet it is more natural to find them reciprocal. Perhaps there is a betrothed somewhere to whom he has sworn allegiance in its most rigid form; is that the reason?"

Mrs. McVeigh smiled. She rather liked to think her son not so susceptible as Frenchmen pretended to be.

"I do not think there are any vows of allegiance," she confessed; "but there is someone at home to whom we have assigned him since they were children."

"Truly? But I fancied the parents did not arrange the affairs matrimonial in your country."

"We do not; that is, not in a definite official way. Still, we are allowed our little preferences, and sometimes we can help or hinder in our own way. But this affair"—and she made a gesture towards the door of her son's room, "this affair is in embryo yet."

"Good settlements?"

"Oh, yes; the girl is quite an heiress and is the niece of his guardian—his guardian that was. Their estates join, and they have always been fond of each other; so you see we have reason for our hopes."

"Excellent!" agreed her friend, "and to conclude, I am to suppose of course she is such a beauty that she blinds his eyes to all the charms arrayed before him here."

"Well, we never thought of Gertrude as a beauty exactly; but she is remarkably good looking; all the Lorings are. I would have had her with me for this visit but that her uncle, with whom she lives, has been very ill for months. They, also, are of colonial French descent with, of course, the usual infusions of Anglo-Saxon and European blood supposed to constitute the new American."

"The new—"

"Yes, you understand, we have yet the original American in our land—the Indian."

"Ah!" with a gesture of repulsion; "the savages; and then, the Africans! How brave you are, Claire. I should die of fear."

Mrs. McVeigh only smiled. She was searching through

a portfolio, and finally extracted a photograph from other pictures and papers.

"That is Miss Loring," she said, and handed it to the Countess, who examined it with critical interest.

"Very pretty," she decided, "an English type. If she were a Parisian, a modiste and hairdresser would do wonders towards developing her into a beauty of the very rare, very fair order. She suggests a slender white lily."

"Yes, Gertrude is a little like that," assented Mrs. McVeigh, and placed the photograph on the mantel beside that of the very charming, piquant face of a girl resembling Mrs. McVeigh. It was a picture of her daughter.

"Only six weeks since I left her; yet, it seems like a year," she sighed; and Fitzgerald Delaven, who had entered from the Lieutenant's room, sighed ponderously at her elbow.

"Well, Dr. Delaven, why are you blowing like a bellows?" she asked, with a smile of good nature.

"Out of sympathy, my lady," replied the young Irishman.

"Now, how can you possibly sympathize understandingly with a mother's feelings, you Irish pretender?" she asked with a note of fondness in her tones. "I sigh because I have not seen my little Evilene for six weeks."

"And I because I am never likely to see that lovely duplicate of yourself at all, at all! Ah, you laugh! But have you not noticed that each time I am allowed to enter this room I pay my devotions to that particular corner of the mantel?"

"A very modern shrine," observed the Countess; "and why should you not see the original of the picture some day. It is not so far to America."

"True enough, but I'll be delving for two years here in the medical college," he replied with lamentation in his tone.

"And after that I'll be delving for a practice in some modest corner of the world, and all the time that little lady will be counting her lovers on every one of her white fingers, and, finally, will name the wedding day for a better boy than myself, och hone! och hone!"

Both the ladies laughed over his comical despair, and when Lieutenant McVeigh entered and heard the cause of it he set things right by promising to speak a good word for Delaven to the little girl across the water.

"You are a trump, Lieutenant; sorry am I that I have no sister with which to return the compliment."

"She might be in the way," suggested the Countess, and made a gesture towards the other picture. "You perceive; our friend need not come abroad for charming faces; those at home are worth courting."

"True for you, Madame;" he gave a look askance at the Lieutenant, and again turned his eyes to the photograph; "there's an excuse for turning your back on the prettiest we have to offer you!" and then in an undertone, he added: "Even for putting aside the chance of knowing our so adorable Marquise."

The American did not appear to hear or to appreciate the spirit of the jest regarding the pictures, for he made no reply. The Countess, who was interested in everybody's affairs, wondered if it was because the heiress was a person of indifference to him, or a person who was sacred; it was without doubt one or the other for which the man made of himself a blank wall, and discouraged discussion.

Her carriage was just then announced; an engagement with Mrs. McVeigh was arranged for the following morning, and then the Countess descended the staircase accompanied by the Lieutenant and Delaven. She liked to make progress through all public places with at least two men in attendance; even a youthful lieutenant and an untitled medical student were not to be disdained, though she would, of course, have preferred the Lieutenant in a uniform, six feet of broad shouldered, good-looking manhood would not weigh in her estimation with the glitter of buttons and golden cord.

The two friends were yet standing on the lower step of the hotel entrance, gazing idly after her carriage as it turned the corner, when another carriage containing two ladies rolled softly towards their side of the street, as if to stop at a jeweler's two doors below.

Delaven uttered a slight exclamation of pleasure, and stepped forward as if to speak, or open the door of their carriage. But the occupants evidently did not see him, and, moreover, changed their minds about stopping, for the wheels were just ceasing to revolve when the younger of the ladies leaned forward, spoke a brief word, and the driver sent the horses onward at a rapid trot past the hotel, and Delaven stepped back with a woeful grimace.

"Faith! no chance to even play the lackey for her," he grumbled. "There's an old saying that 'God is good to the Irish;' but I don't think I'm getting my share of it this day; unless its by way of being kept out of temptation, and sure, its never a Delaven would pray for that when the temptation is a lovely woman. Now wasn't she worth a day's journey afoot just to look at?"

He turned to his companion, whose gaze was still on the receding carriage, and who seemed, at last, to be aroused to interest in something Parisian; for his eyes were alight, his expression, a mingling of delight and disappointment. At Delaven's question, however, he attempted nonchalance, not very successfully, and remarked, as they re-entered the house, "There were two of them to look at, which do you mean?"

"Faith, now, did you suppose for a minute it was the

dowager I meant? Not a bit of it! Madame Alain, as I heard some of them call her, is the 'gem of purest ray serene.' What star of the heavens dare twinkle beside her?"

"Don't attempt the poetical," suggested the other, unfeelingly. "I am to suppose, then, that you know her—this Madame Alain?"

"Do I know her? Haven't I been raving about her for days? Haven't you vowed she belonged to the type abhorrent to you? Haven't I had to endure your reflections on my sanity because of the adjectives I've employed to describe her attractions? Haven't you been laughing at your own mother and myself for our infatuation?—and now—"

He stopped, because the Lieutenant's grip on his shoulder was uncomfortably tight, as he said:

"Shut up! Who the devil are you talking about?"

"By the same power, how can I shut up and tell you at the same time?" and Delaven moved his arm, and felt of his shoulder, with exaggerated self-pity. "Man! but you've got a grip in that fist of yours."

"Who is the lady you call Madame Alain?"

"Faith, if you had gone to her home when you were invited you'd have no need to ask me the question this day. Her nearest friends call her Madame Alain, because that was the given name of her husband, the saints be good to him! and it helps distinguish her from the dowager. But for all that she is the lady you disdained to know—Madame la Marquise de Caron."

McVeigh stared at him moodily, even doubtfully. .

"You are not trying to play a practical joke, I reckon?" he said at last; and then without waiting for a reply, walked over to the office window, where he stood staring out, his hands in his pockets, his back to Delaven, who was eyeing

4

him calmly. Directly, he came back smiling; his moody fit all gone.

"And I was idiot enough to disdain that invitation?" he asked; "well, Fitz, I have repented. I am willing to do penance in any agreeable way we can conjure up, and to commence by calling tomorrow, if you can find a way."

Delaven found a way. Finding the way out of, or into difficulties was one of his strong points and one he especially delighted in, if it had a flavor of intrigue, and was to serve a friend. Since his mother's death in Paris, several years before, he had made his home in or about the city. He was without near relatives, but had quite a number of connections whose social standing was such that there were few doors he could not find keys to, or a password that was the equivalent. His own frank, ingenuous nature made him quite as many friends as his social and diplomatic connections; so that despite the fact of a not enormous income, and that he meant to belong to the professions some day, and that he was by no means a youth on matrimony bent—with all these drawbacks he was welcomed in a social way to most delightful circles, and when he remarked to the dowager that he would like to bring his friend, the Lieutenant, at an early day, she assured him they would be welcome.

She endeavored to make them so in her own characteristic way, when they called, twenty-four hour later, and they spent a delightful twenty minutes with her. She could not converse very freely with the American, because of the difficulties of his French and her English, but their laughter over mistakes really tended to better their acquaintance. He was conscious that her eyes were on him, even while she talked with Delaven, whose mother she had known. He would have been uncomfortable under such surveillance

but for the feeling that it was not entirely an unkindly regard, and he had hopes that the impression made was in his
favor.

Loris Dumaresque arrived as they were about to take their
departure, and Lieutenant McVeigh gathered from their
greeting that he was a daily visitor—that as god-son he was
acting as far as possible in the stead of a real son, and that
the dowager depended on him in many ways since his return
to Paris.

The American realized also that the artist would be called
a very handsome man by some people, and that his gaiety
and his self confidence would make him especially attractive
to women. He felt an impatience with women who liked
that sort of impudence. Delaven did not get a civil word
from him all the way home.

Madame la Marquise—Madame Alain—had not appeared
upon the scene at all.

CHAPTER V.

"But he is not at all bad, this American officer," insisted
the dowager; "such a great, manly fellow, with the deference
instinctive, and eyes that regard you well and kindly. Your
imagination has most certainly led you astray; it could not
be that with such a face, and such a mother, he could be the
—horrible! of that story."

"All the better for him," remarked her daughter-in-law.
"But I should not feel at ease with him. He must be some
relation, and I should shrink from all of the name."

"But, Madame McVeigh—so charming!"

"Oh, well; she only has the name by accident, that is, by
marriage."

The dowager regarded her with a smile of amusement.

"Shall you always regard marriage as merely an accident?" she asked. "Some day it will be presented to you in such a practical, advantageous way that you will cease to think it all chance."

"Advantageous?" and the Marquise raised her brows; "could we be more happy than we are?" The old face softened at the words and tone.

"But I shall not be always with you," she replied; and then—"

"Alain knew," said the girl, softly. "He said as a widow I could have liberty. I would need no guardian; I could look after all my affairs as young girls could not do. Each year I shall grow older—more competent."

"But there is one thing Alain did not foresee: that your many suitors would rob you of peace until you made choice of some particular one. These late days I have felt I should like the choice to be made while I am here to see."

"Maman! you are not ill?" and in a moment she was beside the couch.

"No; I think not; no, no, nothing to alarm you. I have only been thinking that together—both of us to plan and arrange—yet I need Loris daily. And if there should be only one of us, that remaining one would need some man's help all the more, and if it were you, who then would the man be? You perceive! It is wise to make plans for all possibilities."

"There are women who live alone."

"Not happy women," said the dowager in a tone, admitting of no contradiction; "the women who live alone from choice are cold and selfish; or have hurts to hide and are heart-sick of a world in which their illusions have been destroyed; or else they have never known companionship, and so never feel the lack of it. My child, I will not have you like any of these; you were made to enjoy life, and life to the young should mean—well, I am a sentimentalist. I married the one man who had all my affection. I approve of such marriages. If the man comes for whom you would care like that, I should welcome him."

"He will never come, Maman," and the smile of the Marquise someway drifted into a sigh. "I shall live and die the widow of Alain."

The dowager embraced her. "But for all that I do not approve," she protested. "Your reasons for not marrying do not convince me, and I promise my support to the most worthy who presents himself. Have you an ideal to which nothing human may reach?"

"For three years your son has seemed ideal to me," said the Marquise, after a moment's hesitation. The dowager regarded her attentively.

"He was?" she asked; "your regard for him does you credit; but, amber eyes, it is not for a man who has been dead a year that a woman blushes as you blush now."

"Oh!" began the Marquise, as if in protest; and then feeling that the color was becoming even more pronounced, she was silent.

The dowager smiled, well pleased at her cleverness.

"There was sure to be some one, some day," she said, nodding sagaciously; "when you want to talk of it I will listen, my Judithe. I could tell it in the tone of your voice as you sang or laughed; yes, there is nothing so wonderful in that," she explained, as the girl looked up, startled. "You have always been a creature of aims, serious, almost ponderous. Suddenly you emerge like sunshine from the shadows; you are all gaiety and sudden smiles; unconsciously you sing low songs of happiness; you suggest brightness

and hope; you have suddenly come into your long-delayed
girlhood. You give me affectionate glimpses of the woman
God meant you to be some day. It can only be a man who
works such a miracle in an ascetic of nineteen years. When
the lucky fellow gathers courage to speak, I shall be glad to
pass judgment on him."

The Marquise was silent. The light, humorous tone of
the dowager had disarmed her; yet she had of her own
accord, and influenced by some wild mood, told Dumaresque
all that was only guesswork to the friend beside her. How
could she have confessed it to him? She had wondered at
herself that she had dared, and after all it had been so entirely useless; it had not driven away the memory of the
man at Fontainbleau, even for one little instant.

Madame Blanc entered with some message for the dowager, and the question of marriage, also the more serious
one of love, were put aside for the time.

But Judithe was conscious that she was under a kindly
surveillance, and suspected that Dumaresque, also, was
given extra attention. Her confession of that unusual fascination had made them better comrades, and the dowager
was taking note that their tone was more frank, and their
attitude suggested some understanding. It was like a comedy for her to watch them, feeling so sure that their sentiments were very clear and that she could see the way it
would all end. Judithe would coquette with him awhile,
and then it would be all very well; and it would not be like a
stranger coming into the family.

The people who came close enough to see her often, realized that the journey back to Paris had not been beneficial
to the dowager. It had only been an experiment through
which she had been led to open her house, receive her
friends, introduce her daughter; but the little excitement

of that had vanished, and now that the routine of life was
to be followed, it oppressed her. The ghosts of other days
came so close—the days when Alain had been beside her.
At times she regretted Rome, but the physician forbade her
return there until autumn. She had fancied that a season
in the old house at Fontainbleau would serve as a restora-
tive to health—the house where Alain was born; but it was
a failure. Her days there were days of tears, and sad, far-
away memories. So to Paris she went with the assertion
that there alone, life was to be found. She meant to live
to the last minute of her life, and where so well as in the one
city inexhaustible?

"Maman is trying to frighten me into marriage," thought
the Marquise after their conversation; "she wants some
spectacular ceremony to enliven the house for a season, and
cure her ennui; Paris has been a disappointment, and Loris
is making himself necessary to her."

She was thinking of the matter, and of the impossibility
that she should ever marry Loris, when a box of flowers was
brought—one left by a messenger, who said nothing of
whence they came, and no name or card attached suggested
the sender.

"For Maman," decided the Marquise promptly.

But Madame Blanc thought not.

"You, Madame, are the Marquise."

"Oh, true! but the people who would send me flowers
would not be so certain their own names would not be forgotten. I have no old, tried, and silent friends to remember me so."

While she spoke she was lifting out the creamy and blush-
tinted roses; Maman should see them arranged in the prettiest vase, they must go up with the chocolate—she would
take it herself!

So she chattered while Madame Blanc arranged the tray. But suddenly the chatter ceased. The Marquise had lifted out the last of the roses, and under the fragrant screen lay the cause of the sudden silence.

It was a few sprays of dew-wet forget-me-nots! Her heart seemed to stop beating.

Forget-me-not! there was but one person who had any association in her mind with that flower. Did this have a meaning relating to him? or was it only chance?

She said nothing to Madame Blanc about the silent message in the bottom of the box.

All that day she moved as in a dream. At times she was oppressed by the terror of discovery, and again it was with a rebellious, delicious feeling of certainty that he had not forgotten! He had searched for her—found her! She meant to ignore him if they should meet; certainly she must do that! His assurance in daring to—yet—yes, she rather liked the daring—still——!

She remembered some one saying that impertinence gained more favors from women than respect, and he—yes, certainly he was impertinent; she must never recognize him, of course—never! Her cheek burned as she fancied what he must think of her—a girl who made friends with strangers in the park! Yet she was glad that since he had not let her forget, he also had been forced to remember.

She told herself all this, and much more; the task occupied so much of her time that she forgot to go asleep that night, and she saw the morning star shine out of the blue haze beyond the city, and it belonged to a dawn with a meaning entirely its own. Never before or after was a daybreak so beautiful. The sun wheeled royally into view through the atmosphere of her first veritable love romance.

CHAPTER VI.

Even the card of Lieutenant McVeigh could not annoy her that morning. He came with some message to the dowager from his mother. At any other time the sound of his name would have made a discord for her. The prejudices of Judithe were so decided, and so independent of all accepted social rules, that the dowager hoped when she did choose a husband he would prove a diplomat—they would need one in the family.

"Madame Blanc, will you receive the gentleman?" she asked. "Maman has not yet left her room, and I am engaged."

And for the second time the American made his exit from the Caron establishment without having seen the woman his friends raved about. Descending the steps he remembered the old saw that a third attempt carried a charm with it. He smiled, and the smile suggested that there would be a third attempt.

The Marquise looked at the card he left, and her smile had not so much that was pleasant in it.

"Maman, my conjecture was right," she remarked as she entered the room of the dowager; "your fine, manly American was really the youth of my Carolina story."

"Carolina story?" and the dowager looked bewildered for a moment; when one has reached the age of eighty years the memory fails for the things of today; only the affairs of long ago retain distinctness.

"Exactly; the man for whom Rhoda Larue was educated, and of whom you forbade me to speak—the man who bought her from Matthew Loring, of Loringwood, Carolina."

"You are certain?"

"Here is the name, Kenneth McVeigh. It is not likely there are two Kenneth McVeighs in the same region. How small the world is after all! I used to fancy the width of the ocean was as a barrier between two worlds, yet it has not prevented these people from crossing, and coming to our door!"

She sank into a seat, the card still in her hand.

"Judithe," said the dowager, after watching her moody face thoughtfully, "my child, I should be happier if you banished, so far as possible, that story from your memory. It will have a tendency to narrow your views. You will always have a prejudice against a class for the wrong done by an individual. Put it aside! It is a question outside of your life, outside of it always unless your sympathies persist in dragging you into such far-away abuses. We have the Paris poor, if you must think and do battle for the unfortunate. And as to the American, consider. He must have been very young, perhaps was influenced by older heads. He may not have realized—"

The Marquise smiled, but shook her head. "You are eloquent, Maman, but you do not convince me. He must be very handsome to have won you so completely in one interview. For me, I do not believe in his ignorance of the evil nor in his youthful innocence. I think of the women who for generations have been the victims of such innocence, and I should like to see your handsome young cadet suffer for his share of it!"

"Tah!" and the dowager put out her hand with a gesture

of protest and a tone of doubt in her voice. "You say so Judithe, but you could not see any one suffer, not even the criminal. You would come to his defense with some philosophical reason for the sin—some theory of pre-natal influence to account for his depravity. Collectively you condemn them; individually you would pardon every one rather than see them suffer—I mean, than stand by and actually see the suffering."

"I could not pardon that man," insisted the Marquise; "Ugh! I feel as if for him I could have the hand of Judithe as well as the name."

"And treat him a-la-Holofernes? My child, sometimes I dislike that name of Judithe for you; I do not want you to have a shadow of the character it suggests. I shall regret the name if it carries such dark influences with it. As for the man—forget him!"

"With all my heart, if he keeps out of my way," agreed the Marquise; "but if the old Jewish god of battles ever delivers him into my hands—!" She paused and drew a deep breath.

"Well?"

"Well—I should show him mercy such as the vaunted law-giver, the chosen of the Lord, the man of meekness, showed to the conquered Midianites—no more!" and her laugh had less of music in it than usual. "I instinctively hate the man, Kenneth McVeigh—Kenneth McVeigh!— even the name is abhorrent since the day I heard of that awful barter and sale. It seems strange, Maman, does it not, when I never saw him in my life—never expected to hear his name again—that it is to our house he has found his way in Paris; to our house, where an unknown woman abhors him. Ah!" and she flung the card from her. "You are right, Maman; I am too often conquered by my own moods and feelings. The American need be nothing to us."

The dowager was pleased when the subject was dropped. She had seen so many battles fought, in theory, by humanitarians who are alive to the injustice of the world. But her day was over for race questions and creeds. Judithe was inspiring in her sympathies, but the questions that breathe living flame for us at twenty years, have burned into dead ashes at eighty.

"Tah! I would rather she would marry and let me see her children," she grumbled to Madame Blanc; "if she does not, I trust her to your care when I am gone. She is different since we reached Paris—different, gayer, and less of the student."

"But no more in touch with society," remarked the attentive companion; "she accepts no invitations, and goes only to the galleries and theatres."

"Um!—pictured people, and artificial people! Both have a tendency to make her an idealist instead of a realist."

To Dumaresque she made the same remark, and suggested he should help find attractions for her in real life.

"She is too imaginative, and I do not want her to be of the romantic women; the craze for romance in life is what fills the columns of the journals with new scandals each month."

"Madame Judithe is safe from that sort of romance," declared her god-son. "Yet with her face and those glorious eyes one should allow her some flights in the land of the ideal. She suggests all old Italy at times, but she has never mentioned her family to me."

"Because it was a topic which both Alain and I forbade her, when she was younger, to discuss. Naturally, she has not a joyous temperament and memories of her childhood can only have an unhappy effect, which accounts for our decision of the matter. Her father died before she could re-

member him, and the mother, who was of Greek blood, not
long after. A relative who arranged affairs left the daughter penniless. At the little chateau Levigne she was of great
service to me when she was but sixteen. Madam Blanc,
who tried to reach me in time, declares the child saved my
life. It was a dog—a mad one. I was on the lawn when he
broke through the hedge, snapped Alain's mastiff, Ponto,
and came straight for me. I was paralyzed with terror; then,
just as he leaped at me, the child swung a heavy chair over
her head. Tah! She looked like a young tigress. The dog
was struck helpless, his back broken. The gardener came
and killed him, and Ponto, too, was killed, when he showed
that the bite had given him the poison. Ah, it was terrible,
that day. Then I wrote Alain and we decided she should
never leave us. I made over to her the income of the little
Lavigne estate, thus her education was carried on, and when
we went to Rome—well, Alain was not satisfied until he
could do even more for her."

The old lady helped herself to snuff and sighed. Her listener wondered if, after all, that death-bed marriage had been
entirely acceptable to the mother. Some suggestion of his
thought must have come to her, for she continued:

"Not that I disapproved, you must understand. No
daughter could be more devoted. I could not be without
her now. But I had a hope—a mother's foolish hope—that
perhaps it might be a love affair; that the marriage would
renew his interest in life and thus accomplish what the physicians could not do—save him."

"Good old Alain," said Dumaresque, with real feeling
in his tones. "He deserved to live and win her. I can
imagine no better fortune for a man."

"But it was an empty hope, and a sad wedding," continued the dowager, with a sigh. That was, to her, a day of

gloom, which to others is the one day to look forward to through girlhood and backward to from old age. Oh, yes; it is not so much to be wondered at that she is a creature of moods and ideals outlined on a background of shadow."

The voice of the Marquise sounded through the hall and up the stairs. She was singing, joying as a bird. The eyes of the two met, and Dumaresque laughed.

"Oh! and what is that but a mood, too?" demanded the dowager; "a mood that is pleasant, I grant you, and it has lasted longer than usual—ever since we came to Paris. I enjoy it, but I like to know the reason of things. I guess at it in this case; yet it eludes me."

Dumaresque raised his brows and smiled as one who invites further confidences. But he received instead a keen glance from the old eyes, and a question:

"Loris, who is the man?"

"What! You ask me?"

"There is no other to ask; you know all the men she has met; you are not a fool, and an artist's eye is trained to observe."

"It has not served me in this case, my god-mother."

"Which means you will not tell. I shall suspect it is yourself if you conspire to keep it from me."

"Pouf! When it is myself I shall be so eager to let it be known that no one will have time to ask a question."

"That is good," she said approvingly. "I must rest now. I have talked so long; but a word, Loris; she likes you, she trusts you, and that—well, that goes far."

And all the morning her assurance made for him hours of brightness. The stranger of Fontainbleau had drifted into the background, and should never have real place in their lives. She liked and trusted *him*; and that would go far.

He was happy in imagining the happiness that might be, forgetful of another lover, one among the poets, who avowed that the happiness of the future was the only real happiness of the world.

He was pleased that his god-mother had confided to him these little facts of family history. He remembered how intensely eager the dowager had been for Alain's marriage, years before, that there might be an heir; and he remembered, in part, the cause—her detestation of a female relative whose son would inherit the Marquisate should a son be born to her, and Alain die without children. He could see how eagerly the dowager would have consented to a marriage with even the poorest of poor relations if both the Marquisate and Alain might be saved by it.

Poor Alain! He remembered the story of why he had remained single; a story of love forbidden, and of a woman who entered a convent because, in the world, she could not live with her lover, and would not live with the man whose name she bore. It was an old story; she had died long ago, but Alain had remained faithful. It had been the one great passion he had known of, outside of a romance, and the finale of it was that the slight girlish protegee was mistress of his name and fortune, though her heart had never beat the faster for his glance.

And the Greek blood doubtless accounted for her readiness of speech in different tongues; they were so naturally linguists—the Greeks. He had met her first in Rome, and fancied her an Italian. Delaven had asked if she were not English; and now in the heart of France she appeared to him entirely Parisian.

A chameleon-like wife might have her disadvantages, he thought, as he walked away after the talk with his god-mother; yet she would not be so apt as others to bore one

with sameness. At nineteen she was charming; at twenty-
five she would be magnificent.

The streets were alive that morning with patriotic groups
discussing the victory of the French troops at Magenta.
The first telegrams were posted and crowds were gathered
about them.

Dumaresque passed through them with an unusually
preoccupied air. Then a tall man, leaning against a pillar
and viewing the crowd, bowed to him in such a way as to
arrest his attention. It was the American, of the smiling,
half sleepy eyes, and the firm mouth. The combination appealed to Dumaresque as an artist; also the shape of the
head, it was exceedingly good, strong; even his lounging attitude had the grace suggestive of strength. He remembered seeing somewhere the head of a young lion painted
with just those half closed, shadowy eyes. Lieutenant Mc-
Veigh was regarding him with something akin to their
watchfulness, the same slow gaze travelling from the feet
to the head as they approached each other; it was deliberate
as the measuring of an adversary, and its finale was a
smile.

"Glad to see a man," he remarked. "I have been listening
to the jabbering and screeches of the crowd until they seem
only manikins."

Dumaresque laughed. "You come by way of England,
I believe; do you prefer the various dialects of that land
of fog?"

"No, I do not; have a cigar?" Dumaresque accepted the
offer. McVeigh himself lighted one and continued:

"Their stuffiness lacks the picturesque qualities possessed
by even the poorest of France, and then they bore one with
their wranglings for six-pences, from Parliament down to
peasant. They are always at it in Brittania the gem of the

ocean, wrangling over six-pences, and half-pennies and can-
dle ends."

"You are finding flaws in the people who call you cousin,"
remarked the artist.

"Yes, I know they do,' said the other, between puffs.
"But I can't imagine a real American helping them in their
claims for relationship. Our history gives us no cause for
such kindly remembrances."

"Unless on the principle that one has a kindly regard for
a man after fighting with him and not coming out second
best," remarked Dumaresque. "I have an errand in the next
street; will you come?"

McVeigh assented. They stalked along, chattering and
enjoying their cigars until they reached a florists, where Dumaresque produced a memorandum and read off a list of
blossoms and greenery to be delivered by a certain date.

"An affair for the hospitals to be held in the home of
Madame Dulac, wife of General Dulac," he explained;
"it is to be all very novel, a bazaar and a ball. Madame is
an old friend of my god-mother, the dowager Marquise de
Caron, whom you have met."

McVeigh assented and showed interest.

"We have almost persuaded Madame Alain, her daughter,
to preside over one of the booths. Ah! It will be a place
to empty one's pockets; you must come."

"Not sure about invitations," confessed McVeigh, frankly. "It is a very exclusive affair, I believe, and a foreigner
will be such a distinctive outsider at such gatherings."

"We will undertake to prevent that," promised Dumaresque, "and in the interests of charity you will find both
dames and demoiselles wonderfully gracious to even a lonely, unattached man. If you dance you can win your own
place."

8

"Oh, yes; we all dance in our country; some of us poorly, perhaps; still, we dance."

"Good! You must come. I am assisting, after a fashion, in planning the decorations, and I promise to find you some one who is charming, and who speaks your language delightfully."

There was some further chat. McVeigh promised he would attend unless his mother had made conflicting engagements. Dumaresque informed him it was to be a fancy dress affair; uniforms would be just the thing; and he parted with the American much more pleased with him than in the salons where they had met heretofore.

Kenneth McVeigh sauntered along the avenue, tall, careless, reposeful. His expression was one of content, and he smiled as he silently blessed Loris Dumaresque, who had done him excellent service without knowing it—had found a method by which he would try the charm of the third attempt to see the handsome girl who had passed them that day in the carriage.

He entered the hotel late that night. Paris, in an unofficial way, was celebrating the victory of Magenta by shouting around bon-fires, laughing under banners, forming delegations no one remembered, and making addresses no one listened to.

Late though it was, Mrs. McVeigh had not retired. From a window she was looking out on the city, where sleep seemed forgotten, and her beautiful eyes had a seriousness contrasting strangely with the joyous celebrations of victory she had been witnessing.

"What is it, mother?" he asked, in the soft, mellow tones of the South, irresistible in their caressing qualities. The mother put out her hand and clasped his without speaking.

"Homesick?" he ventured, trying to see her face as he

drew a chair closer; "longing for that twelve-year-old baby of yours? Evilena certainly would enjoy the hubbub."

"No, Kenneth," she said at last; "it is not that. But I have been watching the enthusiasm of these people over a victory they have helped win for Italy's freedom—not their own. We have questions just as vital in our country; some day they must be settled in the same way; there seems no doubt of it—and then—"

"Then we will go out, have our little pass at each other, and come back and go on hoeing our corn, just as father did in the Mexican campaign," he said with an attempt at lightness; but she shook her head.

"Many a soldier left the corn fields who never came back to them."

"Why, mother, what is it, dear? You've been crying, crying here all alone over one war that is nothing to us, and another that may never happen; come! come!" He put his arm about her as if she were a child to be petted. Her head sank on his shoulder, though she still looked away from him, out into the brilliantly lighted street.

"It was not the—the political justice or injustice of the wars," she confessed after a little; "it was not of that I was thinking. But a woman screamed out there on the street. They—the people—had just told her the returns of the battle, and her son was among the killed—poor woman! Her only son, Kenneth, and—"

"Yes, dear, I understand." He drew her closer and lifting her head from her lap, placed it on his shoulder. She uttered a tremulous little sigh of content. And then, with his arms about her, the mother and son looked out on Paris after a victory, each thinking of their own home, their own capital cities, and their own vague dread of battles to be in the future.

CHAPTER VII.

As morning after morning passed without the arrival of other mysterious boxes of flowers or of significant messages, the Marquise began to watch Loris Dumaresque more than was usual with her. He was the only one who knew; had he, educated by some spirit of jest, been the sender of the blossoms?

And inconsistent as it may appear when one remembers her avowed fear of discovery, yet from the moment that suspicion entered her mind the charm was gone from the blossoms and the days to follow, and she felt for the first time a resentment towards Monsieur Incognito.

Her reason told her this was an inevitable consequence, through resentment forgetfulness would come.

But her heart told her—?

Her presence at the charitable fete held by Madame la General at the Hotel Dulac was her first response, in a social way to the invitations of her Parisian acquaintances. A charity one might support without in any way committing oneself to further social plunges. She expected to feel shy and strange; she expected to be bored. But since Maman wished it so much—!

There is nothing so likely to banish shyness as success. The young Marquise could not but be conscious that she attracted attention, and that the most popular women of the court who had been pleased to show their patronage by attendance, did not in the least eclipse her own less pre-

tentious self. People beseiged Madame Dulac for intro-
ductions, and to her own surprise the debutante found herself enjoying all the gay nothings, the jests, the bright sentences tossed about her and forming a foundation for compliments delicately veiled, and the flattering by word or
glance that was as the breath of life to those people of the
world.

She was dressed in white of medieval cut. Heavy white
silk cord was knotted about the slender waist and touched
the embroidered hem. The square neck had also the simple finish of cord and above it was the one bit of color; a
flat necklace of etruscan gold fitted closely about the white
throat, holding alternate rubies and pearls in their curiously
wrought settings. On one arm was a bracelet of the same
design; and the linked fillet above her dark hair gleamed,
also, with the red of rubies.

It was the age of tarletan and tinsel, of delicate zephyrs
and extremes in butterfly effects. Hoop-skirts were persisted in, despite the protests of art and reason; so, the
serenity of this dress, fitting close as a habit, and falling in
soft straight folds with a sculpturesque effect, and with the
brown-eyed Italian face above it, created a sensation.

Dumaresque watched her graciously accepting homage
as a matter of course, and smiled, thinking of his prophecy
that she would be magnificent at twenty-five;—she was so
already.

Some women near him commented on the simplicity of
her attire.

"Oh, that is without doubt the taste of the dowager; failing to influence the politics of the country she consoled
herself with an attempt to make a revolution in the fashions
of the age."

"And is this sensation to illustrate her ideas?" asked another. "She has rather a good manner—the girl—but the dress is a trifle theatrical, suggestive of the pages of tragedies and martyred virgins."

"Suggestive of the girl Cleopatra before she realized her power," thought the artist as he passed on. He knew that just those little remarks stamped her success a certainty, and was pleased accordingly. The dowager had expressed her opinion that Judithe would bury herself in studies if left to herself, perhaps even go back to the convent. He fancied a few such hours of adulation as this would change the ideas of any girl of nineteen as to the desirability of convents.

He noticed that the floral bower over which she presided had little left now but the ferns and green things; she had been adding money to the hospital fund. Once he noticed the blossoms left in charge of her aides while she entered the hall room on the arm of the most distinguished official present, and later, on that of one of the dowager's oldest friends. She talked with, and sold roses to the younger courtiers at exorbitant prices, but it was only the men of years and honors whom she walked beside.

Madame Dulac and Dumaresque exchanged glances of approval; as a possible general in the social field of the future, she had commenced with the tactics of absolute genius. Dumaresque wondered if she realized her own cleverness, or if it was because she honestly liked best to talk or listen to the men of years, experience, and undoubted honors.

Mrs. McVeigh was there, radiant as Aurore and with eyes so bright one would not fancy them bathed in tears so lately, or the smooth brow as containing a single anxious motherly thought. But the Marquise having heard that story of the son, wondered as she looked at her if the handsome mother had not many an anxious thought the world never suspected.

She was laughing frankly to the Marquise over the future just read in her palm by a picturesque Egyptian, who was one of the novelties added to Madame Dulac's list for the night.

Nothing less than an adoring husband had been promised her, and with the exception of a few shadowed years, not a cloud larger than the hand of a man was to cross the sky of her destiny.

"I am wishing Kenneth had come—my son, you know. Something has detained him. I certainly would have liked him to hear that promise of a step-father. Our Southern men are not devoid of jealousy—even of their mothers."

Then she passed on, a glory of azure and silver, and the Marquise felt a sense of satisfaction that the son had not come; the prejudice she felt against that unabashed American would make his presence the one black cloud across the evening.

While she was thinking of him the party about her separated, and she took advantage of a moment alone to slip unperceived into the alcove back of the evergreens. It seemed the one nook unappropriated by the glittering masses of people whose voices, near and far, suggested the murmur of bees to her as she viewed it from her shadowy retreat, while covered from sight herself.

The moonlight was shining through the window of the little alcove screened by the tall palms. The music of a tender waltz movement drifted softly across to her and made perfect her little retreat. She was conscious that it had all been wonderfully and unexpectedly perfect; the success, the adulation, had given her a new definite faith in herself. How Maman would have enjoyed it. Maman, who would want every little detail of the pleasant things said and done. She wondered if it was yet too early to depart, she might reach home before the dowager slept, and tell her all the glories of it.

So thinking, she turned to enter again the glare of light to find Madame Dulac, or Madame Blanc, who had accompanied her, to tell them.

But another hand pushed aside the curtain of silk and the drooping fronds of gigantic fern. Looking up she saw a tall, young man, wearing a dark blue uniform, who bowed with grace, and stood aside that she might pass if she chose. He showed no recognition, and there was the pause of an instant. She could feel the color leave her face. Then, with an effort, she raised her eyes, and tried to speak carelessly, but the voice was little more than a whisper, in which she said:

"You!"

His face brightened and grew warm. The tone itself told more than she knew; a man would be stupid who could not read it, and this one, though youthful, did not look stupid.

"Madame Unknown," he murmured, in the voice she had not been able to forget, "I am not so lost here as at Fontainbleau. May I ask some one to present me to your notice?"

At that she smiled, and the smile was contagious.

"You may not," she replied frankly, recovering herself, and assuming a tone of lightness to conquer the fluttering in her throat. "The list of names I have had to remember this evening is most formidable, another one would make the last feather here," and she tapped her forehead significantly. "I was just about to flee from it all when——"

She hesitated and looked about her in an uncertain way.

He at once placed a chair for her. She allowed her hand to rest on the back of it as if undecided.

"You will not be so unkind?" he said; and his words held a plea. She answered it by seating herself.

"Well?"

At the interrogation he smiled.

"Will you not allow me, Madame, to introduce myself?"

"But, Monsieur Incognito, consider; I have remembered you best because you have not done so; is was a novelty. But all those people whose names were spoken to me this evening—pouf! and she blew a feathery spray of fern from her palms, "they have all drifted into oblivion like that. Do you wish, then, to be presented and—to follow them?"

"I refuse to follow them there—from you."

His tones were so low, so even, so ardent, that she looked startled and drew her breath quickly.

"You are bold, Monsieur," and though she strove to speak haughtily she was too much of a girl to be severe when her eyes met his.

"Why not?" he asked, growing bolder as she grew more timid. "You grant me one moment out of your life; then you mean to close the gates against me—if you can. In that brief time I must condense all that another man should take months to say to you. I have been speaking to you daily, however, for six weeks and—"

"Monsieur! Six weeks?"

"Every day," he assented, smiling down at her. "Of course you did not hear me. I was very confidential about it. I even tried to stop it entirely when I was allowed to believe that Mademoiselle was Madame."

"But it is quite true—she is Madame."

"Certainly; yet you let me think—well, I forgive you for it now, since I have found you again."

"Monsieur!"—she half arose.

"Will Mademoiselle have her fortune told?" asked a voice beside them, and the beringed Egyptian pushed aside the palms, "or Monsieur, perhaps?"

"Both of us," he assented with eagerness; that is, if Mademoiselle chooses." He dropped two pieces of gold in the beaded purse held out. "Come," he half whispered to the Marquise, "let me see if oblivion is really the doom fate reads against me."

She half put out her hand, thinking that after all it was only a part of the games of the night—the little amusements with which purses were filled for charity; then some sudden after thought made her draw it back.

"You fear the decision?" he asked.

She did not fear the decision he meant, but she did fear—

"No, Monsieur, I am not afraid. Oh, yes; she may read my palm, it is all a jest, of course."

The Egyptian held the man's hand at which she had not yet glanced. She took the hand of the Marquise.

"Pardon, Madame, it is no jest, it is a science," she said briefly, and holding their hands, glanced from one to the other.

"Firm hands, strong hands, both," she said, and then bent over that of the Marquise; as she did so the expression of casual interest faded from her face; she slowly lifted her head and met the gaze of the owner.

"Well, well? Am I to commit murders?" she asked; but her smile was an uneasy one; the gaze of the Egyptian made her shrink.

"Not with your own hand," said the woman, slowly studying the well-marked palm; "but you will live for awhile surrounded by death and danger. You will hate, and suffer for the hate you feel. You will love, and die for the love you will not take—you—"

But the Marquise drew her hand away petulantly.

"Oh! I am to die of love, then?—I!" and her light laugh was disdainful. "That is quite enough of the fates for one evening;" she regarded the pink palm doubtfully. "See, Monsieur, it does not look so terrible; yet it contains all those horrors."

"Naturally it would not contain them," said the Egyptian. "You will force yourself to meet what you call the horrors. You will sacrifice yourself. You will meet the worst as the women of '93 ascended the guillotine—laughing."

"Ah, what pictures! Monsieur, I wish you a better fortune."

"Than to die of love?" he asked, and met her eyes; "that were easier than to live without it."

"Chut!—you speak like the cavalier of a romance."

"I feel like one," he confessed, "and it rests on your mercy whether the romance has a happy ending.

She flashed one admonishing glance at him and towards the woman who bent over his hand.

"Oh, she does not comprehend the English," he assured her; "and if she does she will only hear the echo of what she reads in my hand."

"Proceed," said the Marquise to the Egyptian, "we wait to hear the list of Monsieur's romances."

"You will live by the sword, but not die by the sword," said the woman. "You will have one great passion in your life. Twice the woman will come in your path. The first time you will cross the seas to her, the second time she comes to you—and—ah!—"

She reached again for the hand of the Marquise and compared them. The two young people looked, not at her, but at each other.

In the eyes of the Marquise was a certain petulant rebellion, and in his the appealing, the assuring, the ardent gaze that met and answered her.

"It is peculiar—this," continued the woman. "I have never seen anything like it before; the same mark, the same, Mademoiselle, Monsieur; you will each know tragedies in your experience, and the lives are linked together."

"No!"—and again the Marquise drew her hand away. "It is no longer amusing," she remarked in English, "when those people think it their duty to pair couples off like animals in the ark."

Her face had flushed, though she tried to look indifferent. The Egyptian had stepped back and was regarding her curiously.

"Do not cross the seas, Mademoiselle; all of content will be left behind you."

"Wait," and the Monsieur Incognito put out his hand. "You call the lady 'Mademoiselle,' but your guess has not been good;" and he pointed to a plain ring on the hand of the Marquise.

"I call her Mademoiselle because she never has been a wife, and—she never will be a wife. There are marriages without wedding rings, and there are wedding rings without marriages; pardon!—" and passing between the ferns and palms she was gone.

"That is true!" half whispered the Marquise, looking up at him; "her words almost frighten me."

"They need not," and the caress in his eyes made her drop her own; "all your world of Paris knows the romance of your marriage. You are more of a celebrity than you may imagine; my knowledge of that made me fear to approach you here."

"The fear did not last long," and she laughed, the coquetry of the sex again uppermost. "For how many seconds did you tremble on the threshold?"

"Long enough to avoid any friends who had planned to present me."

"And why?"

"Lest it might offend to have the person thrust on you whom you would not know among less ceremonious surroundings."

"Yet you came alone?"

"I could not help that, I *had* to see you, even though you refused to recognize me; I had to see you. Did I not prophecy there in the wood that we should meet again? Even the flowers you gave me I—"

"Monsieur, no more!" and she rose from the chair with a certain decision. "It was a thoughtless, childish farce played there at Fontainbleau. But—it is over. I—I have felt humiliated by that episode, Monsieur. Young ladies in France do not converse with strangers. Pray go back to England and forget that you found one so indiscreet—oh! I know what you would say, Monsieur," as he was about to speak. "I know many of these ladies of the court would only laugh over such an episode—it would be but a part of their amusements for the day; but I, I do not belong to the court or their fashions. I am only ashamed, and ask that you forget it. I would not want any one to think—I mean that I—"

She had commenced so bravely with her wise, firm little speech, but at the finale she wavered and broke down miserably.

"Don't!"—he broke in as a tear fell on the fan she held;

"you make me feel like a brute who has persecuted you; don't cry. Come here to the window; listen to me. I—I loved you that first day; you just looked at me, spoke to me and it was all over with me. I can't undo it. I can go away, and I *will*, rather than make you unhappy; but I can't forget you. I have never forgotten you for an hour. That was why. Oh, I know it is the wildest, maddest, most unpardonable thing I am saying to you. Your friends would want to call me out and shoot me for it, and I shall be happy to give them the chance," he added, grimly. "But don't, for Heaven's sake, think that my memory of you would be less than respectful. Why, I—I adore you. I am telling it to you like a fool, but I only ask you to not laugh until I am out of hearing. I—will go now—and do not even ask your forgiveness, because—well I can't honestly say I am sorry."

Sorry! She thought of those days when she had wakened to a new world because his eyes and his voice haunted her; she heard him acknowledge the same power, and he spoke of forgiveness as though convicted of a fault. Well, she had not been able to prevent the same fault, so, how dared she blame him? He need not know, of course, how well she had remembered; yet she might surely be a little kind for all that.

"Monsieur Incognito!"

Her voice had an imperious tone; she remembered she must not be too kind. He was already among the palms, in the full light of the salon, and he was boy enough for all the color to leave his face as he heard the low command. She had heard him declare his devotion, yet she had recalled him.

"Madame," he said, and stood stubbornly the width of the alcove from her, though he was conscious of all tender words rushing to his lips. She was so adorable; a woman in mentality, but the veriest girl as to the emotions his words had awakened.

"Monsieur," she said, without looking at him, "I do not truly believe you meant to offend me; therefore I have nothing to forgive."

"You angel!" he half whispered, but she heard him.

"No, I am not that," and she flashed a quick glance at him, "only I think I comprehend you, and to comprehend is to forgive, is it not? I—I cannot listen to the—affection you speak of. Love and marriage are not for me. Did not the Egyptian say it? Yes; that was quite true. But I can shake hands in good-bye, Monsieur Incognito. Your English people always do that, eh? Well, so will I."

She held out her hand; he took it in both his own and his lips touched it.

"No! no!" she said softly, and shook her head; "that is not an English custom." He lifted his head and looked at her.

"Why do you call me English?" he asked, and she smiled, glad to break that tenseness of feeling by some commonplace.

"It was very simple, Monsieur; first it was the make of your hat, I read the name of the maker in the crown that day in the park; then you spoke English; you said you had just arrived from England; and the English are so certain to get lost unless they go in groups—therefore!"

She had enumerated all those reasons on her white fingers. She glanced at him, with an adorable smile as a finale, so confident she had proven her case.

"And you French have no fondness for the English people," he said slowly, looking at her. "I wear an American uniform tonight; suppose I am an American? I am tempted to disobey and tell you who I am, in hopes you will not send me into exile quite so soon."

"No, no, *no*!" she breathed hurriedly. "You must go; and you must remain Monsieur Incognito; thus it will be only a comedy, a morsel of romance. But if I knew you well—ah! I do not know what it would be then. I am afraid to think. Yes, I confess it, Monsieur, you make me afraid. I tell myself you are a foreign ogre, yet when you speak to me—ah!"

She put out her hands as he came close. But he knelt at her feet, kissing her hands, her wrists, the folds of her dress, then lifted his face glowing, ardent, to her own.

"I shall make you love me some day," he whispered; "not now, perhaps, but some day."

She stared at him without a word. She had received proposals of marriage, dignified, ceremonious affairs submitted to her by the dowager, but from this stranger came the first avowal of love she had ever listened to. A stranger; yet he held her hand; she felt herself drawn towards him by a force she could not combat. Her other arm was over the back of a chair, slowly she lifted it, then he felt her hand touch his hair and the touch was a caress.

"My queen!"

"Co—now," she said so lowly it was almost a whisper. He arose, pressed her hand to his lips and turned away, when a woman's voice spoke among the palms:

"Did you say in this corner, Madame? I have not found him; Kenneth!"

"It is my mother," he said softly, and was about to draw back the alcove draperies when the Marquise took a step towards him, staring strangely into his face.

"*Your Mother*!" and her tones expressed only doubt and

dread. "No, no! Why, I—I know the voice; it is Madame McVeigh; she called Kenneth, her son—"

He smiled an affirmative.

"Yes; you will forgive me for having my name spoken to you after all? But there seems to be no help for it. So you see I am not English despite the hat, and my name is Kenneth McVeigh."

His smile changed to quick concern as he noticed the strange look on her face, and the swaying movement towards the chair. He put out his hand, but she threw herself back from him with a shuddering movement of repulsion.

And a moment later the palms parted beside Mrs. McVeigh, and she was startled at sight of her son's face.

"Kenneth! Why, what is wrong?"

"A lady has fainted there in the alcove," he said, in a voice which sounded strange to her; "will you go to her?"

"Fainted? Why, Kenneth!—"

"Yes; I think it is the Marquise de Caron."

CHAPTER VIII.

The dowager was delighted to find that the one evening of complete social success had changed her daughter-in-law into a woman of society. It had modified her prejudices. She accepted invitations without her former protests, and was only careful that the people whom she visited should be of the most distinguished.

Dumaresque watched her with interest. There seemed much of deliberation back of every move she made. The men of mark were the only ones to whom she gave encouragement, and she found several so responsive that there was

6

no doubt, now, as to whether she was awake to her own power—more, she had a mind to use it. She was spoken of as one of the beauties of the day.

The McVeighs had gone to Italy, the mother to visit a relative, the son to view the late battle fields on the other side of the Pyrences and acquaint himself with military matters wherever he found them.

He had called on the Marquise the day following the fete at the Hotel Dulac. She had quite recovered her slight indisposition of the preceding evening, and there had been no hesitation about receiving him. She was alone, and she met him with the fine, cool, gracious manner reserved for the people who were of no importance in her life.

Looking at her, listening to her, he could scarcely believe this could be the girl who had provoked him into a declaration of love less than a day ago, and in whose eyes he had surprised a fervor responding to his own. She called him Lieutenant McVeigh, with an utter disregard of the fact that she had ever called him anything else.

When in sheer desperation he referred to their first meeting, she listened with a chill little smile.

"Yes," she agreed; "Fontainbleau was beautiful in the spring time. Maman was especially fond of it. She, herself, had been telling a friend lately of the very unconventional meeting under the bushes of the Mademoiselle and Monsieur Incognito, and he—the friend—had thought it delightfully amusing, good enough for the thread of a comedy."

Then she sent some kindly message to Mrs. McVeigh, but refused to see the wonder—the actual pain—in the eyes where before she had remembered those half slumberous smiles, or that brief space of passionate pleading. He interrupted some cool remark by rising.

"It is scarcely worth while—all this," he said, abruptly. "Had you closed your doors against me after last night I should have understood—I should have gone away adoring you just the same. But to open them, to receive me, and then—"

His voice trembled in spite of himself. All at once he appeared so much more boyish than ever before—so help-less in a sort of misery he could not account for, she turned away her head.

"With the ocean between us my love could not have hurt you. You might have let me keep that." He had recovered control of his voice and his eyes swept over her from head to foot like blue lightning. "I bid you good-day, Madame."

She made an inclination of the head, but did not speak. She had reached the limit of her self control. His words, *"You might have let me keep that,"* were an accusation she dared not discuss.

When the door closed behind him she could see nothing, for the blur of tears in her eyes. Madame La Marquise received no other callers that day.

In the days following she compared him with the cour-tiers, the diplomats, the very clever men whom she met, and told herself he was only a boy—a cadet of twenty-two. Why should she remember his words, or forget for one instant that infamy with which his name was connected?

"He goes on his knees to me only because he has grown weary of the slave-women of the plantations," she told her-self in deepest disgust. Sometimes she would look curiously at the hands once covered by his kisses. And once she threw a withered bunch of forget-me-nots from her window, at night, and crept down at daybreak next morning and found it, and took it back to her room.

It looked as though the boy was holding his own despite the diplomats.

When she saw him again it was at an auction of articles donated for a charity under the patronage of the Empress, and open to the public. Cotton stuffs justled my lady's satins, and the half-world stared at short range into the faces whose owners claimed coronets.

Many leading artists had donated sketches of their more pretentious work. It was to that department the Marquise made her way, and entering the gallery by a side door, found that the crowd had separated her from the Countess Biron and the rest of their party.

Knowing that sooner or later they would find her there, she halted, examining some choice bits of color near the door. A daintily dressed woman, who looked strangely familiar, was standing near with apparently the same intent. But she stood so still; and the poise of her head betrayed that she was listening to something. The something was a group of men back of them, where the black and white sketches were on exhibition. The corridor was not wide, and their conversation was in English and not difficult to understand if one gave attention. The Marquise noted that Dumaresque was among them, and they stood before his donation of sketches, of which the principal one was a little study of the octoroon dancer, Kora.

Then in a flash she understood who the person was who listened. She was the original of the picture, drawn there no doubt by a sort of vanity to hear the artistic praise, or personal comment. But a swift glance showed her it had been a mistake; the dark brows were frowning, the full lip was bitten nervously, and the small ungloved hand was clenched.

The men were laughing carelessly over some argument,

not noticing that they had a listener; the people moving along the corridor, single and in groups, hid the two who remained stationary, and whose backs were towards them. It was most embarrassing, and the Marquise was about to move away when she heard a voice there was no mistaking —the voice she had not been able to forget.

"No, I don't agree with you;" he was saying, "and you would not find half so much to admire in the work if the subject were some old plantation mammy equally well painted. Come over and see them where they grow. After that you will not be making celebrities of them."

"If they grow many like that I am most willing, Monsieur."

"I, too. When do we start? I can fancy no land so well worth a visit but that of Mohammed."

The first speaker uttered an exclamation of annoyance, but the others laughed.

"Oh, we have seen other men of your land here," remarked Dumaresque. "They are not all so discreet as yourself. We have learned that they do not usually build high walls between themselves and pretty slaves."

"You are right," agreed the American. "Sorry I can't contradict you. But these gorgeous Koras and Phrynes remind me of a wild blossom in our country; it is exquisite in form, beautiful to the eye, but poison if touched to the lips. It is called the yellow jasmine."

"No doubt you are right," remarked one of the men as Kora dropped her veil over her face. "You are at all events poetical."

"And the reason of their depravity?"

"The fact that they are the outgrowth of the worst passions of both races—at least so I have heard it said by men who make more of a study of such questions that I."

A party of people moved between the two women and
the speakers. The Marquise heard Kora draw a sobbing
breath. She hesitated an instant, her own eyes flashing, her
cheeks burning. *He* to sit in judgment on others—he!"

Then she laid her hand on the wrist of Kora.

"Come with me," she said, softly, in English, and the
girl with one glance of tear-wet eyes, obeyed.

The Marquise opened the door beside her, a few steps
further and another door led into an ante-room belonging
to a portion of the building closed for repairs.

"Why do you weep?" she asked briefly, but the kindly
clasp of her wrist told that the questioner was not without
sympathy, and the girl strove to compose herself while staring at the other in amazement.

"You—I have seen you—I remember you," she said,
wonderingly, "the Marquise de Caron!"

"Yes;" the face of the Marquise flushed, "and you are
the dancer—Kora. Why did you weep at their words?"

"Since you know who I am, Madame, I need not hesitate
to tell you more," she said, though she *did* hesitate, and
looked up, deprecatingly, to the Marquise, who stood a few
paces away leaning against the window.

There was only one chair in the room. Kora perceived
for the first time that it had been given to her while the
Marquise stood. She arose to her feet, and with a deference
that lent a subtile grace to her expression, offered it to her
questioner.

"No; resume your seat;" the command was a trifle imperious, but it was softened the next instant by the smile
with which she said: "A dear old lady taught me that to
the burdened horse we should always give the right of way.
We must make easier the way of those who bear sorrows.
You have the sorrow today—what is it?"

"I am not sure that you will understand, Madame," and the girl's velvety black eyes lifted and then sought the floor again. "But you, perhaps, heard what they said out there, and the man I—I—well, he was there."

The lips of the Marquise grew a trifle rigid, but Kora was too much engaged with her own emotion to perceive it.

"I suppose I shouldn't speak of him to a—a lady who can't understand people who live in a different sort of world. But you mean to be kind, and I suppose have some reason for asking?" and she glanced at the lady in the window. "So—"

The Marquise looked at her carefully; yes, the girl was undeniably handsome; a medium sized, well-turned figure, small hands and feet, graceful in movement, velvety oriental eyes, and the deep cream complexion over which the artists had raved. She had the manner of one well trained, but was strangely diffident before this lady of the other world. The Marquise drew a deep breath as she realized how attractive she could be to a man who cared.

"You are a fool," she said, harshly, "to care for a man who speaks so of your people."

"Oh, Madame!" and the graceful form drooped helplessly. "I knew you could never understand. But if folks only loved where it was wise to love, all the trouble of the world would be ended."

The hand of the Marquise went to her throat for an instant.

"And then it is true, all they said there," continued Kora; "that is why—why I had let you see me cry; what he said is true—and I—I belong in his country where the yellow jasmine grows. There are times when I never stop to think —weeks when I am satisfied that I have money and a fine apartment. Then, all at once, in a minute like this, I see that it does not weigh down the one drop of black blood in my hand there. Sometimes I would sell my soul to wipe it out, and I can't! I can't!"

Her emotions were again overwhelming her. The Marquise watched her clench the shapely hands with their tapering fingers and many rings, the pretty graceful bit of human furniture in an establishment for such as *he*!

"An oriental prince was entertained by the Empress last week," she remarked, abruptly. "His mother was a black woman, yours was not."

"I know; I try to understand it—all the difference that is made. I can't do it; I have not the brain. I can only"— and she smiled bitterly—"only learn to dance a little, and you don't need brain for that. My God! How can they expect us to have brain when our mothers and grandmothers had to live under laws forbidding a slave to dispute any command of a white man? Madame, ladies like you—ladies of France—could not understand. I could not tell you. Sometimes I think money is all that can help you in this world. But even money can't kill the poison he spoke of. We might be free for generations but the curse would stay on us, because away back in the past our people had been slaves."

"So have the ancestors of those men you listened to," said the Marquise, and the girl looked at her wonderingly.

"*They*! Why, Madame!"

"It is quite true. Everyone of them is the descendant of slaves of the past. Every ancient race was at some time the slaves of some stronger nation. Many of the masters of to-day are the descendants of people who were bought and sold with the land for hundreds of years. Think of that when they taunt you with slavery!"

"Oh! Madame!"

"And remember that every king and queen of Egypt for centuries, every one told of in their bibles and histories, would look black beside the woman who was your mother! Chut! do not look so startled! The Caucassian of today is now believed by men of science to be only a bleached negro. To be sure, it has taken thousands of years, and the ice-fields and cave dwellings of the North to do the bleaching. But man came originally from the Orient, the very womb of the earth from which only creatures of color come forth."

"You!—a white lady! a noble! say this to comfort me; why?" asked the girl. She had risen again and stood back of the chair. She looked half frightened.

"I say it because, if you study such questions earnestly, you will perceive how the opinion of those self-crowned judges will dwindle; they will no longer loom above you because of your race. My child, you are as royal as they by nature. It is the cultivation, the training, the intellect built up through generations, by which they are your superiors today. If your own life is commendable you need not be ashamed because of your race."

Kora turned her head away, fingering the rings on her pretty hands.

"You—it is no use trying to make a lady like you understand," she muttered, "but you know who I am, and it is too late now!"

She attempted to speak with the nonchalance customary to her, but the entire interview, added to the conversation in the corridor, had touched depths seldom stirred, and never before appealed to by a woman. What other woman would have dared question her like that? And it was not that she had been awed by the rank and majesty in which this Marquise moved; she, Kora—who had laughed in the face of a Princess whose betrothed was seen in Kora's carriage! No; it was not the rank, it was the gentle, yet slightly imperious womanliness, back of which could be felt a fund of sympathy new and strange to her; it appealed to her as the reasoning of a man would appeal; and man was the only compelling force hitherto acknowledged by Kora.

The Marquise looked at her thoughtfully, but did not speak. She was too much of a girl herself to understand entirely the nature before her or its temptations. They looked, really, about the same age, yet for all the mentality of the Marquise, she knew Kora was right—the world of emotions that was an open book to the bewitching octoroon was an unknown world to her.

"The things I do not understand I will not presume to judge," she said, at last, very gently; "but is there no one anywhere in this world whose affection for you would be strong enough to help you live away from these people who speak of you as those men spoke, yet who are themselves accountable for the faults over which they laugh together."

"Oh, what you have said has turned me against that Trouvelot—that dandy!" she said, with a certain vehemence. "He is only a Count of yesterday, after all; I'll remember that! Still; it is all the habit of life, Madame, and I never new any other. Look here; when I was twelve I was told by an old woman to be careful of my hands, of my good looks every way, for if I was handsome as my mother, I would never need to do housework; that was the beginning! Well!" and she smiled bitterly, "I have not had to do it, but it was through no planning of theirs."

"And your mother?"

"Dead; and my father, too. He was her master."

"It is that spendthrift—Trouvelot, you care for?"

"Not this minute," confessed the girl; "but," and she
shrugged her shoulders, "I probably shall tomorrow! I
know myself well enough for that; and I won't lie—to you!
You saw how he could make me cry? It is only the man
we care for who can hurt us."

The Marquise did not reply; she was staring out of the
window. Kora, watching her, did not know if she heard.
She had heard and was angry with herself that her heart
grew lighter when she heard the name of Kora's lover.

"I—I will not intrude longer, Madame," said the girl at
last. "What you've said will make me think more. I
never heard of what you've told me today. I wish there
were women in America like you; oh, I wish there were!
There are good white ladies there, of course, but they don't
teach the slaves to think; they only tell them to have faith!
They teach them from their bible; and all I could ever remember of it was: 'Servants, obey your masters;' and I
hated it. So you see, Madame, it is too late for me; I don't
know any other life; I—"

"I will help you to a different life whenever you are willing to leave Paris," said the Marquise.

"*You* would do that, Madame?"

Kora dropped into the chair again, covering her face with
her hands. After a little she looked up, and the cunning of
her class was in her eyes.

"Is it to separate me from *him*?" she asked, bluntly. "I
know they want him to marry; are you a friend of his family?"

The Marquise smiled at that.

"I really do not know if he has a family," she replied. "I
am interested because it seems so pitiful that a girl should
never have had a chance to live commendably. It is not
too late. In your own country a person of your intelligence

and education should be able to do much good among the children of the free colored people. You would be esteemed. You—"

"Esteemed!" Kora smiled skeptically, thinking no doubt of the half-world circle over which she was a power in her adopted city; she, who had only to show herself in the spectacle to make more money than a year's earnings in American school teaching. She knew she could not really dance, but she did pose in a manner rather good; and then, her beauty!

"I was a fool when I came here—to Paris," she said woefully. "I thought everybody would know I was colored, so I told. But they would not know," and she held out her hand, looking at the white wrist, "I could have said I was a West Indian, a Brazilian, or a Spanish Creole—as many others do. But it is all too late. America was never kind to my people, or me. You mean to be kind, Madame; but you don't know colored folks. They would be the first to resent my educational advantages; not that I know much; books were hard work for me, and Paris was the only one I could learn to read easy. As for America, I own up, I'm afraid of America."

The Marquise thought she knew why, but only said:

"If you change your mind you can let me know. I have a property in New Orleans. Some day I may go there. I could protect you if you would help protect yourself." She looked at the lovely octoroon with meaning, and the black velvety eyes fell under that regard.

"You can always learn where I am in Paris, and if you should change your mind—" At the door she paused and said kindly: "My poor girl, if you remain here he will break your heart."

"They usually do when a woman loves them, Madame,"

replied Kora, with a sad little smile; she had learned so much in the book of Paris.

The friends of the Marquise were searching for her when she emerged from the ante-room. The Countess Biron confessed herself in despair.

"In such a mixed assembly! and all alone! How was one to know what people you might meet, or what adventures."

"Oh, I am not adventurous, Countess," was the smiling reply; "and let me whisper: I have been talking all of the time with one person, one very pretty person, and it has been an instructive half hour."

"Pretty? Well, that is assurance as to sex," remarked Madame Choudey, with a glance towards one of the others of the party.

"And if you will watch that door you will be enlightened as to the individual," said the Marquise.

Three pair of eyes turned with alertness to the door. At that moment it opened, and Kora appeared. The lace veil no longer hid her beautiful eyes—all the more lovely for that swift bath of tears. She saw the Marquise and her friends, but passed as if she had never seen one of them before; Kora had her own code.

"Are you serious, Judithe de Caron?" gasped the Countess Helene. "Were you actually—conversing—with that —demi-mondaine?"

"My dear Marquise!" purred Madame Choudey, "when she does not even *pretend* to be respectable!"

"It is because she does not pretend that I spoke with her. Honesty should receive some notice."

"Honesty! Good heavens!" cried Madame Ampere, who had not yet spoken, but who expressed horror by her eyes,

"where then do you find your standards for such judgment?"

"Now, listen!" and the Marquise turned to the three with
a quizzical smile, "if Kora lived exactly the same life mor-
ally, but was a ruler of the fashionable world, instead of the
other one; if she wore a crown of state instead of the tinsel
of the varieties, you would not exclaim if she addressed me."

"Oh, I must protest, Marquise," began Madame Ampere
in shocked remonstrance, but the Marquise smiled and
stopped her.

"Yesterday," she said slowly, "I saw you in conversation
with a man who has the panels of his carriage emblazoned
with the Hydrangea—also called the Hortensia."

The shocked lady looked uncomfortable.

"What then? since it was the Emperor's brother."

"Exactly; the brother of the Emperor, and both of them
the sons of a mother beside whom beautiful Kora is a thing
of chastity."

"The children could not help the fact that they were all
half-brothers," laughed the Countess Helene.

"But this so-called Duke could help parading the doubtful honor of his descent; yet who fails to return his bow?
And I have yet to learn that his mother was ignored by the
ladies of her day. Those Hortensias on his carriage are
horrible to me; they are an attempt to exalt in a queen the
immorality condemned in a subject."

"Ah! You make my head swim with your theories," confessed the Countess. "How do you find time to study them
all?"

"They require no study; one meets them daily in the
street or court. The difficulty is to cease thinking of them
—to enjoy a careless life when justice is always calling
somewhere for help."

"I refuse to be annoyed by the calls, yet am comfortable," said Madame Choudey. "The people who imagine they hear justice calling have had, too often, to follow the calls into exile."

"That is true," agreed her friend; "take care Marquise! Your theories are very interesting, but, truly, you are a revolutionist."

Their little battle of words did not prevent them parting with smiles and all pleasantry. But the Countess Biron, to whose house the Marquise was going, grimaced and looked at her with a smile of doubt when they were alone.

"Do you realize how daring you are Judithe?—to succeed socially you should not appeal to the brains of people, but to their vanities."

"Farewell, my social ambitions!" laughed the Marquise. "Dear Countess, pray do not scold! I could not help it. Why must the very respectable world see only the sins of the unfortunate, and save all their charity for the heads with coronets? Maman is not like that; she is always gentle with the people who have never been taught goodness; though she is severe on those who disgrace good training. I like her way best; and Alain? Well, he only told me to do my own thinking, to be sure I was right before I spoke, and to let no other consideration weigh at all."

"Yes! and he died in exile because he let no worldly consideration weigh," said the Countess Helene grimly.

CHAPTER IX.

At the entrance to the gallery the Marquise saw Dumaresque on the step, and with him Kenneth McVeigh. She entered the carriage, hoping the Countess would not perceive them; but the hope was in vain, she did, and she motioned them ·both to her to learn if Mrs. McVeigh had also unexpectedly returned.

She had not. Italy was yet attractive to her, and the Lieutenant had come alone. He was to await her arrival, whenever she chose, and then their holiday would be over. When they left Paris again it would be for America.

He smiled in the same lazy, yet deferential way, as the Countess chatted and questioned him. He confessed he did not remember why he had returned; at least he could not tell in a crowd, or with cynical Dumaresque listening to him.

"Invite him home, and he will vow it was to see you," said the artist.

"I mean to," she retorted; "but do not judge all men by yourself, Mousier Loris, for I suspect Lieutenant McVeigh has a conscience."

"I have," he acknowledged, "too much of one to take advantage of your invitation. Some day, when you are not tired from the crowds, I shall come, if you will allow me."

"No, no; come now!" insisted the Countess, impulsively; "you will rest me; I assure you it is true! We have been with women—women all morning! So take pity on us.

We want to hear all about the battle grounds and fortresses you were to inspect. The Marquise, especially, is a lover of wars."

"And of warriors?" queried Dumaresque; but the Countess paid no attention to him.

"Yes, she is really a revolutionist, Monsieur; so come and enlighten us as to the latest methods of those amiable patriots."

The Marquise had given him a gracious little bow, and had politely shown interest in their remarks to such an extent that the Countess did not notice her silence. But during the brief glance she noticed that the blue eyes had dark circles under them, but they were steady for all that. He looked tired, but he also looked more the master of himself than when they last met; she need fear no further pleading.

The Countess prevailed, and he entered the carriage. Dumaresque was also invited, but was on some committee of arrangements and could not leave.

As they were about to drive away the Marquise called him.

"Oh, Monsieur Loris, one moment! I want the black and white sketch of your Kora. Pray have it bid in for me."

It was the first time she had ever called him Loris, except in her own home, and as a partial echo of the dowager. His eyes thanked her, and Kenneth McVeigh received the benefit both of her words and the look.

"But, my dear Marquise, it will give me pleasure to make you something finer of the same subject."

"No, no; only the sketch. I will value it as a souvenir of—well—do not let any one else have it."

Then she bowed, flashed a rare smile at him, and they wheeled away with McVeigh facing her and noting with his

7

careless smile every expression of her coquetry. He had
gone away a boy—so she had called him; but he had come
back man enough to hide the hurts she gave him, and willing to let her know it.

Someway he appeared more as he had when she met him
first under the beeches; then he had seemed so big, so
strong, so masterful, that she had never thought of his
years. But she knew now he was younger than he looked.

She had plenty of time to think of this, and of many other
things, during the drive.

The Countess monopolized the young officer with her
questions. He endeavored to make the replies she invited,
and neither of them appeared to note that the share of the
Marquise was limited to an interested expression, and an
occasional smile.

She studied his well-formed, strong hands, and thought
of the night they had held her own—thought of all the impetuous, passionate words; try as she would to drive them
away they came back with a rush as his cool, widely different tones fell on her ear. What a dissembler the fellow
was! All that evil nature which she knew about was hidden under an exterior so engaging! *"If one only loved
where it was wise to love, all the sorrows of the world would
be ended,"* those words of the pretty figureante haunted her,
with all their meaning beating through her brain. What a
farce seemed the careless, empty chatter beside her! It
grew unbearable, to feel his careless glance sweep across
her face, to hear him laugh carelessly, to be conscious of the
fact that after all he was the stronger; he could face her
easily, graciously, and she did not dare even meet his eyes
lest he should, after all, see; the thought of her weakness
frightened her; suppose he should compel her to the truth.
Suppose—

She felt half hysterical; the drive had never before been so long. She feared she must scream—do something to break through this horrible chain of circumstances, linking them for even so short a space within touch of each other. And he was the man she had promised herself to hate, to make suffer, to—

Some one did scream; but it was the Countess. Out of a side street came a runaway team, a shouting man heralding their approach. At that point street repairs had left only a narrow carriage-way, and a wall of loose stone; there was no time to get out of the way; no room to turn. There was a collision, a crash! The horses of the Countess leaped aside, the right front wheel struck the heap of stone, flinging the driver from his seat. He fell, and did not move again.

At that sight the Countess uttered a gasp and sank to the bottom of the carriage. The Marquise stooped over her only for an instant, while the carriage righted itself and all four wheels were on a level once more; the horses alone had been struck, and were maddened with fear, and in that madness lay their only danger now.

She lifted her head, and the man opposite, in her instant of shrinking, had leaped over the back of the seat to secure the lines of the now thoroughly wild animals.

One line was dragging between them on the ground. Someway he maintained his footing on the carriage pole long enough to secure the dragging line, and when he gained the driver's seat the Marquise was beside him.

She knew what lay before them, and he did not—a dangerous curve, a steep embankment—and they had passed the last street where they could have turned into a less dangerous thoroughfare.

People ran out and threw up their hands and shouted.

She heard him fling an oath at them for adding fury to the maddened animals.

"It is no use," she said, and laid her hand on his. He turned and met her eyes. No veil of indifference was between them now, no coquetry; all pretense was swept aside and the look they exchanged was as a kiss.

"You love me—now?" he demanded, half fiercely.

"Now, and always, from the first hour you looked at me!" she said, with her hand on his wrist. His grip tightened on the lines, and the blood leaped into his face.

"My love, my love!" he whispered; and she slipped on her knees beside him that she might not see the danger to be faced.

"It is no use, Kenneth, Kenneth! There is the bank ahead —they cannot stop—it will kill us! It is just ahead!"

She was muttering disjointed sentences, her face averted, her arms clasping him.

"Kill us? Don't you believe it!" And he laughed a trifle nervously. "Look up, sweetheart; the danger is over. I knew it when you first spoke. See! They are going steady now."

They were. He had gained control of them in time to make the dangerous curve in safety. They were a quarter of the way along the embankment. Workmen there stared at the lady and gentleman on the coachman's seat, and at the rather rapid gait; but the real danger was over.

They halted at a little cafe, which was thrown into consternation at sight of a lady insensible in the bottom of the carriage; but a little wine and the administrations of the Marquise aided her recovery, and in a short time enabled her to hear the account of the wild race.

The driver had a broken arm, and one of the horses was slightly injured. Lieutenant McVeigh had sent back about the man, and secured another team for the drive home. He was now walking up and down the pavement in front of the cafe, in very good spirits, and awaiting the pleasure of the Countess.

They drove home at once; the Countess voluably grateful to Kenneth, and apparently elated over such a tremendous adventure. The young officer shared her high spirits, and the Marquise was the only silent member of the party. After the danger was passed she scarcely spoke. When he helped her into the carriage the pressure of his hand and one whispered word sent the color sweeping over her face, leaving it paler than before. She scarcely lifted her eyes for the rest of the drive, and after retiring for a few moments' rest, apparently, broke down entirely; the nervous strain had proven rather trying, and she was utterly unable—to her own regret—to join them at lunch.

Lieutenant McVeigh begged to withdraw, but the Countess Biron, who declared she had never been the heroine of a thrilling adventure, before, insisted that she at least was quite herself again, and would feel cheated if their heroic deliverer did not remain for a lunch, even though it be a tete-a-tete affair; and she, of course, wanted to hear all the details of the horror; that child, Judithe, had not seemed to remember much; she supposed she must have been terribly frightened. "Yet, one never knew how the Marquise would be effected by *any* thing! She was always surprising people; usually in delightful ways, of course."

"Of course," assented her guest, with a reminiscent gleam and a wealth of absolute happiness in the blue eyes. "Yes, she is rather surprising at times; she surprised me!"

*   *   *   *   *

"Judithe, my child, it was an ideal adventure," insisted the Countess, an hour after the Lieutenant had left her, and she had repaired to the room where the Marquise was supposed to be resting. Her nervousness had evidently not yet abated, for she was walking up and down the floor.

"An absolutely ideal adventure, and a heroic foreigner to the rescue! What a god-send that I invited him! And I really believe he enjoyed it. I never before saw him so gay, so charming! There are men, you know, to whom danger is a tonic, and my friend's son is like that, surely. Did he not seem at all afraid?"

"Not that I observed."

"Did he not say anything?"

"Y—yes; he swore at the people who shouted and tried to stop the horses."

"You should not have let yourself hear that," said the Countess, reproachfully. "I thought he was so perfect, and was making my little romance about him—or could, if you would only show a little more interest. Ah! at your age I should have been madly in love with the fine fellow, just for what he did today; but *you*! Still, it would be no use, I suppose. He is fiancee, you know. Yes; the mother told me; a fine settlement; I saw her picture—very pretty."

"American—I suppose?"

"Oh, yes; their lands join, and she is a great heiress. The name—the name is Loring—Genevieve? No—Gertrude, Mademoiselle Gertrude Loring. Ah! so strong he was, so heroic. If she loves him she should have seen him today."

"Yes," agreed the Marquise, with a curious little smile, "she should."

* * * * *

Two hours later she was on her knees beside the dowager's couch, her face hidden and all her energy given to one plea:

"Maman—Maman! Do not question me; only give me your trust—let us go away!"

"But the man—tah! It is only a fancy; why should you leave for that? Whoever it is, the infatuation grew quickly and will die out the same way—so—"

"No! If I remain I cannot answer for myself. I am ashamed to confess it, but—listen, Maman—but put your arms around me first; he is not worthy, I know it; yet I love him! He vows love to me, yet he is betrothed; I know that, *also*; but I have no reason left, and my folly will make me go to him if you do not help me. Listen, Maman! I—I will do all you say. I will marry in a year—two years—when this is all over. I will obey you in everything, if you will only take me away. I cannot leave you; yet I am afraid to stay where he is."

"Afraid! But, Judithe, my child, no one shall intrude upon you. Your friends will protect you from such a man. You have only to refuse to see him, and in a little while—"

"Refuse! Maman, what can I say to make you understand that I could never refuse him again? Yet, oh, the humiliation! Maman, he is the man I despised—the man I said was not fit to be spoken to; it was all true, but when I hear his voice it makes me forget his unworthiness. Listen, Maman! I—I confessed to him today that I loved him; yet I know he is the man who by the laws of America is the owner of Rhoda Larue, and he is now the betrothed of her half-sister; I heard the name of his fiancee today, and it told me the whole story. He is the man! *Now*, will you take me away?"

The next morning the dowager, Marquise de Caron, left her Paris home for the summer season. Her destination was indefinitely mentioned as Switzerland. Her daughter-in-law accompanied her.

And to Kenneth McVeigh, waiting impatiently the hour
when he might go to her, a note was given:

"MONSIEUR:

"My words of yesterday had no meaning. I was frightened and irresponsible. When you read this I will have left
Paris. By not meeting again we will avoid further mistakes
of the same nature.

"This is my last word to you.

"JUDITHE CARON."

For two weeks he tried in vain to find her. Then he was
recalled to Paris to meet his mother, who was ready for
home. She was shocked at his appearance, and refused to
believe that he had not been ill during her absence, and had
some motherly fears regarding Parisian dissipations, from
which she decided to remove him, if possible. He acknowledged he would be glad to go—he was sick of Europe any
way.

The last day he took a train for Fontainbleau, remained
two hours under the beeches, alone, and got back to Paris
in time to make the train for Havre.

After they had got comfortably established on a home-
ward-bound vessel, and he was watching the land line grow
fainter over the waters, Mrs. McVeigh came to him with
a bit of news read from the last journal brought aboard.

The dowager, Marquise de Caron, had established herself
at Geneva for the season, accompanied by her daughter, the
present Marquise, whose engagement to Monsieur Loris
Dumaresque had just been announced.

CHAPTER X.

Long before the first gun had been fired at Fort Sumpter, Madame la Marquise was able to laugh over that summertime madness of her's, and ridicule herself for the wasted force of that infatuation.

She was no longer a recluse unacquainted with men. The prophecy of Madame, the dowager, that if left alone she would return to the convent, had not been verified. The death of the dowager occurred their first winter in Paris, after Geneva, and the Marquise had not yet shown a predilection for nunneries.

She had seen the world, and it pleased her well enough; indeed, the portion of the world she came in contact with did its best to please her, and with a certain feverish eagerness she went half way to meet it.

People called her a coquette—the most dangerous of coquettes, because she was not a cold one. She was responsive and keenly interested up to the point where admirers declared themselves, and proposals of marriage followed; after *that*, every man was just like every other one! Yet she was possessed of an idea that somewhere there existed a hitherto undiscovered specimen who could discuss the emotions and the philosophies in delightful sympathy, and restrain the expression of his own personal emotions to tones and glances, those indefinite suggestions that thrill yet call for no open reproof—no reversal of friendship.

So, that was the man she was seeking in the multitudes—

and on the way there were surely amusements to be found!

Dumaresque remonstrated.   She defended herself with the avowal that she was only avenging weaker womanhood, smiled at, won, and forgotten, as his sex were fond of forgetting.

"But we expect better things of women," he declared warmly; "not a deliberate intention of playing with hearts to see how many can be hurt in a season.   Judithe, you are no longer the same woman.   Where is the justice you used to guage every one by?   Where the mercy to others weaker than yourself?"

"Gone!" she laughed lightly; "driven away in self-defense!   I have had to put mercy aside lest it prove my master.   The only safeguard against being too warm to all may be to be cool to all.   You perceive that would never—never do.   So—!"

"End all this unsatisfied, feverish life by marrying me," he pleaded.   "I will take you from Paris.   With all your social success you have never been happy here; we will travel.   You promised, Judithe, and—"

"Chut! Loris; you are growing ungallant.   You should never remember a woman's promise after she has forgotten it.   We were betrothed—yes.   But did I not assure you I might never marry?   Maman was made happy for a little while by the fancy; but now?—well, matrimony is no more appealing to me than it ever was, and you would not want an indifferent wife.   I like you, you best of all those men you champion, but I love none of you!   Not that I am lacking in affection, but rather, incapable of concentrating it on one object."

"Once, it was not so; I have not forgotten the episode of Fontainbleu."

"That? Pouf! I have learned things since then, Loris.

I have learned that once, at least, in every life love seems to have been born on earth for the first time; happy those whom it does not visit too late! Well! I, also, had to have my little experience; it had to be *some* one; so it was that stranger. But I have outgrown all that; we always ougrow those things, do we not? I compare him now with the men I have known since, and he shrinks, he dwindles! I care only for intellectual men, and the artistic temperament. He had neither. Yes, it is true; the girlish fancies appear ridiculous in so short a time."

Dumaresque agreed that it was true of any fancy, to one of fickle nature.

"No, it is not fickleness," she insisted. "Have you no boyish loves of the past hidden away, each in their separate nook of memory? Confess! Are you and the world any the worse for them? Certainly not. They each contributed a certain amount towards the education of the emotions. Well; is my education to be neglected because you fear I shall injure the daintly-bound books in the human library? I shall not, Loris. I only flutter the leaves a little and glance at the pictures they offer, but I never covet one of them for my own, and never read one to the finale, hence—"

Dumaresque left soon after for an extended artistic pilgrimage into northern Africa, and people began to understand that there would be no wedding. The engagement had only been made to comfort the dowager.

Judithe de Caron regretted his departure more than she had regretted anything since the death of the woman who had been a mother to her. There was no one else with whom she could be so candid—no man who inspired her with the same confidence. She compared him with the

American, and told herself how vastly her friend was the superior.

Had McVeigh been one of the scholarly soldiers of Europe, such as she had since known—men of breadth and learning, she could have understood her own infatuation. But he was certainly provincial, and not at all learned. She had met many cadets since, and had studied them. They knew their military tactics—the lessons of their schools. They flirted with the grissettes, and took on airs; they drank and had pride in emptying more glasses and walking straighter afterwards than their comrades. They were very good fellows, but heavens! how shallow they were! So *he* must have been. She tried to remember a single sentence uttered by him containing wisdom of any sort whatever—there had not been one. His silences had been links to bind her to him. His glances had been revelations, and his words had been only: "I adore you."

So many men had said the same thing since. It seemed always the sort of thing men said when conversation flagged. But in those earlier days she had not known that, hence the fact that she—well, she knew now!

Twice she had met that one-time bondwoman, Kora, and the meeting left her thoughtful, and not entirely satisfied with herself.

How wise she could be in advice to that pretty butterfly! How plainly she could work out a useful life to be followed by—some one else!

Her more thoughtful moods demanded: Why not herself? Her charities of the street, her subscriptions to worthy funds, her patronage of admirable institutions, all these meant nothing. Dozens of fashionables and would-be fashionables did the same. It was expected of them.

Those charities opened a door through which many entered the inner circles.

She had fitful desires to do the things people did not expect. She detested the shams of life around her in that inner circle. She felt at times she would like to get them all under her feet—trample them down and make room for something better; but for what? She did not know. She was twenty-one, wealthy, her own mistress, and was tired of it all. When she drove past laughing Kora on the avenue she was more tired of it than ever.

"How am I better than she but by accident?" she asked herself. "She amuses herself—poor little bondslave, who has only changed masters! I amuse myself (without a master, it is true, and more elegantly, perhaps), but with as little usefulness to the world."

She felt ashamed when she thought of Alain and his mother, who seemed to have lived only to help others. They had given over the power to her, and how poorly she had acquitted herself!

Once—when she first came with the dowager to Paris—the days had been all too short for her plans and dreams of usefulness; how long ago that seemed.

Now, she knew that the owner of wealth is the victim of multitudinous schemes of the mendicant, whether of the street corner or the fashionable missions. She had lost faith in the efficacy of alms. No cause came to her with force enough to re-awaken her enthusiasms. Everything was so tame—so old!

One day she read in a journal that the usefulness of Kora as a dancer was over. There had been an accident at the theatre, her foot was smashed; not badly enough to call for amputation, but too much for her ever to dance again.

The Marquise wondered if the fair-weather friends would

desert her now. She had heard of Trouvelot, an exquisite who followed the fashions in everything, and Kora had succeeded in being the fashion for two seasons. She was just as pretty, no doubt—just as adorable, but—

As the weeks of that winter went by rumors from the Western world were thick with threats of strife. State after State had seceded. The South was marshalling her forces, training her men, urging the necessity of defending State rights and maintaining their power to govern a portion as ably as they had the whole of the United States during the eighty years of its governmental life. The North, with its factories, its foreign commerce, and its manifold requirements, had bred the politicians of the country. But the South, with its vast agricultural States, its wealth, and its traditions of landed ancestry, had produced the orators—the statesman—the men who had shone most brilliantly in the pages of their national history.

From the shores of France one could watch some pretty moves in the games evolving about that promise of civil war; the creeping forward of England to help widen the breach between the divided sections, and the swift swinging of Russian war vessels into the harbors of the Atlantic—the silent bear of the Russias facing her hereditary English foe and forbidding interference, until the lion gave way with low growlings, not daring to even roar his chagrin, but contenting himself with night-prowlings during the four years that followed.

All those wheels within wheels were discussed around the Marquise de Caron in those days. Her acquaintance with the representatives of different nations and the diplomats of her own, made her aware of many unpublished moves for advantage in the game they surveyed. The discussion of them, and guesses as to the finale, helped to awake her

from the lethargy she had deplored. Remembering that
the McVeighs belonged to a seceding state, she asked many
questions and forgot none of the replies.

"Madame La Marquise, I was right," said a white mous-
tached general one night at a great ball, where she appeared.
"Was it not a rose you wagered me? I have won. War
is declared in America. In South Carolina, today, the Confederates won the first point, and secured a Federal fort."

"General! they have not dared!"

"Madame, those Southerons are daring above everything.
I have met them. Their men are fighters, and they will be
well officered."

Well officered! She thought of Kenneth McVeigh, he
would be one of them; yes, she supposed that was one thing
he could do—fight; a thing requiring brute strength, brute
courage!

"So!" said the Countess Biron, who seldom was acquainted with the causes of any wars outside those of court
circles, "this means that if the Northern States should re-
taliate and conquer, all the slaves would be free?"

"Not at all, Countess. The North does not interfere with
slavery where it exists, only protests against its extension
to greater territory."

"Oh! Well; I understood it had something to do with
the Africans. That clever young Delaven devoted an entire hour to my enlightment yesterday. And my poor
friend, Madame McVeigh, you remember her, Judithe?
She is in the Carolinas. I tremble to think of her position
now; an army of slaves surrounding them, and, of course,
only awaiting the opportunity for insurrection."

"And Louisiana seceded two months ago," said the Marquise, and then smiled. "You will think me a mercenary
creature," she declared, "but I have property in New Orleans

which I have never seen, and I am wondering whether its value will rise or fall because of the proposed change of government."

"You have never seen it?"

"No; it was a purchase made by my husband from some home-sick relative, who had thought to remain there, but could not live away from France. I have promised myself to visit it some day. It would be exceedingly difficult to do so now, I suppose, but how much more spirited a journey it would be; for each side will have vessels on guard all along the coast, will they not?"

"There will at least be enough to deter most ladies from taking adventurous pilgrimages in that direction. I shall not advise you to go unless under military escort, Marquise."

"I shall notify you, General, when my preparations are made; in the meantime here is your rose; and would not my new yacht do for the journey?"

So, jesting and questioning, she accepted his arm and made the circle of the rooms. Everywhere they heard fragments of the same topic. Americans were there from both sections. She saw a pretty woman from Alabama nod and smile, but put her hands behind her when a hitherto friendly New Yorker gave her greeting.

"We women can't do much to help," she declared, in those soft tones of the South, "but we can encourage our boys by being pronounced in our sympathies. I certainly shall not shake hands with a Northerner who may march with the enemy against our men; how can I?"

"Suppose we talk it over and try to find a way," he suggested. Then they both smiled and passed on together. Judithe de Caron found herself watching them with a little ache in her heart. She could see they were almost, if not quite, lovers; yet all their hopes were centered on opposite victories. How many—many such cases there must be!

* * * * *

Before spring had merged into summer, a lady, veiled, and giving no name, was announced to the Marquise. Rather surprised at the mysterious call, she entered the reception room, and was again surprised when the lifted veil disclosed the handsome face of the octoroon, Kora.

She had lost some of her brilliant color, and her expression was more settled, it had less of the butterfly brightness.

"You see, Madame, I have at last taken you at your word."

The Marquise, who was carefully noting the alteration in her, bowed, but made no remark. The face of the octoroon showed uncertainty.

"Perhaps—perhaps I have waited too long," she said, and half rose.

"No, no; you did right to come. I expected you—yes, really! Now be seated and tell me what it is."

"First, that you were a prophetess, Madame," and the full lips smiled without merriment. "I am left alone, now that I have neither money nor the attraction for the others. He only followed the crowd—to me, and away from me!"

"Well?"

"Well, it is not about *that* I come! But, Madame, I am going to America; not to teach, as you advised, but I see now a way in which I can really help."

"Help whom?"

Her visitor regarded her with astonishment; was it possible that she, the woman whose words had aroused the first pride of race in her, the first thought of her people unlinked with shame! That she had so soon forgotten? Had

8

she remembered the pupil, but failed to recall the lesson taught?

"You have probably forgotten the one brief conversation with which you honored me, Madame. But I mean the people we discussed then—my people."

"You mean the colored people."

"Certainly, Madame."

"But you are more white than colored."

"Oh, yes; that is true, but the white blood would not count in America if it were known there was one drop of black blood in my mother. But no one need know it; I go from France, I will speak only French, and if you would only help me a little."

She grew prettier in her eagerness, and her eyes brightened. The Marquise smiled at the change enthusiasm made.

"You must tell me the object for which you go."

"It is the war, Madame; in time this war must free the colored folks; it is talked of already; it is said the North will put colored soldiers in the field; that will be the little, thin edge of the wedge, and if I could only get there, if you would help me to some position, or a recommendation to people in New Orleans; any way so that people would not ask questions or be curious about me—if you would only do that madame!"

"But what will you do when there?"

The girl glanced about the room and spoke more softly.

"I am trusting you, Madame, without asking who you side with in our war, but even if you are against us I—I trust you! They tell me the South is the strongest. They have been getting ready for this a long time. The North will need agents in the South. I have learned some things here—people talk so much. I am going to Washington.

From there I will go south. No one will know me in New Orleans. I will change my name, and I promise not to bring discredit on any recommendation you may give me."

"It is a plan filled with difficulties and dangers. What has moved you to contemplate such sacrifices?"

"You, Madame!" The Marquise flushed slightly. "From the time you talked to me I wanted to do something, be something better. But, you know, it seemed no use; there was no need of me anywhere but in Paris. That is all over. I can go now, and I have some information worth taking to the Federal government. The South has commissioners here now. I have learned all they have accomplished, and the people they have interested, so if I had a little help—"

"You shall have it!" declared the Marquise. "I have been dying of ennui. Your plan is a cure for me—better than a room full of courtiers! But if I give you letters it must be to my lawyers in New Orleans—clever, shrewd men— and I should have to trust you entirely, remember."

"I shall not forget, Madame."

"Very good; come tomorrow. What can you do about an establishment such as mine? Ladies maid? Housekeeper? Governess?"

"Any of those; but only governess to very small children."

"Come tomorrow. I shall have planned something by then. I have an engagement in a few minutes, and have no more time today. By the way, have you ever been in Georgia or South Carolina?"

Kora hesitated, and then said: "Yes, Madame."

"Have you any objection to going back there?"

The octoroon looked at her in a startled, suspicious way.

"I hesitate to reply to that, Madame, for reasons! I

don't mind telling you, though, that there *is* one place in America where I might be claimed, if they knew me. I am not anxious to visit that place."

"Naturally! Tomorrow at eleven I will see you, and you can tell me all about it. If I am to act as your protectress I must know all you can tell me—*all*! It is the only way. I like the mystery and intrigue of the whole affair. It promises new sensations. I will help you show that government that you are willing to help your people. Come tomorrow."

A few days later the Marquise set her new amusement on foot by bidding adieu to a demure, dark eyed, handsome girl, who was garbed most sedately, and whose letters of introduction pronounced her—oh, sentiment or irony of women—Madame Louise Trouvelot, an attache of the Caron establishment, commissioned by the Marquise to inspect the dwellings on the Caron estate in New Orleans, and report as to whether any one of them would be suitable for a residence should the owner desire to visit the city. If none should prove so, Louise Trouvelot, who comprehended entirely the needs of the Marquise, was further commissioned to look up such a residence with a view to purchase, and communicate with the Marquise and with her American lawyers, who were to give assistance to Louise Trouvelot in several business matters, especially relating to her quest.

CHAPTER XI.

ON THE SALKAHATCHIE.

Scarce a leaf quivered on the branches of the magnolias, or a tress of gray-green moss on the cypress boughs. All the world of the Salkahatchie was wrapped in siesta. The white clouds drifting on palest turquoise were the only moving things except the water flowing beneath, and its soft swish against the gunnels of the floating wharf made the only sound.

The plantation home of Loringwood, facing the river, and reached through the avenue of enormous live oaks, looked an enchanted palace touched with the wand of silence.

From the wide stone steps to the wide galleries, with their fluted pillars, not a murmur but the winged insects droning in the tangled grasses, for the wild luxuriance of rose tree and japonica, of lawn and crape myrtle, betrayed a lack of pruning knives in the immediate season past; and to the south, where the rice fields had reached acre beyond acre towards the swamps, there were now scattered patches of feathering young pine, creeping everywhere not forbidden to it by the hand of man.

Spring time and summer time, for almost a century, had been lived through under its sloping, square, dormer-windowed roof. But all the blue sky and brilliant sunshine above could not save it from a suggestion of autumn, and the shadows lengthening along the river were in perfect keeping with the entire picture—a picture of perpetual afternoon.

"Row-lock," "Row-lock," sounded the dip and click of paddles, as a boat swept close to the western bank, where the shadows fell. Two Afro-Americans bent in rythmic motion—bronze human machines, whose bared arms showed nothing of effort as they sent the boat cutting through the still water.

A middle aged woman in a voluminous lavender lawn and carrying a parasol of plaid silk-green, with faded pink bars, sat in the after part of the boat, while a slight brown-haired girl just in front amused herself by catching at branches of willows as they passed.

"Evilena, honey, you certainly are like to do yourself a hurt reaching out like that, and if you *should* go over!"

"But I shan't, Aunt Sajane. Do you reckon I'd risk appearing before Gertrude Loring in a draggled gown just when she has returned from the very heart of the civilized world? Goodness knows, we'll all look dowdy enough to her."

Aunt Sajane (Mistress Sarah Jane Nesbitt) glanced down at her own immaculate lawn, a little faded but daintily laundered, and at her own trim congress-gaitered feet.

"Oh, I didn't mean you," added the girl, laughing softly. "Aunt Sajane, I truly do believe that if you had nothing but gunny sacks for dresses you'd contrive to look as if you'd just come out of a bandbox."

"I'd wear gunny sacks fast enough if it was to help the cause," agreed Aunt Sajane, with a kindly smile. "So would you, honey."

"Honey" trailed her fingers in the waters, amber tinted from the roots of the cypress trees.

"If a letter from mama comes today we will just miss it."

"Only by a day. Brother Gideon will send it."

"But suppose he's away somewhere on business, or up

there at Columbia on state councils or conventions, or whatever they are, as he is just now?"

"Then Pluto will fetch it right over," and she glanced at one of the black men, who showed his teeth for an instant and bent his head in assent.

"Don't see why Judge Clarkson was *ever* named Gideon," protested the girl. "It's a hard, harsh sort of name, and he's as—as—"

"Soft?" queried the judge's sister, with an accompaniment of easy laughter. The youngest of the two oarsmen grinned. Pluto maintained a well-bred indifference.

"No!" and the girl flung a handful of willow leaves over the lavender lawn. "He is—well—just about right, the judge is; so gentle, so considerate, so altogether magnificent in his language. I've adored him as far back as when he fought the duel with the Northern man who reflected some way on our customs; that was starting a war for his state all alone, before anyone else thought of it, I reckon. I must have been very little then, for I just recollect how he used to let me look in his pockets for candy, and I was awfully afraid of the pistols I thought he must carry there to shoot people with," and she smiled at the childish fancy. "I tell you, Aunt Sajane, if my papa had lived there's just one man I'd like him to favor, and that's our judge. But he didn't, did he?"

"No, he didn't," said Aunt Sajane. "The McVeigh men were all dark, down to Kenneth, and he gets his fairness from your ma." Then she added, kindly, "the judge will be very proud of your admiration."

"Hope he'll care enough about it to hurry right along after us. He does put in a powerful lot of his time in Charleston and Columbia lately," and the tone was one of childish complaint.

"Why, honey, how you suppose our soldier boys would be provided for unless some of the representative men devote their time to the work? It's a consolation to me that Gideon is needed for civil service just now, for if he wasn't he wouldn't be so near home as he is; he'd be somewhere North with a regiment, and I reckon that wouldn't suit you any better."

"No, it wouldn't," agreed the girl, "though I do like a man who will fight, of course. *Any* girl does."

"Oh, Honey!"

"Yes they do, too. But just now I don't want him either fighting or in legislature. I want him right along with us at Loringwood. If he isn't there to talk to Mr. Loring it won't be possible to have a word alone with Gertrude all the time we stay. How he *does* depend on her, and what an awful time she must have had all alone with him in Paris while he was at that hospital, or whatever it was."

"Not many girls so faithful as Gertrude Loring," agreed Aunt Sajane. "Not that he has ever shown much affection for her, either, considering she is his own brother's child. But she certainly has shown a Christian sense of duty towards him. Well, you see, they are the only ones left of the family. It's natural, I suppose."

"*I* would think it natural to run away and leave him, like Aleck and Scip did.

Aunt Sajane cast a warning glance towards the two oarsmen.

"Well, I would," insisted the girl. "I wonder no more of them ran away when they thought he was coming home. How he must have raved! *I* shouldn't wonder if it prostrated him again. You know old Doctor Allison said it was just a fit of temper caused—"

"Yes, yes, honey; but you know we are to sleep under his roof tonight."

"I'll sleep under Gertrude's half of it," laughed the girl. "It's no use reminding me of my bad manners, Aunt Sajane. But as long as I can remember anyone, I've had two men in my mind. One always grunted at me and told me to take my doll somewhere else or be quiet. That was Kenneth's guardian, Matthew Loring. The other man always had sugar kisses in his pocket for me and gave me my first dog and my only pony. That was Judge Clarkson. You see if my judge had not been so lovely the other would not have seemed so forbidding. It was the contrast did it. I wonder—I wonder if he ever had a sweetheart?"

"Gideon Clarkson? Lots of them," said his sister, promptly.

"I meant Mr. Loring."

"Nonsense, honey, nonsense."

"And nonsense means no," decided the girl. "I thought it would be curious if he had," then an interval of silence, broken only by the dip of the oars. "Gertrude's note said a Paris doctor is with them, a friend of Kenneth and mama. Well, I only hope *he* isn't a crusty old sweetheartless man. But of course he is if Mr. Loring chose him. I'm wild to know how they got through the blockade. Oh, dear, how I wish it was Ken!"

"I don't suppose you wish it any more than the boy himself," said Aunt Sajane, with a sigh. "There's a good many boys scattered from home, these days, who would be glad to be home again."

"But not unless they gain what they went for," declared the girl in patriotic protest.

The older woman sighed, and said nothing. Her enthusiasms of a year ago had been shrouded by the crape of a mourning land; the glory of conquest would be compensation, perhaps, and would be gained, no doubt. But the price to be paid chilled her and left her without words when Evilena revelled in the glories of the future.

"Loringwood line," said Pluto, motioning towards a great ditch leading straight back from the river.

Evilena shrugged her shoulders with a little pretense of chill, and laughed.

"That is only a reminder of what I used to feel when Gertrude's uncle came to our house. I wonder if this long dress will prevent him from grunting at me or ordering me out of the room if I talk too much."

"Remember, Evilena, he has been an invalid for four years, and is excusable for almost any eccentricity."

"How did you all excuse his eccentricities before he got sick, Aunt Sajane?"

Receiving no reply, the girl comforted herself with the appreciative smile of the oarsmen, who were evidently of her mind as to the planter under discussion, and a mile further they ran the boat through the reeds and lily pads to the little dock at Loringwood.

Mrs. Nesbitt shook out the folds of her crisp lawn, adjusted her bonnet and puffs and sighed, as they walked up the long avenue.

"I can remember when the lily pads never could get a chance to grow there on account of the lot of company always coming in boats," she said, regretfully, "and I've heard that the old Lorings lived like kings here long ago; wild, reckless, magnificent men; not at all like the Lorings now; and oh, my, how the place has been neglected of late. Not a sign of life about the house. Now, in *Tom* Loring's time—"

They had reached the foot of the steps when the great

double doors swung back and a woman appeared on the threshold and inclined her head in greeting.

"Well, Margeret, I am glad to see some one alive," declared Mrs. Nesbitt; "the place is so still."

"Yes; just look at Pluto and Bob," said Evilena, motioning towards the boatmen. "One would think a ghost had met them at the landing, they are so subdued."

The brown eyed, grey haired woman in the door glanced at the two colored men who were following slowly along a path towards the back of the house.

"Yes, Miss Lena, it is quiet," she agreed. "Please step in Mistress Nesbitt. I'll have Raquel show you right up to your rooms, for Miss Loring didn't think you could get here for an hour yet, and she felt obliged to ride over to the north corner, but won't be gone long."

"And Mr. Loring—how is he?"

"Mr. Loring is very much worn out. He's gone asleep now. Doctor says he's not to be seen just yet."

"Oh, yes; the doctor. I'll see him directly after I've rested a little. He speaks English, I hope. Are you coming up, honey?"

"Not yet. I'll keep a lookout for Gertrude."

Margeret had touched a bell and in response a little black girl had appeared, who smiled and ducked her head respectfully.

"Howdy, Miss Sajane? Howdy, Miss Lena?" she exclaimed, her black eyes dancing. "I dunno how come it come, I nevah heerd you all, for I done got—"

"Raquel, you show Mistress Nesbitt to the west room," said the quiet tones of Margeret, and Raquel's animation subsided into wordless grins as she gathered up the sunshade, reticule and other belongings, and preceded Mistress Nesbitt up the stairs.

"If there's anything I can do for you just send Raquel for me."

"Thank you, Margeret. I'll remember."

Margeret crossed the hall to the parlor door and opened it.

"If you'd rather rest in here, Miss Lena—"

"No, no; I'll go look for Gertrude. Don't mind me. I remember all the rooms well enough to make myself at home till she comes."

Margeret inclined her head slightly and moved along the hall to the door of the dining room, which she entered.

Evilena looked after her with a dubious smile in the blue-gray eyes.

"I wonder if I could move as quietly as that even with my feet *bare*," and she tried walking softly on the polished oak floor, but the heels of her shoes would persist in giving out little clicking sounds as Margeret's had not.

"It's no use. No living person with shoes on could walk silently as that woman. She's just a ghost who—*a-gh-gh*!"

Her attempt at silent locomotion had brought her to the door of the library, directly opposite the dining room. As she turned to retrace her steps that door suddenly opened and a hand grasped her shoulder.

"Oh, ho! This time I've caught you, have I? you—oh, murder!"

Her half uttered scream had been checked by the sound of a voice which memory told her was not that of her bug-bear, the invalid master of the house. It was, instead, a strange gentleman, who was young, and even attractive; whose head was a mass of reddish curls, and whose austere gaze changed quickly to an embarrassed stare as her hat slipped back and he saw her face. The girl was the first. to recover herself.

"Yes, you certainly did catch me this time," she gasped.

"My dear young lady, I'm a blundering idiot. I beg your pardon most humbly. I thought it was that Raquel, and I—"

"Oh, Raquel?" and she backed to the opposite wall, regarding him with doubt and question in her eyes.

"Exactly. Allow me to explain. Raquel, in company with some other imps of all shades, have developed an abnormal interest in the unpacking of various boxes today, and especially a galvanic battery in here, which—"

"Battery? In *there*?" and Evilena raised on her tip-toes to survey the room over his shoulder. "I know some boys of Battery B, but I never saw them without uniforms."

"Uniform, is it? Well, now, you see, I've only been a matter of hours in the country, and small chance to look up a tailor. Are—are they a necessity to the preservation of life here?"

He spoke with a doubtful pretense of timidity, and looked at her quizzically. She smiled, but made a little grimace, a curve of the lips and nod of the head conveying decision.

"You will learn it is the only dress for a man that makes life worth living, for him, around here," she replied. "Every man who is not superannuated or attached to the state government in some way has to wear a uniform unless he wants his loyalty questioned."

The un-uniformed man smiled at her delightful patriotic frankness.

"Faith, now, I've no objection to the questions if you are appointed questioner. But let me get you a chair. Even when on picket duty and challenging each new comer, you are allowed a more restful attitude than your present one, I hope. You startled me into forgetting—"

"*I* startled *you*? Well!"

"Oh, yes. I was the one to do the bouncing out and nabbing you, wasn't I? Well, now, I can't believe you were the more frightened of the two, for all that. Have this chair, please; it is the most comfortable. You see, I fancied Raquel had changed under my touch from dusky brown to angelic white. The hat hid your face, you know, until you turned around, and then—"

"Well?" At the first tone of compliment she had forgotten all the strangeness of their meeting, and remembered only the coquetry so naturally her own. With or without the uniform of her country, he was at least a man, and there had been a dearth of men about their plantation, "The Terrace," of late.

"Well," he repeated after her, "when you tipped the hat back I thought in a wink of all the fairy stories of transformation I used to hear told by the old folks in Ireland."

"Do you really mean that you believe fairy stories?" Her tone was severe and her expression chiding.

"On my faith I believed them all that minute."

Her eyes dropped to the toe of her slipper. It was all very delightful, this tete-a-tete with the complimentary unknown, and to be thought a fairy! She wished she had gone up with Aunt Sajane and brushed her hair. Still—

"I was sure it was Mr. Loring who had hold of me until I looked around," she confessed, "and that frightened me just as much as the wickedest fairy or goblin could ever do."

"Indeed, now, would it?"

She glanced around to see if her indiscreet speech had been overheard and then nodded assent.

"Oh, you needn't smile," she protested; and his face at once became comically grave. "*You* didn't have him for a bug-a-boo when you were little, as I did. That doctor of his gave orders that no one was to see him just now, and

I am glad Gertrude will be back before we are admitted. With Gertrude to back me up I could be brave as—as—"

"A sheep," suggested the stranger.

"I was going to say a lion, but lions are big, and I'm not very."

"No, you are not," he agreed. "Sad, isn't it?"

Then they both laughed. She was elated, bubbling over with delight, at meeting some one in Loringwood who actually laughed.

"Gertrude's note last night never told us she had company, and I had gloomy forebodings of Uncle Matthew and Uncle Matthew's doctor, to whom I would not dare speak a word, and the relief of finding real people here is a treat, so please don't mind if I'm silly."

"I shan't—when you are," he agreed, magnanimously. "But pray enlighten me as to why you will be unable to exchange words with the medical stranger? He's no worse a fellow than myself."

"Of *course* not," she said, with so much fervor that her listener's smile was clearly a compromise with laughter. "But a doctor from Paris! Our old Doctor Allison is pompous and domineering enough, and he never was out of the state, but this one from Europe, he is sure to oppress me with his wonderful knowledge. Indeed, I don't know who he *will* find to talk to here, now, except Judge Clarkson. The judge will be scholarly enough for him."

"And does he, also, oppress you with his professional knowledge?"

Evilena's laugh rang out clear as a bird's note.

"The Judge? Never! Why I just love him. He is the dearest, best—"

"I see. He's an angel entirely, and no mere mortal from Paris is to be mentioned in the same breath."

"Well, he is everything charming," she insisted. "You would be sure to like him."

"I wish I could be as sure you might change your mind and like the new-comer from Paris."

"Do you? Oh, well, then, I'll certainly try. What is he like, nice?"

"I really can't remember ever having heard any one say so," confessed the stranger, smiling at her.

"Well," and Evilena regarded him with wide, astonished eyes, "no one else likes him, yet you hoped I would. Why, I don't see how—"

The soft quick beat of horse hoofs on the white shelled road interrupted her, or gave opportunity for interrupting herself.

"I hope it's Gertrude. Oh, it *is*! You dear old darling."

She flounced down the steps, followed by the man, who was becoming a puzzle. He gave his hand to Miss Loring, who accepted that assistance from the horse block, and then he stepped aside that the embrace feminine might have no obstacle in its path.

"My dear little girl," and the mistress of Loringwood kissed her guest with decided fondness. "How good of you to come at once—and Mrs. Nesbitt, too? I'm sorry you had to wait even a little while for a welcome, but I just had to ride over to the quarters, and then to the far fields. Thank you, doctor, for playing host."

"*Doctor*?" gasped Evilena, gripping Miss Loring's arm. There was a moment of hesitation on the part of all three, when she said, reproachfully, looking at the smiling stranger, "Then it was you all the time?"

"Was there no one here to introduce you?" asked Miss Loring, looking from one to the other. "This is Dr. Delavan, dear, and this, doctor, is Kenneth's sister."

"Thanks. I recognized her at once, and I trust you will forgive me for not introducing myself sooner, mademoiselle, but—well, we had so many other more interesting things to speak of."

Evilena glanced at him out of the corner of her eye, and with her arm about Gertrude walked in silence up the steps. She wanted time to think over what awful things she had said to him, not an easy thing to do, for Evilena said too many things to remember them all.

Margeret was in the hall. Evilena wondered by what occult messages she learned when any one ascended those front steps. She took Miss Loring's riding hat and gloves.

"Mistress Nesbitt is just resting," she said, in those soft even tones. "She left word to call her soon as you got back —she'd come down."

"I'll go up and see her," decided Miss Loring. "Will you excuse us, doctor? And Margaret, have Chloe get us a bit of lunch. We are all a little tired, and it is a long time till supper."

"I have some all ready, Miss Gertrude. Was only waiting till you got back."

"Oh, very well. In five minutes we will be down."

Then, with her arm about Evilena, Miss Loring ascended the wide stairway, where several portraits of vanished Lorings hung, none of them resembling her own face particularly.

She was what the Countess Biron had likened her to when the photograph was shown—a white lily, slender, blonde, with the peculiar and attractive combination of hazel eyes and hair of childish flaxen color. Her features were well formed and a trifle small for her height. She had the manner of a woman perfectly sure of herself, her position and her own importance.

9

Her voice was very sweet. Sometimes there were high, clear tones in it. Delaven had admired those bell-like intonations until now, when he heard her exchange words with Margeret. All at once the mellow, contralto tones of the serving woman made the voice of the lovely mistress sound metallic—precious metal, to be sure, nothing less than silver. But in contrast was the melody, entirely human, soft, harmonious, alluring as a poet's dream of the tropics.

CHAPTER XII.

"How that child is petted on, Gideon," and Mrs. Nesbitt looked up from her work, the knitting of socks, to be worn by unknown boys in gray. Even the material for them was growing scarce, and she prided herself on always managing, someway, to keep her knitting needles busy. At present she was using a coarse linen or tow thread, over which she lamented because of its harshness.

Miss Loring, who appeared very domestic, with a stack of household linen beside her, glanced up, with a smile.

"Rather fortunate, isn't it, considering—" an arch of the brows and a significant expression were allowed to finish her meaning. Mrs. Nesbitt pursed up her lips and shook her head.

"I really and truly wonder sometimes, Gertrude, if it's going on like this always. Ten years if it's a day since he commenced paying court there, and what she allows to do, at least is more than I can guess."

"Marry him, no doubt," suggested Gertrude, inspecting a sheet carefully, and then proceeding to tear it in widths designated by Dr. Delaven for hospital bandages. "She certainly esteems him very highly."

"Oh, esteem!" and Mrs. Nesbitt's tone was dubious.

"Well, people don't think much of getting married these days, where there is fighting and mourning everywhere."

The older lady gave her a quick glance over the tow yarn rack, but the fair face was very serene, and without a trace of personal feeling on the subject.

"Yes, that's so," she admitted, "but I used to think they were only waiting till Kenneth came of age, or until he graduated. But my! I didn't see it make a spec of difference. They danced together at the party given for him, and smiled, careless as you please, and now the dancing is ended, they keep on friendly and smiling, and I'm downright puzzled to know what they do mean."

"Maybe no more than those two, who are only amusing themselves," said Gertrude, with a glance towards the lawn where Evilena and Delaven were fencing with long stalks of a wild lily they had brought from the swamps, and when Evilena was vanquished by the foe her comforter was a white-haired gentleman, inclined to portliness, and with much more than an inclination to courtliness, whom Evilena called "My Judge."

It was two weeks after the descent of Aunt Sajane and Evilena upon Loringwood. The former, after a long consultation with Dr. Delaven, had returned to her own home, near the McVeigh plantation, and putting her household in order for a more prolonged visit than at first intended, she had come back to be near Gertrude in case—

None of them had put into words to each other their thought as to Matthew Loring's condition, but all understood the seriousness of it, and Gertrude, of course, must not be left alone.

Dr. Delaven had meant only to accompany the invalid home, consult with their local physician, and take his departure after a visit to Mrs. McVeigh, and possibly a sight of their new battlefield beside Kenneth, if his command was not too far away.

Kenneth McVeigh was Col. McVeigh now, to the great delight of the sister, who loved men who could fight. On his return from Paris he had, at his own request, and to the dismay of his family, been sent to the frontier. At the secession of his state he was possessed of a captaincy, which he resigned, returned home, and in six weeks tendered a regiment, fully equipped at his own expense, to the Confederate government. His offer had been accepted and himself made a colonel. His regiment had already seen one year of hard service, were veterans, with a colonel of twenty-five—a colonel who had been carried home wounded unto death, the surgeons said, from the defeat of Fort Donaldson. He had belied their prophecies of death, however, and while not yet equal to the rigors of camp life, he had accepted a commission abroad of decided importance to his government, and became one of the committee to deal with certain English sympathizers who were fitting out vessels for the Confederate navy.

Mrs. McVeigh had been called to Mobile by the serious illness of an aged relative and had been detained by something much less dreary, the marriage of her brother, who had command of a garrison at that point.

Thus barred from seeing either of his former Parisian friends, Delaven would have gone back to Charleston, or else gone North or West to view a new land in battle array.

But Mr. Loring's health, or Miss Loring's entreaties had interfered with both those plans. He could not desert a young lady on an isolated plantation with only the slaves about her, and a partial paralytic to care for, especially when all the most capable physicians were at military posts, and no one absolutely reliable nearer than Charleston.

So he had promised to stay, and had advised Miss Loring to induce Mrs. Nesbitt to remain until a few weeks' rest and the atmosphere of home would, he hoped, have a beneficial influence on the invalid.

All his suggestions had been carried out. Aunt Sajane (who had not a niece or nephew in the world, yet was "aunt" to all the young folks) was to remain, also Evilena, until the return of Mr. McVeigh, after which they all hoped Mr. Loring could be persuaded to move up the river to a smaller estate belonging to Gertrude, adjoining The Terrace, as the nearness of friends would be a great advantage under the circumstances. The isolation of Loringwood had of late become oppressive to its mistress, who strongly advocated its sale. They had enough land without, and she realized it was too large a tract to be managed properly or to profit so long as her uncle was unable to see to affairs personally. But above all else, the loneliness of it was irksome since her return.

"Though we never did use to think Loringwood isolated, did we, Gideon?" asked Mrs. Nesbitt, who remembered the house when full of guests, and the fiddles and banjos of the colored musicians always ready for dance music.

"Relentless circumstances over (he called it ovah, and Delaven delighted in the charming dialect of the South, as illustrated by the Judge) which we have no control have altered conditions through this entire (entiah) commonwealth. But, no. I should not call Loringwood exactly isolated, with the highway of the Salkahatchie at its door."

"But when no one travels the highway?" said Delaven, whose comments had aroused the discussion. "No one but black hunters in log canoes have I seen come along it for a week, barring yourselves. Faith, I should think their presence alone would be enough to give a young lady nervous chills, the daily and nightly fear of insurrection."

The Judge smiled, indulgently, willing to humor the fancies of foreigners, who were not supposed to understand American institutions.

"Your ideas would be perfectly sound, my dear sir, if you were dealing with any other country, where the colored man is the recognized servant of the land and of the land owners. But we of the South, sir, understand their needs and just the proper amount of control necessary to be enforced for mutual protection. They have grown up under that training until it is a part of themselves. There are refractory blacks, of course, just as there are worthless demoralized whites, but I assure you, sir, I voice the sentiments of our people when I state that the families of Southern planters feel much more secure when guarded by their colored folk than they would if surrounded by a troop of Northern soldiery. There have been no cases where white women and children have had reason to regret having trusted to the black man's guardianship, sir. In that respect I believe we Southrons hold a unique place in history. The evils of slavery, perfectly true in many lands, are not true here. The proofs of it are many. Their dependence on each other is mutual. Each understands and respects that fact, sir, and the highest evidence of it is shown when the master marches to meet their common enemy, and leaves his wife and children to the care of the oldest or most intelligent of his bondsmen.

"I tell you, sir, the people of Europe cannot comprehend the ties between those two races, because the world has seen nothing like it. The Northern people have no understanding of it, because, sir, their natures are not such as to call forth such loyalty. They are a cold, unresponsive people, and the only systematic cruelty ever practiced against the colored folks by Americans has been by the New England slavers, sir. The slave trade has always been monopolized by the Northern folks in this country—by the puritanical New Englanders who used to sell the pickaninnies at so much a pound, as cattle or sheep are sold.

"They are no longer able to derive a profit from it, hence their desire to abolish the revenue of the South. I assure you, sir, if the colored man could endure the climate of their bleak land there would be no shouting for abolition."

It was only natural that Delaven should receive a good deal of information those days from the Southern side of the question. Much of it was an added education to him—the perfect honesty of the speakers, the way in which they entered heart and soul into the discussion of their state's rights, the extreme sacrifices offered up, the lives of their sons, the wealth, the luxury in which they had lived, all given up without protest for the cause. Women who had lived and ruled like queens over the wide plantations, were now cutting their living expenses lower and lower, that the extra portion saved might be devoted to their boys at the front. The muslins and linens for household purposes were used as Gertrude Loring was using them now; everything possible was converted into bandages for hospital use.

"I simply don't dare let the house servants do it," she explained, in reply to the Judge's query. "They could do the work, of course, but they never have had to practice economy, and I can't undertake to teach it to them as well as myself, and to both at the same time. Oh, yes, Margeret is capable, of course, but she has her hands full to watch those in the cook house."

Her smile was very bright and contented. It hinted
nothing of the straightened circumstances gradually surrounding them, making a close watch in all directions absolutely necessary. Affairs were reaching a stage where
money, except in extravagant quantities, was almost useless. The blockade had raised even the most simple articles to the price of luxuries. All possessions, apart from
their home productions, must be husbanded to the utmost.

"You are a brave little woman, Miss Gertrude," said the
Judge, bowing before her with a certain reverence. "All the
battles of this war are not fought to the sound of regimental
music, and our boys at the front shoot straighter when they
have at home women like you to guard. Our women of the
South are an inspiration—an inspiration!"

No courtier of storied Castile could have rivaled the
grace of manner with which the praise was spoken, so
thought Delaven, for all his mental pictures of Castillian
courtesies revealed them as a bit theatrical, while the Judge
was sincerity itself.

As he spoke, the soft sound of wheels was heard in the
hall, and Matthew Loring, in his invalid chair, was rolled
slowly out on the veranda by his man, Ben. Margeret
followed with a light robe over her arm, and a fan.

"Not there, Ben," she said, in the low tone of one giving
an order entirely personal and not intended to be heard by
the others, "the draught does seem to coax itself round that
corner, and—"

"Not a bit of it," broke in the master of Loringwood, abruptly. "No more draught there than anywhere else. It's
all right, Ben, wheel me to that railing."

Margeret silently spread the robe over his knees, laid the
fan in his lap, adjusted the cushion back of his head, and

re-entered the house with a slight gesture to Ben, who followed her.

"She's a puzzle entirely," remarked Delaven, who was watching them from the rustic seat nearest the steps. Evilena was seated there, and he stood beside her.

"Margeret? Why?" she asked, in the same low tone.

I'll tell you. Not thirty minutes ago I told her he could be brought out and have his chair placed so that the sun would be on his limbs, but not on his head. Now, what does she do but pilot him out and discourage him from going to just the corner that was best."

"And you see the result," whispered the girl, who was laughing. "Margeret knows a lot. Just see how satisfied he is, now, the satisfaction of having had to fight some one. If he knew it was anybody's orders, even yours, he would not enjoy that corner half so much. That is the sweet disposition of our Uncle Matthew."

Overhanging eyebrows of iron-gray were the first thing to arrest attention in Matthew Loring's face. They shadowed dark expressive eyes in a swarthy setting. His hair and mustache were of the same grey, and very bushy. He had the broad head and square jaw of the aggressive type. Not a large man, even in his prime, he looked almost frail as he settled back in his chair. He was probably sixty, but looked older.

"Still knitting socks, Mistress Nesbitt?" he inquired, with a caustic smile. "Charming occupation. Do you select that quality an' color for any beauties to be found in them? I can remember seeing your mother using knitting needles on this very veranda thirty—yes, forty years ago. But I must say I never saw her make anything heavier than lace. And what's all this, Gertrude? Do you entertain your visitors these days by dragging out the old linen for their inspection? Why are you dallying with the servants' tasks?"

"No; it is my own task, uncle," returned his niece, with unruffled serenity. "Not a very beautiful one, but consoling because of its usefulness."

"Usefulness—huh! In your mother's day ladies were not expected to be useful."

"Alas for us that the day is past," said the girl, tearing off another strip of muslin.

"Now, do you wonder that I adore my Judge?" whispered Evilena to Delaven.

CHAPTER XIII.

Despite his natural irritability, to which no one appeared to pay much attention, Mr. Loring grew almost cordial under the geniality and hopefulness emanating from Judge Clarkson, whom he was really very glad to see, and of whom he had numberless queries to ask regarding the hostilities of the past few months.

The enforced absence abroad had kept him in a highly nervous condition, doing much to counteract the utmost care given him by the most learned specialists of Europe. Half his fortune had been lost by those opening guns at Sumter. His warehouses, piled with great cotton bales for shipment to England, had been fired—burned to the ground. The capture of Beaufort, near which was another plantation of his, had made further wreck for him, financially, and whatever the foreign doctors might to with his body, his mind was back in Carolina, eager, questioning, combative. He was burning himself up with a fever of anxiety.

"It is all of no use, Mademoiselle," said the most distinguished specialist whom she had consulted, "Monsieur, your uncle will live for many years if but the mind is composed—no shocks, no heavy loads to carry. But the mind, you perceive—it is impossible for him to allow himself to be composed away from his country. We have done all that can be done here. To return to his own land under the care of a competent physician, of course, would be now the best arrangement I could suggest. He may live there for many years; here, he will most certainly die."

At Loring's request Dr. Delaven was the physician who had been approached with the proposal to accompany him to Carolina. Why, it would be hard to guess, for they were totally unlike in every way—had not, apparently, a single taste in common. But the physician in charge of the hospital approved his judgment.

"It is a most wise one, Monsieur Loring. Dr. Delaven has shown as his specialty cases similar to your own, and has proven most successful. Withal, he is adventurous. He will enjoy the new country, and he is of your own language. All I could do for you he can do, perhaps more; for I am old, while he is young and alive with enthusiasms with which to supplement his technical knowledge."

Gertrude only delayed their departure long enough to write Col. McVeigh, who was in London. He secured for them transportation to Nassau under the guardianship of an official who would take most extreme care that the party be conveyed from there by some blockade runner to be depended upon. And that the Federal blockade often failed of its purpose was evidenced by the fact that they were quietly landed one night in a little inlet south of Charleston, which they reached by carriage, and rested there a few days before attempting the journey overland.

The doctors were correct as to the beneficial results of the home coming of Loring. It acted like a tonic and the thought of outwitting the Yankees of that blockade pleased him immensely. He never gave a thought to the girl who watched with pale face and sleepless eyes through that dash for the shore. Delaven mentally called him a selfish brute.

The visit of Judge Clarkson was partially an affair of business, but after a private interview with Delaven he decided to dismiss all idea of business settlements until later. Nothing of an annoying or irritating nature must be broached to the convalescent just yet.

The Judge confessed that it was an affair over which Mr. Loring had been deeply chagrined—a clear loss of a large sum of money, and perhaps it would be safer, under the circumstances, to await Col. McVeigh's return. Col. McVeigh was equally interested, and neither he nor the Judge would consent to risk an attack similar to that experienced by Mr. Loring during the bombardment of Port Royal entrance. He was at that time on his Beaufort plantation, where the blue coats overran his place after they landed, and it was known to have been nothing else than a fit of rage at their victory, and rage at the planters who fled on all sides of him, which finally ended in the prostration for which the local physicians could find no remedy. Then it was that Gertrude took him abroad, with the result described. It was understood the prostration had taught him one useful lesson—he no longer cultivated the rages for which he had been locally famous. As he was unable to stamp and roar, he compromised on sneers and caustic retorts, from which he appeared to derive an amount of satisfaction tonical in its effects.

The Judge was giving Delaven the details of the Beaufort affair when Ben wheeled his master into the room. There

was an awkward pause, a slight embarrassment, but he had
caught the words "Port Royal entrance," and comprehended.

"Huh! Talking over that disaster, Judge?" he remarked.
"I tell you what it is, you can't convey to a foreigner anything of the feeling of the South over those misfortunes;
to have Sherman's tramps go rough-shod over your lawns
and rest themselves with braggadocio at your tables—the
most infernal riff-raff—"

"One moment," interposed the Judge, blandly, with a
view to check the unpleasant reminiscences. "Did I not
hear you actually praise one of those Yankees?—in fact,
assert that he was a very fine fellow?"

"Yes, yes; I had forgotten him. A Yankee captain; ordered the blue-coats to the right-about when he found there
was only a sick man and a girl there; and more than that,
so long as those scavengers were ashore and parading
around Beaufort he kept men stationed at my gates for safeguard duty. A fine fellow, for a Yankee. I can only account for it by the fact that he was a West Point graduate,
and was thus thrown, to a certain extent, into the society
and under the influences of our own men. Kenneth, Col.
McVeigh, had known Monroe there—his name was Monroe—Captain John Monroe—at Beaufort his own men called
him Captain Jack."

> "Just as she was stepping on ship board:
>   'Your name I'd like to know?'
> And with a smile she answered him,
>   'My name is Jack Monroe!'"

sang a fresh voice outside the window, and then the curtain was pushed aside and Evilena's brown head appeared.

"I really could not help that, Mr. Loring," she said, laughingly. "The temptation was too great. Did you never whistle 'Jack Monroe' when you were a boy?"

"No, I can't say I ever did," he replied, testily.

"It's intensely interesting," she continued, seating herself on the window sill and regarding him with smiling interest, made bold by the presence of her champion, the Judge. "Aunt Sajane taught it to me, an old, old sailor song. It's all about her sweetheart, Jack, not Aunt Sajane's sweetheart, but the girl's. Her wealthy relatives separate them by banishing him to the wars somewhere, and she dressed up in boy's clothes to follow him.

> " 'She went unto a tailor
>   And dressed in men's array,
>   And thence unto a sailor
>   And paid her fare away.' "

recited Evilena, with uplifted finger punctuating the sentences. "Wasn't she brave? Well, she found him, and they were married. There are seven verses of it."

"I—I should think that quite enough," he remarked, dropping his head forward and looking at her from under the overhanging brows. "Do you mean to sing them all to me?"

"Perhaps, some day," she promised, showing all her teeth and dropping the curtain.

> "So now this couple's married,
>   Despite their bitter foe,
>   And she's back again in England
>   With her darling, Jack Monroe."

The two visitors laughed outright as this information was wafted to them from the veranda, the old song growing more faint as the singer circled the house in search of Gertrude.

"A true daughter of the South, Dr. Delaven," said the Judge, with a tender cadence betraying how close to his heart was his pride in all Southern excellence—"child and woman in one, sir—a charming combination."

"Right you are, Judge, in that; may their numbers never be less."

Evilena had found Gertrude and at once confessed her daring.

"Don't know how I ever did have courage to pop my head in there. Aunt Sajane—but he talked of Jack Monroe just as I passed the window, and I pretended I thought he meant the old song (I do wonder if he ever—*ever* sang or whistled?) Then I told him what it was all about, and promised to sing it to him some day, and I know by the sort of smile he had that he wanted to order me out of the room as he used to when I was little."

"Lena, Lena!" and Gertrude shook her head admonishingly at the girl, though she smiled at the recital.

"Oh, you are an angel, Gertrude; so you never have temptations to do things for pure mischief. But I wish you'd tell me who this Jack Monroe is."

"A Federal officer who was of service to us when Beaufort was taken."

"A *Yankee*!"—and her horror was absolute. "Well, I should not think you'd accept service from such a person."

"Honey!" said Aunt Sajane, in mild chiding.

"We had no choice," said Gertrude, quietly; "afterwards we learned he and Kenneth had been friends at West Point; so he was really a gentleman."

"And in the *Yankee Army*?" queried the irrepressible. "Good-bye, Jack Monroe, I shan't sing you again."

"You might be faithful to one verse for Gertrude's sake," ventured Aunt Sajane.

"Gertrude's sake?"

"Why, yes; he protected them from the intrusion of the Yankees."

"Oh—h! Aunt Sajane, I really thought you were going to ferret out a romance—a Romeo and Juliet affair—their families at war, and themselves—"

"Evilena!"

"When Gertrude says 'Evilena' in *that* tone I know it is time to stop," said the girl, letting go the kitten she was patting, and putting her arm around Gertrude. "You dear, sensible Gertrude, don't mind one word I say; of course I did not mean it. Just as if we did not have enough Romeo's in our own army to go around."

The significant glance accompanying her words made Gertrude look slightly conscious.

"You are a wildly romantic child," she said, smoothing the chestnut tinted waves of the girl's hair, "and pray, tell us how many of our military Romeos are singing 'Sweet Evilena,' and wearing your colors?"

Dr. Delaven passed along the hall in time to hear this bantering query, and came opposite the door when this true daughter of the South was counting all the fingers of one pretty hand.

"Just make it a half dozen," he suggested, for I'm wearing yet the sunflower you gave me," and he pointed to the large daisy in his buttonhole.

"No, I'm always honest with Gertrude, and she must have the true number. We are talking of military men, and all others are barred out."

"So you informed me the first day of our acquaintance," he assented, arranging the daisy more to his liking.

"And I've never forgiven you for that first day," she retorted, nodding her head in a way suggestive of some dire punishment waiting for him in the future. "It was dreadful, the way he led me on to say things, Aunt Sajane, for how was I to guess he was the doctor? I was expecting a man like—well, like Dr. Allison, only more so; very learned, very severe, with eye glasses through which he would examine us as though we were new specimens discovered in the wilds of America. I certainly did not expect to find a frivolous person who wore daisies, and—oh!" as she caught a glimpse of some one coming up the path from the landing —"there comes Nelse. Gertrude, *can't* I have him in here?"

"May I ask if Nelse is one of the five distinguished by your colors?" asked Delaven.

"Nelse is distinguished by his own colors, which is a fine mahogany, and he is the most interesting old reprobate in Carolina—a wizard, if you please—a sure enough voodoo doctor, and the black historian of the Salkahatchie. May I call him?"

"I really do not think uncle likes to have him around," said Gertrude, dubiously; "still—oh, yes, call him if you like. Don't let him tire you with his stories; and keep him out of uncle's way. He would be sure to tell him about those late runaways."

"I promise to stand guard in that case myself, Miss Loring; for I have a prejudice against allowing witch-doctors access to my patients."

Mrs. Nesbitt arose as if to follow Gertrude from the room, hesitated, and resumed her chair.

"When I was a girl we young folks were all half afraid of Nelse—not that he ever harmed any one," she confessed. "The colored folks said he was a wizard, but I never did give credit to that."

10

"Aunt Chloe, she says he is!"

"Oh, yes; and Aunt Chloe sees ghosts, and talks with goblins, to hear her tell the story; but that old humbug is just as much afraid of a mouse as—as I am."

"Nelse is a free nigger," explained Evilena, turning from the window after having motioned him to enter. "He was made free by his old master, Marmaduke Loring, and the old rascal—I mean Nelse, bought himself a wife, paid for her out of his jockey earnings, and when she proved a disappointment what do you think he did?"

Delaven could not get beyond a guess, as the subject of her discourse had just then appeared in the door.

He was a small, black man, quite old, but with a curious attempt at jauntiness, as he made his three bows with his one hand on his breast, the other holding his cane and a jockey cap of ancient fashion. It contrasted oddly with the swallow-tailed coat he wore, which had evidently been made for a much larger man; the sleeves came to his finger tips, and the tails touched his heels. The cloth of which it was made was very fine dark blue, with buttons of brass. His waistcoat of maroon brocade came half way to his knees. Warm as the day was he wore a broad tie of plaid silk arranged in a bow, above which a white muslin collar rose to his ears. He was evidently an ancient beau of the plantations in court dress.

"Yo' servant, Miss Sajane, Miss Lena; yo' servant, Mahstah," he said with a bow to each. "I done come pay my respects to the family what got back. I'm powerful glad to heah they got safe ovah that ocean."

"Oh, yes; you're very thankful when you wait two whole weeks before you come around to say 'howdy.' Have you moved so far into the swamp you can't even hear when the family comes home? Sit down, you're tired likely. Tell us all the news from your alligator pasture."

"My king! Miss Lena, you jest the same tant'lizin' little lady. Yo' growen' up don't make you outgrow nothen' but yo' clothes. My 'gatah pasture? I show yo' my little patch some o' these days—show yo' what kind 'gatahs pasture theah; why, why, I got 'nigh as many hogs as Mahs Matt has niggahs these days."

"Yes, and he hasn't so many as he did have," remarked Mrs. Nesbitt, significantly. "You know anything about where Scip and Aleck are gone?"

"Who—me? Miss Sajane? You think I keep time on all the runaway boys these days? They too many for me. It sutenly do beat all how they scatter. Yo' all hear tell how one o' Cynthy's boys done run away, too? Suah as I tell you—that second boy, Steve! Ole Mahs Masterson got him dogs out fo' him—tain't no use; nevah touched the track once. He'll nevah stop runnen' till he reach the Nawth an' freeze to death. I alles tole Cynthy that Steve boy a bawn fool."

"Do you mean your son Steve, or your grandson?" queried Mrs. Nesbitt.

"No'm, 'taint little Steve; his mammy got too much sense to let him go; but that gal, Cynthy—humph!" and his disdain of her perceptive powers was very apparent.

"But, Uncle Nelse, just remember Aunt Cynthy must be upwards of seventy. Steve is fifty if he is a day. How do you suppose she could control him, even if she knew of his intention, which is doubtful."

"She nevah would trounce that rascal, even in his youngest days," asserted Nelse, earnestly; "and as the 'bush is bent the tree's declined.' I use to kote that scripper to her many's the day, but how much good it do to plant cotton seed on

stony groun' or sow rice on the high lan'? Jes' that much
good scripper words done Cynthy, an' no more."

His tone betrayed a sorrowful but impersonal regret
over the refractory Cynthia, and their joint offspring.
Evilena laughed.

"Where did you get so well acquainted with the scrip-
ture, Nelse?" she asked. I know you never did learn it
from your beloved old Mahs Duke Loring. I want you to
tell this gentleman all about the old racing days. This is
Dr. Delaven (Nelse made a profound bow). He has seen
great races abroad and hunted foxes in Ireland. I want you
to tell him of the bear hunts, and the horses you used to ride,
and how you rode for freedom. The race was so important,
Dr. Delaven, that Marmaduke Loring promised Nelse his
freedom if he won it, and he had been offered three thousand, five hundred dollars for Nelse, more than once."

"Nevah was worth as much to myself as I was to Mahs
Duke," said Nelse, shaking his head. "I tell yo' true, freedom was a sure enough hoodoo, far as I was concerned;
nevah seemed to get so much out o' the horses after I was
my own man; nevah seemed to see so much money as I
owned befo', an' every plum thing I 'vested in was a failure
from the start; there was that gal o' Mahs Masterson's—
that there Cynthy—"

The old man's garrulity was checked by the noiseless entrance of Margeret. He gave a distinct start as he saw her.

"I—I s'lute yo', Miss Retta," he said, sweeping his cap
along the floor and bowing from where he sat. She glanced
at him, bent her head slightly in acknowledgment, but did
not address him.

"Miss Loring asks to see you in the dining room, Mistress Nesbitt," she said softly; then drawing a blind where

the sun was too glaring, and opening another that the breeze might be more apparent, she passed silently out.

The old man never spoke until she disappeared.

"My king!—she get mo' ghost-like every yeah, that Retta," he said, while Evilena gathered up the ball of stocking yard and wound it for Mrs. Nesbitt; "only the eyes o' that woman would tell a body who she is, these days; seems like the very shape o' her face been changed sence she—"

"Nelse," said Mrs. Nesbitt, a trifle sharply, "whatever you do you are not to let Mr. Loring know about those runaways; maybe you better keep out of his sight altogether this visit, for he's sure to ask questions about everything, and the doctor's orders are that he is not to see folks or have any business talks—you understand? and nothing ever does excite him so much as a runaway."

Oh, yes, Miss Sajane, I un'stan'; I'll keep out. Hearen' how things was I jes' come down to see if Miss Gertrude needs any mo' help looken' after them field niggahs. They nevah run away from *me*."

"Well"—and she halted doubtfully at the door—"I'll tell her. And if you want Dr. Delaven to hear about the old racing days, honey, hadn't you better take him into the library where the portraits are? I'm a trifle uneasy lest Mr. Loring should take a notion to come in here. Since he's commenced to walk a little he is likely to appear anywhere but in the library. He never does seem to like the library corner."

Delaven glanced at the library walls as the three advanced thereto—walls paneled in natural cedar, and hung with large gilt frames here and there between the cases of books. "I should think any man would like a room like this," he remarked, especially when it holds one's own family portraits. There is a picture most attractive—a fine make of a man."

"That Mahs Tom Loring, Miss Gertrude's father," explained Nelse. "Jest as fine as he looks theah, Mahs Tom was, and ride!—king in heaven! but he could ride. 'Taint but a little while back since he was killed, twenty yeahs maybe—no, eighteen yeahs come Christmas. He was followen' the houn's, close on, when his horse went down an' Mahs Tom picked up dead, his naik broke. His wife, Miss Leo Masterson, she was, she died some yeahs befo', when Miss Gertrude jest a little missy. So they carried him home from Larue plantation—that wheah he get killed—an' bury him back yonder beside her," and he pointed to a group of pines across the field to the north; "so, after that—"

"Oh, Nelse, tell about live things—not dead ones," suggested Evilena, "tell about the races and your Mahs Duke, how he used to go horseback all the way to Virginia, to the races, and even to Philadelphia, and how all the planters gathered for hundreds of miles, some of the old ones wearing small clothes and buckled shoes, and how—"

"Seems like you done mind them things so well 'taint no use tryen' to rake up the buried reck'lections o' the pas' times," said the old man, rebukingly, and with a certain pomposity. "I reckon now you 'member all the high quality gentlemen. The New Market Jockey Club, an' how they use to meet reg'lar as clock-work the second Tuesday in May and October; an' how my Mahs Duke, with all the fine ruffles down his shirt front, an' his proud walk, an' his voice soft as music, an' his grip hard as steel, was the kingpin o' all the sports—the grandest gentleman out o' Calliny, an' carried his head high as a king ovah all Jerusalem—I reckon you done mind all that theah, Miss Lena."

"I will, next time," laughed the girl, "go on, Nelse, we would rather hear what you remember."

"I don't reckon the names o' the ole time sportin' gentlemen, an' old time jockeys, an' old time stock, would count much with a gentleman from foreign lan's," said the old man, with a deprecating bow to Delaven. "But my Mahs Duke Loring nevah had less than six horses in trainen' at once. I was stable-boy, an' jes' trained up with the colts till Mahs Duke saw I could ride. I sartainly had luck with racin' stock, seein' which he gave me clean charge o' the whole racin' stable; 'sides which, keepen' my weight down to eighty pounds let me in for the jockey work—them was days. I was sent ovah into Kaintucky, an' up Nawth far as Long Island, to ride races fo' otha gentlemen—friends o' Mahs Duke's, an' every big race I run put nigh onto a hundred dollar plump into my own pocket. Money?—my king! I couldn't see cleah how I evah could spend all the money I got them days, cause I didn't have to spend a cent fo' clothes or feed, an' I had mo' presents give to me by the quality folks what I trained horses fer than I could count or reck'lect.

"The ride Miss Lena done tole yo' of—that happen the yeah Mahs Duke imported Lawd Chester, half brother to Bonnie Bell, that won the sweepstakes at Petersburg, an' sire o' Glenalven out o' Lady Clare, who was owned by Mahs Hampton ovah in Kaintucky. Well, sah, the yeah he imported Chester was the yeah he an' Mr. Enos Jackson had the set-to 'bout their two-yeah-olds—leastwise the colts *seemed* to be the cause; but I don't mind tellen', now, that I nevah did take stock in that notion, my own self. Women folks get mixed up even in race fights an' I mind one o' the han'some high steppers o' Philadelphia way down theah that time, an' Mistah Jackson he got a notion his chances mighty good, till long come Mahs Duke an' glance out corner of his eye, make some fine speeches, an'—farwell, Mistah Jackson! Mistah Jackson wa'nt jes' what you'd call the highest quality, though he did own powerful stretches o' lan'—three plantations in Nawth Calliny, 'sides lots o' other property. He had a colt called Darker he 'lowed nothen' could keep in sight of, an' he *was* good stuff—that colt. Mistah Jackson would a had easy riden' fo' the stakes if me an' Mahs Duke hadn't fetch Betty Pride up to show 'em what we could do. Well, the upshot of it was that part on account o' that Nawthen flirtatious young pusson what liked Mahs Duke the best, an' part on account o' Betty Pride, Mistah Jackson act mighty mis- chievous-like, an' twenty minutes afo' time was called I 'scovered that boy, Jim Peters, what was to ride Betty Pride, had been drugged—jest a trifle, not enough to leave him stupid—but too much to leave him ride, bright as he need be that day. He said Mistah Jackson's stable boss had give him a swallow o' apple jack, an' king heaven!—but Mahs Duke turn white mad when I tole him. He say to Jim's brother Mose—Mose was his body servant—'Moses, fetch me my pistols,' jest quiet like that; 'Moses, fetch me my pistols.' Whew!—but I was scared, an' I says, 'No, sah,' I says, 'Mahs Duke, fo' heaven's sake, don't stop the race, an' I'll win it fo' you yet. Mistah Jackson betten nigh bout all he own on Darker; get yo' frien's to take all bets fo' you, an' egg him on. Betty Pride ain't been tampered with!—take my word fo' it, she'll win even with my extra weight—now, Mahs Duke, fo' God's sake,' says I, 'go out theah an' fool them rascals; don't let on you know 'bout their trick; take all theah bets, an' trust me. I trained that colt, an' we'll *win*, Mahs Duke—if we don't—well, sah, you can jest use them pistols on *me*.' I mos' got down on my knees a' beggen' him, an' his blue eyes, like steel, measuren' me an' weighen' my words, then he said: 'I'll risk it, Nelse, but—heaven help yo' if yo' fail me!'

"I knew good enough I'd need *some* powerful help if I come in second, fo' he had a monstrous temper, but kindest man you evah met when things went his way. Well, jest as I was jumpen' into my clothes, an' Mahs Duke had started to the ring, I called out, half joken: 'Oh, Mahs Duke, I'm a dead niggah if I come in second, but what yo' gwine to give me if I come in first?'

"He turned at that an' said, sharp an' quick an' decided— 'Yo' freedom, Nelse.' My king!—that made me shaky, I could scarce get into my clothes. I knew he been offered big money fo' me, many's the time, an' now I was gwine to get it all my own self.

"Mahs Duke done jes' like I begged him—kep' steady an' cool an' take up all Mistah Jackson's bets, and *he* was jest betten wild till he saw who was on Betty Pride, an' I heah tell he come a nigh fainten' when he got sight o' me; but Mahs Duke's look at 'im must a jes' propped him up an' sort o' fo'ced him to brave it out till we come aroun'. It was a sweepstakes an' repeat, an' Betty Pride come in eighteen inches ahead, an' that Nawthen lady what conjure Mistah Jackson so, she fastened roses in Betty Pride's bridle, an' gave me a whole bouquet—with one eye on Mahs Duke all the time, of course, but Lordy!—he wan't thinken' much about ladies jes' that minute. He won ovah thousand dollars in money, 'sides two plantations off Mistah Jackson, who nevah dared enter the jockey club aftah that day. An' Mahs Duke was good as his word 'bout the freedom—he give it to me right theah; that's my Mahs Duke."

"And a fine sort of a man he was, then," commented Delaven, looking more closely at the strong, fine pictured face, and the bushy, leonine shock of tawny hair and the eyes that smiled down with a twinkle of humor in their blue depths. There was a slight likeness to Matthew Loring in the heavy brows and square chin, but the smile of the father was genial—that of the son, sardonic.

"Yes, sah," agreed Nelse, when comment was made upon the likeness, "Mahs Matt favor him a mite, but none to speak of. Mahs Tom more like him in natur'. Mahs Matt he done take mo' likeness to his gran'ma's folks, who was French, from L'weesiana. A mighty sharp eye she got, an' all my Mahs Duke's niggahs walk straight, I tell yo', when she come a visiten' to we all. I heard tell how *her* mother was some sort o' great lady from French court, packed off to L'weesiana 'cause o' some politics like they have ovah theah; an' in her own country she was a princess or some high mightiness, an' most o' her family was killed in some rebeloution—woman, too! All saved her was getten to Orleans, an' *her* daughter, she married ole Matthew Loring, the daddy o' them all, so far back as I know."

The old man had warmed to his task, as floods of reminiscences came sweeping through his memory. He grew more important, and let fall the borrowed cloak of servility; his head was perched a little higher and a trifle askew as he surveyed them. The reflected grandeur of past days was on him, and in comparison modernity seemed common-place. All these brilliant, dashing, elegant men and women of his youth were gone. He was the only human echo left of their greatness, and his diminutive person grew more erect as he realized his importance as a landmark of the past.

"There!" said Evilena, triumphantly, "isn't that as interesting as your Irish romances? Where would you find a landlord of England or Ireland who would make a free gift of three thousand dollars to a servant? They simply could not conceive of such generosity unless it were the gift of a king or a prince, and then it would be put down in their histories for all men to remember."

"True for you," assented Delaven, with the brogue he was fond of using at times when with those elected to comradeship; "true for you, my lady, but you folks who are kings and queens in your own right should be a bit easy on the unfortunates who can be only subjects."

"They don't need to be subjects," she insisted; "they could assert their independence just as we did."

"Oh, sometimes it isn't so bad—this being a subject. I've found life rather pleasant down here in the South, where you are all in training for the monarchy you mean to establish. I don't mind being a subject at all, at all, if it's to the right queen."

"But we didn't come in here to talk politics," she said, hastily. "Uncle Nelse, do tell Dr. Delaven about your freedom days, and all. He is a stranger here and wants to learn all about the country and customs. You've travelled, Nelse, so you can tell him a lot."

"Yes, reckon I could. Yes, sah, I done travelled considerable; the onliest advantage I could conjure up in freedom was goen' wherever the fit took me to go—jes' runnen' roun' loose. My king! I got good an' tiahed runnen, *I* tell yo'. Went cleah out to the Mississippi river, I did—spent all my money, an' started back barefoot, deed I did, an' me worth three thousan' five hundred dollars! Nevah did know how little sense I got till I was free to get myself in trouble if I liked, an' didn't have no Mahs Duke to get me out again. More'n that, seem like I done lost my luck some way—lost races I had no right to lose, till seem like owners they got scary 'bout me, an' when I git far away from my own stamping groun', seem like I wasn't no sort o'

use at all. Bye and bye I fell in with Judge Warner, who
was a great friend o' Mahs Dukes, and I jes' up an' tells him
I done been conjured along o' that freedom Mahs Duke
done give me. My king!—how he did laugh. He offered
me a good berth down on his place, but I say, 'no, sah; all
I want is Mahs Duke an' old Calliny'; so he helps me to
some races an' seems like the very notion o' goen' home
done fetch me good luck right off, 'cause I made good
winnen' on his bay filly, Creole, an' soon as I got some
money I bid far'well to wanderen' an' made fo' home.

"I alles spishuned Mahs Duke know mo' 'bout my travels than he let on, fo' he jes' laughed when he see me an' say:
'All right, Nelse, I been looken' fo' you some time. Now
if yo' done got yo' fill o' seen' the world, 'spose yo' go down
an' look at the new colt I got, an' take yo' ole place in the
stable. Yo' jes' got back in time to spruce up the carriage
team fo' my wedden'.

"Well, sah, yo' could a' knocked me down with a feathah.
Mahs Duke was thirty-five, an' ovah, an' had kep' his own
bachelor place fo' ten yeah, loose an' free. Then all at once
a new family come down heah from Marylan'. They was
the Mastersons, an' a Miss Bar'bra Vaughn come to visit
them, an' it was all ovah with Mahs Duke. She jest won in
a walk—that little lady.

"An' he done took her all the way to Orleans fo' wedden'
trip. I didn't go 'long. I was done tired out with travel
an' 'sides that, I'd been riden' ovah an' back to the Masterson plantation fo' Mahs Duke till I took up with a likely
brown gal they fetched with them from up Nawth, an' of
all niggahs, Nawthen niggahs is the off-scourins o' the
yeath—copy aftah theh masters, I reckon, fo' all the real,
double-distilled quality folks I met up with in all my travels
were gentlemen o' the South, sah. Yes, sah, they may

breed good quality somewheahs up theah, but all o' them sent down heah as samples ain't nowhars with the home-bred article, sah.

"But I didn't know all that them days, an' that Cynthy o' Mistah Masterson's look mighty peart an' talk mighty knowen', an' seem like as we both hed travelled considerable we both hed a heap of talk 'bout; an' the upshot of it was I felt boun' an' sot to buy that gal, if so be they'd give me a fair chance an' plenty o' time. Well, sah, I talk it ovah with Mahs Duke, an' he fix it so I can have Cynthy fo' three hundred dollars.

"Seem like it's a mighty small price to ask fo' a likely young gal like her, but I so conjured with the notion o' buyen' her I nevah stopped to study into the reasons why o' things, special as I had part o' the money right by me to pay; a pocket full o' money gets a man into mo' trouble mostly than an empty one.

"Well, sah, I hadn't owned her no time, till I was mo' sot in my mind than evah as how freedom was a hoodoo. If I hadn't been free I'd nevah took the notion to have a free wife o' my own, an' I'd a been saved a lot o' torment, *I* tell yo'.

"She jest no good no how—that Cynthy. How they got work out o' her ovah on the Masterson plantation I don't know, fo' *I* couldn't. Think she'd even cook vittels fo' her own self if she could help it? No, sah! She too plum lazy. She jes' had a notion that bein' free meant doen' nothen' 'tall fo' no body. It needed a whole meeten' house full o' religion to get along with that gal, 'thout cuss-en' at her, an' as I'd done trained in the race course an' not in a pulpit, seem like I noways fit for the 'casion. But I devilled along with her for three yeahs, and she had two boys by that time—didn't make no sort o' difference. She got worse 'stead o' better o' her worthlessness, but I tried to put up with it till she jest put the cap sheaf on the hull business by getten' religion up thah in the gum tree settlement, an' I drew the line at that, *I* tell yo.' Thah she was, howlen' happy every night in the week 'long-side o' Brother Peter Mosely. Brother Mosely's wife didn't seem to favah their religion no more'n I did; so, seen' as I couldn't follow roun' aftah her with a hickory switch, an' couldn't keep her home or at work no othah way, I just got myself a divorce, an' settled down alone on a patch o' lan' I bought o' Mahs Duke, an' I kep' on looken' aftah his stables long as he kept any. He died just afore young Mahs Tom married Miss Leo Masterson."

"But what of the divorce? Did it improve her religion or cure her laziness?" asked Delaven, who found more of novelty in the black man's affairs than the master's.

"Who—Cinthy? I just sold her right back to Mistah John Masterson fo' twenty-five dollar less than I paid, an' the youngsters they went into the bargain; fo' I tell yo', sah, them Nawthen niggahs is bad stock to manage—if they's big or little; see what happened that Steve o' hern; done run off, he has, an' him ole enough to know bettah. Oh, yes, sah, I up an' I sold the whole batch; that how come I get my money back fo' her, an' stock my little patch o' groun'. Yes, sah, she got scared an' settle down when I done sold her back again. Mahs Masterson he got mo' work out o' her than I could; he knew mo' 'bout managen' them Nawthen niggahs."

"Wouldn't he be a find for those abolitionists?" asked Evilena, laughing. "Nelse, you've been very entertaining, and if your Miss Gertrude needs you to stay about the place we'll steal hours to hear about old times."

"Thanky, Miss Lena; yo' servant, sah; it sartainly does do me good to get in heah an' see all these heah faces again —mighty fine they are. I mind when some o' them was painted. Mahs Duke's was done in Orleans; so was Miss Bar'bra, it's in the parlah. But Mahs Tom—he had an artis' painter come down from Wash'nton to do Miss Gertrude's, once when she just got ovah sick spell—he scared lest she die an' nevah have no likeness; her ma, she died sudden that-a-way. We all use to think it bad luck to get likenesses; I nevah hád none; Mahs Matt navah had none; an' we're a liven' yet. All the rest had 'em took an' wheah are they?"

"Now, Uncle Nelse, you don't mean to say it shortens people's lives to have their picture taken?"

"Don't like to say, Miss Lena, but curious things do happen in this world. That artist man, his name, Mistah Madden, he made Mahs Tom's likeness, an' Mahs Tom got killed! An' all time Mahs Tom's likeness was bein' done, an' all time Miss Gertrude's was a doin', that Mistah Madden he just go 'stracted to print one o' Retta to take 'way with him. All the niggahs jest begged her not to let him, but she only laughed—she laughed most o' the time them days; an' Mahs Tom he sided with Mistah Madden, so she give consent, an' he painted two—one monstrous big one to take 'way with him, an' then a teeny one fo' a breastpin; he give it to Retta 'cause she set still an' let him make the big one. An' now what happened? Within a yeah Mahs Tom, he was killed, an' Retta Caris, she about died o' some crazy brain fever, an' it was yeahs afore she knew her own name again; yes, went 'wildered like—she did; an' that's what two likenesses done to my sutain knowledge."

"Then I've hoodooed Dr. Delaven, for I made a pencil picture of him only this morning."

"And if I should fall down stairs, or into the Salkahatchie, you will know the primal reason for it."

Old Nelse shook him head at such frivolity.

"Jes' 'cause you all ain't afraid don't take yo' no further off danger," he said, soberly. Then he followed Evilena to the kitchen, where his entrance was greeted with considerable respect. When Nelse appeared at Loringwood in his finest it was a sort of state affair in the cook house. He was an honored guest with the grown folks, because the grandeurs he had witnessed and could tell of, and he was a cause of dread to the pickaninnies who were often threatened with banishment to the Unc. Nelse glade, and they firmly believed he immediately sold all the little darkies who put foot in his domain.

"Isn't he delightfully quaint?" asked the girl, rejoining Delaven. "Gertrude never does seem to find him interesting; but I do. She has been used to him always, of course, and I haven't, and she thinks it was awful for him to sell Cynthia, just because she got religion and would not behave. Now, I think it's funny; don't you?"

"Your historian has given me so many side-lights on slavery that I'm dazzled with the brilliancy of them; whether serious or amusing, it is astonishing."

"Only to strangers," said the girl; "to us they are never puzzling; they are only grown-up children—even the wisest —and need to be managed like children. Those crazy abolitionists should hear Nelse on the 'hoodoo' of freedom; I fancy he would astonish them."

"Not the slightest doubt of it," agreed Delaven, who usually did agree with Evilena—except when argument would prolong a tete-a-tete.

CHAPTER XIV.

Gertrude promptly assured old Nelse that the plantation needed no extra caretakers just then, the work was progressing very well since their return. Nelse swept the jockey cap over his feet in a profound bow, and sauntered around the house. The mistress of Loringwood asked Evilena to see if he had gone to his canoe. She did so, and reported that he had gone direct to the stables, where he had looked carefully over all the horses, and found one threatened with some dangerous ailment requiring his personal ministrations. He had announced his intention of staying right there until that horse was "up an' doin' again." At that minute he was seated on a half bushel measure as on a throne from which he was giving his orders, and all the young niggars were fairly flying to execute them.

"It is no use, Gertrude," said Mrs. Nesbitt, with a sigh; "as soon as I saw that vest and your grandfather's coat with the brass buttons, I knew Nelse had come to stay a spell, and stay he will in spite of us."

Which statement gave the man from Dublin another sidelight on the race question!

One of the servants announced a canoe in sight, coming from up the river, and anticipating a probable addition to their visitors, Delaven escaped by a side door, until the greetings were over, and walking aimlessly along a little path back from the river, found it ended at a group of pines surrounded by an iron railing, enclosing, also, the high,

11

square granite and marble abodes of the dead. It was here Nelse had pointed when telling of Tom Loring's sudden death and burial.

He opened the gate, and as he did so noticed a woman at the other side of the enclosure. Remembering how intensely superstitious the colored folks were said to be, he wondered at one of them coming alone into the grove so nearly darkened by the dense covering of pine, and with only the ghostly white of the tombs surrounding her.

He halted and stood silent beside a tree until she arose and turned towards the gate, then he could see plainly the clear, delicate profile of the silent Margeret. Of all the people he had met in this new country, this quiet, pale woman puzzled him most. She seemed to compel an atmosphere of silence, for no one spoke of her. She moved about like a shadow in the house, but she moved to some purpose, for she was a most efficient housekeeper, even the pickaninnies from the quarters—saucy and mischievous enough with any one else—were subdued when Margeret spoke.

After she had passed out of the gate he went over where he had seen her first. Two tombs were side by side, and of the same pattern; a freshly plucked flower lay on one. He read the name beneath the flower; it was, *Thomas Loring, in the thirtieth year of his age*; the other tomb was that of his wife, who had died seven years earlier.

But it was on Tom Loring's tomb the blossom had been laid.

Was it merely an accident that it was the marble on which the fragrant bit of red had been let fall? or—

He walked slowly back to the house, feeling that he had touched on some story more strange than any Evilena had asked him to listen to of the old days, and this one was vital, human, fascinating.

He wondered who she was, yet felt a reluctance to ask. To him she appeared a white woman. Yet an intangible something in Miss Loring's manner to her made him doubt. He remembered hearing Matthew Loring on the voyage complain many times that Margeret would have arranged things for his comfort with more foresight than was shown by his attendants, but when he had reached Loringwood, and Margeret gave silent, conscientious care to his wants, there was never a word of praise given her. He—Delaven —felt as if he was the only one there who appreciated her ministrations; the others took them as a matter of course.

He saw old Nelse hitching along, with his queer little walk, coming from the direction of the stables. He motioned to him, and seated himself on a circular bench, backed by a great, live oak, and facing the river. Nelse proved that his sight was good despite his years, for he hastened his irregular shuffle and drew near, cap in hand.

"Did the canoe from up the river bring visitors?" asked Delaven, producing one cigar which he lighted, and another which he presented to the old man, who received it with every evidence of delight.

"I can't even so much as recollect when I done put my hands on one o' these real Cubas; I thank yo' kindly, sah. We all raise our own patches o' tobacco, and smoke it in pipes dry, so! an' in course by that-a-way we 'bleeged to 'spence with the julicious flavor o' the Cubas. No, sah; ain't no visitors; just Mrs. McVeigh's man, Pluto, done fetched some letters and Chloe—Chloe's cook, heah—she tell me she reckon Miss Gertrude try get Mahstah Matt to go up there fo' good 'fore long, fo' Mrs. McVeigh, she comen' home from Mobile right away, now; done sent word. An' Miss Lena, she jest in a jubilee ovah the letter, fo' her ma gwine fotch home some great quality folks a visiten'.

Judge Clarkson, he plan to start in the mawnen' for Savanna, he gwine meet 'em there."

"And in the meantime we can enjoy our tobacco; sit down. I've been so much interested in your stories of long ago that I want to ask you about one of the present time."

The smile of Nelse broadened. He felt he was appreciated by Miss Gertrude's guests, even though Miss Gertrude herself was not particularly cordial. He squatted on the grass and waited while Delaven took two or three puffs at his cigar before speaking again.

"Now, in the first place, if there is any objection to answering my question, I expect you to tell me so; you understand?" Nelse nodded solemnly, and Delaven continued:

"I have one of the best nurses here that it has ever been my luck to meet. You spoke of her today as in someway deprived of her senses for a long time. I can't quite understand that, for she appears very intelligent. I should like to know what you meant."

"I reckon o' course the pussen to who you pintedly make reference is Retta," said the old man, after a pause.

"You are the only one I've heard call her that—the rest call her Margeret."

"Humph—yes, sah; that Mahstah Matt's doens, I reckon! not but what Marg'ret alles was her real sure-'nough name, but way back, when Mahstah Tom was a liven', no one evah heard tell o' her been' called any name but Retta; an' seem like it suit her them days, but don't quite suit her now so well."

Delaven made no reply, and after another thoughtful pause, the old man continued:

"No, sah; I've been thinken' it ovah middlen' careful, an' I can't see—considerin' as yo's a doctah, an' a 'special friend o' the family—why I ain't free to tell you Retta's story clean

through; an' seen' as yo' have to put a lot o' 'pendance on
her 'bout carryen' out you ordahs fo' Mahstah Matt, seems
to me like a bounden' duty fo' *some* one to tell yo', fo' theah
was five yeahs—yes—six of 'em, when Retta wasn't a 'nigh
this plantation at all. She was stark, raven, crazy—dangerous crazy—an' had to be took away to some 'sylum place;
we all nevah knew where; but when she did come back she
was jest what you see—jest the ghost of a woman, sensible
'nough, seem like, but I mind the time when she try to kill
herself an' her chile, an' how we to know that fit nevah find
her again?"

"She—killed her child?"

"Oh, no, sah; we all took the baby; she wan't but five yeah
ole, from her, an' got the knife out o' her hands; no, no one
got hurt. But I reckon I better go 'way back an' tell yo'
the reason."

"Very well; I was wondering if she was really a colored
person," remarked Delaven.

"Retta's an octoroon, mahstah," said the old man, with
a certain solemnity of tone. "I done heard old Mahstah
Jean Larue swear that if folks are reckoned as horses are,
Retta'd be counted a thoroughbred, 'cause far back as they
can count theah wan't no scrub stock in her pedigree.

"Long 'bout hundred yeahs ago folks come in colony
fashion from some islands 'way on other side the sea. They
got plantations in Florida, an' Mahs Duke he knew some o'
them well. I only rec'lect hearen' one o' the names they
was called—an' mighty hard some o' them was to say!—but
the one I mind was Andros, or Ambrose Lacaris, an' he was
a Greek gentleman; an'—so it was said—Retta was his chile;
his nat'ral daughter, as Mahs Larue call it, an' she was raised
in his home jest like as ef she gwine to be mistress some
day."

Delaven's cigar was forgotten, and its light gone out. The pedigree was more interesting than he had expected. A Greek! All the beauty of the ancient world had come from those islands across the sea. The romances, the poems, the tragedies! and here was one living through a tragedy of today; that flower on the tomb under the pines— it suggested so much, now that he heard what she was.

"Mahs Lacaris, from what I could heah, was much the turn o' my Mahs Duke, but 'thout Mahs Duke's money to back him; an' one day all his business 'rangements, they go smash! an' sheriff come take all his lan' and niggahs fo' some 'surance he'd gone fo' some one. Well, sah, they say he most went 'stracted on head o' that smash up; an' 'special when he found they took stock o' Retta, just like any o' the field hands. But theah wan't no help fo' it, 'cause Retta's mammy was a quadroon gal; jest made a pet o' the chile, an' was so easy goen' he nevah took a thought that anything would ever change his way o' liven'.

"Mahs Tom, he jes' got married to Miss Leo Masterson an' took her down Florida fo' wedden' trip; that how he come to be theah when all Mahs Lacaris' belongings was put up fo' sale. Seem like Mahs Lacaris had hope he could get mo' money back in his own country, an' he was all planned to start, an' he beg Mahs Tom to buy his little Retta an' keep her safe till he come back.

"*Now*, Mahs Tom was powerful good-hearted—jest like his daddy. So he totes the chile home, an' I know Hester (Miss Leo's maid) was ragen' mad about it, 'cause she had to wait on her the whole enduren' trip home, fo' seem like that chile nevah had been taught to wait on herself.

"Well, sah, Massa Lacaris, he nevah did come back; that ship he went in nevah was heard tell of again from that day to this, an' theah wan't nothin' fo' Mahs Tom to do but jest keep her. He did talk about sendin' her 'way to some school, fo' she mighty peart with books, an' then given' her a chance to buy herself if so be she wanted to. But Miss Leo object to that, flat foot down; she hadn't no sort o' use fo' 'ristocrat book-learned niggahs.

"Hester, she heard Miss Leo say them words, an' was mighty glad to tattle 'em! Hester—she was Maryland stock, same as Cynthy. Well, sah, they worried along fo' 'bout a yeah not deciden' jest what to do with that young stray, then Miss Gertrude she come to town an' it did'n take no time to fine out what to do with her, *then*!

"Miss Gertrude wan't no 'special stout chile, an' took a heap o' care an' pamperin' an' when none o' the othahs could do a trick with her, Retta would jest walk in, take her in her arms, an' the wah was ended fo' that time! Fust time Mahs Tom see that performance he laugh hearty, an' then he say, 'Retta, we jest find out what we do need you fo'; yo' gwine to be installed as governess at Lorinwood from this time on.' An' Retta she was powerful pleased an' so happy, she alles a laughen' an' her eyes a shinen'.

"Long 'bout a yeah after that, it was, when Miss Leo die. Mahs Tom, he went way then fo' a long spell, cause the place too lonesome, an' when he come back, Retta, she ovah seventeen, an' she jest manage the whole house fine as she manage that baby, an' all the quality folks what come an' go praise her mightily an' talk 'bout how peart she was.

"Then Mahs Matt, he come up from Orleans, whah he been cutten' a wide swath, if all folks told true, an' fust thing his eyes caught was that gal Retta, an' he up an' tole Mahs Tom what a fool he was not to sell her down in Orleans whah she'd fetch mo' money than would buy six muss gals or housekeepers.

"Mahs Tom cussed at him powerful wicked when he say
that! I heard that my own self—it was down at the stable
an' I was jest putten' a saddle on fo' Mahs Tom, an' then
right in the middle o' his cussin' an' callen' names he stopped
short off an' says—says he: 'Don't you evah open youah
mouth to me 'bout that again so long as yo' live. If Retta
takes care o' my Gertrude till she ten yeahs old, I made up
my mine to give her freedom if she want it, that gal wan't
bought for no slave an' she ain't gwine to be one heah—yo'
un'stan'? You un'stan' if you got any notion o' stayen' at
Lorinwood!' An' then with some more mighty uncivil
sayen's he got in the saddle an' rode like Jehu, an' I don'
reckon Mahs Matt evah did make mention of it again, fo'
they got 'long all good 'nough so long as he stayed.

"Well, sah, haven' to take her part a-way made him think
mo' 'bout the gal I reckon; anyway he say plain to more'n
one that he sure gwine give Retta her freedom.

"He gwine do it jest aftah her chile was bawn, then theah
was some law fusses raised 'bout that time consarnnen'
Mahstahs freen' slaves, an' Mahs Matt was theah then, an'
he not say a word again *freen'* her, only he say, 'wait a spell,
Tom.'

"Retta, she wan't caren' then; she was young an' happy
all day long while her chile that was jest as white as Miss
Gertrude dar be.

"Things went on that-a-way five yeahs, her chile was five
yeahs ole when he start fo' a business visit down to Charleston, an' he say fo' he start that Retta gwine have her freedom
papers fo' Christmas gift. Well, sah, he done been gone two
weeks in Charleston when he start home, an' then Mahs
Larue persuade him to stay ovah night at his plantation fo'
a fox hunt in the mawnen'. Mahs Matt was theah, an' some
othah friends, so he staid ovah an' next we heard Mahs Matt

sent word Mahs Tom killed, an' we all was to be ready to see aftah the relations an' othah quality folks who boun' to come to the funeral.

"An' now, sah, you un'stan' what sort o' shock it was made Retta lose her mind that time. She fainted dead away when she heard it, but then she kind o' pulled herself togethah, as a horse will for a spurt, an' she looked aftah the company an' took Mahs Matt's orders 'bout 'rangements, but we all most scared at the way she look—jest a watching Mahs Matt constant, beggen' him with her eyes to tell her 'bout them freedom papers, but seems like he didn't un'stan', an' when she ask him right out, right 'long side o' dead Mahs Tom, he inform her he nevah heah tell 'bout them freedom papers, Mahs Tom not tole him 'bout them, so she b'long to the 'state o' Loring jest same as she did afore, only now Miss Gertrude owned her 'stead o' Mahs Tom.

"That when she tried to kill herself, an' try to kill the chile; didn't know anybody, she didn't, I tell yo' it make a terrible 'miration 'mongst the quality folks, an' I b'lieve in my soul Mahs Matt would a killed her if he dared, fo' it made all the folks un'stan' jest what he would 'a tried to keep them from.

"An' that, sah, is the whole 'count o' the reason leaden' up to the sickness whah she lost her mine. We all sutten sure Mahs Matt sell her quick if evah her senses done come back, but she really an' truly b'long to Miss Gertrude, an' Miss Gertrude, she couldn't see no good reason to let go the best housekeeper on the plantation, an' that how come she come to stay when she fetched back cured by them doctors. She ain't nevah made a mite o' trouble—jest alles same as yo' see her, but o' course yo' the best judge o' how far to trust her 'bout special medicine an' sech.''

"Yes," agreed Delaven, thoughtfully. He arose and walked back and forth several times. Until now he had only come in contact with the pleasant pastoral side of life, given added interest because, just now, all its peace was encircled by war; but it *was* peace for all that—peace in an eminently Christian land, a land of homes and churchly environment, and made picturesque by the grotesque features and humor of the dark exiles. He had only laughed with them until now and marveled at the gaiety of the troops singing in the rice fields, and suddenly another window had been opened and through it one caught glimpses of tragedies.

"And the poor woman's child?" he asked, after a little.

"Mahs Matt done send her down to Mahs Larue's Georgy plantation, an' we all nevah seen her no mo'. Mahs Larue done sold that Georgy plantation 'bout five yeahs back an' move up fo' good on one his wife own up heah. An' little while back I hear tell they gwine sell it, too, an' flit way cross to Mexico somewhah. This heah war jest broke them up a'ready."

"And the child was sold?—do you mean that?"

"Deed we all nevah got a sure story o' what come o' that baby; only when Retta come back Mahs Matt tell her little Rhoda dead long time ago—dead down in Georgy, an' no one evah heah her ask a word from that day to this. But one Larue's niggahs *tole me*"—and the voice and manner of Nelse took on a grotesquely impressive air—"they done raise a mighty handsome chile 'bout that time what was called Rhoda, an' she went to ferren parts with Mahs Larue an' his family an' didn't nevah come back, no mo', an' Mahs Matt raise some sort o' big row with Mahs Jean Larue ovah that gal, an' they nevah was friends no mo'. To be suah maybe that niggah lied—*I* don't know. But he let on as how

Mars Larue say that gal gwine to fetch a fancy price some day, an' I thought right off how Mahs Matt said Retta boun' to fetch a fancy price in Orleans; an' taken' it all roun' I reckoned it jest as well Retta keep on thinken' that chile died."

Delaven agreed. From the house he could hear the ladies talking, and Evilena's laugh sang out clear as a bird's song. He wondered if they also knew the story of the silent deft-handed bondwoman?—but concluded it was scarcely likely. Mrs. Nesbitt might know something of it, but who could tell Tom Loring's daughter?—and Evilena, of course, was too much of a child.

"I should like to see the picture you spoke of," he said at last, "the small one the painter left."

"I reckon that picture done sent away with little Rhoda's things. I ain't nevah heard tell of it since that time. But it don't look a mite like her now. All the red gone out o' her cheeks an' lips, all the shine out o' her eyes, an' her long brown hair has mo' white than brown in it these days. This woman Marg'ret ain't Retta; they jest as yo' might say two different women;" then, after a pause, "any othah thing you want ask me, sah? I see Jedge Clarkson comen' this way."

"No, that is all; thank you, old fellow."

He left Nelse ducking his head and fingering a new coin, while he sauntered to meet the Judge.

"How much he give you, Uncle Nelse?" asked a guarded voice back of the old man, and he nearly fell over backwards in his fright. A large, middle-aged colored man arose from the tall grass, where he has been hidden under the bank.

"Wha—what you mean— yo' Pluto? What fo' you hide theah an' listen?"

"I wan't hiden'," replied the man, good naturedly. "I jest lay to go sleep in the shade. Yo' come 'long an' talk—

talk so I couldn't help hear it all," and he smiled shrewdly.
"I alles was curious to know the true way 'bout that Mar-
g'ret—I reckon there was a heap that wan't told to neighbors. An' reason why I ask you how much he give you fo'
the story is 'cause I got that picture you tole 'bout. I married Mahs Larue's Rosa what come from Georgy with them.
She been daid ovah a yeah now, but it's some whar 'mongst
her b'longings. Reckon that strange gentleman give me
dollar for it?—the frame is mighty pretty—what you think?"

CHAPTER XV.

"Do tell me every blessed thing about her—a real Marquise—I love titles;" and Evilena clasped her hands rap-
turously.

"Do you, now? Faith, then I'm glad I secured mine before I came over," and the laughing Irish eyes met hers
quizzically.

"Oh, I never meant titles people earn themselves, Mr.
Doctor, for—"

"Then that puts the Judge and Col. Kenneth and myself
on the outside of your fence, does it? Arrah now! I'll be
looking up my pedigree in hopes of unearthing a king—
every true Irishman has a traditional chance of being the
descendant of rulers who ran barefoot, and carried a club
to teach the court etiquette."

She made a mutinous little grimace and refused to discuss his probable ancestors.

"Does not the presence of a French Marquise show how
Europe sides with us?" she demanded, triumphantly.
"Quantities of noblemen have been the guests of the South

lately, and isn't General Wolseley, the most brilliant officer of the British Army, with our General Lee now? I reckon all *that* shows how we are estimated. And now the ladies of title are coming over. Oh, tell me all about her; is she very grand, very pretty?"

"Grand enough for a queen over your new monarchy," replied Delaven, who derived considerable enjoyment from teasing the girl about affairs political—"and pretty? No, she's not that; she's just Beauty's self, entirely."

"And you knew her well in Paris?" asked Evilena, with a hesitating suspicion as to why he had not announced such a wonderful acquaintance before—this woman who was Beauty's self, and a widow. She wondered if she had appeared crude compared with those grand dames he had known and forgotten to mention.

"Oh, yes, I knew her while the old Marquise was living, that was when your mother and Col. Kenneth met her, but afterwards she took to travel for a change, and has evidently taken your South on her way. It will be happiness to see her again."

"And brother Ken knew her, too?" asked the girl, with wide-open eyes; "and *he* never mentioned her, either—well!"

"The rascal!—to deprive you of an account of all the lovely ladies he met! But you were at school when they returned, were you not?—and Ken started off hot foot for the West and Indian fighting, so you see there were excuses."

"And Kenneth does not know you are here still, and will not know the beautiful Marquise is here. Won't he be surprised to see you all?"

"I doubt if I cause him such a shock," decided Delaven; "when he gets sight of Judithe, Marquise de Caron, he will naturally forget at once whether I am in America or Ireland."

"Indeed, then, I never knew Kenneth to slight a friend," said the girl, indignantly.

"But maybe you never saw him face to face with such a temptation to make a man forget the universe."

"Sh—h!" she whispered, softly. Gertrude had come out on the veranda looking for the Judge. Seeing him down at the landing she walked leisurely in that direction.

"You do say such wild, extravagant things," continued Evilena, "that I just had to stop you until Gertrude was out of hearing. I suppose you know she and Kenneth are paired off for matrimony."

"Are they, now? Well, he's a lucky fellow; when are we to dance at the wedding?"

"Oh, they never tell me anything about serious things like that," complained Evilena. "There's Aunt Sajane; she can tell us, if any one can; everybody confides love affairs to her."

"Do they, now? Might I ask how you know?"

"Yes, sir; you may *ask*!" Then she dropped that subject and returned to the first one. "Aunt Sajane, when do you reckon we can dance at Kenneth's wedding—his and Gertrude's? Doctor Delaven and I want to dance."

"Evilena—honey!" murmured Aunt Sajane, chidingly, the more so as Matthew Loring had just crept slowly out with the help of his cane, and a negro boy. His alert expression betrayed that he had overheard the question.

"You know," she continued, "folks have lots to think of these days without wedding dances, and it isn't fair to Gertrude to discuss it, for *I* don't know that there really has been any settled engagement; only it would seem like a perfect match and both families seem to favor it." She glanced inquiringly at Loring, who nodded his head decidedly.

"Of course, of course, a very sensible arrangement. They've always been friends and it's been as good as settled ever since they were children."

"Settled by the families?" asked Delaven.

"Exactly—a good old custom that is ignored too often these days," said Mr. Loring, promptly. "Who is so fit to decide such things for children as their parents and guardians? That boy's father and me talked over this affair before the children ever knew each other. Of course he laughed over the question at the time, but when he died and suggested me as the boy's guardian, I knew he thought well of it and depended on me, and it will come off right as soon as this war is over—all right."

"A very good method for this country of the old French cavaliers," remarked Delaven, in a low tone, to the girl, "but the lads and lassies of Ireland have to my mind found a better."

Evilena looked up inquiringly.

"Well, don't you mean to tell me what it is?" she asked, as he appeared to have dropped the subject. He laughed at the aggrieved tone she assumed.

"Whist! There are mystical rites due to the telling, and it goes for nothing when told in a crowd."

"You have got clear away from Kenneth," she reminded him, hastily. "Did you mean that he was—well, in love with this magnificent Marquise?"

Low as she tried to speak, the words reached Loring, who listened, and Delaven, glancing across, perceived that he listened.

"In love with the Marquise? Bless your heart, we were all of course."

"But my brother?" insisted Evilena.

"Well, now he might have been the one exception—in fact he always did get out of the merely social affairs when he could, over there."

"Showed his good sense," decided Loring, emphatically. "I don't approve of young people running about Europe, learning their pernicious habits and customs; I've had my fill of foreign places and foreign people."

Mrs. Nesbitt opened her lips with a shocked expression of protest, and as promptly closed them, realizing the uselessness of it. Evilena laughed outright and directed an eloquent glance towards the only foreigner.

"Me, is it?" he asked, doubtingly. "Oh, don't you believe it. I've been here so long I'm near a Southerner myself."

"How near?" she asked, teasingly.

"Well, I must acknowledge you hold me at arms length in spite of my allegiance," he returned, and in the laugh of the others, Mr. Loring's tirade against foreigners was passed over.

It was only a few hours since Pluto arrived with the letter from Mobile telling of the early arrival of Mrs. McVeigh and her guest. Noting that the letter had been delayed and that the ladies might even now be in Savannah, Judge Clarkson proposed starting at once to meet them, but was persuaded to wait until morning.

Pluto was also told to wait over—an invitation gladly accepted, as visits to Loringwood were just now especially prized by the neighboring darkies, for the two runaways were yet subjects of gossip and speculation, and Uncle Nelse scattered opinions in the quarters on the absolute foolishness in taking such risks for freedom, and dire prophesies of the repentance to follow.

That his own personal feeling did not carry conviction to his listeners was evidenced by the sullen silence of many who did not think it wise to contradict him. Pluto was the only person to argue with him. But this proved to be the one subject on which Pluto could not be his natural good-natured self. His big black eyes held threatening gleams, rebellious blood throbbed through every vein of his dark body. He championed the cause of the runaways; he knew of none who had left a good master; old man Masterson was unreasonable as Matthew Loring; he did not blame them for leaving such men.

"I got good a mistress—good a master as is in all Carolina," he stated, bluntly, "but you think I stay here to work for any of them if it wan't for my boy?—my Rose's baby? No, I wouldn't! I'd go North, too! I'd never stop till I reached the men who fight against slave states. You all know what keeps me here. I'd never see my boy again. I done paid eighteen dollars towards Rose's freedom when she died. Then I ask Mr. Jean Larue if he wouldn't let that go on the baby. He said yes, right off, an' told me I could get him for hundred fifty dollars; *that* why I work 'long like I do, an' let the other men fight fo' freedom But I ain't contented so long as any man can sell me an' my child."

None of the other blacks made any verbal comment on his feelings or opinions, but old Nelse easily saw that Pluto's ideas outweighed his own with them.

"I un'stan' you to say Mahs Jean Larue promise he keep yo' boy till such time as the money is raised?" he asked, cautiously.

"That's the way it was," assented Pluto. "I ain't been to see him—little Zekal—for nigh on two months now. I'm goen', sure, soon as Mrs. McVeigh come home an' get settled. It's quite a jaunt from our place to Mahs Larue's—thirty good mile."

12

Aunt Chloe poured him out some more rye and corn-meal coffee and insisted on him having more sweet potato pie. She swept an admonishing glance towards the others as she did so. "I did heah some time ago one o' the Larue's gwine way down to the Mexico country," she remarked, carelessly. "I don't reckon though it is this special Larue. I mind they did have such a monstrous flock o' them Larue boys long time back; some got killed in this heah war what's maken' trouble all roun'. How much you got paid on yo' little boy, Pluto?"

"Most thirty dollars by time I make next trip over. Takes mighty long time to save money these days, quarters scarcer than dollars use to be."

His entertainers agreed with him; then the little maid Raquel entered to say Pluto was wanted by Miss Sajane soon as his lunch was over.

And as he walked across the grounds Evilena pointed him out to Delaven.

"That is our Pluto," she said, with a certain note of pride in her tone; "three generations of his family belonged to us. Mama can always go away feeling the whole plantation is safe so long as Pluto is in charge. We never do have trouble with the folks at the quarters as Mr. Loring does. He is so hard on them I wonder they don't all run away; it would be hard on Gertrude, though—lose her a lot of money. Did you know Loringwood is actually offered for sale? Isn't it a shame? The only silver lining to the cloud is that then Gertrude will have to move to The Pines—I don't mean to the woods"—as he turned a questioning glance on her. "I mean to Gertrude's plantation joining ours. It is a lovely place; used to belong to the Masterson tracts, and was part of the wedding dowery of that Miss Leo Masterson Uncle Nelse told of—Gertrude's

mother, you know. It is not grand or imposing like Loringwood, but I heard the Judge say that place alone was
enough to make Gertrude a wealthy woman, and the love-
liest thing about it is that it joins our plantation—lovely for
Gertrude and Kenneth, I mean. Look here, Doctor Delaven, you roused my curiosity wonderfully with that little
remark you made about the beautiful Marquise; tell me
true—were they—did Ken, even for a little while, fall in
love with her?"

She looked so roguishly coaxing, so sure she had stumbled on some fragment of an adventure, and so alluringly
confident that Delaven must tell her the rest, that there is
no telling how much he might have enlightened her if Miss
Loring had not entered the room at that moment through
a door nearest the window where they stood.

Her face was serene and self possessed as ever. She
smiled and addressed some careless remark to them as she
passed through, but Delaven had an uncomfortable feeling
that she had overheard that question, and Evilena was too
frightened to repeat it.

———

CHAPTER XVI.

The warm summer moon wheeled up that evening
through the dusk, odorous with the wild luxuriance of wood
and swamp growths. A carriage rolled along the highway
between stretches of rice lands and avenues of pines.

In the west red and yellow showed where the path of
the sun had been and against it was outlined the gables of an
imposing structure, dark against the sky.

"We are again close to the Salkahatchie," said Mrs. Mc-
Veigh, pointing where the trees marked its course, "and
across there—see that roof, Marquise?—that is Loringwood.
If the folks had got across from Charleston we would stop
there long enough to rest and have a bit of supper. But
the road winds so that the distance is longer than it looks,
and we are too near home to stop on such an uncertainty.
Gertrude's note from Charleston telling of their safe arrival
could say nothing definite of their home coming."

"That, no doubt, depends on the invalid relative," suggested her guest; "the place looks very beautiful in this
dim light; the cedars along the road there are magnificent."

"I have heard they are nearly two hundred years old.
Years ago it was the great show place of the country, but
two generations of very extravagant sportsmen did much to
diminish its wealth—generous, reckless and charming men
—but they planted mortgages side by side with their rice
fields. Those encumbrances have, I fancy, prevented Gertrude from being as fond of the place as most girls would
be of so fine an ancestral home."

"Possibly she lacks the gamester blood of her forefathers
and can have no patience with their lack of the commercial
instinct."

"I really do believe that is just it," said Mrs. McVeigh.
"I never had thought of it in that way myself, but Gertrude
certainly is not at all like the Lorings; she is entirely of her
mother's people, and they are credited with possessing a
great deal of the commercial instinct. I can't fancy a Masterson gambling away a penny. They are much more sensible; they invest."

The cedar avenues had been left a mile behind, and they
had entered again the pine woods where even the moon's
full radiance could only scatter slender lances of light. The

Marquise leaned back with half-shut slumberous eyes, and confessed she was pleased that it would be later, instead of this evening, that she would have the pleasure of meeting the master and mistress of Loringwood—the drive through the great stretches of pine had acted as a soporific; no society for the night so welcome as King Morpheus.

The third woman in the carriage silently adjusted a cushion back of Madame's head. "Thank you, Louise," she said, yawning a little. "You see how effectually I have been mastered by the much remarked languor of the South. It is delightfully restful. I cannot imagine any one ever being in a hurry in this land."

Mrs. McVeigh smiled and pointed across the field, where some men were just then running after a couple of dogs who barked vociferously in short, quick yelps, bespeaking a hot trail before them.

"There is a living contradiction of your idea," she said; "the Southerners are intensity personified when the game is worth it; the game may be a fox chase or a flirtation, a love affair or a duel, and our men require no urging for any of those pursuits."

They were quite close to the men now, and the Marquise declared they were a perfect addition to the scene of moonlit savannas backed by the masses of wood now near, now far, across the levels. Two of them had reached the road when the carriage wheels attracted attention from the dogs, and they halted, curious, questioning.

"Why, it's our Pluto!" exclaimed Mrs. McVeigh; "stop the carriage. Pluto, what in the world are you doing here?"

Pluto came forward smiling, pleased.

"Welcome home, Mrs. McVeigh. I'se jest over Loringwood on errend with yo' all letters to Miss Lena an' Miss Sajane. Letters was stopped long time on the road someway; yo' all get here soon most as they did. Judge Clarkson—he aimen' to go meet yo' at Savannah—start in the mawning at daybreak. He reckoned yo' all jest wait there till some one go fo' escort."

"Evilena is at Loringwood, you say? Then Miss Loring and her uncle have got over from Charleston?"

"Yes, indeedy!—long time back, more'n a week now since they come. Why, how come you not hear?—they done sent yo' word; I *know* Miss Lena wrote you, 'cause she said so. Yes'm, the folks is back, an' Miss Sajane an' Judge over there this minute; reckon they'll feel mighty sorry yo' all passed the gate."

"Oh, but the letter never reached me. I had no idea they were home, and it is too far to go back I suppose? How far are we from the house now?"

"Only 'bout a mile straight 'cross fields like we come after that 'possum, but it's a good three miles by the road."

"Well, you present my compliments and explain the situation to Miss Loring and the Judge. We will drive on to the Terrace. Say I hope to see them all soon as they can come. Evilena can come with you in the morning. Tell Miss Gertrude I shall drive over soon as I am rested a little —and Mr. Loring, is he better?"

"Heap better—so Miss Gertrude and the doctor say. He walks roun' some. Miss Gertrude she mightily taken with Dr. Delaven's cure—she says he jest saved Mahs Loring's life over there in France."

"Dr. Delaven!" uttered the voice of the Marquise, in soft surprise—"*our* Dr. Delaven?" and as she spoke her hand stole out and touched that of the handsome serving woman she called Louise; "is he also a traveller seeking adventure in your South?"

"Did I not tell you?" asked Mrs. McVeigh. "I meant to. Gertrude's note mentioned that her uncle was under the care of our friend, the young medical student, so you will hear the very latest of your beloved Paris."

"Charming! It is to be hoped he will visit us soon. This little woman"—and she nodded towards Louise—"must be treated for homesickness; you observe her depression since we left the cities? Dr. Delaven will be an admirable cure for that."

"Your Louise will perhaps cure herself when she sees a home again," remarked Mrs. McVeigh; "it is life in a carriage she has perhaps grown tired of."

"Madame is pleased to tease me as people tease children for being afraid in the dark," explained Louise. "I am not afraid, but the silence does give one a chill. I shall be glad to reach the door of your house."

"And we must hasten. Remember all the messages, Pluto; bring your Miss Lena tomorrow and any of the others who will come."

"I remember, sure. Glad I was first to see yo' all back—good night."

The other colored men in the background had lost all interest in the 'possum hunt, and were intent listeners to the conversation. Old Nelse, who had kept up to the rest with much difficulty, now pushed himself forward for a nearer look into the carriage. Mrs. McVeigh did not notice him. But he startled the Marquise as he thrust his white bushy head and aged face over the wheel just as they were starting, and the woman Louise drew back with a gasp of actual fear.

"What a stare he gave us!" she said, as they rolled away from the group by the roadside. "That old man had **eyes** like augers, and he seemed to look through me—may I ask if he, also, is of your plantation, Madame?"

"Indeed, he is not," was Mrs. McVeigh's reassuring answer. "But he did not really mean to be impertinent; just some childish old 'uncle' who is allowed special privileges, I suppose. No; you won't see any one like that at the Terrace. I can't think who it could be unless it is Nelse, an old free man of Loring's; and Nelse used to have better manners than that, but he is very old—nearly ninety, they say. I don't imagine he knows his own age exactly— few of the older ones do."

Pluto caught the old man by the shoulder and fairly lifted him out of the road as the carriage started.

"What the matter with yo', anyway, a pitchen' yo'self 'gainst the wheel that-a-way?" he demanded. "Yo' ain't boun' and sot to get run over, are yo'?"

Some of the other men laughed, but Nelse gripped Pluto's hand as though in need of the support.

"Fo' God!—thought I seen a ghost, that minute," he gasped, as the other men started after the dogs again; "the ghost of a woman what ain't dead yet—the ghost o' Retta."

"Yo' plum crazy, ole man," said Pluto, disdainfully. "How the ghost o' that Marg'ret get in my mistress carriage, I like to know?—'special as the woman's as live as any of us. Yo' gone 'stracted with all the talken' 'bout that Marg'ret's story. Now, *I* ain't seen a mite of likeness to her in that carriage at all, I ain't."

"That 'cause yo' ain't nevah see Retta as she used to be. I tell yo' if her chile Rhoda alive at all I go bail she the very likeness o' that woman. My king! but she done scairt me."

"Don't yo' go talk such notions to any other person," suggested Pluto. "Yo' get yo'self in trouble when yo' go tellen' how Mrs. McVeigh's company look like a nigger, yo' mind! Why, that lady the highest kind o' quality—most a queen where she comes from. How yo' reckon Mrs. McVeigh like to hear such talk?"

"Might'nt a' been the highest quality one I meant," protested Nelse, strong in the impression he had received; "it wa' the othah one, then—the one in a black dress."

All three occupants of the carriage had worn dark clothes, in the night all had looked black. Nelse had only observed one closely; but Pluto saw a chance of frightening the old man out of a subject of gossip so derogatory to the dignity of the Terrace folks, and he did not hesitate to use it.

"What other one yo' talken' 'bout?" he demanded, stopping short, "my Mistress McVeigh?"

"Naw!—think me a bawn fool—you? I mean the *otha* one—the number three lady."

"This here moonlight sure 'nough make you see double, ole man," said Pluto, with a chuckle. "Yo' better paddle yo'self back to your own cabin again 'stead o' hunten' ghost women 'round Lorin'wood, 'cause there wan't only two ladies in that carriage—two *live* ladies," he added, meaningly, "an' one o' them was my mistress."

"Fo' Gawd's sake!"

The old man appeared absolutely paralyzed by the statement. His eyes fairly bulged from their sockets. He opened his lips again, but no sound came; a grin of horror was the only describable expression on his face. All the superstition in his blood responded to Pluto's suggestion, and when he finally spoke it was in a ghostly whisper.

"I—I done been a looken' for it," he gasped, "take me home—yo'! It's a sure 'nough sign! Last night ole whippo'will flopped ovah my head. Three nights runnen' a hoot owl hooted 'fore my cabin. An' now the ghost of a woman what ain't dead yet, sot there an' stare at me! I ain't entered fo' no mo' races in this heah worl', boy ; I done covah the track fo' las' time ; I gwine pass undah the line at the jedge stan', I tell yo'. I got my las' warnen'—I gwine home !"

CHAPTER XVII.

Pluto half carried the old man back to Loringwood, while the other darkies continued their 'possum hunt. Nelse said very little after his avowal of the "sign" and its relation to his lease of life. He had a nervous chill by the time they reached the house and Pluto almost repented of his fiction. Finally he compromised with his conscience by promising himself to own the truth if the frightened old fellow became worse.

But nothing more alarming resulted than his decision to return at once to his own cabin, and the further statement that he desired some one be despatched at once for "that gal Cynthy," which was done according to his orders.

The women folk—old Chloe at their head—decided Uncle Nelse must be in some dangerous condition when he sent the command for Cynthia, whom he had divorced fifty years before. The rumors reached Dr. Delaven, who made a visit to Nelse in the cabin where he was installed temporarily, waiting for the boatmen who were delegated to row him home, he himself declining to assist in navigation or any other thing requiring physical exertion.

He was convinced his days were numbered, his earthly labors over, and he showed abject terror when Margeret entered with a glass of bitters Mrs. Nesbitt had prepared with the idea that the old man had caught a chill in his endeavor to follow the dogs on the oppossum hunt.

"I told you all how it would be when I heard of him going," she asserted, with all a prophet's satisfaction in a prophecy verified. "Pluto had to just about tote him home —following the dogs at his age, the idea!"

But for all her disgust at his frivolity she sent the bitters, and Delaven could not comprehend his shrinking from the cup-bearer.

"Come—come, now! You're not at all sick, my man; what in the wide world are you shamming for? Is it for the dram? Sure, you could have that without all this commotion."

"I done had a vision, Mahs Doctor," he said, with impressive solemnity. "My time gwine come, I tell yo'." He said no more until Margeret left the room, when he pointed after her with nervous intensity. "It's that there woman I seen—the ghost o' that woman what ain't dead—the ghost o' her when she was young an' han'some—that's what I seen in the McVeigh carriage this night, plain as I see yo' face this minute. But no such *live* woman wa' in that carriage, sah. Pluto, he couldn't see but two, an' *I* saw three plain as I could see one. Sure as yo' bawn it's a death sign, Mahs Doctor; my time done come."

"Tut, tut!—such palaver. That would be the queerest way, entirely, to read the sign. Now, I should say it was Margeret the warning was for; why should the likeness of her come to hint of your death?"

Nelse did not reply at once. He was deep in thought— a nervous, fidgety season of thought—from which he finally emerged with a theory evidently not of comfort to himself.

"I done been talken' too much," he whispered. "I talk on an' on today; I clar fo'got yo' a plum stranger to we all.

I tell all sorts o' family things what maybe Mahs Duke not
want tole. I talked 'bout that gal Retta most, so he done
sent a ghost what look like Retta fo' a sign. Till day I
die I gwine keep my mouth shut 'bout Mahs Duke's folks,
I tell yo', an' I gwine straight home out o' way o' temptations."

So oppressed was he with the idea of Mahs Duke's displeasure that he determined to do penance if need be, and
commenced by refusing a coin Delaven offered him.

"No, sah; I don' dar take it," he said, solemnly, "an' I
glad to give yo' back that othar dollar to please Mahs Duke,
only I done turned it into a houn' dog what Ben sold me,
and Chloe—she Ben's mammy—she got it from him, a'ready,
an' paid it out fo' a pair candlesticks she been grudgen' ole
M'ria a long time back, so I don' see how I evah gwine get
it. But I ain't taken' no mo' chances, an' I ain't a risken' no
mo' ghost signs. Jest as much obliged to yo' all," and
he sighed regretfully, as Delaven repocketed the coin; but
I know when I got enough o' ghosts."

Pluto had grace enough to be a trifle uneasy at the intense despondency caused by his fiction in what he considered a good cause. The garrulity of old Nelse was verging
on childishness. Pluto was convinced that despite the old
man's wonderful memory of details in the past, he was
entirely irresponsible as to his accounts of the present, and
he did not intend that the McVeigh family or any of their
visitors should be the subject of his unreliable gossip. Pride
of family was by no means restricted to the whites. Revolu-
tionary as Pluto's sentiments were regarding slavery, his
self esteem was enhanced by the fact that since he was a
bondman it was, at any rate, to a first-class family—regular
quality folks, whose honor he would defend under any circumstances, whether bond or free.

His clumsily veiled queries about the probable result of Uncle Nelse's attack aroused the suspicions of Delaven that the party of hunters had found themselves hampered by the presence of their aged visitor, who was desirous of testing the ability of his new purchase, the hound dog, and that they had resorted to some ghost trick to get rid of him.

He could not surmise how the shade of Margeret had been made do duty for the occasion, her subdued, serious manner giving the denial to any practical joke escapades.

But the news Pluto brought of Mrs. McVeigh's home-coming dwarfed all such episodes as a scared nigger who refused to go into details as to the scare, and in his own words was "boun' an' sot" to keep his mouth shut in future about anything in the past which he ever had known and seen, or anything in his brief earthly future which he might know or see. He even begged Delaven to forget immediately the numerous bits of history he, Nelse, had repeated of the Loring family, and Delaven comforted him by declaring that all he could remember that minute was the horse race and he would put that out of his mind at once if necessary.

Nelse was not sure it was necessary to forget *that*, because it didn't in any way reflect discredit on the family, and he didn't in reason see why his Mahs Duke should object to that story unless it was on account of the high-flier lady from Philadelphia what Mahs Duke won away from Mr. Jackson without any sort of trouble at all, and if Mahs Duke was hovering around in the library when Miss Evilena and Mahs Doctor listened to that story, Mahs Duke ought to know in his heart, if he had any sort of memory at all, that he, Nelse, had not told half what he might have told about that Northern filly and Mahs Duke. And taking it all in all Nelse didn't see any reason why Delaven need put that out of his remembrance—especially as it was mighty good running for two-year-olds.

Evilena had peeped in for a moment to say good-bye to their dusky Homer. But the call was very brief. All her thoughts were filled with the folks at the Terrace, and dawn in the morning had been decided on for the ten-mile row home, so anxious was she to greet her mother, and so lively was her interest in the wonderful foreigner whom Dr. Dela-ven had described as "Beauty's self."

That lady had in the meantime arrived at the Terrace, partaken of a substantial supper, and retired to her own apartments, leaving behind her an impression on the colored folks of the household that the foreign guest was no one less than some latter day queen of Sheba. Never before had their eyes beheld a mistress who owned white servants, and the maid servant herself, so fine she wore silk stockings and a delaine dress, had her meals in her own room and was so grand she wouldn't even talk like folks, but only spoke in French, except when she wanted something special, at which time she would condescend to talk "United States" to the extent of a word or two. All this superiority in the maid—whom they were instructed to call "Miss"—reflected added glory on the mistress, who, at the supper table, had been heard say she preferred laying aside a title while in America, and to be known simply as Madame Caron; and laughingly confessed to Mrs. McVeigh that the American Republic was in a fair way to win her from the French Em-pire, all of which was told at once in the kitchen, where they were more convinced than ever that royalty had descended upon them. This fact did not tend to increase their useful-ness in any capacity; they were so overcome by the grandeur and the importance of each duty assigned to them that the wheels of domestic machinery at the Terrace that evening

were fairly clogged by the eagerness and the trepidation of
the workers. They figuratively—and sometimes literally—
fell over each other to anticipate any call which might assure them entrance to the wonderful presence, and were
almost frightened dumb when they got there.

Mrs. McVeigh apologized for them and amused her guest
with the reason:

"They have actually never seen a white servant in their
lives, and are eaten up with curiosity over the very superior
maid of yours, her intelligence places her so high above their
ideas of servitors."

"Yes, she is intelligent," agreed the Marquise, "and much
more than her intelligence, I value her adaptability. As my
housekeeper she was simply perfect, but when my maid grew
ill and I was about to travel, behold! the dignity of the
housekeeper was laid aside, and with a bewitching maid's
cap and apron, and smile, she applied for the vacant position and got it, of course."

"It was stupid of me not to offer you a maid," said Mrs.
McVeigh, regretfully; "I did not understand. But I could
not, of course, have given you any one so perfect as your
Louise; she is a treasure."

"I shall probably have to get along with some one less
perfect in the future," said the other, ruefully. "She was to
have had my yacht refurnished and some repairs made while
I was here, and now that I am safely located, may send
her back to attend to it. She is worth any two men I could
employ for such supervision, in fact, I trust many such
things to her."

"Pray let her remain long enough to gain a pleasant impression of plantation life," suggested Mrs. McVeigh, as
they rose from the table. "I fancied she was depressed by
the monotony of the swamp lands, or else made nervous by

the group of black men around the carriage there at Loringwood; they did look formidable, perhaps, to a stranger
at night, but are really the most kindly creatures."

Judithe de Caron had walked to the windows opening on
the veranda and was looking out across the lawn, light almost as day under the high moon, a really lovely view, though
both houses and grounds were on a more modest scale
than those of Loringwood. They lacked the grandeur suggested by the century-old cedars she had observed along the
Loring drive. The Terrace was much more modern and,
possibly, so much more comfortable. It had in a superlative
degree the delightful atmosphere of home, and although the
stranger had been within its gates so short a time, she
was conscious of the wonder if in all her varied experience
she had ever been in so real a home before.

"How still it all is," remarked Mrs. McVeigh, joining
her. "Tomorrow, when my little girl gets back, it will be
less so; come out on the veranda and I can show you a
glimpse of the river; you see, our place is built on a natural
terrace sloping to the Salkahatchie. It gives us a very good
view."

"Charming! I can see that even in the night time."

"Three miles down the river is the Clarkson place; they
are most pleasant friends, and Miss Loring's place, The
Pines, joins the Terrace grounds, so we are not so
isolated as might appear at first; and fortunately for us our
plantation is a favorite gathering place for all of them."

"I can quite believe that. I have been here two—three
hours, perhaps, and I know already why your friends would
be only too happy to come. You make them a home from
the moment they enter your door."

"You could not say anything more pleasing to my vanity,
Marquise," said her hostess, laughingly, and then checked

herself at sight of an upraised finger. "Oh, I forgot—I do persist in the Marquise."

"Come, let us compromise," suggested her guest, "if Madame Caron sounds too new and strange in your ears, I have another name, Judithe; it may be more easily remembered."

"In Europe and England," she continued, "where there are so many royal paupers, titles do not always mean what they are supposed to. I have seen a Russian prince who was a hostler, an English lord who was an attendant in a gambling house, and an Italian count porter on a railway. Over here, where titles are rare, they make one conspicuous; I perceived that in New Orleans. I have no desire to be especially conspicuous. I only want to enjoy myself."

"You can't help people noticing you a great deal, with or without a title," and Mrs. McVeigh smiled at her understandingly. "You cannot hope to escape being distinguished, but you shall be whatever you like at the Terrace."

They walked arm in arm the length of the veranda, chatting lightly of Parisian days and people until ten o'clock sounded from the tall clock in the library. Mrs. McVeigh counted the strokes and exclaimed at the lateness.

"I certainly am a poor enough hostess to weary you the first evening with chatter instead of sending you to rest, after such a drive," she said, in self accusation. But you are such a temptation—Judithe."

They both laughed at her slight hesitation over the first attempt at the name.

"Never mind; you will get used to it in time," promised the Marquise, "I am glad you call me 'Judithe.'"

Then they said good night; she acknowledged she did feel sleepy—a little—though she had forgotten it until the clock struck.

13

Mrs. McVeigh left her at the door and went on down the hall to her own apartment—a little regretful lest Judithe should be over wearied by the journey and the evening's gossip.

But she really looked a very alert, wide-awake young lady as she divested herself of the dark green travelling dress and slipped into the luxurious lounging robe Mademoiselle Louise held ready.

Her brows were bent in a frown of perplexity very different from the gay smile with which she had parted from her hostess. She glanced at her attendant and read there anxiety, even distress.

"Courage, Louise," she said, cheerily; "all is not lost that's in danger. Horrors! What a long face! Look at yourself in the mirror. I have not seen such a mournful countenance since the taking of New Orleans."

"And it was not your mirror showed a mournful countenance that day, Marquise," returned the other. "I am glad some one can laugh; but for me, I feel more like crying, and that's the truth. Heavens! How long that time seemed until you came."

"I know," and the glance of her mistress was very kind. "I could feel that you were walking the floor and waiting, but it was not possible to get away sooner. Get the other brush, child; there are wrinkles in my head as well as my hair this evening; you must help me to smooth them."

But the maid was not to be comforted by even that suggestion, though she brushed the wavy, dusky mane with loving hands—one could not but read tenderness in every touch she gave the shining tresses. But her sighs were frequent for all that.

"Me of help?" she said, hopelessly. "I tell you true, Marquise, I am no use to anybody, I'm that nervous. I was

afraid of this journey all the time. I told you so before you
left Mobile; you only laughed at my superstitious fears, and
now, even before we reach the place, you see what happened."

"I see," asserted the Marquise, smiling at her, teasingly,
"but then the reasons you gave were ridiculous, Louise; you
had dreams, and a coffin in a teacup. Come, come; it is not
so bad as you fear, despite the prophetic tea grounds; there
is always a way out if you look for paths; so we will look."

"It is all well for you, Marquise, to scoff at the omens;
you are too learned to believe in them; but it is in our
blood, perhaps, and it's no use us fighting against presentiments, for they're stronger than we are. I had no heart to
get ready for the journey—not a bit. We are cut off from
the world, and even suppose you could accomplish anything
here, it will be more difficult than in the cities, and the
danger so much greater."

"Then the excitement will provide an attraction, child,
and the late weeks have really been very dull."

The hair dressing ceased because the maid could not
manipulate the brush and express sufficient surprise at the
same time.

"Heavens, Madame! What then would you call lively if
this has been dull? I'm patriotic enough—or revengeful
enough, perhaps—for any human sort of work; but you
fairly frighten me sometimes the way you dash into things,
and laughing at it all the time as if it was only a joke to you,
just as you are doing this minute. You are harder than iron
in some things and yet you look so delicately lovely—so like
a beautiful flower—that every one loves you, and—"

"Every one? Oh, Louise, child, do you fancy, then, that
you are the whole world?"

The maid lifted the hand of the mistress and touched it to her cheek.

"I don't only love you, I worship you," she murmured. "You took me when I was nothing, you trusted me, you taught me, you made a new woman of me. I wouldn't ever mind slavery if I was your slave."

"There, there, Louise;" and she laid her hand gently on the head of the girl who had sunk on the floor beside her. "We are all slaves, more or less, to something in this world. Our hearts arrange that without appeal to the law-makers."

"All but yours," said the maid, looking up at her fondly and half questioningly, "I don't believe your heart is allowed to arrange anything for you. Your head does it all; that is why I say you are hard as iron in some things. I don't honestly believe your heart is even in this cause you take such risks for. You think it over, decide it is wrong, and deliberately outstrip every one else in your endeavor to right it. That is all because you are very learned and very superior to the emotions of most people;" and she touched the hand of the Marquise caressingly. "That is how I have thought it all out; for I see that the motives others are moved by never touch you; the others—even the high officials—do not understand you, or only one did."

Her listener had drifted from attention to the soft caressing tones of the one time Parisian figurante, whose devotion was so apparent and whose nature required a certain amount of demonstration. The Marquise had, from the first, comprehended her wonderfully well, and knew that back of those feminine, almost childish cravings for expression, there lived an affectionate nature too long debarred from worthy objects, and now absolutely adoring the one she deemed her benefactress; all the more adoring because of the courage and daring, that to her had a fascinating touch of masculinity about it; no woman less masterful, nor less beautiful, could have held the pretty Kora so completely. The dramatic side of her nature was appealed to by the luxurious surroundings of the Marquise, and the delightful uncertainty, as each day's curtain of dawn was lifted, whether she was to see comedy or tragedy enacted before the night fell. She had been audience to both, many times, since the Marquise had been her mistress.

Just now the mistress was in some perplexed quandary of her own, and gave little heed to the flattering opinions of the maid, and only aroused to the last remark at which she turned with questioning eyes, not entirely approving:

"Whom do you mean?" she asked, with a trifle of constraint, and the maid sighed as she selected a ribbon to bind the braid she had finished.

"No one you would remember, Marquise," she said, shaking her head; "the trouble is you remember none of them, though you make it impossible that they should forget you. Many of those fine gallants of Orleans I was jealous of and glad to see go; but this one, truly now, he seemed to me well worth keeping."

"Had he a name?" asked the Marquise, removing some rings, and yawning slightly.

"He had," said the girl, who was unfolding a night robe and shaking the wrinkles from the very Parisian confection of lawn and lace and tiny pink ribbons accenting neck and wrist. When she walked one perceived a slight halt in her step—a reminder of the injury through which her career in Paris had been brought to an end. "He had, my Marquise. I mean the Federal officer, Monroe—Captain Jack, the men called him. Of all the Orleans gentlemen he was the only one I thought fit for a mate for you—the only one I was sorry to see you send away."

"Send? What an imaginative romancer you are! He went where his duty called him, no doubt. I do not remember that I was responsible. And your choice of him shows you are at least not worldly in your selections, for he was a reckless sort of ranger, I believe, with his sword and his assurance as chief belongings."

"You forget, Marquise, his courage."

"Oh, that!" and Judithe made a little gesture of dismissal; "it is nothing in a man, all men should have courage. But, to change the subject, which of the two men have most interest for us tonight, Captain Jack or Dr. Delaven? The latter, I fancy. While you have been chattering I have been making plans."

The maid ceased her movements about the room in the preparations for the night, and, drawing a low stool closer, listened with all attention.

"Since you are afraid here and too much oppressed by your presentiments to be useful"—she accompanied this derogatory statement with an amused smile—"I conclude it best for you to return to the sea-board at once—before Dr. Delaven and the rest pay their duty visit here.

"I had hoped the change in your appearance would place you beyond danger of recognition, and so it would with any one who had not known you personally. Madame McVeigh has been vaguely impressed with your resemblance to Monsieur Dumaresque's picture. But the impression of Dr. Delaven would probably be less vague—his remembrance of you not having been entirely the memory of a canvas."

"That is quite true," agreed the other, with a regretful sigh. "I have spoken with him many times. He came with —with his friend Trouvelot to see me when I was injured. It was he who told me the physicians were propping me up with falsehoods, and taking my money for curing a lameness they knew was incurable. Yes, he was my good friend in that. He would surely remember me," and she looked troubled.

"So I supposed; and with rumors abroad of an unknown in the heart of the South, who is a secret agent for the Federals, it is as well not to meet any one who could suggest that the name you use is an assumed one, it might interfere with your usefulness even more than your dismal presentiments," and she arched her brows quizzically at the maid, who sighed forlornly over the complications suggested. "So, you must leave at once."

"Leave, alone—without you?" and the girl's agitation was very apparent. "Madame, I beg you to find some reason for going with me, or for following at once. I could send a dispatch from Savannah, you could make some excuse! You, oh, Marquise! if I leave you here alone I would be in despair; I would fear I should never, never see you again!"

"Nonsense, child! There is absolutely no ground for your fears. If you should meet trouble in any way you have only to send me word and I will be with you. But your imaginary terrors you must yourself subdue. Come, now, be reasonable. You must go back—it is decided. Take note of all landmarks as we did in coming; if messengers are needed it is much better that you inform yourself of all approaches here. Wait for the yacht at Savannah. Buy anything needed for its refurnishing, and see that a certain amount of repairing is done there while you wait further orders. I shall probably have it brought to Beaufort, later, which would be most convenient if I should desire to give my good friends here a little salt water excursion. So, you perceive, it is all very natural, and it is all decided."

"Heavens, Marquise, how fast you move! I had only got

so far I was afraid to remain, and afraid to excite wonder by leaving; and while I lament, you arrange a campaign."

"Exactly; so you see how easily it is all to be done, and how little use your fears."

"I am so much more contented that I will see everything as you wish," promised the girl, brightly. "Savannah, after all, is not very far, and Beaufort is nearer still. But after all, you must own, my presentiments were not all wrong, Marquise. It really was unlucky—this journey."

"We have heretofore had only good fortune; why should we complain because of a few obstacles now?" asked her mistress. "To become a diplomat one needs to be first a philosopher, and prepared at all times for the worst."

"I could be more of a philosopher myself over these complications," agreed the girl, smiling, "if I were a foreigner of rank seeking amusement and adventure. But the troubles of all this country have come so close home to the people of my race that we fear even to think what the worst might be."

The Marquise held up an admonishing finger and glanced towards the door.

"Of course no one hears, but it is best never to allow yourself the habit of referring to family or personal affairs. Even though we speak a language not generally understood in this country, do not—even to me—speak of your race. I know all, understand it all, without words; and, for the people we have met, they do not doubt you are a San Domingo creole. You must be careful lest they think differently."

"You are right; what a fool I am! My tongue ever runs ahead of my wit. Marquise, sometimes I laugh when I remember how capable I thought myself on leaving Paris, what great things I was to do—I!" and she shrugged her plump shoulders in self derision. "Why, I should have been

discovered a dozen times had I depended on my own wit. I
am a good enough orderly, but only under a capable general," and she made a smiling courtesy to the Marquise.

"Chatterbox! If I am the general of your distinguished
selection, I shall issue an order at once for your immediate
retirement."

"Oh, Marquise!"

"To bed," concluded her mistress, gayly, "go; I shall not
need you. I have work to do."

The girl first unlaced the dark boots and substituted a
pair of soft pink slippers, and touched her cheek to the
slender foot.

"I shall envy the maid who does even that for you when
I am gone," she said, softly. "Now, good rest to you, my
general, and pleasant dreams."

"Thanks; but my dreams are never formidable nor important," was the teasing reply as the maid vanished. The
careless smile gave way to a quick sigh of relief as the
door closed. She arose and walked back and forth across
the room with nervous, rapid steps, her hands clasped back
of her head and the wide sleeves of the robe slipped back,
showing the perfect arms. She seemed a trifle taller than
when in Paris that first springtime, and the open robe revealed a figure statuesque, perfect as a sculptor's ideal, yet
without the statue's coldness; for the uncovered throat and
bosom held delicious dimples where the robe fell apart and
was swept aside by her restless movements.

But her own appearance was evidently far from her
thoughts at that moment. Several of Mrs. McVeigh's very
affectionate words and glances had recurred to her and
brought her a momentary restlessness. It was utterly absurd that it should be so, especially when she had encouraged the fondness, and meant to continue doing so. But

she had not counted on being susceptible to the same feeling for Kenneth McVeigh's mother—yet she had come very near it, and felt it necessary to lay down the limits as to just how far she would allow such a fondness to lead her.

And the fact that she was in the home of her one-time lover gave rise to other complex fancies. How would they meet if chance should send him there during her stay? He had had time for many more such boyish fancies since those days, and back of them all was the home sweetheart she heard spoken of so often—Gertrude Loring.

How very, very long ago it seemed since the meetings at Fontainbleau; what an impulsive fool she had been, and how childish it all seemed now!

But Judithe de Caron told herself she was not the sort of person to allow memories of bygone sentiment to interfere for long with practical affairs. She drew up a chair to the little stand by the window and plunged into the work she had spoken of, and for an hour her pen moved rapidly over the paper until page after page was laid aside.

But after the last bit of memoranda was completed she leaned back, looking out into the blue mists of the night—across his lands luxuriant in all the beauty of summer time and moonlight, the fields over which he had ridden, the trees under which he had walked, with, perhaps, an occasional angry thought of her—never dreaming that she, also, would walk there some day.

"But to think that I *am* actually here—here above all!" she murmured softly. "Maman, once I said I would be Judithe indeed to that man if he was ever delivered into my hands. Yet, when he came I ran away from him—ran away because I was afraid of him! But now—"

Her beautiful eyes half closed in a smile not mirthful, and the sentence was left unfinished.

CHAPTER XVIII.

What embraces, ejaculations and caresses, when Evilena, accompanied by Pluto and the delighted Raquel, arrived at the Terrace next morning! Judithe, who saw from the veranda the rapturous meeting of mother and daughter, sighed, a quick, impatient catching of the breath, and turned to enter the library through the open French windows. Reconsidering her intention, she halted, and waited at the head of the broad steps where Kenneth's sister saw her for the first time and came to her with a pleased, half shy greeting, and where Kenneth's mother slipped one arm around each as they entered the house, and between the two she felt welcomed into the very heart of the McVeigh family feminine.

"Oh, and mama!"—thus exclaimed Evilena as she was comfortably ensconced in the same chair with that lady—"there is so much news to tell you I don't know where to begin. But Gertrude sends love—please don't go, Madame Caron—I am only going to talk about the neighbors. And they are all coming over very soon, and the best of all is, Gertrude has at last coaxed Uncle Matthew (a roguish grimace at the title) to give up Loringwood entirely and come to the Pines. And Dr. Delaven—he's delightful, mama, when he isn't teasing folks—he strongly advises them to make the change soon; and, oh, won't you ask them all over for a few weeks until the Pines is ready? And did you hear about two of their field hands running off? Well, they did. Scip and Aleck; isn't it too bad? and Mr. Loring doesn't know

it yet, no one dares tell him; and Masterson's Cynthia had a
boy run off, too, and went to the Yankees, they suppose.
And old Nelse he got scared sick at a ghost last night while
they were 'possum hunting. And, oh, mama, have you
heard from Ken?—not a word has come here, and he never
even saw Gertrude over there. He must be powerful busy if
he could not stop long enough to hunt friends up and say
'howdy.' "

"Lena, Lena, child!" and the mother sank back in her
chair, laughing. "Have they enforced some silent system of
existence on you since I have been down at Mobile? I declare, you fairly make my head swim with your torrent of
news and questions. Judithe, does not this young lady ful-
fill the foreign idea of the American girl—a combination of
the exclamation and interrogation point?"

Evilena stopped further criticism by kisses.

"I will be good as goodness rather than have Madame
Caron make up her mind I am silly the very first day," she
promised, "but, oh, mama, it *is* so good to have you to talk
to, and so delightful of Madame to come with you"—this
with a swift, admiring side glance at their visitor—"and, altogether, I'm just in love with the world today."

Later she informed them that Judge Clarkson would
probably drive over that evening, as he was going to Columbia or Savannah—she had forgotten which—and had to
go home first. He would have come with her but for a business talk he wanted to have, if Mr. Loring was able, this
morning.

"Gertrude coaxed him to stop over and settle something
about selling Loringwood. She's just grieving over the
wreck and ruin there, and Mr. Loring never will be able to
manage it again. They've been offered a lot of money for it
by some Orleans people, and Gertrude wants it settled.

Aunt Sajane is going to stay until they all come to the Pines."

"If Judge Clarkson should be going to Savannah you could send your maid in his charge, since she is determined to leave us," suggested Mrs. McVeigh.

"She would, no doubt, be delighted to go under such escort," said Judithe, "but her arrangements are made to start early in the morning; it is not likely your friend would be leaving so soon. Then, madamoiselle has said she is not sure but that it is to some other place he goes."

"Columbia?—yes; and more than likely it *is* Columbia," assented Mrs. McVeigh. "He is there a great deal during these troublous times."

A slight sigh accompanied the words, and Judithe noticed, as she had done often before, the lack of complaint or bewailings of the disasters so appalling to the South, for even the victories were so dearly bought. There was an intense eagerness for news from the front, and when it was read, the tears were silent ones. The women smiled bravely and were sure of victory in the end. Their faith in their men was adorable.

Evilena undertook to show the Marquise around the Terrace, eagerly anxious to become better acquainted with the stranger whose beauty had won her quite as quickly as it had won her brother. Looking at her, and listening to the soft tones with the delicious accent of France, she wondered if Ken had ever really dared to fall in love with this star from a foreign sky, or if Dr. Delaven had only been teasing her. Of course one could not help the loving; but brave as she believed Ken to be, she wondered if he had ever dared even whisper of it to Judithe, Marquise de Caron; for she refused to think of her as simply Madame Caron even though she did have to say it. The courtesy shown to her own demo-

cratic country by the disclaiming of titles was altogether
thrown away on Evilena, and she comforted herself by whis-
pering softly the given name *Zhu-dctte—Zhudcttc*, delighted
to find that the French could make of the stately name a
musical one as well.

Raquel came breathlessly to them on the lawn with the
information that "Mistress McVeigh ast them to please come
in de house right off case that maid lady, Miss Weesa, she
done slip on stairs an' hurt her foot powerful."

"Thanks, yes; I will come at once," said Miss Weesa's
mistress in so clear and even a tone that Evilena, who was
startled at the news, was oppressed by a sudden fear that all
the warmth in the nature of her fascinating Marquise was
centered in the luminous golden brown eyes.

As Judithe followed the servant into the house there came
a swift remembrance of those lamentable presentiments.
Was there, after all, something in the blood akin to the
prescience through which birds and wild things scent the
coming storms?—some atavism outgrown by the people of
intellectual advancement, but yet a power to the children of
the near sun?

Miss Louisa's foot certainly was hurt; it had been twisted
by a fall on the stairs, and the ankle refused to bear the
weight; the attempt to step on it caused her such agony that
she had called for help, and the entire household had responded.

It was Pluto who reached her first, lifting her in his arms
and carrying her to a bed. She had almost fainted from
pain or fright, and when she opened her eyes again it was
to meet those of her mistress in one wild appeal. Pluto
had not moved after placing her on the bed, though the other
darkies had retired into the hall, and Judithe's first impression of the scene was the huge black eyes fairly devouring

the girl's face with his curious gaze. He stepped back as Mrs. McVeigh entered with camphor and bandages, but he saw that pleading, frightened glance.

"Never mind, Louise, it will all be well," said her mistress, soothingly; "this has happened before," she added, turning to Mrs. McVeigh. "It needs stout bandages and perfect rest; in a week it will be forgotten."

"A week!—moaned the girl with pale lips, "but tomorrow —I *must* go tomorrow!"

"Patience, patience! You shall so soon as you are able, Louise, and the less you fret the sooner that may be."

Judithe herself knelt by the bed and removed tenderly the coquettish shoe of soft kid, and, to the horror of the assembled maids at the door, deliberately cut off the silk stocking, over which their wonder had been aroused when the short skirts of Louise had made visible those superfine articles. The pieces of stocking, needless to say, were captured as souvenirs and for many a day shown to the scoffers of neighboring plantations, who doubted the wild tales of luxury ascribed to the foreign magnate whose servants were even dressed like sure enough ladies.

"We must bandage it to keep down the swelling," said Judithe, working deftly as she spoke; "it happened once in New Orleans—this, and though painful, is not really serious, but she is so eager to commence the refurnishing of the yacht that she laments even a day's delay."

Louise did not speak again—only showed by a look her comprehension of the statement, and bore patiently the binding of the ankle.

It was three days before she could move about the room with help of a cane, and during those days of feverish anxiety her mistress had an opportunity to observe the very pointed and musical interest Pluto showed in the invalid

whose language he could not speak. He was seldom out of
hearing or her call and was plainly disturbed when word
came from Loringwood that the folks would all be over in
a few days. He even ventured to ask Evilena if Mr. Loring's
eyesight hadn't failed some since his long sickness, and was
well satisfied, apparently, by an affirmative reply. He even
went so far as to give Louise a slight warning, which she
repeated to her mistress one day after the Judge and Delaven had called, and Louise had promptly gone to bed and to
sleep, ofessing herself too well now for a doctor's attention.

"Pluto is either trying to lay a trap for me to see if I do
know English, or else he is better informed than we guess—
which it is, I cannot say, Marquise," she confided, nervously. "When he heard his mistress say I was to start
Thursday, he watched his chance and whispered: 'Go
Wednesday—don't wait till visitors come, go Wednesday."

"Visitors?—then he means the Lorings, they are to be
here Thursday," and Judithe closed the book she had been
reading, and looked thoughtfully out of the window. Louise
was moving about the room with the aid of a cane, glancing
at her mistress now and then and waiting to hear her opinion.

"I believe I would take his advice, Louise," she said at
last. "I have not noticed the man much beyond the fact
that he has been wonderfully attentive to your wants. What
do you think of him—or of his motives?"

"I believe they are good," said the girl, promptly. "He
is dissatisfied; I can see that—one of the insurrection sort
who are always restless. He's entirely bound up in the issue
of the war, as regards his own people. He suspects me and
because he suspects me tries to warn me—to be my friend.
When I am gone you may need some one here, and of all

I see he is the one to be most trusted, though, perhaps, Dr. Delaven—"

"Is out of the question," and Judithe's decision was emphatic. "These people are his friends."

"They are yours, too, Marquise," said the girl, smiling a little; but no smile answered her, a slight shade of annoyance—a tiny frown—bent the dark brows.

"Yes, I remember that sometimes, but I possess an antidote," she replied, lightly. "You know—or perhaps you do not know—that it is counted a virtue in a Gypsy to deceive a Georgio—well, I am fancying myself a Gypsy. In the Mohammedan it is a virtue to deceive the Christian, and I am a Mohammedan for the moment. In the Christian it was counted for centuries a mark of special grace if he despoil the Jew, until generations of oppression showed the wanderer the real God held sacred by his foes—money, my child, which he proceeded to garner that he might purchase the privileges of other races. So, with my Jewish name as a foundation, I have created an imaginary Jewish ancester whose wrongs I take up against the people of a Christian land; I add all this debt to the debt Africa owes this enlightened nation, and I shall help to pay it."

The eyes of Louise widened at this fantastical reason. She was often puzzled to determine whether the Marquise was entirely serious, or only amusing herself with wild fancies when she touched on pondrous questions with gay mockery.

Just now she laughed as she read dismay in the maid's face.

"Oh, it is quite true, Louise, it is a Christian land—and more, it is the most Christian portion of a Christian land, because the South is entirely orthodox; only in the North will you find a majority of skeptics, atheists, and agnostics. Though they may be scarcely conscious of it themselves,

14

it is because of their independent heterodox tendencies that they are marching today by thousands to war against a slavery not their own—the most righteous motive for a war in the world's history; but it cannot be denied that they are making war against an eminently Christian institution." And she smiled across at Louise, whose philosophy did not extend to the intricacies of such questions.

"I don't understand even half the reasons back of the war," she confessed, "but the thing I do understand is that the black man is likely to have a chance for freedom if the North wins, and that's the one question to me. Miss Evilena said yesterday it was all a turmoil got up by Yankee politicians who will fill their pockets by it."

"Oh, that was after Judge Clarkson's call; she only quoted him in that, and he is right in a way," she added; "there *is* a great deal of political jugglery there without a vestige of patriotism in it, but they do not in the least represent the great heart of the people of the North; *they* are essentially humanitarians. So you see I weigh all this, with my head, not my heart," she added, quizzically, "and having done so—having chosen my part—I can't turn back in the face of the enemy, even when met by smiles, though I confess they are hard weapons to face. It is a battle where the end to be gained justifies the methods used."

"*Ma belle*, Marquise," murmured the girl, in the untranslatable caress of voice and eyes. "Sometimes I grow afraid, and you scatter the fear by your own fearlessness. Sometimes I grow weak, and you strengthen me with reasons, reasons, reasons!"

"That is because the heart is not allowed to hamper the head."

"Oh, you tease me. You speak to me like a guardian angel of my people; your voice is like a trumpet, it stirs echoes in my heart, and the next minute you laugh as though it were all a play, and I were a child to be amused."

" 'And each man in his time plays many parts,' " quoted Judithe, thoughtfully, then with a mocking glance she added: "But not so many as women do."

"There—that is what I mean. One moment you are all seriousness and the next—"

"But, my child, it is criminal to be serious all the time; it kills the real life and leads to melancholia. You would grow morbid through your fears if I did not laugh at them sometimes, and it would never—never do for me to approve them."

She touched the girl's hand softly with her own and looked at her with a certain affectionate chiding.

"You are going away from me, Louise, and you must not go in dread or despondency. It may not be for long, perhaps, but even if it should be, you must remember that I love you—I trust you. I pity you for the childhood and youth whose fate was no choice of yours. Never forget my trust in you; when we are apart it may comfort you to remember it."

The girl looked at her with wide black eyes, into which the tears crept.

"Marquise," she whispered, "you talk as if you might be sending me away for always. Oh, Marquise—"

Judithe raised her hand warningly.

"Be a soldier, child," she said, softly, "each time we separate for even a day—you and I—we do not know that we will ever meet again. These are war times, you know."

"I know—but I never dreaded a separation so much; I wish you were not to remain. Perhaps that Plutos' words made me more nervous—it is so hard to tell how much he guesses, and those people—the Lorings—"

"I think I shall be able to manage the Lorings," said her mistress, with a reassuring smile, "even the redoubtable Matthew—the tyrannical terror of the county; so cheer up, Louise. Even the longest parting need only be a lifetime, and I should find you at the end of it."

"And find me still your slave," said the girl, looking at her affectionately. "That's a sort of comfort to think, Marquise; I'm glad you said it. I'll think of it until me meet again."

She repeated it Wednesday morning when she entered the boat for the first stage of her journey to Savannah, and the Marquise nodded her comprehension, murmured kindly words of adieu, and watched the little vessel until a bend in the river hid it from view, when she walked slowly back to the house. Since her arrival in America this was the first time she had been separated from the devoted girl for more than a day, and she realized the great loss it would be to her, though she knew it to be an absolutely necessary one.

As for Louise, she watched to the last the slight elevation of the Terrace grounds rising like an island of green from the level lands by the river. When it finally disappeared— barred out by the nearer green of drooping branches, she wept silently, and with a heavy heart went downward to Pocotaligo, oppressed by the seemingly groundless fear that some unknown evil threatened herself or the Marquise —the dread lest they never meet again.

CHAPTER XIX.

"Hurrah! Hurrah! for Southern rights Hurrah!
Hurrah! for the bonney blue flag,
    That bears the single star!"

Evilena was singing this stirring ditty at the top of her
voice, a very sweet voice when not overtaxed, but Dilsey,
the cook, put both hands to her ears and vowed cooking
school would close at once if that "yapping" was not
stopped; she could not for the life of her see why Miss
Lena would sing that special song so powerful loud.

"Why, Dilsey, it is my shout of defiance," explained
the girl, stirring vigorously at a mass in a wooden bowl
which she fondly hoped would develop into cookies for that
evening's tea, when the party from Loringwood were expected. "It does not reach very far, but I comfort myself
by saying it good and loud, anyway. That Yankee general
who has marched his followers into Orleans fines everybody—even if its a lady—who sings that song. I can't make
him hear me that far off, but I do my best."

"Good Lawd knows you does," agreed Dilsey. "But
when you want to sing in this heah cookhouse I be 'bleeged
if yo' fine some song what ain't got no battles in it. Praise
the Lawd, we fur 'nough away so that Yankee can't trouble
we all."

"Madam Caron saw him once," said the amateur cook,
tasting a bit of the sweetened dough with apparent pleas-

ure, "but she left Orleans quick, after the Yankees came. Of course it wouldn't be a place for a lady, then. She shut her house up and went straight to Mobile, and I just love her for it."

"Seems to me like she jest 'bout witched yo' all," remarked Dilsey; "every blessed nigger in the house go fallen' ovah theyselves when her bell rings, fo' feah they won't git thah fust; an' Pluto, he like to be no use to any one till aftah her maid, Miss Louise, get away, he jest waited on her, han' an' foot."

Dilsey had heretofore been the very head and front of importance in the servants' quarters on that plantation, and it was apparent that she resented the comparative grandeur of the Marquise's maid, and especially resented it because her fellow servants bowed down and paid enthusiastic tribute to the new divinity.

"Well, Dilsey, I'm sure she needed waiting on hand and foot while she was so crippled. I know mama was mighty well pleased he *was* so attentive; reckon maybe that's why she let him go riding with Madame Caron this morning."

"Pluto, he think plenty o' hisself 'thout so much pamperen," grumbled Dilsey. "Seem like he counted the whole 'pendence o' the family since Mahs Ken gone."

Evilena prudently refrained from expressing an opinion on the subject, though she clearly perceived that Dilsey was possessed of a fit of jealousy; so she proceeded to flatter the old soul into a more sunny humor lest dinner should go awry in some way, more particularly as regarded the special dishes to which her own little hands had added interest.

She was yet in the cookhouse when the guests arrived, and doffing the huge apron in which she was enveloped, skurried into the house, carrying with her the fragrance of cinnamon and sweet spices, while a dust of flour on curls and chin gave her a novel appearance, and the confession that she had been cooking was not received with the acclamation she had expected, though there was considerable laughter about it. No one appeared to take the statement seriously except Matthew Loring, who took it seriously enough to warn Margeret he would expect her to supervise all dishes he was to partake of. His meals were affairs not to be trifled with.

Margeret and Ben had accompanied the party. Others of the more reliable house servants of Loringwood, were to commence at once work at the Pines, and Gertrude was almost enthusiastic over the change.

"You folks really live over her," she declared to Mrs. McVeigh, "while at Loringwood—well, they tell me life used to be very gay there—but I can't remember the time. It seems to me that since the day they carried papa in from his last hunting field the place has been under a cloud. Nothing prospers there, nobody laughs or sings; I can't be fond if it, and I am so glad to get away from it again."

"Still, it is a magnificent estate," said Mrs. McVeigh, thoughtfully; "the associations of the past—the history of your family—is so intimately connected with it, I should think you would be sorry to part with it."

"I should not!" said Gertrude, promptly, "the money just now would do me a great deal more good than family records of extravagance which all the Lorings but Uncle Matthew seem to have been addicted to; and he is the exact opposite, you know."

Mrs. McVeigh did know. She remembered hearing of him as a one-time gamester long ago in New Orleans, a man without the conviviality of his father or his brother Tom; a man who spent money in dissipations purely selfish, carrying the spirit of a speculator even into his pursuit of social enjoyment. Then, all at once, he came back to Loringwood, settled down and became a model in deportment and plantation management, so close a calculator of dimes as well as dollars that it was difficult to believe he ever had squandered a penny, and a great many people refused to credit those ancient Orleans stories at all. Kenneth's father was one of them.

"I don't believe I am very much of a Loring, anyway," continued Gertrude with a little sigh. "They were a wild, reckless lot so far back as I can learn, and I—well, you couldn't call me wild and reckless, could you?"

Mrs. McVeigh smiled at the query and shook her head. "Not the least little bit, and we are glad of it." She walked over to the window looking across the far fields where the road showed a glimpse of itself as it wound by the river. "I thought I saw some one on horseback over there, and every horseman coming our way is of special interest just now. I look for word from Kenneth daily—if not from the boy himself; he has had time to be home now. His stay has already been longer than he expected."

Gertrude joined her and gave her attention to the head of the road.

"It may be your visitor from France, Evilena said she had gone riding. Of course you know we are all eager to meet her. Dr. Delaven sings her praises to us until it has become tantalizing."

"We should have driven over to see you but for that accident to her maid—the poor thing, except a few words, could only speak her own language, and we could not leave her entirely to the servants. Madame Caron seemed quite impressed with the brief glance she got of Loringwood, and when she heard it was likely to be sold she asked a great

many interested questions concerning it. She is wealthy
enough to humor her fancies, and her latest one is a Carolina plantation near enough to water for her yacht, which
Mobile folks say is the most beautiful thing—and the Com-
bahee would always be navigable for so small a craft, and the
Salkahatchie for most of the year."

"She certainly must be able to humor any sort of fancy
if she keeps a yacht of her own; that will be a new departure
for a woman in Carolina. It sounds very magnificent."

"It is; and it suits her. That is one reason why I thought
she might be the very best possible purchaser for Loringwood. She would resurrect all its former glories, and establish new ones."

Matthew Loring entered the sitting room, moving somewhat haltingly with the help of a cane. Gertrude arranged
a chair near the window, in which he seated himself slowly.

"Do you feel tired after the ride, Uncle?"

"No," he said, fidgetting with the cushion back of his
head, and failing to adjust it to suit him, either let it fall
or threw it on the floor. Gertrude replaced it without a
word, and Mrs. McVeigh smiled quietly, and pretended not
to see.

"I think I can promise you a pleasant visitor, Mr. Loring," she remarked, turning from the window. "A gentleman just turned in at our gate, and he does look like
Judge Clarkson."

Gertrude left the room to join the others who were talking
and laughing in the arbor, a few steps across the lawn. Mrs.
McVeigh busied herself cutting some yellowing leaves from
the plants on the stand by the window. Loring watched her
with a peculiar peering gaze. His failing sight caused him
to pucker his brows in a frown when he desired to inspect
anything intently, and it was that regard he was now di-

recting toward Mrs. McVeigh, who certainly was worth looking at by any man.

The dainty lace cap she wore had tiny bows of violet showing among the lace, and it someway had the effect of making her appear more youthful instead of adding matronliness. The lawn she wore had violet lines through it, and the flowing sleeves had undersleeves of sheer white gathered at the wrist. The wide lace collar circled a throat scarcely less white, and altogether made a picture worth study, though Matthew Loring's view of it was rather blurred because of the failure of vision which he denied whenever opportunity offered; next to paralysis there was nothing he dreaded so much as blindness, and even to Delaven he denied—uselessly—any tendency in that direction.

"Hum!" he grunted, at last, with a cynical smile; "if Gid Clarkson keeps up his habit of visiting you regularly, as he has done for the past ten years, you ought to know him a mile away by this time."

"Oh!"—Mrs. McVeigh was refastening her brooch before the mirror, "not ten years, quite."

"Well, long enough to be refused three times to my certain knowledge; why, he doesn't deny it—proud to let the country know his devotion to the most charming of her sex," and he gave an ironical little nod for which she exchanged one of her sweetest smiles.

"Glad you looked at me when you said that," she remarked, lightly; "and we do depend on Judge Clarkson so much these days I don't know what I ever would do if his devotion dwindled in the least. But I fancy his visit this morning is on your account instead of mine."

At that moment the white hat of Clarkson could be seen above the veranda railing, and Mrs. McVeigh threw open the glass doors as he appeared at the top of the steps with an immense boquet held with especial care—the Judge's one hobby in the realm of earth-grown things was flowers.

He bowed when he caught sight of the mistress of the Terrace, who bestowed on him a quaint courtesy such as the good nuns of Orleans taught their pupils thirty years before, she also extended her hand, which he kissed—an addition to fine manners the nuns had omitted—probably they knew how superfluous such training would be, all Southern girls being possessed of that knowledge by right of birth.

"Good morning, Judge."

"Mistress McVeigh!" Loring uttered an inarticulate exclamation which was first cousin to a grunt, as the Judge's tone reached his ear, and the profound bow was robbed of its full value by the Judge straightening, and glancing sideways.

"My delight, Madame, at being invited over this morning is only to be expressed in the silent language of the blossoms I bring. You will honor me by accepting them?"

"With very great pleasure, Judge; here is Mr. Loring."

"Heartily pleased to see you have arrived," and the Judge moved over and shook hands. "I came within bowing distance of Miss Gertrude as I entered, so I presume she has induced you to come over to the Pines for good. Your position, Mr. Loring, is one to be envied in that respect. Your hours are never lonely for lack of womanly grace and beauty in your household;" he glanced at Mrs. McVeigh, who was arranging the flowers in a vase, "I envy you, sir, I envy you."

"Oh, Gertrude is well enough, though we don't unite to spoil each other with flattering demonstrations," and he smiled cynically at the other two, and peered quizzically at Mrs. McVeigh, who presented him with a crimson beauty of a rose, for which he returned a very gracious, "Thank you," and continued: "Yes, Gertrude's a very good girl, though it's a pity it wasn't a boy, instead, who came into the Loring family that day to keep up the old name. And what about that boy of yours, Mistress McVeigh? When do you expect him home?"

"Very soon, now. His last message said they hoped to reach Charleston by the twentieth—so you see the time is short. I am naturally intensely anxious—the dread of that blockade oppresses me."

"No need, no need," and Loring's tone was decided and reassuring. "We got out through it, and back through it, and never a Yankee in sight; and those men on a special commission will be given double care, you may be sure."

"Certainly; the run from Nassau has kept the mail service open almost without a break," assented Clarkson, "and we have little reason for anxiety now that the more doubtful part of the undertaking has been successfully arranged."

"Most successfully; he writes that the English treat our people with extreme consideration, and heartily approve our seceding."

"Of course they do, and why shouldn't they?" demanded Loring. "I tell you, they would do much more than give silent sympathy to our cause if it were not that Russia has chosen to send her warships into Yankee harbors just now on guard against the interference of any of our friends, especially against Great Britain's interference, which would be most certain and most valuable."

"Quite true, quite true," assented the Judge, with a soothing tone, calculated to allay any combative or excited mood concerning that or any other subject; "but even their moral support has been a wonderful help, my dear sir, and the securing of an important addition to our navy from them just now means a very great deal I assure you; once let us gain a foothold in the North—get into Washington—and she will be the first to acknowledge us as a power—a sovereign power, sir !"

"I don't understand the political reasons of things," confessed their hostess, "but I fear Kenneth has imbibed the skepticism of the age since these years of military associations; he suggests that England's motive is really not for our advantage so much as her own. I dislike to have my illusions dispelled in that respect; yet I wonder if it *is* all commercialism on their part."

"Most assuredly," said the Judge. "England's policy has always been one of selfishness where our country was concerned. We must not forget she was the bitterest foe of our fathers. She has been sent home from our shores badly whipped too often to feel much of the brotherly love she effects just now for her own purposes. We must not expect anything else. She is of help to us now for purposes of revenue, only, and we will have to pay heavy interest for all favors. The only thought of comfort to us in the matter is that our cause is worth paying that interest for."

Loring acknowledged the truth of the statements, and Mrs. McVeigh sighed to think of the duplicity of the nation she had fancied single-hearted. And to a woman of her trustful nature it was a shock to learn that the British policy contained really none of the sweetly domestic and fraternal spirit so persistently advertised.

To change the conversation the Judge produced a letter just received—a proposal for Loringwood at Mr. Loring's own price.

"Already?" asked Mrs. McVeigh; and Loring, who realized that his own price was a remarkably high one, showed surprise at the ready acceptance of it.

"The offer is made by a law firm in New Orleans, Hart
& Logan," continued Clarkson. "But the real purchaser is
evidently some client of theirs."

"Well, I certainly hope the client will prove a pleasant
personage if he is to locate at Loringwood," remarked Mrs.
McVeigh. "Some one in New Orleans? Possibly we know
them."

"I am led to believe that the property is desired for some
educational institution," said Clarkson, handing the letter
to Loring, who could not decipher two lines of the fine script,
but refrained from acknowledging it.

"I must say the offer pleases me greatly." He nodded his
head and uttered a sigh of satisfaction; "a school or semi-
nary, no doubt, I like that; so will Gertrude. Speak to her,
and then write or telegraph the acceptance, as they prefer.
This is remarkably quick work; I feared it would be a long
while before a purchaser could be found. This is most fortunate."

"Then I congratulate you, Mr. Loring," said Mrs. Mc-
Veigh, who was grateful to the Judge for bringing news
likely to make the entertainment of the invalid an easier
affair. "But your fortunate offer from New Orleans dispels
a hope I had that my friend, Madame Caron, might buy it.
She seemed quite impressed with it. I was just saying so
to Gertrude."

"Yes, we've all been hearing considerable about this
charming foreigner of yours, who is daring enough to cross
to a war-ridden country to pay visits."

"She owns a fine property in New Orleans, but left there
in disgust when the Yankees took possession. I was delighted to find her in Mobile, and persuaded her to come
along and see plantation life in our country. We met her

first in Paris—Kenneth and I. He will be delightfully surprised to find her here."

"No doubt, no doubt," but Loring's assent was not very hearty; he remembered those first comments on her at Loringwood. "Dr. Delaven, also, was among her Parisian acquaintances, so you will have quite a foreign colony at the Terrace."

"I was much pleased with that fine young fellow, Dr. Delaven," remarked the Judge, "and really consider you most fortunate to secure his services—a very superior young man, and possessed, I should say, of very remarkable talent, and of too gay a heart to be weighed down with the importance of such special knowledge, as is too often the case in young professional men—yes, sir; a very bright young man."

Mrs. McVeigh, hearing laughter, had stepped out on the veranda, and smiled in sympathy with the couple who appeared on the step. The very talented young man just mentioned was wreathed in blossoms and wild vines; he carried Aunt Sajane's parasol, and was guided by reins formed of slender vines held in Miss Evilena's hands; the hat he wore was literally heaped with flowers, and he certainly did not appear to be weighed by the importance of any special knowledge at that moment. At sight of the Judge, Evilena dropped her improvised lines and ran to him.

"Oh, Judge, it is right kind of you to come over early today. Aunt Sajane is coming, she was down to the river with us; she laughed too much to walk fast. We were getting wild flowers for decorating—and here is Dr. Delaven."

"Yes, I'm one of the things she's been decorating," and he entered from the veranda, shook hands with Clarkson, and stood for inspection. "Don't I look like a lamb decked

for the sacrifice? But faith it was the heart of a lion I needed to go into the moccasin dens where she sent me this day.
The blossoms desired by your daughter were sure to grow in
the wildest swamps."

"I didn't suppose a bog-trotter would object to that,"
remarked the girl, to Loring's decided amusement.

"Lena!" and at the look of horror on her mother's face
she fled to the veranda.

"Ah—Mrs. McVeigh, I'm not hurt at all, but if she had
murthered me entirely your smile would give me new life
again; it's a guardian angel you are to me."

"You do need assistance," she replied, endeavoring to
untwine the vines twisted about his shoulders, "now turn
around."

He did, spinning in top fashion, with extended arms, while
Evilena smiled at the Judge from the window. His answering smile grew somewhat constrained as his hostess deliberately put her pretty arm half way around the young
man's shoulder in her efforts to untangle him.

"I say, Judge, isn't it in fine luck I am?— the undoing of
Delaven!"

But the Judge did not respond. He grew a trifle more
ceremonious as he turned from the window.

"Mistress McVeigh, I shall step out on the lawn to meet
my sister and Miss Loring, and when you have concluded
your present task, would you permit me to see the autumn
roses you were cultivating? As a lover of flowers I certainly
have an interest in their progress."

"Autumn roses—humph!" and Loring smiled in a grim
way only discernible to Delaven, who had grown so accustomed to his sardonic comments on things in general that
they no longer caused surprise.

"Of course, Judge; I'll show them to you myself," and Mrs. McVeigh let fall the last of the vines and joined him at the window—"so charming of you to remember them at all."

"Don't you want to go along and study the progress of autumn roses?" asked Evilena, peering around the window at Delaven, who laughed at the pretended demureness and timidity with which she invested the question.

"Not at this moment, my lady. Autumn roses, indeed!—while there's a wild flower in sight—not for the O'Delavens!"

And the O'Delaven's bright Irish eyes had so quizzical a smile in them the girl blushed and was covered with confusion as with a mantle, and gathering the blossoms in her arms seated herself ostentatiously close to Mr. Loring's chair while she arranged them, and Delaven might content himself with a view of one pink ear and a delicious dimple in one cheek, which he contemplated from the lounging chair back of her, and added to his occupation by humming, very softly, a bit of the old song:

"Ten years have gone by and I have not a dollar;
Evilena still lives in that green grassy hollow;
And though I am fated to marry her never,
I'm sure that I'll love her for ever and ever!"

"For ever and ever! I say, Miss Evilena, how do you suppose the fellow in the song could be so dead sure of himself, for ever and ever?"

"Probably he wasn't an Irishman," suggested the girl, bending lower over the blossoms that he might not see her smiling.

"Arrah, now, I had conjured up a finer reason that that entirely; it had something to do with the charms of your

15

namesake, but I'll not be telling you of it while you carry a nettle on your tongue to sting poor harmless wanderers with."

His pondrous sigh was broken in on by her laughter, and the beat of hoofs on the drive. While they looked at each other questioningly the voice of Judithe was heard speaking to Pluto, and then humming the refrain of Evilena's favorite, "Bonnie Blue Flag," she ran up to the veranda where Mrs. McVeigh met her.

"Oh, what a glorious gallop I had. Good morning, Judge Clarkson. How glad I am that you came right over soon as you got home. You are to us a recruit from the world whom we depend on to tell us all about doings there, and it is so good of you."

"It argues no virtue in a man, Madame, that he comes where beauty greets him," and the Judge's bow was a compliment in itself.

"Charming—is it not, Madame McVeigh? Truly your Southern men are the most delightful in the world."

"Ah, Madame," and Delaven arose from his chair with a lugubrious countenance, "for how am I to forgive you for adopting the fancy that Ireland is out of the world entirely?"

Judithe laughed frankly and put out her hand; she was exceedingly gay and gracious that morning; there was a delightful exhileration in her manner, and it was contagious. Matthew Loring half turned in his chair and peered out at the speaker as she turned to Delaven.

"Not out of the world of our hearts, Dr. Delaven, and for yourself, you really should not have been born up where the snow falls. You really belong to the South—we need you here."

"Faith, it was only a little encouragement I was needing, Marquise. I'll ask the Judge to prepare my naturalization papers in the morning."

"Other friends have arrived during your ride, Judithe," and her hostess led her into the sitting room. "Allow me to present our neighbor, Mr. Loring, of the Loringwood you admired so greatly."

"And with such good reason," said Judithe, with gracious bend of her head, and a charming smile. "I have looked forward to meeting you for some time, Mr. Loring, and your estate really appealed to me—it is magnificent. After riding past it I was conscious of coveting my neighbor's goods."

"It is our loss, Madame, that you did ride past," and Loring really made an effort to be cordial and succeeded better than might have been expected. He was peering at her from under the heavy brows very intently, but she was outlined against the flood of light from the window, and it blurred his vision, leaving distinct only the graceful, erect form in its dark riding habit. "Had you entered the gates my neice would have been delighted to entertain you."

"What a generous return for my envy," exclaimed Judithe. "The spirit of hospitality seems ever abroad in your land, Mr. Loring."

He smiled, well pleased, for his pride in his own country, his own state, was very decided. He lifted the forgotten rose from the arm of his chair.

"I will have to depend on our friend, the Judge, to present you fine phrases in return for that pretty speech, Madame; I can only offer a substitute," and to Evilena's wide-eyed astonishment he actually presented the rose to the Marquise.

"She simply has bewitched him," protested the girl to
Delaven, later. "I never knew him to do so gallant a thing
before. I could not have been more surprised if he had
proposed marriage to her before us all."

Delaven confessed he, too, was unprepared for so much
amiability, but then he admitted he had known men to do
more astonishing things that that, on short notice, for a
smile from Madame Judithe.

She accepted the rose with a slight exclamation of pleasure.

"You good people will smother me with sweets and per-
fumes," she protested, touching her cheek with the beautiful flower; then, as she was about to smell it, they were astonished to see it flung from her with a faint cry, followed by
a little laugh at the consternation of the party.

"How unpardonable that I discover a worm at the heart
of your first friendly offering to me, Mr. Loring;" and her
tones were almost caressing as she smiled at him; "the poor,
pretty blossom, so lovely, and so helpless in the grasp of its
enemy, the worm."

Pluto had entered with a pitcher of water which he placed
on the stand. He had witnessed the episode of the rose, and
picked it up from where it had been tossed.

"Margeret told me to see if you wanted anything, Mr.
Loring," he said, gently, and Mr. Loring's answer was decided, brusque and natural.

"Yes, I do; I want to go to my room; get my stick. Mistress McVeigh, if you have no objection to me breaking up
your party, I would like to have Judge Clarkson go along;
we must settle these business matters while I am able."

"At your service, sir, with your permission, Madame,"
and the Judge glanced at Mrs. McVeigh, who telegraphed a
most willing consent as she passed out on the veranda after

Evilena and Delaven. Judithe stood by the little side table, slowly pulling off her gauntlets, when she was aware that the colored man Pluto was regarding her curiously, and she perceived the reason. He had looked into the heart of the rose, and on the floor where it had fallen, and had found no living thing to cause her dread of the blossom.

He dropped his eyes when she looked at him, and just then a bit of conversation came to him as the Judge offered his arm to Loring and assisted him to rise.

"I certainly am pleased that you feel like looking into the business matters," Clarkson was saying, "and the Rhoda Larue settlement cannot be postponed any longer; Colonel McVeigh may be back any time now, and we must be ready to settle with him."

Loring made some grumbling remark in which "five thousand dollars" was the only distinguishable thing, and then they passed out, and Pluto followed, leaving the Marquise alone, staring out of the window with a curious smile; she drew a deep breath of relief as the door closed.

CHAPTER XX.

Mrs. McVeigh entered the sitting room some time after and was astonished to find her still there and alone.

"Why, Judithe, I fancied you had gone to change your habit ages ago, and here you are, plunged in a brown study."

"No—a blue and green one," was the smiling response. "Have you ever observed what a paintable view there is from this point? It would be a gem on canvas; oh, for the talent of our Dumaresque!"

"Your Dumaresque," corrected Mrs. McVeigh. "I never
can forgive you, quite, for sending him away; oh, Helene
wrote me all about it—and he *was* such a fine fellow."

"Yes, he was," and Judithe gave a little sigh ending in a
smile; "but one can't keep forever all the fine fellows one
meets, and when they are so admirable in every way as
Dumaresque, it seems selfish for one woman to capture
them."

Mrs. McVeigh shook her head hopelessly over such an
argument, but broke a tiny spray of blossom from a plant
and fastened it in the lapel of Judithe's habit.

"It is not so gorgeous as the rose, but it is at least free
from the pests."

Judithe looked down at the blossom admiringly. "I trust
Mr. Loring will forgive my panic—I fear it annoyed him."

"Oh, no—not really. He is a trifle eccentric, but his in-
validism gains him many excuses. There is no doubt but
that you made a decided impression on him."

"I hope so," said Judithe.

Margeret entered the room just then, and with her
hand on the door paused and stared at the stranger who
was facing her. Judithe, glancing up, saw a pair of strange
dark eyes regarding her. She noticed how wraith-like
the woman appeared, and how the brown dress
she wore made the sallow face yet more sallow. A narrow
collar and cuffs of white, and the apron, were the only sharp
tones in the picture; all the rest was brown—brown hair
tinged with grey rippling back from the broad forehead,
brown eyes with a world of patience and sadness in them
and slender, sallow-looking hands against the white apron.

She looked like none of the house servants at the Terrace—in fact Judithe was a trifle puzzled as to whether she
was a servant at all. She had not a feature suggesting col-

ored blood, was much more Caucasian in appearance than Louise.

It was but a few seconds they stood looking at each other, when Margeret made a slight little inclination of her head and a movement of the lips that might have been an apology, but in that moment the strange woman's face fairly photographed itself on Judithe's mind—the melancholy expression of it haunted her afterwards.

Mrs. McVeigh, noticing her guest's absorbed gaze, turned and saw Margeret as she was about to leave the room.

"What is it, Margeret?" she asked, kindly, "looking for Miss Gertrude?"

"Yes, Mistress McVeigh; Mr. Loring wants her."

"I think she must have gone to her room, she and Mistress Nesbitt went upstairs some time ago."

Margeret gently inclined her head, and passed out with the noiseless tread Evilena had striven to emulate in vain that day at Loringwood.

"One of Miss Loring's retainers?" asked Judithe; "I fancied they only kept colored servants."

"Margeret *is* colored," explained Mrs. McVeigh, "that is," as the other showed surprise, "although her skin does not really show color, yet she is an octoroon—one-eighth of colored ancestry. She has never been to the Terrace before, and she had a lost sort of appearance as she wandered in here, did she not? She belongs to Miss Loring's portion of the estate, and is very capable in her strange, quiet way. There have been times, however, when she was not quite right mentally—before we moved up here, and the darkies rather stand in awe of her ever since, but she is entirely harmless."

"That explains her peculiar, wistful expression," suggested
Judithe. "I am glad you told me of it, for her melancholy
had an almost mesmeric effect on me—and her eyes!"

All the time she was changing her dress for lunch those
haunting eyes, and even the tones of her voice, remained
with her.

"Those poor octoroons!" and she sighed as she thought of
them, "the intellect of their white fathers, and the bar of their
mothers' blood against the development of it—poor soul,
poor soul—she actually looks like a soul in prison. Oh!"—
and she flung out her hands in sudden passion of impotence. "What can one woman do against such a multitude?
One look into that woman's hopeless face has taken all the
courage from me. Ah, the resignation of it!"

But when she appeared among the others a little later,
gowned in sheer white, with touches of apple green here
and there, and the gay, gracious manner of one pleased
with the world, and having all reason to believe the world
pleased with her, no one could suspect that she had any
more serious problem to solve than that of arranging her
own amusements.

Just now the things most interesting to her were the affairs of the Confederacy. Judge Clarkson answered all her
questions with much good humor, mingled with amusement,
for the Marquise, despite her American sympathies, would
get affairs hopelessly mixed when trying to comprehend
political and military intricacies; and then the gallant Judge
would explain it all over again. Whether from Columbia
or Charleston, he was always in touch with the latest returns, hopes, plans of the leaders, and possibilities of the
Southern Confederacy, together with all surreptitious assistance from foreign sources, in which Great Britain came

first and Spain close behind, each having special reasons of their own for widening the breach in the union of states.

From Mobile there came, also, through letters to Mrs. McVeigh, many of the plans and possibilities of the Southern posts—her brother being stationed at a fort there and transmitting many interesting views and facts of the situation to his sister on her more Northern plantation.

Thus, although they were out of the whirl of border and coast strife, they were by no means isolated as regards tidings, and the fact was so well understood that their less fortunate neighbors gathered often at the Terrace to hear and discuss new endeavors, hopes and fears.

"I like it," confessed Judithe to Delaven, "they are like one great family; in no country in the world could you see such unanimous enthusiasm over one central question. They all appear to know so many of the representative people; in no other agricultural land could it be so. And there is one thing especially striking to me in comparison with France—in all this turmoil there is never a scandal, no intrigues in high places such as we are accustomed to in a court where Madame, the general's wife, is often quite as much of a factor in the political scene as the general himself; it is all very refreshing to a foreigner."

"Our women of the South," said the Judge, who listened, "are more of an inspiration because they are never associated in our minds with any life but that of the home circle and its refining influences. When our women enter the arena, it is only in the heart and memory of some man whose ideals, Madame, are higher, whose ambitions are nobler, because she exists untouched by the notoriety attaching itself to the court intrigues you mention, the notoriety too often miscalled fame."

"Right you are, Judge," said Delaven, heartily. "After all, human nature is very much alike whether in kingdom or republic, and men love best the same sort of women the world over."

Matthew Loring entered the room just then, leaning on the arm of Gertrude, whose fair hair made harmony with the corn-colored lawn in which she looked daintily pretty, and as the two ladies faced each other the contrasted types made a most effective picture.

"You have not met the Marquise de Caron?" he asked of Gertrude; and then with a certain pride in this last of the Lorings, he continued: "Madame la Marquise, allow me to present my niece, Miss Loring."

The blue eyes of the Carolina girl and the mesmeric amber eyes of the Parisian met, with the slight conventional smile ladies favor each other with, sometimes. There was decided interest shown by each in the other—an interest alert and questioning. Judithe turned brightly to Loring:

"In your democratic land, my dear sir, I have dispensed with 'La Marquise.' While here I am Madame Caron, very much at your service," and she made him a miniature bow.

"We shall not forget your preference, Madame Caron," said Gertrude, "it is a pretty compliment to our institutions." Then she glanced at Delaven, "did we interrupt a dissertation on your favorite topic, Doctor?"

"Never a bit; it's yourself is an inspiration to continue the same topic indefinitely," and he explained the difference Madame Caron had noticed in political matter with and without the feminine element.

"For all that, there *are* women in the political machines here, also," said Loring, testily—"too many of them, secret agents, spies, and the like. Gertrude, what was it Captain Masterson reported about some very dangerous person of that sort in New Orleans?—a woman whose assistance to the Yankees was remarkable, and whose circle of acquaintances was without doubt the very highest—did he learn her name?"

"Why, no, Uncle Matthew; don't you remember he was finding fault with *our* secret agents because they had not established her identity—in fact, had only circumstantial evidence that it was a woman, though very positive evidence that the person belonged to the higher social circle there."

"Faith, I should think the higher circle would be in a sorry whirl just then—not knowing which of your neighbors at dinner had a cup or dagger for you."

"The daggers were only figurative," said the Judge, "but they were none the less dangerous, and the shame of it! each innocent loyal Southerner convinced that a traitor had been made as one of themselves—trusted as is the nature of Southerners when dealing with friends, just as if, in this Eden-like abode, Mistress McVeigh should be entertaining in any one of us, supposed to be loyal Southerners, a traitor to his country."

"How dreadful to imagine!" said Judithe, with a little gesture of horror, "and what do they do with them—those dangerous serpents of Eden?"

"It isn't nice at all to hear about, Madame Caron," spoke Aunt Sajane, who was, as usual, occupied with the unlovely knitting. "It gave me chills to hear Phil Masterson say how that spy would be treated when found—not even given time for prayers!"

"Captain Masterson is most loyal and zealous, but given to slight extravagancies in such matters," amended the Judge. "No woman has ever suffered the extreme penalty of military law for spy work, in this country, and especially would it be impossible in the South. Imprisonment indefinitely and the probable confiscation of all property would no doubt be the sentence if, as in this suspected case, the traitoress were a Southern woman of means. But that seems scarcely credible. I have heard of the affair mentioned, but I refuse to believe any daughter of the South would so employ herself."

"Thank you, Judge," said Gertrude, very prettily; "any daughter of the South would die of shame from the very suspicion against her."

"Who is to die?" asked Mrs. McVeigh, coming in; "all of you, and of hunger, perhaps, if I delay tea any longer. Come right on into the dining room, please, and let me hear this discussion of Southern daughters, for I chance to be a daughter of the South myself."

Captain Philip Masterson, from an adjoining plantation, arrived after they were seated at the table, and was taken at once into the dining room, where Judithe regarded with interest this extremist who would not allow a secret agent of the North time for prayers. He did not look very ferocious, though his manner had a bluntness not usual in the Southern men she had met—a soldier above and beyond everything else, intelligent, but not broad, good looking with the good looks of dark, curly hair, a high color, heavy mustache, which he had a weakness for caressing as he talked, and full, bold eyes roaming about promiscuously and taking entire advantage of the freedom granted him at the Terrace, where he had been received as neighbor since boyhood. He was a cousin of Gertrude's, and it was not difficult to see that she was the first lady in the county to him, and the county was the center of Philip Masterson's universe.

He was stationed at Charleston and was absent only for some necessary business at Columbia, and hearing Judge Clarkson was at the Terrace he had halted long enough to greet the folks and consult the Judge on some legal technicality involved in his journey.

Pluto, who had seen that the Captain's horse had also been given refreshment, came thoughtfully up the steps, puzzling his head over the perfect rose cast aside on a pretense. It puzzled him quite as much as the problem of Louise; and the only key he could find to it was that this very grand lady knew all about the identity of Louise, and knew why she had hurried away so when old Nelse recognized her.

He wished he had that picture of Margeret, brought by Rosa from Georgia. But it was still with a lot of Rosa's things over at the Larue plantation, with the child. He counted on going over to see the boy in a week at the furthest.

As he reached the top of the steps he could see Margeret through the open window of the sitting room. Her back was towards him, and she was so absorbed in regarding the party in the dining room that he approached unnoticed, and she turned with a gasp as of fear when he spoke:

"You're like to see more gay folks like that over here than you have at Loringwood," he remarked. "I reckon you glad to move."

"No," she said, and went slowly towards the veranda; then she turned and looked at him questionably, and with an interest seldom shown for anyone.

"You—you heard news from Larue plantation?" she asked, hesitatingly.

"Who, me? No, I aint had no news. I aint"—then he stopped and stared at her, slowly comprehending what news *might* come from there. "Fo' God's sake, tell me! My Zekal; my—"

She lifted her finger for silence and caught his arm.

"They hear you—they will," she said, warningly, "come in here."

She opened the door into the library and he followed; she could feel his hand tremble, and his eyes were pleading and full of terror. The light chatter and laughter in the dining room followed them.

"Sick?" and his eyes searched her face for reply, but she slowly shook her head and he caught his breath in a sob, as he whispered: "Daid! My baby, oh—"

"Sh-h! He's alive—your boy. It's worse than that, maybe—and they never let you know! Mr. Larue had gone down to Mexico, and the overseer has published all his slaves to be sold—all sold, and your child—your little boy—"

"God A'mighty!"

He was silent after that half-whispered ejaculation. His face was covered with his hands, while the woman stood regarding him, a world of pity in her eyes.

"They can't sell Zekal," he said, at last, looking up. "Mahs Larue tole me plain he give me chance. I got some o' the money, that eighteen dollah I paid on Rosa's freedom —that gwine be counted in—then I got most nine dollah 'sides that yet, an' I gwine Mahs Jean Larue an' go down my knees fo' that boy, I will! He only pickaninny, my Zekal, an' I promise Rosa 'fore she died our boy gwine be free; so I gwine Mahs Larue, I—"

Margeret shook her head.

"He's gone, I tell you—gone to Mexico, more miles away than you could count; sold to the sugar plantation and left the colored folks for lawyer and overseer to sell. They all to be sold—a sale bill came to Loringwood yesterday. Men like overseers and lawyers never take account of one little pickaninny among a hundred. One same as another to them —one same as another!"

Her voice broke and she covered her face with her hands, rocking from side to side, overcome by memories of what had been. Pluto looked at her and realized from his own misery what hers had been. Again the laughter and tinkle of tea things drifted in to them; some one was telling a story, and then the laughter came more clearly. Pluto listened, and his face grew hard, brutish in its sullen hate.

"And they can laugh," he muttered, sullenly, "while my baby—my Rosa's baby—is sold to the traders, sold away where I nevah can find him again; sold while the white folks laugh an' make merry," and he raised his hand above his head in a fury of suppressed rage. "A curse on every one of them! a curse—"

Margeret caught his arm with a command to silence.

"Hush! You got a kind master—a kind mistress. The people who laugh at that table are not to blame on account of Rosa's master, who holds your child."

"You stand up fo' the race that took yo' chile from yo?" he demanded, fiercely. "That held yo' a slave when yo' was promised freedom? That drove yo' wild fo' years with misery? The man is in that room who did all that, an' yo' stan' up fo' him along of the rest?"

He paused, glowering down at her as if she, too, were white enough to hate. When she spoke it was very quietly, almost reprovingly.

"My child died. What good was freedom to me without her? Where in all this wide world would I go with my freedom if I had it? Free and alone? No," and she shook her head sadly, "I would be like a child lost from home—

helpless.   The young folks laughing there never hurt me —never hurt you."

The people were leaving the dining room. Captain Masterson, who had time for but a brief call, was walking along the veranda in low converse with the Judge. Judithe had separated herself from the rest and walked through the sitting room into the library, when she halted, surprised at those two facing each other with the air of arrested combat or argument. She recovered her usual manner enough to glance at the clock, and as her eyes crossed Margeret's face she saw traces of tears there.

"It is time, almost, for the mail up from Pocotaligo today, is it not, Pluto?" she said, moving towards a book-case. Receiving no reply, she stopped and looked at him, at which he recovered himself enough to mutter, "Yes, mist'ess," and turned towards the door, his trembling tones and the half-groping movement as he put his hand out before him showed he was laboring under some emotion too intense for concealment, and involuntarily she made a gesture of command.

"Wait! You have grief—some sad misfortune?" and she glanced from his face to that of Margeret, questioningly. "Poor fellow—is it a death?"

"No death, and nothing to trouble a white lady with," he said, without turning, and with hopeless bitterness in his voice; "not fit to be told 'long side o' white folks merry-maken', only—only Rosa, my boy's mother, died yeah ago ovah on Larue plantation, an' now the chile hisself—my Rosa's baby—gwine to be sold away—gwine to be sold to the traders!"

His voice broke in a sob; all the bitterness was drowned in the wave of grief under which his shoulders heaved, and his broken breaths made the only sound in the room, as

Judithe turned questioningly to Margeret, who bent her head in confirmation of his statement.

"But," and the questioner looked a trifle bewildered, "a little child, that would not mean a great expense, surely if your mistress, or your master, knew, they would help you."

Margeret shook her head, and Pluto spoke more calmly.

"Not likely ; this war done crippled all the folks in money ; that way Mahs Jean Larue sell out an' go ovah in Mexico ; that why Loren'wood up fo' sale to strangers ; that why Judge Clarkson done sell out his share in cotton plantation up the river ; ain't *nobody* got hundreds these days, an' lawyers won't take promises. I done paid eighteen dollars on Rosa when she died, but I ain't got no writin'," he went on, miserably, "that was to go on Zekal, an' I have 'nigh onto nine dollars 'sides that. I gwine take it ovah to Mahs Larue nex' week, sure, an' now—an'—now—"

His words were smothered in a sigh ; what use were words, any way? Judithe felt that Margeret's eyes were on her face as she listened—wistful, questioning eyes! Would the words be of no use?

"The Jean Larue estate," she said, meditatively, seating herself at the table and picking up a pen, "and your wife was named Rosa?"

"Yes'm." He was staring at her as a man drowning might stare at a spar drifting his way on a chance wave ; there was but the shadow of a hope in his face as he watched with parted lips the hand with the pen—and back of the shadow what substance!

"And she is dead—how long?"

"A yeah gone now."

"And Mr. Larue asks how much for her child?"

16

"Hundred 'n' fifty dollar—this what he *said*, but, God knows, lawyers got hold o' things now, maybe even more 'n that now, an' anyway—"

His words sounded vague and confused in his own ears, for she was writing, and did not appear to hear.

"Where is this Larne place?" she asked, glancing up. "I heard of a Jean Larue plantation across in Georgia—is this it?"

"No'm," and he turned an eager look of hope towards Margeret at this pointed questioning, but her expression was unchanged; she only looked at the strange lady who questioned and showed sympathy.

"No, mist'ess, this Mahs Jean Larue did stay on they Georgy plantation till five yeah back, then they move ovah to Callina again; that how I come to meet up with Rosa. Larue place down river towards Beaufort—a whole day's walken'."

"What did you say this child was named?" she asked, without ceasing the movement of the pen over the white paper.

"His name *Ezekal*, but we ain't nevah call him anything but Zekal—he's so little yet."

"And when is this sale to be?"

Pluto looked helplessly towards Margeret.

"Tomorrow week, Madame Caron," she said, speaking for the first time, though her steady gaze had almost made Judithe nervous. It had a peculiar, appealing quality, which Judithe, with a little grimace, assured herself was so appealing it was compelling; it left her no choice but to do what she was doing and for which she could take no credit whatever to herself—the wistful eyes of the pale-faced bondwoman did it all.

"In a week there is plenty of time to arrange it," she said, turning kindly to Pluto. "You can rest in peace about your Rosa's boy. I will attend to it at once, and the traders shall never have him."

Margeret drew a sharp, inward breath of relief.

"Yo' mean *you'll* buy him in?" and Pluto's voice was scarcely more than a whisper. "Yo' mean I'll have a chance, maybe, to buy him back some day?"

"Not 'some day,' my good fellow," and Judithe folded the paper she had been writing; "from the day he is bought from the Larue estate he will have his freedom. He will never be bought or sold again."

The man stared at her, helplessly. No hope of his had ever reached so high as *that*! He tried to speak—failed— and his face was covered by his sleeve, as he went slowly out of the room.

"Don't—don't you think Pluto ain't thankful, Madame Caron," said the soft tones of Margeret, and they were not quite steady tones, either. Judithe did not look up for fear she should see tears in the melancholy, dark eyes; "that black boy just so thankful he can't speak. He'll worship you for what you've done for him, and well he may."

There was a soft rustle beside her—the presence of lips on her hand, and then Judithe was alone in the room, and stronger than when she had entered it so short a while since, braced by the certainty that here, at least, she had been of use—practical use her own eyes could see, and all the evening a bird sang in her heart, and the grateful touch of the bondwoman's lips gave her more pleasure than she could remember through the same tribute of any courtier.

CHAPTER XXI.

When Pluto brought her mail, an hour later, he tried to express more clearly in words the utter happiness showing through every feature of his dark face, but she stopped him with a little gesture.

"I see you are glad—no need to tell it," she remarked, briefly; "if you want to thank me do it by helping any of your people whom you find in trouble. There are many of them, no doubt."

And when Mrs. McVeigh thanked her for doing what she could not have done on such short notice, Judithe put the question aside quite as lightly.

"The man is a very good groom," she remarked. "I enjoyed my ride the more today for having him along to answer all my curious questions of the country. I meant to give him 'backsheesh,' as the Orientals call it, so why not select what the fellow most wants—even though it be a pickaninny?"

"Well, he certainly is singing your praises down in the cook-house. I even heard several 'hallelujas' from Aunt Dilsey's particular corner. Judge Clarkson has endorsed the check and will send a white man horseback with it to Larues in the morning. Pluto starts tonight on foot across country —says he can't sleep, any way—he's so happy. The women are arguing already as to which shall have the special care of Zekal. Altogether, you have created a sensation in the household, and we all love you for it."

"What further recompense to be desired? It really is not worth so much of praise."

"Kenneth will not think so when he comes home," and Kenneth's mother slipped her arm around the girl's shoulder affectionately, not noticing how her careless expression changed at mention of the name.

"Oh! Will he, then, be interested in such small things as pickaninnies?" and her light words belied the look in her eyes.

"Will he? Well, I should think so! You have done just what he would want done—what he would do if it were possible. For two generations the McVeighs have neither bought nor sold slaves"—Judithe's eyes shot one disdainful flash—"just kept those inherited; but I'm sure that boy of mine would have broken the rule for his generation in this case, and he'll be so grateful to you for it. Pluto was his playmate and respected monitor as a child, and Pluto's Zekal certainly will have a place in his affections."

Judithe picked up one of several letters, over which she had glanced, and remarked that she would expect a visitor within a week—possibly in a day or two, the master of her yacht, which from a letter received, she learned had reached Savannah before Louise. A storm had been encountered somewhere along the southern coast, and he would submit the list of damages—not heavy, yet needing a certain amount of refitting.

"Fortunate Louise did go down," she said, with a certain satisfaction, as she laid down the communication. "She will be perfectly happy, even hobbling around with a cane, if she is only buying things; she delights in spending money;" then, after a pause, "I presume Col. McVeigh's return is still uncertain?"

"Yes, rather; yet I fancy each morning he will come before night, and each night that he may waken me in the morning. I have been living in that delightful hopefulness for a week."

Lena called them and they went out to the rustic seat circling the great live oak at the foot of the steps. The others were there, and the Judge was preparing to drive the three miles home with his sister. Now that the invalid was better, and the wanderer returned from Mobile, Aunt Sajane bethought herself of the possible sixes and sevens of her own establishment, and drove away with promises of frequent visits on both sides.

Long after the others had retired for the night Judithe's light burned, and there was little of the careless butterfly of fashion in her manner as she examined one after another of the letters brought her by the last mail, and wrote replies to some she meant to take to the office herself during her early morning ride; it was so delightful to have an errand, and Pluto had shown her the road. After all the others were done she picked up again the communication she had shown to Mrs. McVeigh—the report from the yacht master, and from the same envelope extracted a soft silken slip of paper with marks peculiar—apparently mere senseless scratches of a thoughtless pen, but it was over that paper and the reply most of the evening was spent. It was the most ancient method of secret writing known to history, yet, apparently, so meaningless that it might pass unnoticed even by the alert, or be turned aside as the ambitious scrawlings of a little child.

Each word as deciphered she had pencilled on a slip of paper, and when complete it read:

"Courant brings word McV. is likely to be of special interest. If he travels with guard we can't interfere on road from coast, and you will be only hope. A guard of Federals will be landed north of Beaufort and await your orders. Messenger will communicate soon as movements are known. You may expect Pierson. We await your orders or any suggestions."

There was no signature. Her orders or suggestions were written in the same cipher, and required much more time and thought than had been given to the buying and freeing of Pluto's pickaninny, after which she destroyed all unnecessary writings, and retired with the satisfied feeling of good work done and better in prospect, and in a short time was sleeping the calm, sweet sleep of a conscienceless child.

She rode even further next morning than she had the preceding day, when Pluto was her guide, and she rode as straight east as she could go towards the coast. When she met colored folk along the road she halted, and spoke with them, to their great delight. She asked of the older ones where the road led to, and were the pine woods everywhere along it, and what about swamps and streams to ford, etc., etc. Altogether, she had gained considerable knowledge of that especial territory by the time she rode back to the Terrace and joined the rest at the late breakfast. She had been in the saddle since dawn, and recounted with vivacity all the little episodes of her solitary constitutional; the novelty of it was exilarating. That it appeared a trifle eccentric to a Southerner did not suggest itself to her; all her eccentricities were charming to the McVeigh household, and Delaven lamented he had not been invited as proxy for Pluto, and amused the breakfast party by anecdotes of hunting days in Ireland, and the energy and daring of the ladies who rode at dawn there.

Several times during the day Judithe attempted to have a tete-a-tete with Mrs. McVeigh, and learn more about Miss

Loring's silent maid, who was the first person she saw on
her return from the ride that morning. The absolute self-
effacement of an individual whose repose suggested self-re-
liance, and whose well shaped head was poised so admirably
as to suggest pride, made the sad-faced servant a fascinating personality to any one interested in questions concerning her race. No other had so won her attention since she
made compact with Kora in Paris.

But Mistress McVeigh was a very busy woman that day.
Pluto's absence left a vacancy in the establishment no other
could fill so intelligently. Miss Loring had promptly attached herself as general assistant to the mistress of the
house. Delaven noticed how naturally she fell into the position of an elder daughter there, and, remembering Evilena's
disclosures at Loringwood, and Matthew Loring's own
statement, he concluded that the wedding bells might sound
at any time after Kenneth's return, and he fancied they had
been delayed, already, three years longer than suited the
pleasure of her uncle.

Delaven, as well as Judithe, was attracted by the personality of Margeret. In the light, or the shadow, of the sad
story he had listened to, she took on a new interest, an
atmosphere of romance surrounded her. He pictured what
her life must have been as a child, amid the sunshine of
Florida, the favorite of her easy-living, easy-loving Greek
father, the sole relic of some pretty slave! As she walked
silently along the halls of the Terrace, he tried to realize
Nelse's description of her gayety, once, in the halls of Loringwood. And when he observed the adoring eyes with
which she regarded the Marquise after the pickaninny episode, he understood it was another child she was thinking of
—a child who should have been freed, and was not, and the
feelings of Pluto were as her own.

Two entire days passed without Pluto's return. There was some delay, owing to the absence of the overseer from the Larue estate; then, Zekal was ailing, and that delayed him until sundown of the second day, when he took the child in his arms—his own child now—and with its scanty wardrobe, and a few sundry articles of Rose's, all saved religiously by an old "aunty," who had nursed her—he started homeward on his long night tramp, so happy he scarce felt the weight of the boy in his arms, or that of the bundle fastened with a rope across his shoulders. He had his boy, and the boy was free! and when he thought of the stranger who had wrought this miracle his heart swelled with gratitude and the tears blinded him as he tramped homeward through the darkness.

The first faint color of dawn was showing in the east when he walked into Dilsey's cook-house and showed the child asleep in his arms.

What a commotion! as the other house servants mustered in, sleepily, and straightway were startled very wide awake indeed, and each insisted on feeling the weight of the newcomer, just, Dilsey said, as if there never was a child seen on that plantation before. And all had cures for the "brashy" spell the little chap had been afflicted by, and which seemed frightened away entirely, as he looked about him with eyes like black beads. All the new faces, and the petting, were a revelation to Zekal.

Dilsey put up with it till everything else seemed at a standstill in the morning's work, when she scattered the young folks right and left to their several duties, got Pluto an excellent breakfast, and gave the child in charge of one of the mothers in the quarters till "mist'ess" settled about him.

"Yo' better take his little duds, too, Lucy," suggested Pluto, as the boy was toddling away with her, contentedly,

rich in the possession of two little fists full of sweet things;
"they're tied up in that bandana—not the blue one! That
blue one got some o' his mammy's things I gwine look over;
maybe might be something make him shirts or aprons, an'
if there is a clean dress in that poke I—I like to have it put
on 'im 'fore she sees him—Madame Caron, an', an' Mist'ess,
o' course! I like her to see he's worth while."

Then he asked questions about what all had been done in
his absence, and learned there had been company coming
and going so much Mahs Loring had his meals in his own
room, "'cause o' the clatter they made." Margeret had been
over at the Pines with Miss Loring to see about the work already commenced there, and Madame Caron and Miss Lena
and Dr. Delaven just amused themselves.

He learned that the mail had been detained and no one
had gone for it, and, tired though he was, started at once.
He had noticed Madame Caron's mail was of daily importance, and it should not be neglected by him even if company
did make the others forgetful.

He was especially pleased that he had gone, when the
postmaster handed over to him, besides several other letters
and papers, a large, important-looking envelope for the
Marquis de Caron—a title difficult for Pluto to spell;
though he recognized it at sight.

The lady herself was on the veranda, in riding garb, when
he presented himself, and she smiled as she caught sight of
that special envelope among the rest.

"Margeret tells me you brought back the boy," she said,
glancing up, after peering in the envelope and ascertaining
its contents, "and, Pluto, you paid me for Zekal when you
brought this letter to me—so the balance is even."

Pluto made no comment—only shook his head and smiled. He could not comprehend how any letter, even a big one, could balance Zekal.

She retired to her room to examine the other letters, while Pluto placed the mail for the rest at their several places on the breakfast table.

Judithe unfolded the large enclosure and gave a sigh of utter content as her eyes rested on the words there. They conveyed to the Marquise de Caron, of France, an estate in South Carolina outlined and described and known as Loringwood. The house was sold furnished as it stood, and there followed an inventory of contents, excepting only family china and portraits.

"Not such an unlucky journey, after all, despite the coffins in the tea cups," and she smiled at the fearful fancies of Louise, as she laid the paper aside; for the time it had made her forget there were other things equally important.

There was another letter, without signature. It said: "McVeigh is in Charleston, detained by official matters. Pierson leaves with particulars. Mail too irregular to be reliable. Your latest word from Columbia most valuable; we transmitted it as you suggested. Your location fortunate. The Powers at W. delighted with your success, but doubtful of your safety—unhealthy climate except for the natives! Report emancipation will be proclaimed, but nothing definite heard yet."

She removed her habit and joined the rest at the breakfast table, clad in the daintiest of pink morning gowns, and listened with pleased surprise to Mrs. McVeigh's information that her son, the Colonel, might be expected at any time. They had passed the blockade successfully, reached Charleston two nights before; were detained by official matters, and hoped, surely, to reach home within twenty-four hours after

the letter. His stay, however, would have to be brief, as he
must move north at once with his regiment.

And in the midst of the delight, Judithe created a sensation by remarking:

"Well, my good people, I am not going to allow the
Colonel all the surprise. I have had one of my own this
morning, and I can scarcely wait to share it with you. It is
the most astonishing thing!" and she glanced around at the
expectant faces.

"If it's of interest to you, it will be the wide world's worth
to us," affirmed Delaven, with exaggerated show of devotion, at which she laughed happily, and turned to her
hostess.

"You remember I informed you in Mobile I meant to sell
my Orleans property, as I would not occupy it under exist-
ing rule;" to which explanation Matthew Loring actually
beamed commendation, "well, I left it in the hands of my
business man with orders to invest the money from the sale
in some interior plantations not under Federal control. I
wanted a house furnished, colonial by choice—some histori-
cal mansion preferred. The particular reason for this is, I
have no relatives, no children to provide for, and the fancy
has come to me for endowing some educational institution in
your land, and for such purpose a mansion such as I suggested would, in all ways be preferable. Well, they forwarded me a list of properties. I sent them back unread lest
I should covet them all, for they all would cost so little!
I repeated to them the description Madame McVeigh had
given me of your ancestral home, my dear sir, and told them
to secure me a property possessing just such advantages as
yours does—near enough to the coast for yachting, and far
enough from cities to be out of social chains, except the
golden one of friendship," she added, letting her eyes rest

graciously on her listeners. "Well, can you surmise the result of that order?"

Each looked at the other in wonder; her smile told half
the truth.

"I am afraid to put my surmise in words," confessed Mrs.
McVeigh, "for fear of disappointment."

"I'm not!" and Evilena flourished her napkin to emphasize her delight, "its Loringwood! Oh, oh, Madame Caron,
you've bought Loringwood!"

Margeret was entering the room with a small tray containing something for Mr. Loring, whose meals she prepared personally. Delaven, who was facing her, saw her
grow ashen, and her eyes closed as though struck a physical
blow; a glass from the tray shivered on the floor, as he
sprang up and saved her from falling.

"What ails you, Margeret?" asked Gertrude, with the ring
of the silver sounding through her tones. "There—she is
all right again, Dr. Delaven. Don't come into the dining
room in future unless you feel quite well. Uncle can't endure crashes, or nervous people, about him."

"I know; I beg pardon, Miss Gertrude, Mistress Mc-
Veigh," and Margeret's manner was above reproach in its
respectful humility, though Delaven observed that the firm
lips were white; "the kitchen was very warm. I—I was
faint for a minute."

"Never mind about the glass, Caroline will pick it up,"
said Mrs. McVeigh, kindly; "you go lay down awhile, it *is*
very warm in the kitchen. Dilsey always will have a tremendous fire, even to fry an egg on; go along now—go rest
where its cool."

Margeret bent her head in mute acknowledgment of the
kindness, and passed out of the room. Mr. Loring had

pushed his plate away with an impatient frown, signifying that breakfast was over for him, any way.

Delaven, noticing his silence and the grim expression on his face, wondered if he, too, was doubtful of that excuse uttered by the woman. The kitchen, no doubt, was warm, but he had seen her face as she heard Evilena's delighted exclamation; it was the certainty that Loringwood was actually sold—Loringwood, and that grave under the pines? Possibly she had fostered hope that it might not be yet— not for a long time, and the suddenness of it had been like a physical shock to the frail, devoted woman. He had reasoned it out like that, and his warm, Irish heart ached for her as she left the room, and, glancing about the table, he concluded that only Matthew Loring and himself suspected the truth, or knew the real reason of her emotion, though the eyes of the Marquise did show a certain frank questioning as they met his own.

"Margeret's fit just frightened the plantation away for a minute," resumed Evilena, "but do own up, Madame Caron, *is* it Loringwood?"

"Yes," assented Judithe, "the letter from my lawyer, this morning, informs me it is really Loringwood."

"I am very much pleased to hear it, Madame," and Matthew Loring's tone was unusually hearty. "Since we part with it at all, I am pleased that no scrub stock gets possession. The place is perfectly adapted to the use you have planned, and instead of falling into neglect, the old home will become a monument to progress."

"So I hope," replied Judithe, with a subtle light, as of stars, in the depths of her eyes; "I am especially delighted to find that the old furnishings remain; it would be difficult for me to collect articles so in keeping with the entire scheme of arrangement, and it would make a discord to introduce new things from the shops."

"You will find no discords of *that* sort at Loringwood," said Gertrude, speaking for the first time; "and, I hope, not many of any kind. Many of the heavy, massive old things I disliked to part with, but they would be out of place at the Pines, or, in fact, in any house less spacious. Like uncle, I am pleased it goes into the keeping of one who appreciates the artistic fitness of the old-fashioned furnishings."

"Which she has never seen yet," supplemented Evilena, as Judithe received this not very cordial compliment with a little bow and a brilliant smile.

"We will remedy that just as soon as we can secure an invitation from the present lady of the manor," she said, in mock confidence to Evilena, across the table, at which the rest laughed, and Mr. Loring declared that now she was the lady of the manor herself, and his one regret was that he and his niece were not there to make her first entrance a welcome one.

"That would certainly add to the pleasure of the visit," and her smile was most gracious. "But even your wish to welcome me makes it all the more delightful. I shall remember it when I first enter the door."

Gertrude made an effort to be cordial, but that it was an effort Mrs. McVeigh easily discerned, and when they were alone, she turned to her in wonder:

"What is it, dear? Are you displeased about the sale? I feel so responsible for it; but I fancied it would be just what you would want."

"So it is, too; but—oh, I had no idea it could all be settled so quickly as this!"

"When people never hesitate to telegraph, even about trifles, and Judithe never does, they can have business affairs moved very quickly," explained Mrs. McVeigh; "but what possible reason have you.for objecting to the settlement?"

"I don't object, but—you will think me silly, perhaps— but, I am sorry it is out of our hands before Kenneth returns. I should like to have him go over the old place, just once, before strangers claim it."

"Never mind, dear, the nearer you are to the Terrace the better the Kenneth will like it, and the Pines is a great improvement in that way."

"Yes; still it was at Loringwood I first saw him. Do you remember? You folks had just moved here from Mobile; it was my tenth birthday, and I had a party. Kenneth was the beau of the whole affair, because he was a new-comer, and a 'town boy,' and, I remember, we compared ages and found that he was three months older than I, and for a long time he assumed superior airs in consequence," and she smiled at the remembrance. "Well, Uncle Matthew is delighted, and I suppose I should be. It ends all our money troubles for awhile, any way. Now, what are you planning for Kenneth's home coming? All the people will want to see him."

"And so they shall. We certainly can depend on him for tomorrow night, and we will have a party. Pluto shall start with the invitations at once."

And Pluto did, just as soon as he had brought Zekal around for an inspection, which proved so entirely satisfactory that Evilena threatened to adopt him right away. He should be her own especial boy soon as he was big enough to run errands, which statement appeared to make an impression on Zekal not anticipated, for he so delighted to gaze on the pretty young white lady who petted him, that he objected lustily to being removed from the light of her countenance; and Delaven gave him a coin and informed him that he felt like himself, often. This remark, made in the presence of Madame Caron, who laughed, brought on a tilt at hostilities between himself and Miss Evilena, who declared he was mocking her, and trying to render her ridiculous in the eyes of the only foreigner she admired excessively! He endeavored to persuade her to extend the last by warbling "Sweet Evilena," which she declared she could not endure to hear for three distinct reasons.

"Let's hear them," he suggested, continuing the low humming:

> "Ten years have gone by
> And I have not one dollar;
> Evilena still lives
> In that green grassy hollow."

"There! what sort of man would he be, any way?" she demanded, "a man who couldn't earn a dollar in ten years!"

"Arrah, now! and there's many a one of us travels longer and finds less, and never gets a song made about him, either; so, that's your first reason, is it?"

"And a very good one, too!" affirmed the practical damsel; "do you want to hear the second?"

"An' it please your sovereign grace!"

"Well, it doesn't, for you can't sing it," and she emphasized the statement by flaunting her garden hat at every word.

"Me, is it? Ah, now, listen to that! I can't sing it, can't I? Well, then, I'll practice it all day and every day until you change your mind about that, my lady!"

"I shan't; for I've heard it sung so much better—and by a boy *who wore a uniform*—and that's the third reason."

After that remark she walked up the steps very deliberately, and was very polite to him when they met an hour later, which politeness was the foundation for a feud lasting

17

forty-eight hours; she determined that his punishment
should be nothing *less* than that; it would teach him not to
make her a laughing stock again. He should find he had
not an Irish girl to tease, and—and make love to—especially
before other folks!

And to shorten the season of her displeasure, he evolved
a plan promising to woo the dimples into her cheeks again,
for, if nothing but a uniformed singer was acceptable to her,
a uniformed singer she should have. For the sake of her
bright eyes he was willing to humor all her reasonable fancies—and most of her unreasonable ones. The consequences of this particular one, however, were something he
could not foresee.

CHAPTER XXII.

The O'Delaven, as he called himself when he was in an
especially Irish mood, was Mistress McVeigh's most devoted servant and helper in the preparations for the party.
In fact, when Judge Clarkson rode over to pay his respects,
a puzzled little frown persistently crept between his brows
at the gallantry and assiduity displayed by this exile of Erin
in carrying out the charming lady's orders, to say nothing of
the gayety, the almost presumption, with which he managed
affairs to suit his own fancy when his hostess was not there
to give personal attention; and the child Evilena was very
nearly, if not quite ignored, or at any rate, was treated in a
condescending manner almost parental in its character, and
which he perceived was as little relished by the girl as by
himself.

He was most delighted, of course, to learn who was the purchaser of Loringwood—it was such an admirable trans-action he felt everybody concerned was to be congratulated; even war news was forgotten for a space.

All the day passed and no Kenneth! His mother decided he would be there the following morning, and, with flags draped over walls, and all the preparations complete for his reception, she retired, weary and happy from the day's labors.

Judithe eyed those flags with the same inscrutable smile sometimes given to Matthew Loring's compliments. She pointed to them next morning, when Delaven and herself stood in the hall waiting for their horses. She had accepted him as cavalier for the time, and they were going for a ride in the cool of the morning before the others were stirring.

Margeret was in sight, however—Judithe wondered if she *ever* slept—and she came to them with delicious coffee and crisp toast, and watched them as they rode away.

It was while sipping the steaming coffee the flags were noticed, and Judithe remarked: "Those emblems mean so much down here, yet I never hear you discuss them, or what they stand for. Your nation is one always in rebellion against its unsympathetic governess. I should think you would naturally tend towards the seceders here."

"I do—towards several, individually," and he looked at her over the rim of the cup with quizzical blue eyes. "But I find three factions here instead of two, and my people have been too long under the oppressor for me not to appreciate what freedom would mean to these serfs in the South, and how wildly they long for it. No; I like the Southerners better than the Northerners, because I know them better; but in the matter of sympathy, faith! I forget both the warring factions and only think of Sambo and Sambo's wife and children."

Judithe raised her finger, as Margeret entered with the toast and quietly vanished.

"I was afraid she would hear you. I fancy they must feel sensitive over the situation; speak French, please. What was it the Judge was saying about emancipation last evening? I noticed the conversation was changed as Mr. Loring grew—well, excited."

"Oh, the old story; rumors again that the Federal government mean to proclaim freedom for the blacks. But when it was done in two states by the local authorities, it was vetoed at Washington; so it is doubtful after all if it is true, there are so many rumors afloat. But if it is done there will be nothing vague about it. I fancy it will be said so good and loud that there will be a panic from ocean to ocean."

"Insurrection?"

"No; the Judge is right; there is a peculiar condition of affairs here precluding the possibility of that unless in isolated instances, a certain personal sympathy between master and slave which a foreigner finds difficult of comprehension."

"What about the runaways?" she asked, with a little air of check, "several of them have escaped the sympathetic bonds in that way; in fact, they tell me Mr. Loring, or his niece, has lately lost some very valuable live stock through that tendency."

"Whisper now!—though I believe it is a very open secret in the community, the gentleman in question, my dear Marquise, is one of the isolated instances. If you are studying social institutions in this country you must make a note of that, and underline it with red ink. He is by no means the typical Southerner. He is, however, a proof of the fact that it is a dangerous law which allows every one possessing wealth an almost unlimited power over scores of human beings. To be sure, he is mild as skim-milk these days of convalescence, but there are stories told of the use he made of power when he dared, that would warrant the whole pack taking to their heels if they had the courage. They are not stories for ladies' ears, however, and I doubt if Miss Loring herself is aware of them. But in studying the country here, don't forget that my patient is one in a thousand—better luck to the rest."

"So!" and she arose, drawing on her glove slowly, and regarding him with a queer little smile; "you *have* been giving thought to something besides the love songs of this new country? Your ideas are very interesting. I shall remember them, even without the red ink."

Then they mounted the impatient horses and rode out in the pink flush of the morning—the only hours cool enough for the foreigners to exercise at that season. They were going no place in particular, but when the cross-country road was reached leading to Loringwood, she suddenly turned to him and proposed that he conduct her to her new purchase—introduce her to Loringwood.

"With all the pleasure in life," he assented gaily, somewhat curious to see how she would like the "pig in a poke," as he designated her business transaction.

When they reached the gate she dismounted and insisted on walking through the long avenue she had admired. He was going to lead the horses, but she said, "No, tie them to the posts there, they were both well behaved, tractable animals; she could speak for her mount at any rate. Pluto had told her it was Col. McVeigh's favorite, trained by himself.

She wore a thin silken veil of palest grey circling her hat, covering her face, and the end fastened in fluffy loops on her bosom. Her habit was of cadet grey, with a military dash of braid on epaulettes and cuff; the entire costume was perfect in its harmonious lines, and admirably adapted to the girlish yet stately figure. Delaven, looking at her, thought that in all the glories of the Parisian days he had never seen la belle Marquise more delightful to the eye than on that oft-to-be-remembered September morning.

She was unusually silent as they walked along the avenue, but her eyes were busy and apparently pleased at the prospect before her, and when they reached the front of the house she halted, surveyed the whole place critically, from the lazy wash of the river landing to the great pillars of the veranda, and drew a little breath of content.

"Just what I expected," she remarked, in reply to his question. "I hope the river is not too shallow. Can we go in? I should like to, but not as the owner, please. They need not know of the sale until the Lorings choose to tell them."

Little Raquel had opened the door, very much pleased at their arrival. She informed them "Aunt Chloe laid up with some sort of misery, and Betsey, who was in the cookhouse, she see them comen' an' she have some coffee for them right off," and she was proceeding with other affairs of entertainment when Judithe interrupted:

"No coffee, nothing for me. Now, Doctor, if you want to show me the library; you know we must not linger, this is to be a busy day at the Terrace."

They had gone through the lower rooms, of which she had little to say. He had shown her the dashing portrait of Marmeduke Loring and given her a suggestion of the character as heard from Nelse. He had shown her the pretty, seraphic portrait of Gertrude as a little child, and the fair, handsome face of Tom Loring, as it looked down from the canvas with a smile for all the world in his genial eyes.

They had made no further progress when Raquel appeared upon the scene again with a request from Aunt Chloe, "Would Mahs Doctor come roun' an' tell her jest what ailed her most, she got so many cu'eous compercations."

He followed to see what the complications were, and thus it happened that Judithe was left alone to look around her new possessions.

But she did not look far. After a brief glance about she returned to the last portrait, studying the frank, handsome face critically.

"And thou wert the man," she murmured. "Why don't such men bear faces to suit their deeds, that all people may avoid the evil of them? Fair, strong, and appealing!" she continued, ennumerating the points of the picture, "and a frank, honest gaze, too; but the painter had probably been false in that, and idealized the face. Yet I have seen eyes that were as honest looking, cover a vile soul, so why not this one?"

The eyes that were as honest looking were the deep sea-blue eyes she had described once to Dumaresque, confessing with light mockery their witchcraft over her; she thanked God those days were over. She had now something more to dream over than sentimental fancies.

She heard the quick beat of horse hoofs coming up the avenue and stopping at the door; then, a man's voice:

"Good morning, Jeff—any of our folks over from the Terrace?"

"Yes, sah; good mawn, sah; leastwise I jest saw Miss Gertrude go in; they all stayen' ovah at Terrace; I reckon

she rode back for something. I reckon you find her in
library; window's open thah."

The man's voice replied from the hall, "All right," and he
opened the door.

"Good morning, little woman," he said, cheerily, boyishly.
"When I saw Hector at the gate with the side saddle I
thought—"

What he thought was left unfinished. The slender figure
in grey turned from the window, and throwing back the
veil with one hand extended the other to him, with an
amused smile at his mistake.

"*Judithe!*" He had crossed the room; he held her hand in
both of his; he could not otherwise believe in the reality of
her presence. In dreams he had seen her so often thus, with
the smile and the light as of golden stars deep in the brown
eyes.

"Welcome to Loringwood, Col. McVeigh," she said,
softly.

"Your welcome could make it the most delightful home-
coming of my life," he said, looking down at her, "if I dared
be sure I was quite welcome to your presence."

"I am your mother's guest," and she met his gaze with
cordial frankness; "would that be so if—oh, yes, you may
be very sure I am pleased to see you home again, and especially pleased to see you here."

"You are? Judithe, I beg pardon," as she raised her
brows in slight question. "I am not accountable this morning, Marquise; with a little time to recover myself in, I may
grow more rational. To find you here is as much a surprise as though I had met you alone at sea in an open
boat."

"Alone—at sea—in an open boat," she repeated, with a
curious inflection; "but you perceive, Col. McVeigh, the sit-

uation is not at all like that. I am under my own roof tree, and a very substantial one it is," with a comprehensive glance about the imposing apartment; "and you are the first guest I have welcomed here—I am much pleased that it happened so." When he stared at this bit of information she continued: "I have just made purchase of the estate from your friends, the Lorings—this is my first visit to it, and you are my first caller. You perceive I am really your neighbor, Monsieur."

His eyes were bent on her with mute question; it all seemed so incredible that she should come there at all—to his country, to his home. He had left France cursing her coquetry; he had, because of her, gone straight to the frontier on his return to America, and lived the life of camps ever since; he had fancied no woman would ever again hold the sway over him she had held for that one brief season. Yet the graciousness of her tone, the frank smile in her eyes, and the touch of her hand—the beautiful hand!—

Delaven came in, and there were more explanations; then, to the regret of Raquel and Betsey, they left for the Terrace without partaking of the specially prepared coffee. Col. McVeigh had ridden from the coast with a party of the state guard, who were going to the river fortifications. Seeing his own saddle horse at the gate he had let them go on to the Terrace without him, while he stopped, thinking to find his mother or sister there.

The new mistress of Loringwood listened with an interested expression to this little explanation, and no one would have thought there was any special motive in leaving the horse tied there on the only road he would be likely to come, or that his statement that he traveled with a party of military friends conveyed a distinct message to her of work to be done.

She did not fail to notice that Col. McVeigh was a much handsomer man than the lieutenant had been. He appeared taller, heavier—a stalwart soldier, who had lost none of his impetuousness, and had even gained in self confidence, but for all that the light of boyhood was in his eyes as he looked at her, and she, well satisfied that it was so, rode happily to the Terrace beside him, only smiling when he pointed out a clump of beeches and said he never passed without thinking of the trees at Fontainbleau.

"And," with a little mocking glance, "do the violets and forget-me-nots also grow among the bushes here?"

"Yes;" and he returned her mocking look with one so deliberate that her eyes dropped, "the forget-me-not is hardy in my land, you know; it lives always if encouraged."

"Heavens!—will the man propose to me again before we reach the house or have breakfast?" she thought, and concluded it more wise to drop such dangerous topics. Until her expected messenger came she could not quite decide what was to be done or what methods employed.

"Forget-me-nots, is it?" queried Delaven, in strict confidence with himself; "oh, but you've been clever, the pair of you, to get so far as forget-me-nots, and no one the wiser; then aloud he said, "I've an idea that the best beloved man on the plantation this day will be the one who announces your coming, Colonel; so if you'll look after Madame la Marquise—"

And then he dashed ahead congratulating himself on the way he was helping the Colonel.

"It's well to have a friend at court," he decided, "and its myself may need all I can get—for pill boxes are a bad balance for plantations, Fitz; faith, they'll be flung to the moon at first tilt."

The two left alone had three miles to go and seemed likely to make the journey in silence. She was a trifle dismayed at Delaven's desertion, and could find no more light words. She attempted some questions concerning the blockade, but his replies showed his thoughts were elsewhere.

"It is no use," he said, abruptly. "I have only forty-eight hours to remain; I may not see you again for a year, perhaps, never, for I go at once to the front. There is only one thought in my mind, and you know what it is."

"To conquer the Yankees?" she hazarded.

"No, to conquer some pride or whim of the girl who confessed once that she loved me."

"Take my advice, Monsieur," she said with a cool little smile. "No doubt you have been fortunate enough to hear those words many times—I should think it quite probable," and she let her eyes rest approvingly for a moment on his face; "but it is well to consider the girls who make those avowals before you place full credence on the statement—not that they *always* mean to deceive," she amended, "but those three words have a most peculiar fascination for girlhood—they like to use them even when they do not comprehend the meaning."

He shook his head as he looked at her.

"It is no use, Madame la Marquise," he said, and the ardent eyes met her own and made her conscious of a sudden fear. "You reason it out very well—philosophy is one of your hobbies, isn't it? I always detested women with hobbies—the strong-minded woman who reasons instead of feeling; and now you are revenging the whole army of them by making me feel beyond reason. But you shan't evade me by such tactics. Do you remember what your last spoken words to me were, three years ago?"

Her face paled a little, she lifted the bridle to urge her horse onward, but he laid his hand on her wrist.

"No, pardon me, but I must speak to you—day and night I have thought of them, and now that you are here—oh, I know you sent me away—that is, you hid from me; and why, Judithe? I believe on my soul it was because you meant those words when you said: *"I love you now, and from the first moment you ever looked at me!"* I told myself at first, when I left France, that it was all falsehood, coquetry—but I could not keep that belief, for the words rang too true—you thought you were going over that bank to death, and all your heart was in your voice and your eyes. That moment has come back to me a thousand times since; has been with me in the thick of battle, singing through my ears as the bullets whistled past. *'I love you now, and from the first moment you ever looked at me.'* It is no use to pretend you did not mean those words then. I know in my heart you did. You were bound in some way, no doubt, and fancied you had no right to say them. The announcement of your engagement suggested that. But you are free now, or you would not be here, and I must be heard."

"Be satisfied then," she replied, indifferently, though her hand trembled on the bridle, "you perceive you have, thanks to your stronger arm, an audience of one."

"You are angry at my presumption—angry at the advantage I have taken of the situation?" he asked. "I grant you are right; but remember, it is now or perhaps never with me; and it is the presumption of love—a woman should forgive that."

"They usually do, Monsieur," she replied, with a little shrug and glance of amusement. For one bewildered instant she had lost control of herself, and had only the desire to flee; but it was all over now, she remembered another point to be made in the game—something to postpone the finale until she had seen Pierson.

"It is not just to me," he said, meeting her mocking glance with one that was steadfast and determined. "However your sentiments have changed, I know you cared for me that day, as I have cared for you ever since, and now that you have come here—to my own country, to my mother's house, I surely may ask this one question: Why did you accept the love I offered, and then toss it away almost in the same breath?"

"I may reply by another question," she said, coolly. "What right had you to make any offers of love to me at any time? What right have you now?"

"What right?"

"Yes; does your betrothed approve? Is that another of the free institutions in your land of liberties?"

"What do you mean?—my betrothed?"

"Your betrothed," she said, and nodded her head with that same cool little smile. "I heard her name that evening of the drive you remember so well; our friend, the Countess Helene, mentioned it to me—possibly for fear my very susceptible heart might be won by your protection of us," and she glanced at him again, mockingly. "You had forgotten to mention it to me, but it really does not matter, I have learned since then that gentlemen absolutely cannot go around reciting the lists of former conquests—it is too apt to prevent the acquisition of new ones. I did not realize it then—there were so many things I could not realize; and I felt piqued at your silence; but," with an expressive little gesture and a bright smile, "I am no longer so. I come to your home; I clasp hands with you; I meet your bride-elect, Miss Loring—she is remarkably pretty, Monsieur, and I am quite prepared to dance at your wedding; therefore—"

"Marquise, on my honor as a man," he did not see the scornful light in her eyes as he spoke of his honor; "there has never been a word of love between Gertrude Loring and myself; it is nothing but family gossip dating from the time we were children, and encouraged by her uncle for reasons entirely financial. We have both ignored it. We are all fond of her, and I believe my mother at one time did hope it would be so arranged, but I hope she wins a better fellow than myself; she cares no more for me than I for her."

They had turned into the Terrace grounds. Evilena was running out to meet them. She was so close now she could hear what he said if it were not for her own swiftness.

"Judithe! One word, a look; you believe me?"

She said nothing, but she did flash one meaning glance at him, and then his sister was at the stirrup and he swung out of the saddle to kiss her.

CHAPTER XXIII.

"Of course we are anxious to hear all you dare tell us about the success of your mission over there," said his mother, an hour later, when the riders had done justice to a delightful breakfast. "Are all the arrangements made by our people entirely satisfactory?"

"Entirely, mother. This is the twenty-second of September, isn't it? Well, it is an open secret now. The vessel secured goes into commission today, and will be called the Alabama."

"Hurrah for the Alabama!" cried Evilena, who was leaning on the back of her brother's chair. He put his arm around her and turned to Judithe.

"Have you become acquainted with the patriotic ardor of my little sister?" he asked. "I assure you we have to fight these days if we want to keep the affections of our Southern girls."

Gertrude smiled across the table at him.

"I can't fancy you having to fight very hard battles along that line, Monsieur," replied Judithe, in the cool, half mocking tone she had adopted for all questions of sentiment with him; and Gertrude, who saw the look exchanged between them, arose from the table.

"Uncle Matthew asked to see you when you have time, Kenneth."

"Thanks, yes; I'll go directly. Mother, why not ask the boys of the guard to stop over for your party? They are of Phil Masterson's company—all Carolina men."

"Of course, I shall invite them personally," and she left the room to speak to the men who were just finishing breakfast under an arbor, and congratulating themselves on the good luck of being travelling companions of Colonel McVeigh.

Evilena waltzed around the table in her delight at the entire arrangement; boys in uniform; the longed-for additions to the festivities, and they would have to be a formidable lot if she could not find one of their number worth dancing with; she would show Dr. Delaven that other men did not think her only a baby to be teased!

"Now, Madame Caron, we can show you a regular plantation jubilee, for the darkies shall have a dance at the quarters. You'll like that, won't you?"

"Anything that expresses the feminine homage to returning heroes," replied Judithe, with a little bow of affected humility, at which Colonel McVeigh laughed as he returned it. She passed out of the door with his sister and he stood looking after her, puzzled, yet with hope in his eyes. His impetuousness in plunging into the very heart of the question at once had, at any rate, not angered her, which was a great point gained. He muttered an oath when he realized that but for the Countess Biron's gossip they might never have been separated, for she did love him then—he knew it. Even today, when she would have run away from him again, she did not deny *that*! Forty-eight hours in which to win her—and his smile as he watched her disappear had a certain grim determination in it. He meant to do it. She had grown white when he quoted to her her own never forgotten words. Well, she should say them to him again! The hope of it sent the blood leaping to his heart, and he turned away with a quick sigh.

Gertrude, who had only stepped out on the veranda when she left the table, and stood still by the open glass door, saw the lingering, intense gaze with which he followed the woman she instinctively disliked—the woman who was now mistress of Loringwood, and had made the purchase as carelessly as though it were a new ring to wear on her white hand—a new toy to amuse herself with in a new country; the woman who threw money away on whims, had the manner of a princess, and who had aroused in Gertrude Loring the first envy or jealousy she had ever been conscious of in her pleasant, well-ordered life. From the announcement that Loringwood had passed into the stranger's possession her heart had felt like lead in her bosom. She could not have explained why—it was more a presentiment of evil than aught else, and she thought she knew the reason of it when she saw that look in Kenneth McVeigh's eyes—a look she had never seen there before.

And the woman who had caused it all was walking the floor of her own apartment in a fever of impatience. If the man she expected would only come—then she would have work to do—definite plans to follow; now all was so vague, and those soldiers staying over, was it only a chance invitation, or was there a hidden purpose in that retained guard? Her messenger should have arrived within an hour of Colonel McVeigh, and the hour was gone.

As she passed the mirror she caught sight of her anxious face in it, and halted, staring at the reflection critically.

"You are turning coward!" she said, between her closed teeth. "You are afraid to be left to yourself an hour longer—afraid because of this man's voice and the touch of his hand. Aren't you proud of yourself—you! He is the beast whose name you hated for years—the man for whom that poor runaway was taught the graces and accomplishments of white women—in this house you heard Matthew Loring mention the price of her and the portion to be forfeited to Kenneth McVeigh because the girl was not to be found. Do you forget that? Do you think I shall let you forget it? I shan't. You are to do the work you came here to do. You are to have no other interest in the people of this house."

She continued her nervous walk back and forth across the room. She put aside the grey habit and donned a soft, pretty house-gown of the same color. Her hands were trembling. She clasped and unclasped them with a despairing gesture.

"It is not love," she whispered, as though in wild argument against the fear of it. "Not love—some curse in the blood—that is what it is. And to think that after three

18

years—three years!—it all comes back like this. Oh, you fool, you fool! Love," she continued, in more clear, reasoning tones, speaking aloud slowly as though to impress it on her mind, as a child will repeat a lesson to be learned; "love must be based on respect—what respect can you have for this buyer of young girls?—this ardent-eyed animal who has the good fortune, to be classed as a gentleman. Love in a woman's heart should be her religion; what religion could be centered on so vile a creature? To look up to such a man, how low a woman would have to sink."

Evilena knocked at the door to show some little gift brought by her brother from across the ocean, and Judithe turned to her feverishly, glad of some companionship to drive away her dread and suspense until the expected messenger arrived—the minutes were as long as hours, now!

Colonel McVeigh had scarcely more than greeted Loring when Pluto announced Captain Masterson and some other gentleman. Evilena saw them coming from the window and reported there were two soldiers besides Captain Masterson, and a man in blue clothes, who aroused her curiosity mightily. They were out of range before Judithe reached the window, but her heart almost stopped beating for an instant; the man she expected wore a blue yachting suit, and this sudden gathering of soldiery at the Terrace?

Colonel McVeigh greeted Masterson cordially and turned to the others. Two were men in Confederate uniform, just outside the door, and the third was a tall man in the uniform of a Federal Captain. His left wrist was bandaged. He was smiling slightly as McVeigh's glance became one of doubt for an instant, and then brightened into unmistakable recognition.

"By Jove, this is a surprise!" and he shook hands cordially with the stranger. "Captain Monroe, I am delighted to see you in our home."

"Thank you; I'm glad to get here," replied Monroe, with a peculiar look towards Masterson, who regarded the cordial greeting with evident astonishment, "I had not expected to call on you this morning, but—Captain Masterson insisted."

He smiled as he spoke—a smile of amusement, coolly careless of the amazement of Masterson, and the inquiry in the glance of McVeigh.

"Colonel McVeigh, he is a prisoner," said Masterson, in reply to that glance, and then, as the prisoner himself maintained an indifferent silence, he explained further, "We caught sight of him galloping ahead of us through the pines, a few miles back. Realizing that we were near enough to the coast for the Federals to send in men for special service, we challenged him, got no explanation except that he rode for his own pleasure; so I put him under arrest."

"Well, well! Since luck has sent you into our lines I'm glad it has done us a good turn and sent you to our home," said McVeigh, though he still looked mystified at the situation. "I've no doubt satisfactory explanations can be made, and a parole arranged."

"That's good of you, Colonel," said the prisoner, appreciatively; "you are a good sort of friend to meet when in trouble—brother Fred used to think so up at the Point; but in this case it really isn't necessary—as I have one parole."

He drew a paper from an inner pocket and passed it to McVeigh, who looked relieved.

"Yes, certainly, this is all right," and he looked inquiringly at Masterson, "I don't understand—"

Neither did that officer, who turned in some chagrin to to prisoner, who glanced from one to the other in evident indifference.

"May I ask," said Masterson, with cold courtesy, "why you did not state when taken prisoner that you were paroled?"

"Certainly," and the easy nonchalence of the other was almost insolent; evidently Masterson had not picked up an affinity. "I was coming your way; had been riding alone for several hours, and feared I should be deprived of the pleasure of your society if I allowed you to know how harmless I was."

He paused for a moment—smiled in a quizzical way at McVeigh, and continued: "Then I heard your orderly mention Colonel McVeigh, whose place you were bound for, and I did not object in the least to being brought to him for judgment. But since you see I am paroled, as well as crippled," and he motioned to the arm which he moved carefully, "incapable in any way of doing harm to your cause, I trust that a flag of truce will be recognized by you," and he extended his hand in smiling unconcern.

But to Captain Masterson there was something irritating in the smile, and he only bowed coldly, ignoring the flag of truce, upon which Captain Monroe seemed quietly amused as he turned to McVeigh and explained that he was wounded and taken prisoner a month before over in Tennessee by Morgan's cavalry, who had gathered in Johnson's brigade so effectively that General Johnson, his staff, and somewhere between two and three hundred others had been taken prisoners. He, Monroe, had found a Carolina relative badly wounded among Morgan's boys, had secured a parole, and brought the young fellow home to die, and when his own wound was in a fair way to take care of itself he had left the place—a plantation south of Allendale, and headed for the coast to connect with the blockading fleet instead of making the journey north through Richmond.

It was a very clear statement, but Masterson listened to it suspiciously, without appearing to listen at all. McVeigh who had known both Monroe and his family in the North, and was also acquainted with the Carolina family mentioned, accepted the Federal's story without question, and invited him to remain at the Terrace so long as it suited him to be their guest.

"I have only two days at home until I leave for my regiment," he explained; "but my mother has enough pleasant people here to make your visit interesting, I hope. She will be delighted to welcome you, and some Beaufort acquaintances of yours are here—the Lorings."

Captain Monroe showed interest in this information, and declared it would give him pleasure to stop over until McVeigh left for the front.

"Good! and you, Captain Masterson?"

Masterson glanced coldly towards Monroe, evidently desirous of a private interview with McVeigh. But seeing little chance of it without a pointed request, he took two packets from a case carefully fastened in his pocket, and presented them.

"I am detailed to convey to you some important papers, and I congratulate you on your promotion to Brigadier-General," he said, with a bow.

"Brigadier? Well, well; they are giving me a pleasant reception," and his face showed his pleasure as he looked at the papers. "Thank you, Captain Masterson. By the way, how much time have you?"

"Until tomorrow night; I meant to ride over to the plantation after delivering this."

"The ladies won't hear to that when they get sight of you. They are giving a party tonight and need all the uniforms we can muster; a squad of your men on their way to the forts below have stopped over for breakfast, and they've even captured them, and you'll be welcome as the flowers of May."

Masterson glanced at Monroe and hesitated. "Those men are needed at one of the fortifications," he said guardedly; "they had better take some other time for a party. With your permission I'll send them on, and remain in their place with one orderly, if convenient."

"Certainly; glad to have you; give your own orders about the men. I do not know that they have accepted the invitation to linger, I only know that the ladies wanted them to."

He rang for Pluto, who was given orders concerning rooms for Captain Monroe, and for Captain Masterson, who left to speak with the men waiting orders without. He made a gesture towards the packet in McVeigh's hand and remarked: "I have reason apart from the commission to think the contents are important. Our regiment is to be merged in your brigade, and all pressed to the front. Towards what point I could not learn at Columbia, but your information will doubtless cover all that, General."

"Colonel will answer until I find my brigade," said McVeigh, with a smile. "You stay over until I learn, since we are to go together, and I will look them over soon as possible."

He himself showed Monroe the room he was to occupy, to the chagrin of Pluto, who was hanging about in a fever of curiosity and dread at sight of a Northern soldier—the first he had ever seen, and the rumor that he was brought there a prisoner suggested calamities to the army through which, alone, his own race dared hope for freedom; and to hear the two men chat and laugh over West Point memories was an aggravation to him, listening, as he was, for the news of today, and the serious questions involved. Only once had there been allusion to the horrors of war—when McVeigh inquired concerning his former classmate, Monroe's brother, Fred, and was told he had been numbered with the dead at Shiloh. The door was open and Pluto could hear all that was said—could see the bronzed face of the Northerner, a face he liked instinctively though it was not exactly handsome—an older face than McVeigh's. He was leaving West Point as the young Southerner entered—a man of thirty years, possibly—five of them, the hard years of the frontier range. A smile lit up his face, changing it wonderfully. His manner was neither diffident nor over-confident—there was a certain admirable poise to it. His cool, irritating attitude towards the zealous Masterson had been drawn out by the innate antagonism of the two natures, but with McVeigh only the cordial side was appealed to, and he responded with frank good will.

Pluto watched them leave the room and enter the apartments of Mr. Loring, where Mrs. McVeigh, Miss Gertrude and Delaven were at that time, and the latter was entertained by seeing one of the Northern wolves welcomed most cordially by the Southern household. Fred Monroe had been Kenneth's alter-ego during the West Point days. Mrs. McVeigh had photographs of them together, which she brought out for inspection, and Kenneth had pleasant memories of the Monroe home where he had been a guest for a brief season after graduation; altogether it was an interesting incident of the war to Delaven, who was the one outsider. He was sorry the Marquise was not there to observe.

The Marquise was, however, making observations on her

own account, but not particularly to her satisfaction. She walked from one window to another watching the road, and the only comforting view she obtained was the departure of the squad of soldiers who had breakfasted in the arbor. They turned south along the river, and when they passed through the Terrace gates she drew a breath of relief at the sight. They would not meet Pierson, who was to come over the road to the east, and they would leave on the place only the orderlies of Colonel McVeigh and Captain Masterson, and the colored men whose quarters were almost a half mile in the rear of the Terrace. She was glad they were at that distance, though she scarcely knew why. Pierson's delay made her fear all sorts of bungling and extreme measures—men were such fools!

Evilena had flitted away again to .ook up a dress for the party, and did not return, so she was left alone. She heard considerable walking about and talking in the rooms below and on the veranda. No one came along her corridor, however, so she could ask no questions as to the latest arrivals. For reasons of her own she had dispensed with a personal attendant after the departure of Louise; there was no maid to make inquiries of.

An hour passed in this feverish suspense, when she went to the mirror with an air of decision, arranged her hair becomingly, added a coral brooch to the lace at her throat, slipped some glimmering rings on her white fingers, and added those little exquisite touches to the toilet which certain women would naturally linger over though it be the last hour on earth.

Then she opened the door and descended the stairs, a picture of beauty and serenity—a trifle of extra color in the cheeks, perhaps, but it would be a captious critic who would object to the added lustre.

Captain Monroe certainly did not, as he halted in the library at sight of her, and waited to see if she passed out on the veranda, or—

She looked out on the veranda; no one was there; with an impatient sigh she turned, pushed the partly opened door of the library back, and was inside the room before she perceived him. Involuntarily she shut the door back of her.

"Oh—h!" and she held out her hand with a quick, pretty gesture of surprise and pleasure—well met, Captain Jack!"

He took the hand she offered and looked at her with a certain questioning directness.

"I hope so, Madame Caron," and the gaze was so steady, his grasp so firm, that she drew her hand away with a little laugh that was a trifle nervous.

"Your voice and face reassure me! I dare breathe again!" she said, with a mock sigh of relief; "my first glimpse of your uniform made me fear a descent of the enemy."

"Have you need to fear any special enemy here?" he asked, bluntly. She put her hand out with a little gesture of protest as she sank back into the chair he offered.

"Why should you be so curious on a first meeting?" she asked, with a quizzical smile. "But I will tell you, Monsieur, for all that; I am, of course, very much afraid of the Northern armies. I left Orleans rather than live under the Federal government, if you please! I have bought a very handsome estate a few miles from here which, of course, binds my interests more closely to the South," and she flashed a meaning, mocking glance up at him. "Do not look so serious, my friend, it is all very beautifully arranged; I had my will made as soon as the deed was signed, of course; no matter what accidents should happen to me, all my Southern properties will be held intact to carry on the plans for which they were purchased. I am already building my monuments," and she unfurled a silken fan the color of her corals and smiled across it at him.

Their backs were towards the window. She was seated in the deep chair, while he stood near her, leaning on the back of another one and looking down in her face. Pluto, who was still hovering around with the hope of getting speech with a "sure enough Lincum man," had come noiselessly to the open window and only halted an instant when he saw the stranger so pleasantly occupied, and heard the musical voice of Madame Caron say "My friend." It was to him the sweetest voice in the world now, and he would gladly have lingered while she spoke, but the rest of the words were very soft and low, and Miss Loring was moving towards him coming slowly up the steps, looking at him as though the veranda was no place for a nigger to lounge when unemployed—a fact he was well enough aware of to walk briskly away around the corner of the house, when he found her eye on him.

She had reached the top of the steps and was thinking the colored folks at the Terrace were allowed a great many privileges, when she heard the low tones of a man's voice. Supposing it was Kenneth and possibly his mother, she stepped softly towards the window. Before she reached it she perceived her mistake—the man wore a blue uniform, and though she could not see Madame Caron, she could see the soft folds of her dress, and the white hand moving the coral fan.

Disappointed, and not being desirous of joining the woman whose charm evidently enthralled every one but herself, she stepped quietly back out of range, and passed on along the veranda to the sitting room, where Evilena was deeply engaged over the problem of a dress to be draped and trimmed for the party. And the two talked on within the closed doors of the library, the man's voice troubled, earnest; the woman's, careless and amused.

"I shall tell you what I wish, Captain Jack," she said, tapping the fan slowly on the palm of her hand and looking up at him, "I am most pleased to see you, but for all that I wish you had not come to this particular house, and I wish you would go away."

"Which means," he said, after a pause, "that you are in some danger?"

"Oh, no! if it were that," and her glance was almost coquettish, "I should ask you to remain as my champion."

"Pardon, Madame," and he shook his head, doubtfully, "but I remember days in New Orleans, and I know you better than that."

She only raised her brows and smiled. He watched her for a moment and then said: "Colonel McVeigh is a friend; I should not like to think that your presence means danger to him."

"What an idea!" and she laughed heartily; "am I grown such a thing of terror that I dare not enter a door lest danger follow? Who could be oppressed with political schemes in this delightful life of the plantation? It is really Eden-like; that is why I have purchased one of the places for my own; it is worth seeing. If you remain I shall invite you over; shall you?"

"For some reason you wish I would not; if I only knew what the reason is!"

"A few months ago you did not question my motives," she said, reprovingly; then in a lower tone, "Your commander has never questioned, why should you? Your President has sent me messages of commendation for my independent work. One, received before I left Mobile, I should like you to see," and she rose from the chair. He put out his hand to stop her.

"Not if it has connection with any plot or plan of work against the people on this side of the line; remember, I am on parole."

"Oh, I shall respect your scruples," she said, lightly. "But you need have no dread of that sort. I would not keep by me anything dangerous; it is not compromising to the Marquise de Caron in any way." She halted at the door and added, "Will you wait?"

"Yes, I will wait," he said; "but I can't approve, and I don't need the evidence of any one else in order to appreciate your value," he added, grimly; "but be careful, remember where you are."

"I could not forget it if I tried, Captain Jack," she declared, with a peculiar smile, of which the meaning escaped him until long after.

That ride from Loringwood in the morning, and the nervous expectancy after, had evidently tended to undermine her own self-confidence and usual power of resource, for when she returned to the room a few minutes later, and found Gertrude and her uncle there, she halted in absolute confusion—could not collect her thoughts quickly enough for the emergency, and glanced inquiringly towards Monroe, as one looks at a stranger, while he, after one look as she entered, continued some remark to Mr. Loring.

For an instant Gertrude's eyes grew narrow as she glanced from one to the other; then she recovered her usual sweet manner, as she turned to Judithe:

"Pardon me, I fancied you two had met. Madame Caron, permit me to present Captain Monroe, one of our recent acquisitions."

Both bowed; neither spoke. Colonel McVeigh entered at that moment. He had changed the grey travelling suit in which he arrived, for the grey uniform of his regiment, and Judithe, however critical she tried to be, could not but acknowledge that he was magnificent; mentally she added, "Magnificent animal; but what of the soul, the soul?"

There was no lack of soul in his eyes as he looked at her and crossed the room, as though drawn by an invisible chain, and noted, as a lover ever notes, that the dress she wore had in its soft, silvery folds, a suggestion of sentiment for the cause he championed.

But when he murmured something of his appreciation, she dropped her eyes to the fan she held, and when she glanced slowly up it was in a manner outlawing the tete-a-tete.

"I realize now, Colonel McVeigh, that you are really a part of the army," she remarked in the tone of one who makes the conversation general. "You were a very civilian-looking person this morning. I have, like your Southern ladies, acquired a taste for warlike trappings; the uniform is very handsome."

"Thanks; I hope you will find my next one more becoming, since it is to be that of Brigadier-General."

Although Matthew Loring's sight was impaired, his locomotion slow, and his left hand and arm yet helpless, his sense of hearing was acute enough to hear the words even across Monroe's conversation, for his sunken eyes lit up as he twisted his head towards the speaker:

"What's that, Kenneth? You to command a brigade?"

"So they tell me," assented McVeigh. "The commission just reached me."

"Good enough! Do you hear that, Gertrude? A Brigadier-General at twenty-five. Well, I don't see what more a man could want."

"I do," he said, softly, to Judithe, so softly that she felt rather than heard the words, to which his eyes bore witness. Then he turned to reply to Mr. Loring's questions of military movements.

"No, I can't give you much special information today," and he smiled across at Monroe, when Loring found fault with the government officials who veiled their plans and prospects from the taxpayers—the capitalists of the South who made the war possible. "But the instructions received lead me to believe a general movement of much importance is about to be made in our department, and my opportunities will be all a soldier could wish."

"So you have become a Brigadier-General instead of the Lieutenant we knew only three years ago," and Judithe's eyes rested on him graciously for an instant, as Monroe and Gertrude helped Loring out to the wheeled chair on the lawn. "You travel fast—you Americans! I congratulate you."

She had arisen and crossed the room to the little writing desk in the corner. He followed with his eyes her graceful walk and the pretty fluttering movements of her hands as she drew out note paper and busied herself rather ostentatiously. He smiled as he noticed it; she was afraid of a tete-a-tete; she was trying to run away, if only to the farther side of the room.

"I shall consider myself a more fit subject for congratulation if you prove more kind to the General than you were to the Lieutenant."

"People usually are," she returned lightly. "I do not fancy you will have much of unkindness to combat, except from the enemy."

Evilena entered the room humming an air, and her brother remarked carelessly that the first of the enemy to invade their domain was not very formidable at present, though Captain Jack Monroe had made a fighting record for himself in the western campaign. Judithe did not appear particularly interested in the record of the Northern campaign, but Evilena, who had been too much absorbed in the question of wardrobe to keep informed of the late arrivals, fairly gasped at the name.

"Really and truly, is that Yankee here?" she demanded, "right here in the house? Caroline said it wasn't a Yankee —just some friend of yours."

"So he is."

"And—a—*Yankee*?"

He nodded his head and smiled at her. Judithe had picked up a pen and was writing. Evilena glanced towards her for assistance in this astonishing state of affairs, but no one appeared to be shocked but herself.

"Well!" she said, at last, resignedly, "since we are to have any Yankee here, I'm glad its the one Gertrude met at Beaufort. I've been conjuring up romances about them ever since, and I am curious to see if he looks like the Jack Monroe in the song."

"Not likely," said her brother, discouragingly, "he is the least romantic hero for a song you can imagine; but if you put on your prettiest dress and promise not to fight all the battles of the war over with him, I'll manage that you sit beside him at dinner and make romances about him at closer range, if you can find the material."

"To think of *me* dressing my prettiest for a Yankee! and oh, Ken, I can't dress so astonishingly pretty, either. I'm really," and she sighed dejectedly, "down to my last party dress."

"Well, that's better than none."

"None!" she endeavored to freeze him with a look, but his smile forbade it, and she left the room, singing

"Just as she stepped on ship board,
    'Your name I'd like to know?'
And with a smile she answered,
    'My name is Jack Monroe.'"

"Thanks; glad to find so charming a namesake," said a deep voice, and she looked up to see a tall man gazing down at her with a smile so kindly she should never have guessed he was a Yankee but for the blue uniform.

"Oh!" she blushed deliciously, and then laughed. There really was no use trying to be dignified with a stranger after such a meeting as that.

"I never did mean to steal your name, Captain Monroe," she explained, "for you are Captain Monroe?"

"Yes, except when I am Jack," and then they both smiled.

"Oh, I've known Jack was your name, too, for this long time," she said, with a little air of impressing him with her knowledge; "but I couldn't call you that, except in the song."

"May I express the hope that you sing the song often?" he asked, with an attempt at gravity not entirely successful.

"But you don't know who I am, do you?" and when he shook his head sadly she added, "but of course you've heard of me; I'm Evilena."

"Evilena?"

"Evilena McVeigh," she said, with a trifle of emphasis.

"Oh, Kenneth's sister?" and he held out his hand. "I'm delighted to know you."

"Thank you." She let her hand rest in his an instant, and then drew it away, with a little gasp.

"There! I've done it after all."

"Anything serious?" he inquired.

She nodded her head; "I've broken a promise."

"Not past repair, I hope."

"Oh, it's only a joke to you, but it really is serious to me. When the boys I know all started North with the army I promised I'd never shake hands with a Yankee."

"Promised them all?" he asked, and without waiting for a reply, he continued: "Now, that's a really extraordinary coincidence; I entertained the same idea about Johnnie Rebs."

"Really?" and she looked quite relieved at finding a companion in iniquity; "but you did shake hands?"

"Yes."

"Are you sorry?"

"No; are you?"

"N—no."

And when Delaven went to look for Evilena to tell her they were to have lunch on the lawn (Mrs. McVeigh had installed him as master of ceremonies for the day), he found her in the coziest, shadiest nook on the veranda, entertaining a sample copy of the enemy, and assuring him that the grey uniforms would be so much more becoming than the blue.

CHAPTER XXIV.

Noon. Colonel McVeigh had been at the Terrace already a half day, and no sign had come from Pierson—no message of any sort. Judithe called Pluto and asked if the mail did not leave soon for down the river, and suggested that when he took it to the office he would ask the man in charge to look carefully lest any letters should have been forgotten from the night before.

"Yes'm, mail go 'bout two hours now," and he looked up at the clock. "I go right down ask 'bout any letters done been fo'got. But I don' reckon any mail to go today; folks all too busy to write lettahs."

"No; I—I—I will have a letter to go," and she turned toward the desk. "How soon will you start?"

"Hour from now," said Pluto, "that will catch mail all right;" and with that she must be content. At any other time she would have sent him at once without the excuse of a letter to be mailed. Those easy-going folk who handled the mail might easily have overlooked some message—a delay of twenty-four hours would mean nothing in their sleepy lives. But today she was unmistakably nervous—all the more reason for exceeding care.

She had begun the letter when Colonel McVeigh came for her to go to lunch; she endeavored to make an excuse—she was not at all hungry, really, it appeared but an hour since the breakfast; but perceiving that if she remained he would remain also, she arose, saying she would join their little festival on the lawn long enough for a cup of tea, she had a letter to get ready for the mail within an hour.

She managed to seat herself where she could view the road to the south, but not a horseman or footman turned in at the Terrace gate. She felt the eyes of Monroe on her; also the eyes of Gertrude Loring. How much did they know or suspect? She was feverishly gay, though penetrated by the feeling that the suspended sword hung above her. Pierson's non-appearance might mean many things appalling—and Louise!

All these chaotic thoughts surging through her, and ever

beside her the voice of Kenneth McVeigh, not the voice alone, but the eyes, at times appealing, at times dominant, as he met her gaze, and forbade that she be indifferent.

"Why should you starve yourself as well as me?" he asked, softly, when she declined the dishes brought to her, and made pretense of drinking the cup of tea he offered.

"You—starving?" and the slight arching of the dark brows added to the note of question.

"Yes, for a word of hope."

"Really? and what word do you covet?"

"The one telling me if the Countess Biron's gossip was the only reason you sent me away."

Mrs. McVeigh looked over at the two, well satisfied that Kenneth was giving attention to her most distinguished guest. Gertrude Loring looked across to the couple on the rustic seat and felt, without hearing, what the tenor of the conversation was. Kenneth McVeigh was wooing a woman who looked at him with slumbrous magnetic eyes and laughed at him. Gertrude envied her the wooing, but hated her for the laughter. All her life Kenneth McVeigh had been her ideal, but to this finished coquette of France he was only the man of the moment, who contributed to her love of power, her amusement. For the girl, who was his friend, read clearly the critical, half contemptuous gleams, alternating at times the graciousness of Madame Caron's dark eyes. She glanced at Monroe, and guessed that he was no more pleased than herself at the tete-a-tete there, and that he was quite as watchful.

And the cause of it all met Colonel McVeigh's question with a glance, half alluring, half forbidding, as she sipped the tea and put aside the cup.

"How persistent you are," she murmured. "If you adopt the same methods in warfare I do not wonder at your rapid promotions.   But I shan't encourage it a moment longer; you have other guests, and I have a letter to write."

She crossed to Mrs. McVeigh, murmured a few words of excuse, exchanged a smile with Evilena, who declared her a deserter from their ranks, and then moved up the steps to the veranda and passed through the open window into the library, pausing for a little backward glance ere she entered; and the people on the lawn who raised their glasses to her, did not guess that she looked over their heads, scanning the road for the expected messenger.

Looking at the clock she seated herself, picked up the pen, and then halted, holding her hand out and noting the trembling of it.

"Oh, you fool!   You *woman*!" she said, through her closed teeth.

She commenced one letter, blotted it in her nervous impatience, turned it aside and commenced another, when Captain Monroe appeared at the window with a glass of wine in his hand.

"Why this desertion from the ranks?" he asked, jestingly, yet with purpose back of the jest.   She recognized, but ignored it.

"That you might be detailed for special duty, perhaps, Captain Jack," she replied, without looking around.

"I have to look up stragglers," and he crossed to the desk where she sat.   "I even brought you a forgotten portion of your lunch."

She looked up at that, saw the glass, and shook her head; "No, no wine for me."

"But it would be almost treasonable to refuse this," he insisted.   "In the first place it is native Carolina wine we are asked to take; and in the second, it is a toast our bear of the swamps—Mr. Loring—has proposed, 'our President.'

I evaded my share by being cup-bearer to you." He offered the glass and looked at her, meaningly, "Will you drink?"

"Only when you drink with me," she said, and smiled at the grim look touching his face for an instant.

"To the President of the Southern Confederacy?" he asked.

"No!—to *our* President!"

She took the glass, touched the wine to her lips, and offered the remainder to him, just as Colonel McVeigh entered from the lawn. He heard Captain Monroe say, "With all my heart!" as he emptied the glass. The scene had such a sentimental tinge that he felt a swift flash of jealousy, and realized that Monroe was a decidedly attractive fellow in his own cool, masterful way.

"Ah! a tryst at mid-day?" he remarked, with assumed lightness.

"No; only a parley with the enemy," she said, and he passed out into the hall, picking up his hat from the table, where he had tossed it when he entered in the morning.

Monroe walked up to the window and back again. She heard him stop beside her, but did not look up.

"I have almost decided to take your advice, and remain only one night instead of two," he said, at last. "I can't approve what you are doing here. I can't help you, and I can't stay by and be witness to the enchantment which, for some reason, you are weaving around McVeigh."

"Enchantment?"

"Well, I can't find a better word just now. I can't warn him; so I will leave in the morning."

"I really think it would be better," she said, looking up at him frankly. "Of all the American men I have met I value your friendship most; yes, it is quite true!" as he uttered a slight exclamation. "But there are times when even our good angels hamper us, and just now I am better, much better, alone."

"If I could help you—"

"You could not," she said hastily. Even without the barrier of the parole, you could not. But I cannot talk. I am nervous, not myself today. You saw how clumsy I was when I brought the letter to show?—and after all did not get to show it. Well, I have been like that all day. I have grown fearful of everything—distrustful of every glance. Did you observe the watchfulness of Miss Loring on the lawn? Still, what does it matter?"

She leaned her head on her hands for a few moments. He stood and looked at her somberly, not speaking. When she turned towards him again it was to ask in a very different tone if he would touch the bell—it was time for Pluto to start with the mail. When he entered she found that a necessary address book had been left in her own apartments.

"You get the mail bag while I go for it, Pluto," she said after tossing the papers about in a vain search; "and Captain Monroe, will you look over this bit of figures for me? It is an expense list for my yacht, I may need it today and have a wretched head for business details of that sort. I am helpless in them."

Then she was gone, and Monroe, with a pencil, noted the amount, corrected a trifling mistake, and suddenly became conscious that the grave, most attentive, black man, was regarding him in a manner inviting question.

"Well, my man, what is it?" he asked, folding up the paper, and speaking with so kindly a smile that Pluto stumbled eagerly into the heart of questions long deferred.

"Jes' a word, Mahs Captain. Is it true you been took prisoner? Is it true the Linkum men are whipped?

"Well, if they are they don't know it; they are still fighting, any way."

"If—if they win," and Pluto looked around nervously as he asked the question, "will it free us, Mahs Captain? We niggahs can't fine out much down heah. Yo' see, sah, fust off they all tell how the Nawth free us sure if the Nawth won the battles. Then—then word done come how Mahsa Linkum nevah say so. Tell me true, Mahs Captain, will we be free?"

His eagerness was so intense, Monroe hesitated to tell him the facts. He understood, now, why the dark face had been watching him so hungrily ever since his arrival.

"The men who make the laws must decide those questions, my man," he said, at last. In time freedom certainly will be arranged for—but—"

"But Mahsa Linkum ain't done said it yet—that it, Mahsa?"

"Yes, that's it."

"Thank yo', sah," and Monroe heard him take a deep breath, sad as tears, when he turned into the hall for the mail bag.

A stranger was just coming up the steps, a squarely built, intelligent-eyed man, with a full dark beard; his horse, held by one of the boys under a shade tree, showed signs of hard riding, and the fact that he was held instead of stabled, showed that the call was to be brief.

The servants were clearing away the lunch things. Mrs. McVeigh had entered the house. Delaven and Gertrude were walking beside Loring's chair, wheeled by Ben, along the shady places. Evilena was coming towards them from across the lawn, pouting because of an ineffectual attempt to catch up with Ken, whom she fancied she saw striding along the back drive to the quarters, but he had walked too fast, and the hedge had hidden him. She came back disappointed to be asked by Delaven what sort of uniform she was pursuing this time, to which he very properly received no reply except such as was vouchsafed by silent, scornful lips and indignant eyes.

Masterson, who was walking thoughtfully alone, noted this distribution of the people as the stranger dismounted, inquired of Caroline for Madame Caron, and was received by Pluto at the door. The man wore a dark blue suit, plain but for a thin cord of gold on collar and sleeve. He did not recognize it as a uniform, yet instinctively associated it with that other blue uniform whose wearer had caused him an annoyance he would not soon forget. He was there alone now with Madame Caron for whom this stranger was asking. He wondered if Colonel McVeigh was there also, but concluded not, as he had seen him on the western veranda with his hat on. All these thoughts touched him and passed on as he stood there looking critically at the dusty horse.

At the same moment he heard the thud, thud of another horse turning in at the Terrace gates; the rider was leaning forward as though urging the animal to its utmost. At sight of Masterson he threw up his hand to attract attention, and the others on the lawn stared at this second tumultuous arrival and the haste Captain Masterson made to hear what he had to say—evidently news of importance from the coast or the North.

Loring hoped it meant annihilation of some Yankee stronghold, and Evilena hoped it did not mean that Kenneth must leave before the party.

*   *   *   *   *   *   *

The man whom Pluto showed into the library with the information that Madame Caron would be down at once, glanced about him quickly, and with annoyance, when he found there was another man in the room. But the instant Monroe's face was seen by him, he uttered an exclamation of pleasure.

"By Jove! Captain Jack?" and he turned to him eagerly, after noting that Pluto had left the door.

"I don't think I know you, sir, though you evidently know one of my names," and his tone was not particularly cordial as he eyed the stranger.

"Don't you remember the night run you made on the yacht *Marquise*, last March?" and the man's tone was low and hurried. "I had no beard then, which makes a difference. This trip is not quite so important, but has been more annoying. "I've been followed, have doubled like a hare for hours, and don't believe I've thrown them off the track after all. I have a message to deliver; if I can't see Madame alone at once you get it to her."

"Can't do it; don't want to see it!" and Monroe's tone was quick and decided as the man's own. "I am on parole."

"Parole!" and the stranger looked at him skeptically. "Look here, you are evidently working with Madame, and afraid to trust me, but it's all right. I swear it is! I destroyed the message when I saw I was followed, but I know the contents, and if you will take it—"

"You mistake. I have absolutely no knowledge of Madame's affairs at present."

"Then you won't take it?" and the man's tones held smothered rage. "So, when put to the test, Captain Jack Monroe is afraid to risk what thousands are risking for the cause, at the front and in secret—a life!"

"It is just as well not to say 'afraid,' my good fellow,"

and Monroe's words were a trifle colder, a shade more deliberate. "Do you know what a parole means? I excuse
your words because of your present position, which may
be desperate. If you are her friend I will do what I can
to save you; but the contents of the dispatch I refuse
to hear."

Judithe entered the door as he spoke, and came forward
smilingly.

"Certainly; it was not intended that you should. This is
the captain of my yacht, and his messages only interest me."

"Madame Caron!" and Monroe's tones were imploring,
"Consider where you are. Think of the risks you run!"

"Risks?" and she made a little gesture of disdain. She
felt so much stronger now that the suspense was over—
now that the message was really here. "Risks are fashionable just now, Monsieur, and I always follow the fashions."

He shook his head hopelessly; words were of no use. He
turned away, and remembering that he still held the slip
with her account on, he halted and handed it to the stranger,
who was nearest him.

"I presume these figures were meant for the master of
your yacht," he remarked, without looking at her, and
passed out on the veranda, where he halted at sight of Masterson running up the steps, and the dusty rider close behind.

Judithe had seated herself at the desk and picked up
the pen. But as Monroe stepped out on the veranda she
turned impatiently:

"The despatch?" and she held out her hand.

"I was followed—I read and destroyed it."

"Its contents?"

"Too late, Madame," he remarked, in a less confidential
tone, as he laid the slip Monroe had given him on the

desk. He had seen Masterson at the door and with him the other rider!

Judithe did not raise her head. She was apparently absorbed in her task of addressing an envelope.

"I will speak with you directly," she said, carelessly sealing the letter. He bowed and stood waiting, respectfully. Glancing up, she saw Captain Masterson, who had entered from the veranda, and bestowed on him a careless, yet gracious smile. Pluto brought the mail bag in from the hall, and she dropped the letter in, also a couple of papers she took from the top of the desk.

"There, that is all. Make haste, please, Pluto," and she glanced at the clock. "I should not like that letter to miss the mail; it is important."

"Yes'm, I gwine right away now," and he turned to the door, when Masterson stepped before him, and to his astonishment, took the bag from his hand.

"You can't take this with you," he said, in a tone of authority. "Go tell Colonel McVeigh he is needed here on business most important."

Pluto stared at him in stupid wonder, and Judithe arose from her chair.

"Go, by all means, Pluto," she said, quietly, "Captain Masterson's errand is, no doubt, more important than a lady's could be," and she moved towards the door.

"I apologize, Madame Caron, for countermanding your orders," said Masterson, quickly, "but circumstances make it necessary that no person and no paper leave this room until this man's identity is determined," and he pointed to the messenger. "Do you know him?"

"Certainly I know him; he is in my employ, the sailing master of my yacht."

Pluto came in again and announced, "Mahs Kenneth

not in the house; he gone somewhere out to the quarters."
Masterson received the news with evident annoyance. There
was a moment of indecision as he glanced from the stranger
to Monroe, who had sauntered through the open window,
and across to Judithe, who gave him one glance which he
interpreted to mean she wished he was somewhere else.
But he only smiled and—remained.

"There is only one thing left for me to do in Colonel
McVeigh's absence," said Masterson, addressing the group
in general, "and that is to investigate this affair myself, as
every minute's delay may mean danger. Madame Caron,
we are forced to believe this man is a spy." Judithe smiled
increduously, and he watched her keenly as he continued:
"More, he is associated with a clever French creole called
Louise Trouvelot, who says she is your maid and who is
at present under surveillance in Savannah, and they both
are suspected of being only agents for a very accomplished
spy, who has been doing dangerous work in the South
for many months. I explain so you will comprehend that
investigation is necessary. This man," and he pointed to
the other stranger, who now stepped inside, "has followed
him from the coast under special orders."

"What a dangerous character you have become!" said
Judithe, turning to her messenger with an amused smile.
"I feared that beard would make you look like a pirate,
but I never suspected *this* of you—and you say," she added,
turning to Masterson, "that my poor maid is also under
suspicion? It is ridiculous, abominable! I must see to it
at once. The girl will be frightened horribly among such
evidences of your Southern chivalry," and she shrugged
her shoulders with a little gesture of disdain. "And what,
pray, do you intend doing with my sailor here?"

The man had been staring at Masterson as though astounded at the accusations. But he did not speak, and the Confederate agent never took his eyes off him.

"Ask him his name," he suggested, softly, to Masterson, who took paper and pencil from the desk and handed it to the suspect. "Write your name there," he said, and when it was quickly, good naturedly done, the self-appointed judge read it and turned to Judithe.

"Madame Caron, will you please tell me this man's name?" and the messenger himself stared when she replied, haughtily:

"No, Captain Masterson, I will not!"

"Ah, you absolutely refuse, Madame?"

"I do; you have accused my employe of being a spy, but your attitude suggests that it is not he, but myself, whom you suspect."

"Madame, you cannot comprehend the seriousness of the situation," and Masterson had difficulty in keeping his patience. "Every one he speaks with, everything concerning him is of interest. These are war times, Madame Caron, and the case will not admit of either delays or special courtesies. I shall have to ask you for the paper he placed in your hands as I entered the room."

Judithe picked up the paper without a word and reached it to him, with the languid air of one bored by the entire affair.

He glanced at it and handed it back. As he did so he perceived an unfinished letter on the desk. In a moment his suspicions were aroused; that important letter in the mail bag!

"You did not complete the letter you were writing?"

"No," and she lifted it from the desk and held it towards him. "You perceive! I was so careless as to blot the paper; do you wish to examine that?"

His face flushed at the mockery of her tone and glance. He felt it more keenly, that the eyes of Monroe were on him. The task before him was difficult enough without that additional annoyance.

"No, Madame," he replied, stiffly, "but the situation is such that I feel justified in asking the contents of the envelope you sealed and gave to the servant."

"But that is a private letter," she protested, as he took it from the mail bag; "it can be of no use to any government or its agents."

"That can best be determined by reading it, Madame. It certainly cannot go out in this mail unless it is examined."

"By you?—oh!" And Judithe put out her hand in protest.

"Captain Masterson!"

"Sir!" and Masterson turned on Monroe, who had spoken for the first time. As he did so Judithe deliberately leaned forward and snatched the letter from his hand.

"You shall not read it!" she said, decidedly, and just then Evilena and her brother came along the veranda, and with them Delaven. Judithe moved swiftly to the window before any one else could speak.

"Colonel McVeigh, I appeal to you," and involuntarily she reached out her hand, which he took in his as he entered the room. "This—gentleman—on some political pretense, insists that I submit to such examinations as spies are subject to. I have been accused in the presence of these people, and in their presence I demand an apology for this attempt to examine my private, personal letters."

"Captain Masterson!" and the blue, steel of McVeigh's eyes flashed in anger and rebuke. But Masterson, strong in his assurance of right, held up his hand.

"You don't understand the situation, Colonel. That man is suspected of being the assistant to a most dangerous, unknown spy within our lines. He has been followed from Beaufort by a Confederate secret service agent, whom he tried to escape by doubling on the road, taking by-ways, riding fully twenty miles out of his course, to reach this point unobserved."

For the first time the suspected man spoke, and it was to Judithe.

"That is quite true, Madame. I mean that I rode out of my way. But the reason of it is that I came over the road for the first time; there were no sign-boards up, and my directions had not been explicit enough to prevent me losing my way. That is my only excuse for not being here earlier. I am not landsman enough to make my way through the country roads and timber."

"You perceive, Colonel McVeigh, the man is in my employ, and has come here by my orders," said Judithe, with a certain impatience at the density of the accuser.

"That should be credential enough," and McVeigh's tone held a distinct reprimand as he frowned at Masterson's senseless accusation, but that officer made a gesture of protest. He was being beaten, but he did not mean to give up without a hard fight.

"Colonel, there were special reasons for doubt in the matter. Madame Caron, apparently, does not know even the man's name. I asked him to write it—here it is," and he handed McVeigh the paper. "I asked her to name him—she refused!"

"Yes; I resented the manner and reason for the question," assented Judithe; "but the man has been the master of my yacht for over a year, and his name is Pierson—John T. Pierson."

"Correct," and McVeigh glanced at the paper on which the name was written. "Will you also write the name of Madame Caron's yacht, Mr. Pierson?" and he handed him a book and pencil. "Pardon me," and he smiled reassuringly at Judithe, "this is not the request of suspicion, but faith." He took the book from Pierson and glanced at the open page and then at her—"the name of your yacht is?—"

"*The Marquise*," she replied, with a little note of surprise in her voice, as she smiled at Evilena, who had slipped to her side, and understood the smile. Evilena and she had made plans for a season of holidays on that same yacht, as soon as the repairs were made. Colonel McVeigh tossed the book indignantly on the table.

"Thank you, Madame! Captain Masterson, this is the most outrageous thing I ever knew an officer to be guilty of! You have presumed to suspect a lady in my house—the guest of your superior officer, and you shall answer to me for it! Mr. Pierson, you are no longer under suspicion here, sir. And you," he added, turning to the Confederate secret agent, "can report at once to your chief that spies are not needed on the McVeigh plantation."

"Colonel McVeigh, if you had seen what I saw—"

"Madame Caron's word would have been sufficient," interrupted McVeigh, without looking at him. And Judithe held out the letter.

"I am quite willing you should see what he saw," she said, with a curious smile. "He saw me, after the arrival of Mr. Pierson, seal an envelope leaving him in ignorance of its contents. The seal is yet unbroken—will you read it?"

"You do not suppose I require proof of your innocence?" he asked, refusing the letter, and looking at her fondly as he dare in the presence of the others.

"But I owe it to myself to offer the proof now," she insisted, "and at the same time I shall ask Mr. Pierson to offer himself for personal search if Captain Masterson yet retains suspicion of his honesty;" she glanced towards Pierson, who smiled slightly, and bowed without speaking. Then she turned to Delaven, who had been a surprised onlooker of the scene.

"Dr. Delaven, in the cause of justice, may I ask you to examine the contents of this letter?" and she tore open the envelope and offered it.

"Anything in the wide world to serve you, Madame la Marquise," he answered, with a shade more than usual of deference in his manner, as he took it. "Are the contents to be considered professionally, that is, confidentially?"

She had taken Evilena by the hand, bowed slightly to the group, and had moved to the door, when he spoke. Monroe, who had watched every movement as he stood there in a fever of suspense for her sake, drew a breath of relief as she replied:

"Oh, no! Be kind enough to read it aloud, or Captain Masterson may include you in the dangerous intrigues here," and, smiling still, she passed out with Evilena to the lawn.

But a few seconds elapsed, when a perfect shout of laughter came from the library. The special detective did not share in it, for he thrust his hands into his pockets with a curse, and Masterson turned to him with a frowning, baffled stare—an absolutely crestfallen manner, as he listened to the following, read in Delaven's best style:

"To Madame Smith,
                "Mobile, Ala.:

"The pink morning gown is perfect, but I am in despair over the night robes! I meant you to use the lace, not the

20

embroidery, on them; pray change them at once, and send at the same time the flounced lawn petticoats if completed. I await reply.

"Judithe de Caron."

CHAPTER XXV.

"Certainly, I apologize," and Masterson looked utterly crushed by his mistaken zeal; "apologize to every one concerned, collectively and individually."

Even McVeigh felt sorry for his humiliation, knowing how thoroughly honest he was, how devoted to the cause; and Mrs. McVeigh was disconsolate over "loyal, blundering Phil Masterson," whom, she could not hope, would remain for the party after what had occurred, and she feared Judithe would keep to her room—who could blame her? Such a scene was enough to prostrate any woman.

But it did not prostrate Judithe. She sent for Mrs. McVeigh, to tell her there must on no account be further hostilities between Colonel McVeigh and Captain Masterson.

"It was all a mistake," she insisted. "Captain Masterson no doubt only did his duty when presented with the statements of the secret service man; that the statements were incorrect was something Captain Masterson could not, of course, know, and she appreciated the fact that, being a foreigner, she was, in his opinion, possibly, more likely to be imposed upon by servants who were not so loyal to the South as she herself was known to be."

All this she said in kindly excuse, and Mrs. McVeigh thought her the most magnanimous creature alive.

Her only anxiety over the entire affair appeared to be

concerning her maid Louise, who, also, was suffering the suspicion attaching to foreigners who were non-residents; it was all very ridiculous, of course, but would necessitate her going personally to Savannah. She could not leave so faithful a creature in danger.

Mrs. McVeigh prevailed upon her to send word with Mr. Pierson to the authorities, and remain herself for two days longer—until Kenneth and his men left for the front, which Judithe consented to do.

Masterson, who for the first time in his life found the McVeighs lacking in cordiality to him (Evilena, even, disposed to look on him as dead and buried so far as she was concerned), felt his loyal heart go out to Gertrude, who was the only one of them all who frankly approved, and who was plainly distressed at the idea of him going at once to join his company.

"Don't go, Phil," she said, earnestly; "something is wrong here—terribly wrong; I can't accuse anyone in particular—I can't even guess what it really means, but, Phil," and she glanced around her cautiously before putting the question, "What possible reason could Madame Caron and Captain Monroe have for pretending they met here as strangers, when it was not a fact?"

Whereupon Gertrude told him of her discovery in that direction.

"I can't, of course, mention it to Kenneth or Mrs. McVeigh, now," she whispered; "they are so infatuated with her, Kenneth in particular. But I do hope you will put aside your personal feelings; make any and every sort of apology necessary, but remain right here until you see what it all means. You may prove in the end that you were not entirely mistaken today. What do you think of it?"

Think! His thoughts were in a whirl. If Madame Caron

and Captain Monroe were secretly friends it altered the whole affair. Monroe, whose conduct on arrest was unusual; who had a parole which might, or might not, be genuine; who had come there as by accident just in time to meet Pierson; who had been in the room alone with Pierson before Madame Caron came down the stairs—he knew, for he had been in sight when she crossed the hall.

He had been a fool—right in theory, but wrong as to the individual. He would remain at the Terrace, and he would start on a new trail!

Mrs. McVeigh was very glad he would remain; she believed implicitly in his profound regret, and had dreaded lest the question be recalled between the two men after they had gone to the front; but, if Phil remained their guest, she hoped the old social relations would be completely restored, and she warned Evilena to be less outspoken in regard to her own opinions.

So, Captain Masterson remained, and remained to such purpose that during the brief hour of Mr. Pierson's stay he was watched very closely, and the watcher was disappointed that no attempt was made at a private interview with Captain Monroe, who very plainly (Masterson thought, ostentatiously) showed himself in a rather unsocial mood, walking thoughtfully alone on the lawn, and making no attempt to speak, even with Madame Caron.

Pierson had a brief interview with her, rendered the more brief that he was conscious of Masterson's orderly lounging outside the window, but plainly within hearing, and the presence of Mrs. McVeigh, who was all interest and sympathy concerning Louise.

When he said: "Don't be at all disturbed over the work to be done, Madame; there is plenty of time in which to complete everything," the others present supposed, of course, he referred to the repairs on the yacht; and when he said, in reply to her admonitions, "No fear of me losing the road again, I shall arrive tonight," they supposed, of course, he referred to his arrival at the coast. Judithe knew better; she knew it meant his return, and more hours of uncertainty for her.

Colonel McVeigh helped to keep those hours from dragging by following up his love-making with a proposal of marriage, which she neither accepted or declined, but which gave her additional food for thought.

All the day Pluto brooded over that scene in the library. He was oppressed by the dread of harm to Madame Caron if some one did not at once acquaint her with the fact that the real spy was Madame's maid, who had fled for fear of recognition by the Lorings. He had been curious as to what motive had been strong enough to bring her back to the locality so dangerous to her freedom. He was puzzled no longer—he knew.

But, how to tell Madame Caron? How could a nigger tell a white lady that story of Rhoda and Rhoda's mother? And if part was told, all must be told. He thought of telling Dr. Delaven, who already knew the history of Margeret, but Dr. Delaven was a friend to the Lorings, and how was a nigger to know what a white man's honor would exact that he do in such a case? And Pluto was afraid to ask it.

Instinctively his trust turned to the blue uniformed "Linkum soldier." No danger of *him* telling the story of the runaway slave to the wrong person. And he was Madame Caron's friend. Pluto had noted how he stepped beside her when Masterson brought his accusation against her, or her agent, Pierson. Monroe had been a sort of divinity to him from the moment the officer in blue had walked up the steps of the Terrace, and Pluto's admiration culminated in the decision that he was the one man to warn Madame Caron of her maid's identity without betraying it to any other.

The lady who caused all this suppressed anxiety was, apparently, care-free herself, or only disturbed slightly over the report concerning Louise. She knew the girl was in no real danger, but she knew, also, that at any hint of suspicion Louise would be in terror until joined by her mistress.

She heard Matthew Loring had sent over for Judge Clarkson to arrange some business affairs while Kenneth was home, and despite Mrs. McVeigh's statement that they neither bought nor sold slaves, she fancied she knew what one of the affairs must be.

Judge Clarkson, however, was not at home—had been called across the country somewhere on business, but Aunt Sajane sent word that they would certainly be over in the evening and would come early, if Gideon returned in time.

But he did not. Several of the guests arrived before them; Colonel McVeigh was employed as host, and the business talk had to be deferred until the following morning.

Altogether, the sun went down on a day heavy with threats and promises. But whatever the rest experienced in that atmosphere of suppressed feeling, Kenneth McVeigh was only responsive to the promises; all the world was colored by his hopes!

And Monroe, who saw clearly what the hopes were, and who thought he saw clearly what the finale would be, had little heart for the festivities afoot—wished himself anywhere else but on the hospitable plantation of the McVeighs, and kept at a distance from the charming stranger who had bewitched the master of it.

Twilight had fallen before Pluto found the coveted opportunity of speaking with him alone. Monroe was striding along the rose arbor, smoking an after-supper cigar, when he was suddenly confronted by the negro who had questioned him about the Federal policy as to slavery.

He had been running along the hedge in a stooping position so as not to be seen from the windows of the dining room, where the other servants were working, and when he gained the shadows of an oleander tree, straightened up and waited.

"Well," remarked Monroe, as he witnessed this maneuver, "what is it?"

Pluto looked at him steadily for an instant, and then asked, cautiously:

"Mahs Captain, you a sure enough friend of Madame Caron?"

"'Sure enough' friend—what do you mean?"

"I mean Madame Caron gwine to have trouble if some sure enough friend don't step in an' tell her true who the spy is they all talk 'bout today."

"Indeed?" said Monroe, guardedly; his first thought was one of suspicion, lest it be some trick planned by Masterson.

"Yes, sah; I find out who that woman spy is, but ain't no one else knows! I can't tell a white lady all that story what ain't noways fitten' fo' ladies to listen to, but—but *somebody* got to tell her, somebody that knows jest how much needs tellin', an' how much to keep quiet—somebody she trusts, an' somebody what ain't no special friend o' the Lorings. Fo' God's sake, Mahsa Captain, won't yo' be that man?"

Monroe eyed him narrowly for an instant, and then tossed away the cigar.

"No fooling about this business, mind you," he said,

briefly; "what has Madame Caron to do with any spy? And what has Matthew Loring?"

"Madame not know she got *anything* to do with her," insisted Pluto, eagerly, "that gal come heah fo' maid to Madame Caron, an' then ole Nelse (what Lorings use to own) he saw her, an' that scare her plum off the place. An' the reason why Mahsa Loring is in it is 'cause that fine French maid is a runaway slave o' his—or maybe she b'long to Miss Gertrude, *I* don' know rightly which it is. Any how, she's Margeret's chile an' ought to a knowed more'n to come a 'nigh to Loring even if she *is* growd up. That why I know fo' suah she come back fo' some special spy work—what else that gal run herself in danger fo' nothen'?"

"You'd better begin at the beginning of this story, if it has one," suggested Monroe, who could see the man was intensely in earnest, "and I should like to know why you are mixing Madame Caron in the affair."

"She bought my baby fo' me—saved him from the trader, Mahsa Captain," and Pluto's voice trembled as he spoke. "Yo' reckon I evah fo'get that ar? An' now seems like as how she's got mixed up with troubles, an' I come to yo' fo' help 'cause yo' a Linkum man, an' 'cause yo' her frien'."

It was twenty minutes later before Pluto completed his eager, hurried story, and at its finish Monroe knew all old Nelse had told Delaven, and more, too, for confidential servants learn many hidden things, and Rosa—afterwards Pluto's wife—knew why Margeret's child was sent to the Larue estate for training. Mistress Larue, whose conscience was of the eminently conventional order, seldom permitting her to contest any decision of her husband, yet did find courage to complain somewhat of the child's charge and her ultimate destination—to complain, not on moral, but on financial grounds—fully convinced that so wealthy a man as Matthew Loring could afford to pay more for her keeping than the sum her husband had agreed to, and that the youth, Kenneth McVeigh, to whose estate the girl was partly sold, could certainly afford more of recompense than his guardian had agreed to.

Pluto told that portion of the story implicating his master with considerable reluctance, yet felt forced to tell it all, that Monroe should be impressed with the necessity of absolute secrecy to every one except Madame Caron, and she, of course, must not hear that part of it.

"Name o' God, no!" burst out Pluto, in terror of what such a revelation would mean. "What yo' reckon Madame Caron think o' we all ef she done heah *that*? Don't reckon his own ma evah heard tell a whisper o' that ar; all Mahs Matt Loring's doin's, that sale was—*must* a been! Mahs Ken wan't only a boy then—not more'n fifteen, so yo' see —"

Monroe made no comment, though he also had a vision of what it would mean if Madame Caron—she of all women! —should hear this evidently true story just as Pluto related it.

He walked along the rose hedge and back again in silence, the colored man regarding him anxiously; finally he said:

"All right, my man. I'll speak to Madame and be careful not to tell her too much. You are all right, Pluto; you did right to come to me."

Some one called Pluto from the window. He was about to go when Monroe asked:

"What about that picture you said your wife had of the girl? Madame Caron may not be easy to convince. You'd better let me have it to show her. Is it a good likeness?"

"'Fore God *I* don' know! I only reckon it is, 'cause

Nelse took her, on sight, fo' Margeret's ghost, which shows it must be the plain image of her! I done been so upset since I got back home with Zekal I nevah had a minute to look ovah Rosa's b'longens', but the likeness is in that bundle somewhere; Rosa alles powerful careful o' that locket thing, an' kep' it put away; don't mind as I evah seen it but once, jest when we fust married. I'd a clean fo'got all 'bout it, only fo' an accident—an' that's the woman now it was painted from."

He pointed to a window where Margeret stood outlined for an instant against the bright background.

"Don't look more like her now, I reckon," he continued, "all her trouble must a' changed her mightily, fo' the ole folks do say she was counted a beauty once. Little Rhoda went a'most crazy when some one stole the locket, so Rosa said; then by and by the gal what took it got scared—thought it was a hoodoo—an' fetched it back, but Rhoda gone away then. My Rosa took it an' kep' it faithful, waiten' fo' that chile to come back, but she nevah come back while Rosa lived."

Monroe was staring still at the figure of Margeret, seen dimly, now, through the window.

"Look here!" he said, sharply, "if the old man recognized the likeness, how comes it that the mother herself did not see it?"

"Why, Margeret she not get here till nex' day after Madame Caron's maid start down the river to take the cars fo' Savannah," explained Pluto. "Then Miss Gertrude come a visiten' an' fetch Margeret along. Yo' see, sah, that woman done been made think her chile dead a long time ago, an' when Margeret went clean 'stracted the word went down to Larues that she dead or dyen'—one! any way my Rosa nevah know'd no different till Larues moved back from

Georgy, so there wan't no one heah to 'dentify her, an' there wan't no one heah to let that gal know she *had* a liven mammy."

Again Caroline called Pluto.

"Go on," said Monroe, "but get me the picture soon as you can. I leave in the morning."

"I be right heah with it in hour's time," promised Pluto; "don' reckon I can slip away any sooner, a sight o' quality folks a' comen'."

CHAPTER XXVI.

As Monroe entered the hall Judithe came down the stairs, a dainty vision in palest rose. She wore armlets and girdle of silver filagree, a silver comb in the dark tresses, and large filagree loops in her ears gave the beautiful face a half-oriental character.

Admire her though he must, he felt an impatience with her, a wonder that so beautiful a being, one so blest with all the material things of life, should forsake harmony, home, and her own land, for the rude contests where men fought, and plotted, and died—died ingloriously sometimes, for the plots and intrigues through which she claimed to find the only escape from ennui.

She saw him, hesitated an instant, and then came towards him, with a suggestion of daring in her eyes.

"I might as well hear the worst, first as last," she said, taking his arm. "Is not the veranda more cool than in here? Come, we shall see. I prefer to be out of hearing of the people while you lecture me for today's mishap."

She glanced up at him with a pretense of dread such as a child might show; she was pleased to be alluringly gracious, but he could feel that she was more nervous than she had ever shown herself before—the strain was telling on her.   Her beautiful eyes were not so slumbrous as usual; they were brilliant as from some inward fever, and, though she smiled and met his sombre gaze with a challenge, she smothered a sigh under her light words.

"I shan't lecture you, Madame Caron; I have no right to interfere with what you call your—amusements," and he glanced down at her, grimly; "but I leave in the morning because by remaining longer I might gain knowledge which, in honor, I should feel bound to report."

"To Colonel—or, shall we say, General—McVeigh?"

He bent his head, and answered: "I have given you warning.   He is my friend."

"And I?" she asked, glancing at him with a certain archness.   He looked down at her, but did not speak.

"And I?" she repeated.

"No," he said, after a pause.   "You, Madame, would have to be something more, or something less.   The fates have decreed that it be less—so," he made a little gesture dismissing the subject.   "Pardon me, but I did not mean to attack you in that fashion.   I came to look for you to ask you a question relating to the very pretty, very clever, maid you had in New Orleans, and whom, I hear, you brought with you on your visit here."

"Oh!   You are curious as to her—and you wish me to answer questions?"

"If you please, though it really does not matter to me. Are you aware that the woman was a runaway slave, and liable to recapture in this particular vicinity?"

"In this particular vicinity?" she repeated, questioningly.

"Yes, if Matthew Loring should once get suspicion of the fact that your maid was really his girl Rosa—no, Rhoda—it would be an awkward fact allied to the episode here to-day," and he made a gesture towards the library window they were just passing.

"Come, we will go down the steps," she suggested. They did so, and were promenading under the trees, lantern lit, on the lawn, when Colonel McVeigh came out on the veranda and felt a momentary envy of Monroe, who was free from a host's duties. They were clear of the steps and of probable listeners before Judithe asked:

"Where did you get this information?"

"From a slave who wanted you warned that you without knowing it, are probably harboring the spy whom Captain Masterson spoke of today."

"Ah, a slave?" she remarked, thoughtfully; and the curious, intense gaze of Margeret was recalled to her, only to be followed by the memory of Pluto's anxiety that Louise should leave before the arrival of the Lorings; it was, then, without doubt, Pluto who gave the warning; but she remembered Zekal, and felt she had little to be anxious over.

"You probably are not aware," he continued, "what a very serious affair it is considered here to assist in hiding a slave of that sort under assumed names or occupations. But if it is discovered it would prove ruinous to you just now."

"In three days I shall be out of the country," she answered, briefly. "I go down to Savannah, secure Louise from this blunder—for there is really nothing to be proven against her as a spy—and then, farewell, or ill, to Carolina. I do not expect to enter it again. My arrangements are all made. Nothing has been forgotten. As to my good Louise, your informer has not been made acquainted with

all the facts. It is true she was a Georgian slave, but is so
no longer. For over a year she has been in possession of
the papers establishing her freedom. Her own money, and
a clever lawyer, arranged all that without any trouble whatever. What Monsieur Loring would do if he knew I had
a maid whose name was assumed, I neither know nor care.
He could not identify her as the girl Rhoda Larue, even if
he saw her. His sight has failed until he could not distinguish you from Colonel McVeigh if across the room. I
learned that fact through Madame McVeigh before leaving
Mobile, so, you perceive, I have not risked so much in making the journey with my pretty maid; and I shall risk no
more when I make my adieus the day after tomorrow."

She laughed, and looked up in his face. He looked down
in her's, but he did not laugh.

"And the estate you have just purchased in order to enjoy
this Eden-like plantation life?"

"The purpose for which it was purchased will be carried
out quite as well without my presence," she said, quietly. "I
never meant to live there."

"Well, that beats me!" he said, halting, and looking
squarely down at her. "You spend thousands to establish
yourself in the heart of a seceding country, and gain the
confidence of the natives, and then toss it all aside as though
it were only a trifle! You must have spent fortunes from
your own pocket to help the Federals!"

"So your President was good enough to say in the letter
I tried to show you—and did not," she replied, and then
smiled, as she added, "but you are mistaken, Captain Monroe; it was only one fortune spent, and I will be recom-
pensed."

"When?"

"When that long-talked-of emancipation is announced."

The bright music of a mazurka stole out of the open windows, and across the level could be seen a blaze of fat pine torches tied to poles and shedding lustre and black pitch over the negro quarters—they also were celebrating "Mahs Ken's" return. Above the dreamy system of the parlor dances they could hear at times the exuberant calls and shouts of laughter where the dark people made merry. Judge Clarkson, who was descending the steps, halted to listen, and drew Monroe's attention to it.

"Happy as children they are, over there tonight," he remarked. "Most contented people on earth, I do believe." He addressed some gallant words to Judithe, and then turned to Monroe.

"Mr. Loring has been inquiring for you, Captain Monroe. You understand, of course, that you are somewhat of a lion and one we cannot afford to have hidden. He is waiting to introduce you to some of our Carolina friends, who appreciate you, sir, for the protection shown a daughter of the South, and from your magnanimous care of a Carolina boy this past month—oh, your fame has preceded you, and I assure you, sir, you have earned for yourself a hearty welcome."

Evilena joined them, followed by Delaven, who asked for a dance and was flouted because he did not wear a uniform. She did present him with a scarlet flower from her boquet, with the remark that if decked with something bright he might be a little less suggestive of funerals, and, attaching herself to Monroe, she left to look up Matthew Loring.

Delaven looked ruefully at the scarlet flower.

"It's a poor substitute for herself," he decided, "but, tell me now, Marquise, if you were fathoms deep in love, as I am this minute, and had so much of encouragement as a flower flung at you, what would you advise as the next move in Cupid's game?"

She assumed a droll air of serious contemplation for an instant, and then replied, in one word:

"Propose."

"I'll do it," he decided; "ah, you are a jewel of a woman to give a man courage! I'll lay siege to her before I'm an hour older. Judge, isn't it you would lend a boy a hand in a love affair? I'm bewitched by one of the fair daughters of the South you are so proud of; I find I am madly jealous of every other lad who leads her onto the dancing floor this night, but every one of them has dollars where I have dimes," and he sighed like a furnace and glanced from one to the other with a comical look of distress; "so is it any wonder I need all the bracing up my friends can give me?"

"My dear sir," said the Judge, genially, "our girls are not mercenary. You are a gentleman, so need fear comparison with none! You have an active brain, a high degree of intelligence, a profession through which you may win both wealth and honors for the lady in question—so why procrastinate?"

"Judge, you are a trump! With you to back me up with that list of advantages, I'll dare the fates."

"I am your obedient servant, sir. I like your enthusiasm —your determination to put the question to the test. I approve of early marriages, myself; procrastination and long engagements are a mistake, sir—a mistake!"

"They are," agreed Delaven, with a decision suggestive of long experience in such matters. "Faith, you two are life preservers to me. I feel light as a cork with one of you on each side—though it was doleful enough I was ten minutes ago! You see, Judge, the lady who is to decide my fate has valued your friendship and advice so long that I count on

you—I really do, now, and if you'd just say a good word
to her—"

"A word! My dear sir, my entire vocabulary is at your
service in an affair of the heart." The Judge beamed on
Delaven and bowed to Madame Caron as though including
her in the circle where Love's sceptre is ever potent.

"Faith, when America becomes a monarchy, I'll vote for
you to be king," and Delaven grasped the hand of the
Judge and shook it heartily; "and if you can only convince
Mrs. McVeigh that I am all your fancy has pictured me,
I'll be the happiest man in Carolina tonight."

"What!" Judge Clarkson dropped his hand as though
it had burned him, and fairly glared at the self-confessed
lover.

"I would that!—the happiest man in Carolina, barring
none," said the reckless Irishman, so alive with his own
hopes that he failed to perceive the consternation in the face
of the Judge; but Judithe saw it, and, divining the cause,
laughed softly, while Delaven continued: "You see, Judge,
Mrs. McVeigh will listen to you and—"

"Young man!" began Clarkson, austerely, but at that
moment the lady in question appeared on the veranda and
waved her fan to Delaven.

"Doctor, as a dancing man your presence in the house
would be most welcome," she said, coming slowly down the
steps towards them.

"Madame, both my feet and my heart are at your disposal," he said, hastening to meet her, and passing on to
find some unpartnered damsels she suggested.

"What a charming young man he is," remarked their
hostess, "and exceedingly skillful in his profession for so
young a physician. Don't you consider him very bright,
Judge?"

21

"I, Madame—I?" and Judithe retired, convulsed at the situation; "on my word, I wouldn't trust him to doctor a sick cat!" Mrs. McVeigh looked astonished at the intensity of his words and was fairly puzzled to see Judithe laughing on the seat under the tree.

"Why, Judge! I'm actually surprised! He is most highly esteemed professionally, and in Paris—"

"Pardon me, but I presume his hair was the same color in Paris that it is here," said the Judge, coldly, "and I have never in my life known a red-headed man who had any sense, or—"

"Oh!" Mrs. McVeigh glanced slowly from the Judge to Judithe and then smiled; "I remember one exception, Judge, for before your hair became white it was—well, auburn, at least."

The Judge ran his fingers through the bushy curls referred to. The man usually so eloquent and ready of speech, was checkmated. He could only stammer something about exceptions to rules, and finally said:

"You will probably remember, however, that my hair was very dark—a dark red, in fact, a—a—brown red."

Judithe, to hide her amusement, had moved around to the other side of the tree circled by the rustic seat. Her hostess turned one appealing glance towards her, unseen by the Judge, who had forgotten all but the one woman before him.

"No matter if he had hair all colors of the rainbow he is not worthy of you, Madame," he blurted out, and Mrs. McVeigh took a step away from him in dismay; in all her knowledge of Judge Clarkson, she had never seen him show quite so intense a dislike for any one.

"Why, Judge! What is the matter tonight?" she asked, in despair. "You mean Dr. Delaven; not worthy of me?"

"He aspires to your hand," blurted out the Judge, angrily. "Such an ambition is a worthy one; it is one I myself have cherished for years, but you must confess I had the courage to ask your hand in person."

"Yes, Judge; but—"

"This fellow, on the contrary, has had the affrontery to come to me—to me! with the request that I use my influence in negotiating a matrimonial alliance with you!"

Mrs. McVeigh stared at him a moment, and then frankly laughed; she suspected it was some joke planned by Evilena. But the indignation of the Judge was no joke.

"Well, Judge, when I contemplate a matrimonial alliance, I can assure you that no one's influence would have quite so much weight as your own;" she had ascended the steps and was laughing; at the top she leaned over and added, "no matter who you employ your eloquence for, Judge;" and with that parting shot she disappeared into the hall, leaving him in puzzled doubt as to her meaning. But the question did not require much consideration. The remembrance of the smile helped clear it up wonderfully. He clasped his hands under his coat tails, threw back his shoulders, walked the length of the veranda and back with head very erect. He was a very fine figure of a man.

"The Irishman's case is quashed," he said, nodding emphatically and confidentially to the oleander bush; "the fact that a woman, and that woman a widow, remembers the color of the plaintiff's hair for twenty years, should convince the said plaintiff if he is a man possessed of a legal mind, that his case is still on the calendar. I'll go and ask for the next dance."

He had scarcely reached the steps when Judithe saw a flutter of white where the shadows were heaviest under the dense green shrubbery. She glanced about her; no one was in hearing. The veranda, for the instant, was deserted, and past the windows the dancers were moving. The music of stringed instruments and of laughter floated out to her. She saw Masterson in the hallway; he was watching Monroe. She saw Kenneth McVeigh speaking to his mother and glancing around inquiringly; was he looking for her? She realized that her moments alone now would be brief, and she moved swiftly under the trees to where the signal had been made. A man had been lying there flat to the ground. He arose as she approached, and she saw he was dressed in Confederate uniform, and that he wore no beard—it was Pierson.

"Why did you leave the place without seeing me again?" she demanded. "This suspense seems to me entirely unnecessary."

"It was the best I could do, Madame," he answered, hurriedly. "Masterson, unknown to the McVeighs, had spies within hearing of every word between us, and to write was too great a risk. His man followed me beyond the second fortification."

"And you eluded him?"

"No; I left him," answered Pierson, grimly. "I wore his uniform back—he did not need it."

Judithe drew a deep, shuddering breath, but made no comment. "Give me the contents of the destroyed despatch," was all she said.

"McVeigh received official notification of promotion today. Important instructions were included as to the movements of his brigade. These instructions must be received by us tonight in order to learn their plans for this wing of the army."

"And you depend on me?"

"No other way to secure them quickly, but some of our

men have been landed north of Beaufort. They are under cover in the swamp and cane brakes awaiting your commands—so if it can't be done quietly there is another way —a raid for any purpose you may suggest, and incidentally these instructions would be among the souvenirs from this especial plantation."

"Colonel McVeigh only remains over tomorrow night. Suppose I succeed, how shall I communicate with you or with the detachment of Federals?"

"I will return tonight after the house is quiet. I shall be in sight of the balcony. You could drop them from there; or, if you have any better plan of your own I will act on it."

She could see Kenneth on the veranda, and knew he was looking for her. The moments were precious now; she had to think quick.

"It may not be possible to secure them tonight; the time is so short; and if not I can only suggest that the commander of the landed troops send a detachment tomorrow, capture Colonel McVeigh and Captain Masterson, and get the papers at the same time. There are also official documents in McVeigh's possession relating to the English commissions for additions to the Confederate Navy. I must go; they are looking for me. You can trust a black man here called Pluto—but do not forget that a detachment of Confederates came today to the fortifications below here, don't let our men clash with them; good bye; make no mistake."

She moved away as she spoke, and the man dropped back unseen into the shadows as she went smilingly forward to meet the lover, whose downfall she was debating with such cool judgment.

And the lover came to meet her with ardent blue eyes aglow.

"Have you fled to the shadows to avoid us all?" he demanded, and then as he slipped her hand through his arm and looked down in her face, he asked, more tenderly, "or may I think you only left the crowd to think over my audacity."

She gave him one fleeting, upward glance, half inviting, half reproving—it would help concentrate his attention until the man in the shadows was beyond all danger of discovery.

"You make use of every pretext to avoid me," he continued, "but it won't serve you; no matter what cool things you say now, I can only hear through your words the meaning of those Fontainbleau days, and that one day in Paris when you loved me and dared to say it. Judithe, give me my answer. I thought I could wait until tomorrow, but I can't; you must tell me tonight; you must!"

"Must?" She drew away from him and leaned against a tall garden vase overrun with clustering vines. They were in the full blaze of light from the windows; she felt safer there where they were likely to be interrupted every minute; the man surely dared not be wildly sentimental in full view of the crowd—which conclusion showed that she was not yet fully aware of what Kenneth McVeigh would dare do where a woman—or the woman was in question.

"An hour ago you said: 'Will you?' Now it is: 'You must!'" she said, with a fine little smile. "How quick you are to assume the tone of master, Monsieur."

"If you said slave, the picture would have been more complete," he answered. "I will obey you in all things except when you tell me to leave you;" he had possessed himself of her hand, under cover of the vines; "it's no use, Judithe, you belong to me. I can't let you go from me again; I won't!"

All of pleading was in his voice and eyes. Moved by some sudden impulse not entirely guileless, she looked full at him and let her hand remain in his.

"Well, since you really cannot," she murmured.

"Judithe! You mean it?" and in an instant both his hands were clasping hers. "You are not coquetting with me this time? Judithe!"

She attempted to draw her hand away, but he bent his head, and kissed the warm palm. Margeret who was lighting an extinguished lantern, saw the caress and heard the low, deep tones. She turned and retraced her steps instead of passing them.

"Do you realize that all who run may read the subject of your discourse?" she asked, raising her brows and glancing after the retreating woman.

"Let them, the sooner they hear it the better I shall be pleased; come, let us tell my mother; I want to be sure of you this time, my beautiful Judithe. What time more fitting than this for the announcement—come!"

"What is it you would tell her?" she asked, looking straight ahead of her into the shadows on the lawn. Her voice sounded less musical than it had a moment before. Her eyes avoided his, and for one unguarded instant the full sculpturesque lips were tense and rigid.

"What is it?" he repeated, "why, that I adore you! that you have been the one woman in the world to me ever since I met you first; that I want you for my wife, and that you—confess it again in words, Judithe—that you love me."

She shook her head slowly, but accompanied that half denial with a bewildering smile.

"Entirely too much to announce in one evening," she decided; "do you forget they have had other plans for you? We must give your family more time to grow accustomed to me and to—your wishes."

"*Our* wishes," he said, correctively, and she dropped her

eyes and bent her head in assent. She was adorable in the
final surrender. He murmured endearing, caressing words
to her, and the warm color merged across her face, and receding, left her a trifle pale. All her indifference had been a
pretense—he knew it now, and it strengthened his protests
against delay. He drew her away from the steps as the
dance ended, and the people came chattering and laughing
out from the brilliantly lit rooms.

"You talk of haste, but forget that I have waited three
years, Judithe; remember that, won't you? Put that three
years to my credit; consider that I wooed you every day of
every year, and I would if I had been given the chance!
You talk of time as if there were oceans of it for us, and you
forget that I have but one more day to be with you—one
day; and then separation, uncertainty. I can't leave you
like that, now that I know you care for me—I won't."

"Oh—h!" and she met his look with a little quizzical smile.
"You mean to resign your commission for the sake of my
society? But I am not sure I should admire you so much
then. I am barbarian enough to like a fighter."

"I should fight all the better for knowing it was a wife I
was leaving behind instead of a sweetheart, Judithe; marry
me tomorrow!"

She made a little gesture of protest, but he clasped her
hand in his and held it close to prevent her from repeat-
ing it. "Why not?" he continued. "No one need know unless you wish; it can be kept secret as the engagement
would be. Then, wherever the fortunes of war may send me,
I can carry with me the certainty of your love. Speak to
me, Judithe! Say yes. I have waited three years; I want
my wife!"

"Your wife! *Your*—oh!"—and she flung out her hands as

though putting the thought away from her. A tear fell on his hand—she was weeping.

"Judithe, sweetheart!" he murmured, remorsefully.

"Tomorrow—not tonight," she half whispered. "I must think, so much is to be considered."

"No! Only one thing is to be considered;" he held her hands and looked in her face, with eyes ardent, compelling; "Only one thing, Judithe, and that is, do you love me—now?"

"Now, and from the first day we ever met," she answered, looking up at him; her eyes were like stars glimmering through the mist of late tears. There came to them both the remembrance of that other avowal, behind those plunging horses in the Paris boulevard. They had unconsciously repeated the words uttered then.

For an instant his arms were about her—such strong, masterful, compelling arms. A wild temptation came to her to remain in that shelter—to let all the world go by with its creeds, its plots, its wars of right and wrong—to live for love, love only, love with him.

"My queen!" he whispered, as her head bent in half avoidance of his caresses even while her hand clasped his closely, convulsively, "it has all been of no use; those three years when you kept me away. It is fate that we find each other again. I shall never let you go from me—never! Do you hear me, Judithe? You are so silent; but words matter little since you belong to me. Do you realize it?—that you must belong to me always!"

The words over which he lingered, words holding all of hope and happiness to him brought to her a swift revulsion of feeling. She remembered those other human creatures who belonged to him—she remembered—

A moment later and he stood alone in the sweet dusk of

the night. She had fairly run from him along the little arbor to the side door, where she vanished unseen by the others. How she was for all her queenly ways! What a creature of moods, and passions, and emotions! The hand on which her tear had fallen he touched to his cheek. Why had she wept at his confession of love for her? She had not wept when the same words were spoken on that never-to-be-forgotten day in Paris!

CHAPTER XXVII.

The love affair of Colonel McVeigh was not the only one under consideration that evening. Delaven was following up the advice of the Judge and Madame Caron to the extent of announcing to Mistress McVeigh during a pause in the dance that his heart was heavy, though his feet were light, and that she held his fate in her hands, for he was madly in love, which statement she had time to consider and digest before the quadrille again allowed them to come close enough for conversation, when she asked the meaning of his mystery.

"First, let me know, Mrs. McVeigh, which you would prefer if you had a choice—to have me for your family physician, or a physician in your family?"

She smiled at the excentric question, but as the dance whisked him off just then she waited for the next installment of his confidence.

"You must tell me, first, what relationship you seek to establish," she demanded, as he came up for his answer.

He looked at her quizzically, and seeing a slight gleam of

humor in her fine eyes, he launched into the heart of the question.

"What relationship? Well, I should say that of husband and wife, if I was not afraid of being premature;" he glanced at her and saw that she was interested and not in the least forbidding. "To be sure, I am poor, while you are wealthy, but I'm willing to overlook that; in fact, I'm willing to overlook anything, and dare all things if you would only consider me favorably—as a son-in-law."

"You are actually serious?"

"Serious, am I—on my faith, it's a life and death affair with me this minute!"

"And my little Evilena the cause?"

"Yes, our Evilena, who does not feel so small as you may imagine. Look at her now. Could a dozen seasons give her more confidence in her own powers than she has this minute by reason of those uniformed admirers?—to say nothing of my own case."

"*Our* Evilena?" and Mrs. McVeigh raised her brows inquiringly—"then you have proposed?"

"Indeed, no! I have not had the courage until tonight; but when I see a lot of lads daft as myself over her, I just whispered in the ear of Delaven that he'd better speak quick. "But I would not propose without asking your permission."

"And if I refused it?"

"You could not be so hard-hearted as that?"

"But suppose I could—and should?"

He caught the gleam of teasing light in her eyes, and smiled back at her:

"I should propose just the same!"

"Well," said Evilena's mother, with a combination of amusement and sympathy in her expression, "you may speak to her and let me know the result."

"I'd get down on my knees to kiss the toe of your slipper, this minute," he whispered, gratefully, "but the Judge would scalp me if I dared; he is eyeing me with suspicion already. As to the result—well, if you hear a serenade in the wee small hours of the night, don't let it disturb you. I've got the guitar and the uniform all ready, and if I fail it will not be because I have overlooked any romantic adjuncts to successful wooing. I'll be under your daughter's window singing 'Sweet Evilena,' rigged out like a cavalier in a picture-book. I'm wishing I could borrow a feather for the hat."

She laughed at the grotesque picture he suggested, but asked what he meant by the uniform, and laughed still more when he told her he was going to borrow one for the occasion from Kenneth, as Evilena had announced her scorn for all ununiformed men, and he did not mean to risk failure in a dress suit. Later he had an idea of applying for a uniform of his own as surgeon in the army.

"If you could introduce *that* into your serenade I have no fear my little girl would refuse you," said Mrs. McVeigh, encouragingly, "at least not more than two or three times."

On leaving Mrs. McVeigh he stumbled against Masterson, who was in the shadow just outside the window within which Monroe was in interested converse with Matthew Loring and some other residents of the county. He had been deliberately, and, in his own opinion, justifiably, a listener to every sentence advanced by the suspected Northerner, whom he felt was imposing on the hospitality of the South only to betray it.

Ernest as his convictions were he had not yet been able to discern the slightest trace of double intent in any of Monroe's remarks, which were, for the most part, of agricultural affairs, foreign affairs, even the possible future of the Seminoles in the Florida swamp; of everything, in fact, but the very vital question of the day surrounding them, which only tended to confirm his idea that the man was remarkably clever, and he despaired of securing sufficient evidence against him in the brief time at his disposal.

He had just arrived at that conclusion when Delaven, high-hearted with hope, saw only the stars over his head as he paced the veranda, and turning the corner stumbled on Masterson.

There was an exclamation, some words of apology, and involuntarily Masterson stepped backward into the stream of light from the open window, and Monroe, looking around, read the whole situation at a glance. Masterson still suspected him, and was listening! Monroe frankly laughed and made a little sound, the mere whisper of a whistle, as he met Masterson's baffled look with one of cool mockery; it was nonchalent to the verge of insolence, and enraged the Southerner, strong in his convictions of right, as a blow could not have done. For a blow a man could strike back, but this mockery!

Delaven walked on, unconscious of the suppressed feeling between the two. Masterson was handicapped by the fact that he dared not again mention his suspicions to the McVeigh family, and he strode down the steps to the lawn, furious at the restraint put upon him, and conscious, now, that surveillance was useless, since the Northerner had been put upon his guard.

His impatience filled him with rage. He was honest, and he was a fighter, but of what use was that since he had blundered? He had dealt clumsy strokes with both hands, but the other had parried each thrust with a foil. He was worsted—the game was up, but he at least meant to let the interloper know that however clever he might be, there were some people, at least, whom he could not deceive.

That was the humor he was in when he saw Monroe excuse himself to Loring, step through the window, and light a cigar, preparatory to a stroll towards the tryst with Pluto.

Masterson watched him sauntering carelessly down the steps. He had removed the cigar and was whistling very softly, unconsciously, as one who is deep in some quandary, but to Masterson it seemed the acme of studious carelessness to ignore his own presence; it seemed insolent as the mocking glance through the window, and it decided him. His shoulders unconsciously squared as he stepped forward.

"Captain Monroe, I want a word with you," and his tone was a challenge in itself. Monroe turned his head, slowly, finished the bar he was whistling in a slightly louder tone— loud enough to distinguish that it was "Rally 'Round the Flag," whistled very badly. Monroe had evidently little music in his soul, however much patriotism he had in his heart.

"Only one, I hope," he said, carelessly, with an irritating smile.

"You may have to listen to several before you get away from here!"

"From—you?" and there was perceptible doubt in the tone; it added to Masterson's conviction of his own impotence. He dared not fight the man unless Monroe gave the challenge, though it was the one thing he wanted to do with all his heart.

"From those in authority over this section," he said, sternly.

"Ah!—that is a different matter."

"You may find it a very serious matter, Captain Monroe."

"Oh, no; I shan't find it, I'm not looking for it," and Monroe softly resumed, *"The Union Forever."*

"If you take my advice," began Masterson, angrily, "you'll"—but Monroe shook his head.

"I shan't, so don't mention it," he said, blandly. Masterson's wordy anger showed him that he was master of the situation, so he only smiled as he added, "advice, you know, is something everybody gives and nobody takes," and Monroe resumed his whistle.

"You think yourself cursedly clever," and it was an effort for Masterson to keep from striking the cool, insolent face. "You thought so today when Madame Caron was suspected instead of yourself."

"Madame Caron!" Monroe ceased the whistle and looked at him with a momentary frown, which Masterson welcomed as a sign of anger.

"Ah, that touches you, does it?"

"Only with wonder that you dare speak of her after your failure to make her the victim of your spies today," and Monroe's tone was again only contemptuous. "First you arrest me, then accuse Madame Caron. Evidently you are out of your sphere in detective work; it really requires considerable cleverness, you know. Yet, if it amuses you—well"—he made a little gesture of indifference and turned away, but Masterson stepped before him.

"You will learn there is enough cleverness here to comprehend why you came to this plantation a willing prisoner," he said, threateningly. Monroe resumed his *Rally Once Again*," and raised his brows inquiringly, "and also why you ignored a former acquaintance with Madame Caron and had to be introduced. Before you are through with this business, Captain Monroe, you'll whistle a different tune."

"Oh, no, I shan't; I don't know any other," said Monroe, amiably, and sauntered away as some of the guests, with gay good nights, came down the steps. The evening, delightful as it had been, fraught with emotion as it had been, was passing. The late hour reminded Monroe that he must no longer delay seeing Pluto if he was to see him at all. They had exchanged glances several times, but the black man's duties had kept him occupied every minute, and they had found no opportunity to speak unobserved.

Judithe stood beside Mrs. McVeigh on the veranda exchanging good nights with some of the people, who expected to be her neighbors in the near future, and who were delighted with the prospect. She had been a decided success with the warm-hearted Southerners, and had entered the rooms a short time after her interview with her host, so gay, so bright, that he could scarcely believe those brilliant eyes were the ones he had seen tear-wet in the dusk. She had not avoided him, but she had made a tete-a-tete impossible; for all that he could only remember the moment when she had leaned upon his breast and confessed that the love was not all on his side; no after attempt at indifference could erase an iota of that!

Monroe stopped to look at her, himself unseen, and as she stood there smiling, gracious, the very star of the evening, he thought he had never before seen her so absolutely sparkling. He had always known her beautiful; tonight she was regal beyond comparison. Always in the years to follow he thought of her as she stood there that night, radiant, dominant, at the very pinacle of success in all things. He never again saw her like that.

As he passed on he relit the cigar, forgotten during his meeting with Masterson, and Pluto, who had been on nettles of anxiety to get away from his duties all the evening, seized the opportunity when no one was looking, and followed closely the light of the cigar as it moved along the hedge past the dining room windows.

He carried the treasured bag holding the dead Rosa's belongings.

"Couldn't get away a mite sooner, not to save me, Mahsa Captain," he said, breathlessly; "had to run now to get 'way from them niggahs in the kitchen, who wanted to know what I was toten. I had this here hid in the pantry whah I had no chance to look through it, so if you'll s'cuse me I jest gwine dump em out right heah; the picture case, it's plum down in the bottom; I felt it."

Monroe smoked in silence while the darky was making the search. He no longer needed the picture in order to convince Madame Caron of the truth of Pluto's story, yet concluded it best that she have possession of so compromising a portrait until her clever maid was out of the country.

He could hear Colonel McVeigh asking for Pluto, and Caroline offering information that "Pluto jest gone out throught the pantry."

"You'd better hurry, my man," suggested Monroe, "they'll be looking for you."

"They will that—folks all gwine home, an' need a sight o' waiten' on; thah's the likeness, Mahs Captain;" he handed him a small oval frame, commenced crowding the other articles hurriedly back into the bag; "fo' God's sake, be careful o' that; I don' want it to fetch harm to that gal, but I don' allow neither fo' Madame Caron to be made trouble if I can help it."

"You're a faithful fellow; there's a coin in exchange for the picture; you'd better go. I'll see you in the morning."

Pluto was profuse in his thanks, while Monroe hunted for a match with which to view the picture.

He struck a light and opened the little closed frame as Pluto started for the side door. An instant later he snapped

22

it shut again, and as the darky reached the steps Monroe's hand was on his shoulder:

"Wait a bit," he said, briefly. "You say that is the picture of Rhoda's mother? Now tell me again what her name is."

"Who?—Margeret? Why, her name Margeret Loring, I reckon, but Nelse did say her right name was 'Caris—Lacaris. Retta Lacaris what she called when she jest a young gal an' Mahs Tom Loring fust bought her."

Monroe repeated the name in order to impress it on his memory. He took a pencil and note book out of his pocket.

Pluto half offered his hand for the little oval frame, for there was enough light where they stood to see it by, but Monroe slipped it with the note book into an inner pocket. "The Colonel will want you; you had better go," he said, turning away, and walking directly from the house he crossed the lawn out of sight and hearing of the departing guests. All the gay chatter jarred on him, oppressed as he was with the certainty of some unknown calamity overhanging those laughing people on the veranda. What it was he did not know, but he would leave in the morning.

He had been gone an hour. He was missed, but no one except Masterson took any special notice of it, and he was wary about asking questions, remembering Colonel McVeigh's attitude in the morning over the disputed question. But as he was enjoying a final cigar with Judge Clarkson on the lawn—the Judge was the very last to leave and was waiting for his horse—all his suspicions were revived with added strength as McVeigh strode hurriedly across the veranda towards them.

"Phil, I was looking for you," and his tone betrayed unusual anxiety reflected in his face as he glanced around to see if there were possible listeners. But the rooms on the first floor were deserted—all dark but for a solitary light in the hall. In the upper rooms little gleams stole out from the sleeping rooms where the ladies had retired for the night.

"Anything wrong, Colonel?" asked Masterson, speaking in a suppressed tone and meeting him at the foot of the steps.

"Who is that with you, the Judge?" asked McVeigh first. "Good! I'm glad you are here. Something astounding has occurred, gentlemen. The papers, the instructions you brought today, together with some other documents of importance, have been stolen from my room tonight!"

"Ah-h!" Masterson's voice was scarcely above a whisper. All his suspicions blazed again. Now he understood Monroe's presence there.

"But, my dear boy," gasped the Judge, thunderstruck at the news, "your commission stolen? Why, how—"

"The commission is the least important part of it," answered McVeigh hopelessly. He was pacing back and forth in decided agitation. "The commission was forwarded me with instructions to take charge of the entire division during the temporary absence of the Major General commanding."

"And you have lost those instructions?" demanded Masterson, who realized the serious consequences impending.

"Yes," and McVeigh halted in his nervous walk, "I have lost those instructions. I have lost the entire plan of movement! It has been stolen from my room—is perhaps now in the hands of the enemy, and I ignorant of the contents! I had only glanced at them and meant to go over them thoroughly tonight. They are gone, and it means failure, court martial, disgrace!"

He had dropped hopelessly on the lower step, his face buried in his hands; the contrast to the joy, the absolute happiness of an hour ago was overwhelming. Masterson stood looking at him, thinking fast, and wondering how much he dared express.

"When did you discover the loss, Colonel?"

"Just now," he answered, rising and commencing again the nervous pacing. "I had gone to my room with Dr. Delaven to find an old uniform of mine he had asked to borrow. Then I found the drawer of my desk open and my papers gone. I said nothing to him of the loss. Any search to be made must be conducted without publicity."

"Certainly, certainly," agreed Judge Clarkson, "but a search, Kenneth, my boy? Where could we begin?"

McVeigh shook his head, but Masterson remembered that Delaven was also an outsider— and Delaven had borrowed a Confederate uniform!

"Colonel," he asked, with a significance he tried ineffectually to subdue, for all subterfuge was difficult to his straightforward nature, "may I ask for what purpose that uniform was borrowed?"

The tone was unmistakable. McVeigh turned as if struck.

"Captain Masterson!"

"Colonel, this is no time to stand on ceremony. Some one who was your guest tonight evidently stole those papers! Most of the guests were old, tried friends, but there were exceptions. Two are foreigners, and one belongs to the enemy. It is most natural that the exceptions be considered first." Clarkson nodded assent to this very logical deduction and Masterson felt assured of his support. "The borrowing of the uniform in itself is significant, but at this time is especially so."

"No, no, no!" and his superior officer waved aside the question impatiently. "Dr. Delaven is above suspicion; he is about to offer his services as surgeon to our cause—talked to me of it tonight. The uniform was for some jest with my sister. It has nothing whatever to do with this."

"What became of the man you suspected as a spy this morning?" asked the Judge, and McVeigh also looked at Masterson for reply.

"No, it was not he," said the latter, decidedly. "He was watched every minute of his stay here, and his stay was very brief. But Colonel McVeigh—Kenneth; even at the risk of your displeasure I must remind you that Dr. Delaven is not the only guest here who is either neutral or pledged to the cause of our enemies—I mean Captain Jack Monroe."

"Impossible!" said McVeigh; but Masterson shook his head.

"If the name of every guest here tonight were mentioned you would feel justified in saying the same thing—impossible, yet it has been possible, since the papers are gone. Who but the Federals would want them? Captain Monroe of the Federal army allowed himself to be taken prisoner this morning and brought to your home, though he had a parole in his pocket! The careless reason he gave for it did not satisfy me, and now even you must agree that it looks suspicious."

McVeigh glanced from one to the other in perplexity. He felt that the Judge agreed with Masterson; he was oppressed by the memory of the accusation against the sailor that morning. Spies and traitors at McVeigh Terrace! He had placed his orderly on guard in the room so soon as he discovered the rifled drawer, and had at once come to Masterson for consultation, but once there no solution of the problem suggested itself. There seemed literally no starting point for investigation. The crowd of people there had made the difficulty greater, for servants of the guests had also been there—drivers and boatmen. Yet who among them could have access to the rooms of the family? He shook his head at Masterson's suggestion.

"Your suspicions against Captain Monroe are without foundation," he said decidedly. "The papers had not yet reached me when he arrived. He had no knowledge of their existence."

"How do we know that?" demanded Masterson. "Do you forget that he was present when I gave you the papers?"

McVeigh stopped short and stared at him. By the thin edge of the wedge of suspicion a door seemed forced back and a flood of revelations forced in.

"By Jove!" he said, slowly, "and he heard me speak of the importance of my instructions!"

"Where is he now?" asked the Judge. "I have not seen him for an hour; but there seems only one thing to be done."

"Certainly," agreed Masterson, delighted that McVeigh at last began to look with reason on his own convictions. "He should be arrested at once."

"We must not be hasty in this matter, it is so important," said McVeigh. "Phil, I will ask you to see that a couple of horses are saddled. Have your men do it without arousing the servants' suspicions. I am going to my room for a more thorough investigation. Come with me, Judge, if you please. I am glad you remained. I don't want any of the others to know what occurred. I can't believe it of Monroe —yet."

"Kenneth, my boy, I don't like to crush any lingering faith you have in your Northern friend," said Clarkson, laying his hand affectionately on McVeigh's arm as they reached the steps, "but from the evidence before us I—I'm afraid he's gone! He'll never come back!"

At that moment a low, lazy sort of whistle sounded across

the lawn, so low and so slow that it was apparently an unconscious accompaniment to reverie or speculation. It was
quite dark except where the light shone from the hall. All
the gaudy paper lanterns had been extinguished, and when
the confidential notes of "Rally 'round the flag, boys," came
closer, and the whistler emerged from the deeper shadows,
he could only distinguish two figures at the foot of the
steps, and they could only locate him by the glow of his
cigar in the darkness.

There was a moment's pause and then the whistler said,
"Hello! Friends or foes?"

"Captain Jack!" said McVeigh, with a note of relief in his
voice, very perceptible to the Judge, who felt a mingling of
delight and surprise at his failure as a prophet.

"Oh, it's you, is it, Colonel?" and Monroe came leisurely
forward. "I fancied every one but myself had gone to bed
when I saw the lights out. I walked away across your fields,
smoking."

The others did not speak. They could not at once throw
aside the constraint imposed by the situation. He felt it as
he neared the steps, but remarked carelessly:

"Cloudy, isn't it? I am not much of a weather prophet,
but feel as if there is a storm in the air."

"Yes," agreed McVeigh, with an abstracted manner. He
was not thinking of the probable storm, but of what action
he had best take in the matter, whether to have the suspected
man secretly watched, or to make a plain statement of the
case, and show that the circumstantial evidence against him
was too decided to be ignored.

"Well, Colonel, you've helped me to a delightful evening,"
continued the unsuspecting suspect. "I shall carry away
most pleasant memories of your plantation hospitality, and
have concluded to start with them in the morning." There

was a slight pause, then he added: "Sorry I can't stay another day, but I've been thinking it over, and it seems necessary for me to move on to the coast."

"Not going to run from the enemy?" asked Clarkson, with a doubtful attempt at lightness.

"Not necessary, Judge; so I shall retreat in good order." He ascended the steps, yawning slightly. "You two going to stay up all night?"

"No," said McVeigh, "I've just been persuading Judge Clarkson to remain; we'll be in presently."

"Well, I'll see you in the morning, gentlemen. Good night."

They exchanged good nights, and he entered the house, still with that soft whisper of a whistle as accompaniment. It grew softer as he entered the house, and the two stood there until the last sound had died away.

"Going in the morning, Kenneth," said the Judge, meaningly. "Now, what do you think?"

"That Masterson is right," answered McVeigh. "He is the last man I should have suspected, but there seems nothing to do except make the arrest at once, or put him secretly under surveillance without his knowledge. I incline to the latter, but will consult with Masterson. Come in."

They entered the hall, where McVeigh shut the door and turned the light low as they passed through. Pluto was nodding. half asleep in the back hall, and his master told him to go to bed, he would not be needed. Though he had formed no definite plan of action he felt that the servants had best be kept ignorant of all movements for the present. Somebody's servants might have helped with that theft, why not his own?

In the upper hall he passed Margeret, who was entering

the room of Miss Loring with a pitcher of water. The hall was dark as they passed the corridor leading to the rooms of Madame Caron, Evilena, Miss Loring and Captain Monroe. Light showed above the doors of Miss Loring and Monroe. The other rooms were already dark.

The two men paused long enough to note those details, then McVeigh walked to the end of the corridor and bolted the door to the balcony. Monroe was still softly whistling at intervals. He would cease occasionally and then, after a few moments, would commence again where he had left off. He was evidently very busy or very much preoccupied. To leave his room and descend the stairs he would have to pass McVeigh's room, which was on the first landing. The orderly was on guard there, within. McVeigh sent him with a message to Masterson, who was in the rear of the building. The man passed out along the back corridor and the other two entered the room, but left the door ajar.

In the meantime a man who had been watching Monroe's movements in the park for some time now crept closer to the house. He watched him enter the house and the other two follow. He could not hear what they said, but the closing of the door told him the house was closed for the night. The wind was rising and low clouds were scurrying past. Now and then the stars were allowed to peep through, showing a faint light, and any one close to him would have seen that he wore a Confederate uniform and that his gaze was concentrated on the upper balcony. At last he fancied he could distinguish a white figure against the glass door opening from the corridor. Assuring himself of the fact he stepped forward into the open and was about to cross the little space before the house when he was conscious of another figure, also in gray uniform, and the unmistakable cavalry hat, coming stealthily from the other side of the house.

The second figure also glanced upwards at the balcony, but was too close to perceive the slender form above moving against one of the vine-covered pillars when the figure draped in white bent over as though trying to decipher the features under the big hat, and just as the second comer made a smothered attempt to clear his throat, something white fell at his feet.

"Sweet Evilena!" he said, picking it up. "Faith, the mother has told her and the darling was waiting for me. Delaven's private post office!" He laid down the guitar and fumbled for a match, when the watcher from the shadows leaped upon him from behind, throttling him that no sound be made, and while he pinned him to the ground with his knee, kept one hand on his throat and with the other tried to loosen the grasp of Delaven's hand on the papers.

"Give me that paper!" he whispered fiercely. "Give it to me or I'll kill you where you lay! Give it to me!"

In the struggle Delaven struck the guitar with the heel of his boot, there was a crash of resonant wood, and a wail of the strings, and it reached the ears of Masterson and the orderly, who were about to enter the side door from the arbor.

Masterson halted to listen whence the crash came, but the orderly's ears were more accurate and he dashed towards the corner.

"Captain," he called in a loud whisper, as he saw the struggling figures, and at the call and the sound of quick steps Pierson leaped to his feet and ran for the shrubbery.

"Halt!" called Masterson, and fired one shot from his revolver. The fugitive leaped to one side as the order rang out and the bullet went whistling past. He had cleared the

open space and was in the shrubbery. The orderly dashed
after him as Masterson caught Delaven, who was scrambling
to his feet, feeling his throat and trying to take a full breath.

"Who are you?" demanded Masterson, shaking him a
trifle to hasten the smothered speech. "Doctor Delaven!
You! Who was that man?"

"It's little I can tell you," gasped the other, "except that
he's some murderous rival who wanted to make an angel
of me. Man, but he has a grip!"

Margeret suddenly appeared on the veranda with a lamp
held high above her head, as she peered downward in the
darkness, and by its light Masterson scanned the appearance of Delaven with a doubtful eye.

"Why did the man assault you?" he demanded, and Delaven showed the long envelope.

"He was trying to rob me of a letter let fall from the
balcony above, bad luck to him!"

At that moment the orderly came running back to say
that the man had got away; a horse had been tied over in
the pines, they could hear the beat of its hoofs now on the
big road.

"Get a horse and follow him," ordered Masterson briefly,
as McVeigh and Clarkson came down the stairs and past
Margeret. "Arrest him, shoot him, fetch him back some
way!" Then he turned again to the would-be cavalier of
romance, who was surveying the guitar disconsolately.

"Doctor Delaven, what are you doing in that uniform?"

"I was about to give a concert," returned that individual,
who made a grotesque figure in the borrowed suit, a world
too large for him.

McVeigh laughed as he heard the reply and surveyed the
speaker. Masterson's persistent search for spies had evidently spoiled Delaven's serenade.

Mrs. McVeigh opened a window and asked what the trouble was, and Masterson assured her it was only an accident—his revolver had gone off, but no one was hurt, on which assurance she said good night and closed the window, while the group stood looking at each other questioningly. Masterson's manner showed that it was something more than an accident.

"What is the meaning of this?" asked McVeigh in a guarded tone; and Masterson pointed to the package in Delaven's hand.

"I think we've found it, Colonel," he said, excitedly. "Doctor Delaven, what is in that envelope?"

"Faith, I don't know, Captain. The fellow didn't give me time to read it."

"Give it to me."

"No, I'll not," returned Delaven, moving towards the light.

"And why not?" demanded Masterson, suspiciously.

"Because it's from a lady, and it's private."

He held the envelope to the light, but there was no name or address on it. He tore off the end and in extracting the contents two papers slipped out and fell on the ground. Masterson picked them up and after a glance waved them triumphantly, while Delaven looked puzzled over the slip in his hands. It was only something about military matters, —the furthest thing possible from a billet-doux.

"I thought myself it was the weightiest one ever launched by Cupid," he remarked as he shook his head over the mystery. But Masterson thrust the papers into McVeigh's hands.

"Your commission and instructions, Colonel!" he said, jubilantly. "What a run of luck. See if they are all right."

"Every one of them," and in a moment the Judge and

Masterson were shaking hands with him, while Delaven stood apart and stared. He was glad they were having so much joy to themselves, but could not see why he should be choked to obtain it for them.

"Understand one thing," said Masterson, when the congratulations were over; "those papers were thrown from that balcony to Dr. Delaven by mistake. The man they were meant for tried to strangle the doctor and has escaped, but the man who escaped, Colonel, was evidently only a messenger, and the real culprit, the traitor, is in your house now, and reached the balcony through that corridor door!"

The wind blew Margeret's lamp out, leaving them, for an instant, in darkness, but she entered the hall, turned up the light there so that it shone across the veranda and down the steps; then she lit the lamp in the library and went softly up the stairs and out of sight.

"Come into the library," suggested McVeigh. "You are right, Phil, there is only one thing to be done in the face of such evidence By Jove! It seems incredible. I would have fought for Jack Monroe, sworn by him, and after all—"

A leisurely step sounded on the stairs and Monroe descended. He wore no coat or vest and was evidently prepared for bed when disturbed.

"What's all the row about?" he asked, yawning. Oh, are you in it, Colonel?"

There was a slight pause before McVeigh said:

"Captain Monroe, the row is over for the present, since your confederate has escaped."

"My—confederate?"

He glanced in inquiry from one to the other, but could see no friendliness in their faces. Delaven looked as puzzled as himself, but the other three regarded him coldly. He tossed his half finished cigar out of the door, and seemed to grow taller, as he turned toward them again.

"May I ask in what way I am linked with a confederacy."

"In using your parole to gain knowledge of our army for the use of the Federal government," answered McVeigh, bluntly.

Monroe made a step forward, but halted, drew a long breath, and thrust his uninjured hand into his pocket, as if to hamper its aggressive tendencies.

"Is it considered a part of Southern hospitality that the host reserves the right to insult his guests?" he asked slowly. Masterson's face flushed with anger at the sweeping suggestion, but McVeigh glanced at him warningly.

"This is not a time for useless words, Captain Monroe, and it seems useless to discuss the rights of the hospitality you have outraged."

"That is not true, Colonel McVeigh," and his tones were very steady as he made the denial. His very steadiness and cool selfcontrol angered McVeigh, who had hoped to see him astonished, indignant, natural.

"Not true?" he demanded. "Is it not true that you were received here as a friend, welcomed as a brother? That you listened this morning when those military dispatches reached me? That you heard me say they were very important? That as soon as they were stolen from my room tonight you announced that you could not prolong your stay, your object in coming having evidently been accomplished? Is it not true that today you managed to divert suspicion from yourself to an innocent lady? The authorities were evidently right who had that sailor followed here; but unknown to her it was not his employer he came here to meet, but *you*, his confederate! He was only the messenger, while you were the real spy—the officer who has broken his parole of honor."

Monroe had listened with set teeth to the accusation, a certain doggedness in his expression as the list of his delinquencies were reviewed, but at the final sentence the clenched hand shot forward and he struck McVeigh a wicked blow, staggering him back against the wall.

"You are a liar and a fool, Colonel McVeigh," he said in a choked voice, his face white with anger.

The Judge and Masterson interposed as McVeigh lunged forward at him, and then he controlled his voice enough to say, "Captain Monroe, you are under arrest."

And the commotion and deep breathing of the men prevented them hearing the soft rustle of a woman's dress in the hall as Judithe slipped away into the darkness of the sitting room, and thence up the back stairs.

She had followed Monroe as he passed her door. She heard all their words, and the final ones: *"Captain Monroe, you are under arrest!"* rang in her ears all night as she tossed sleepless in the darkness. That is what Kenneth McVeigh would say to her if he knew the truth. Well, he should know it. Captain Monroe was sacrificing himself for her. How she admired him! Did he fancy she would allow it? Yet that shot alarmed her. She heard them say Pierson had escaped, but had he retained the papers? If she was quite sure of *that* she would announce the truth at once and clear him. But the morning was so near. She must wait a few hours longer, and then—then Kenneth McVeigh would say to her, *"You are under arrest,"* and after all her success would come defeat.

She had never yet met defeat, and it was not pleasant to contemplate. She remembered his words of love—the adoration in his eye; would that love protect her when he learned

she was the traitor to his home and country? She smiled
bitterly at the thought, and felt that she could see clearly
how *that* would end. He would be patriot first and lover
after, unless it was some one of his own family—some one
whose honor meant his honor—some one—

Then in the darkness she laughed at a sudden
remembrance, and rising from the couch paced feverishly
the length of the room many times, and stood gazing out
at the stars swept by fleecy clouds.

Out there on the lawn he had vowed his love for her,
asked her to marry him—marry him at once, before he
left to join his brigade. She had not the slightest idea of
doing it then; but now, why not? It could be entirely
secret—so he had said. It would merely be a betrothal with
witnesses, *and* it would make her so much a part of the
McVeigh family that he must let Captain Jack go on her
word. And before the dawn broke she had decided her plan
of action. If he said, "*You are under arrest*" to her, it should
be to his own wife!

She plunged into the idea with the reckless daring of a
gamester who throws down his last card to win or lose.
It had to be played any way, so why not double the stakes?
She had played on that principle in some of the most fashionable gaming places of Europe in search of cure for the
ennui she complained of to Captain Jack; so why not in this
more vital game of living pawns?

She had wept in the dark of the garden when his lips had
touched her; she had said, wild, impulsive things; she had
been a fool; but in the light of the new day she set her
teeth and determined the folly was over—only one day remained. Military justice—or injustice—moved swiftly, and
there was a man's life to be saved.

CHAPTER XXVIII.

The sun was just peeping, fiery red and threatening, above the bank of clouds to the east when Delaven was roused from sweet sleep by the apparition of Colonel McVeigh, booted, spurred and ready for the saddle.

"I want you to come riding with me, and to come quick," he said, with a face singularly bright and happy, considering the episode of the night before, and the fact that his former friend was now a prisoner in a cottage back of the dwelling house, guarded by the orderlies.

He had dispatched a courier for a detachment of men from one of the fortifications along the river. He would send Monroe in their charge to Charleston with a full statement of the case before he left to join his brigade—and ere that time :—

Close to his heart lay the little note Pluto had brought him less than an hour before, the second written word he had ever received from Judithe. The first had sent him away from her—but this!

So Delaven dressed himself quickly, ate the impromptu breakfast arranged by the Colonel's order, and joined Judithe at the steps as the horses were brought around.

She was gracious and gay as usual, and replied to his gallant remarks with her usual self-possession, yet he fancied her a trifle nervous, as was to be expected, and that she avoided his gaze, looking over him, past him, every place

23

but in his eyes, at which he did not wonder especially. Of all the women he had known she was the last to associate with a hurried clandestine marriage. Of course it was all explained by the troublous war times, and the few brief hours, and above all by the love he had always fancied those two felt for each other.

They had a five mile ride to the country home of a disabled chaplain who had belonged to McVeigh's regiment—had known him from boyhood, and was home now nursing a shattered arm, and was too well used to these hurried unions of war times to wonder much at the Colonel's request, and only slightly puzzled at the added one of secrecy.

At the Terrace no one was surprised at the early ride of the three, even though the morning was not a bright one. Madame Caron had made them accustomed to those jaunts in the dawn, and Mrs. McVeigh was relieved to learn that Kenneth had accompanied her. Shocked as she was to hear of Monroe's arrest, and the cause of it, she was comforted somewhat that Kenneth did not find the affair serious enough to interfere with a trifle of attention to her guest.

In fact the Colonel had not, in the note hastily scribbled to his mother, given her anything like a serious account of the case. Captain Monroe had for certain military reasons been placed under guard until an escort could arrive and accompany him to Charleston for some special investigations. She was not to be disturbed or alarmed because of it; only, no one was to be allowed to see or speak with him without a special permit. He would explain more fully on his return, and only left the note to explain why Captain Monroe would breakfast alone.

Matthew Loring also breakfasted alone. He was in a most excitable state over the occurrence of the night before, which Judge Clarkson was called on to relate, and concerning which he made all the reservations possible, all of them entirely acceptable to his listeners with the exception of Miss Loring, who heard, and then sent for Phil Masterson.

She was talking with him on the lawn when the three riders returned, and when Kenneth McVeigh bent above Judithe with some laughing words as he led her up the steps, the heart of his girl-playmate grew sick within her. She had feared and dreaded this foreign exquisite from the first ; now, she knew why.

Evilena was also watching for their return and gave Delaven a cool little nod in contrast to the warm greeting given her brother and Madame Caron. But instead of being chilled he only watched his opportunity to whisper:

"I wore the uniform!"

She tossed her head and found something interesting in the view on the opposite side of the lawn. He waited meekly, plucked some roses, which he presented in silence and she regarded with scorn. But as she did not move away more than two feet he took heart of grace and repeated:

"I wore the uniform!"

"Yes," she said, with fine scorn, "wore it in our garden, where you were safe!"

"Arrah! Was I now?" he asked in his best brogue. "Well, it's myself thought I was anything but safe for a few minutes. But I saved the papers, and your brother was good enough to say I'd saved his honor."

"You!"

"Just me, and no other," he affirmed. "Didn't I hold on to those instructions while that Yankee spy was trying to send me to —heaven? And if that was not helping the cause and risking my life, well now, what would you call it?"

"Oh!" gasped Evilena, delightedly, "I never thought of

that. Why, you were a real hero after all. I'm so glad, I—"

Then realizing that her exuberance was little short of caressing, and that she actually had both hands on his arm,
she drew back and added demurely that she would always
keep those roses, and she would like to keep the guitar, too,
just as it was, for her mama agreed that it was a real romance of a serenade—the serenade that was not sung.

After which, he assured her, the serenades under her window should not always be silent ones, and they went in
search of the broken guitar.

Judge Clarkson was pacing the veranda with well con-
cealed impatience. Colonel McVeigh's ride had interfered
with the business talk he had planned. Matthew Loring was
decidedly irritable over it, and he, Clarkson, was the one
who, with Gertrude, had to hear the complaints. But looking in Kenneth's happy face he could not begrudge him
those brief morning hours at Beauty's side, and only asked
his consideration for the papers at the earliest convenient
moment, and at the same time asked if the cottage was really
a safe place for so important a prisoner as Monroe.

"Perfectly safe," decided McVeigh, "so safe that there is
no danger of escape ; and as I think over the whole affair I
doubt if on trial anything in this world can save him."

"Well, I should hate to take his chances in the next," declared the Judge; "it seems so incredible that a man possessed of the courage, the admirable attributes you have always ascribed to him, should prove so unworthy—a broken
parole. Why, sir, it is—is damnable, sir, damnable !"

Colonel McVeigh agreed, and Clarkson left the room
without perceiving that Madame Caron had been a listener,
but she came in, removing her gloves and looking at the
tiny band of gold on her third finger.

"The Judge referred to Captain Monroe, did he not?"

she asked, glancing up at him. "Kenneth"—and her manner was delightfully appealing as she spoke his name in a shy little whisper, "Kenneth, there may be some horrible mistake. Your friend—that was—may be innocent."

"Scarcely a chance of it, sweetheart," and he removed her other glove and kissed her fingers, glancing around first, to see that no one was in sight.

She laughed at his little picture of nervousness, but returned to the subject.

"But if it were so?" she persisted; "surely you will not counsel haste in deciding so serious a matter?"

"At any rate, I mean to put aside so serious a subject of conversation on our wedding morning," he answered, and she smiled back at him as she said:

"On our wedding morning, sir, you should be mercifully disposed towards all men."

"We never class traitors as men," and his fine face grew stern for an instant, "they are vampires, birds of prey. A detail has been sent for to take him to court-martial; there is little doubt what the result will be, and—"

"Suppose," and she glanced up at him with a pretty appeal in her eyes, "that your wife, sir, should ask as a first favor on her wedding day that you be merciful, as the rules of war allow you to be, to this poor fellow who danced with us last night? Even supposing he is most horribly wicked, yet he really did dance with us—danced very well, and was very amusing. So, why not grant him another day of grace? No?" as he shook his head. "Well, Monsieur, I have a fancy ill luck must come if you celebrate our wedding day by hastening a man to meet his death. Let him remain here under guard until tomorrow?"

He shook his head, smilingly.

"No, Judithe."

"Not even for me?"

"Anything else, sweetheart, but not that. It is really out of my power to delay, now, even if I wished. The guard will come for him some time this evening. I, myself, shall leave at dawn tomorrow; so, you see!—"

She glanced at him in playful reproach, a gay irresponsible specimen of femininity, who would ignore a man's treason because he chanced to be a charming partner in the dance.

"My very first request! So, Monsieur, this is how you mean to love, honor and obey me?"

He laughed and caught the uplifted forefinger with which she admonished him.

"I shall be madly jealous in another minute," he declared, with mock ferocity; "you have been my wife two full hours and half of that precious time you have wasted pleading the cause of a possible rival, for he actually did look at you with more than a passing admiration, Judithe, it was a case of witchery at first sight; but for all that I refuse to allow him to be a skeleton at our feast this morning. There comes Phil Masterson for me, I must go; but remember, this is not a day for considerations of wars and retribution; it is a day for love."

"I shall remember," she said, quietly, and walked to the window looking out on the swaying limbs of the great trees; they were being swept by gusts of wind, driving threatening clouds from which the trio had ridden in haste lest a rain storm be back of their shadows. The storm Monroe had prophesied the night before had delayed and grumbled on the way, but it was coming for all that, and she welcomed the coming. A storm would probably delay that guard for which McVeigh had sent, and even the delay of a few hours might mean safety for Captain Monroe; otherwise, she—

She had learned all about the adventures of the papers, and had made her plans. Some time during that day or evening there would be a raid made on the Terrace by Federals in Confederate uniform. They would probably be thought by the inmates a party of daring foragers. and would visit the smoke houses, and confiscate the contents of the pantry. Incidentally they would carry Colonel McVeigh and Captain Masterson back to the coast as prisoners, if the required papers were not found, otherwise nothing of person or property would be molested by them; *and* they would, of course, free Captain Monroe, but force him, also, to go with them until within Federal lines and safety.

She had planned it all out, and knew it would not be difficult. The coast was not far away, a group of men in Confederate uniform could ride across the country to the Salkahatchie, at that point, unobserved. The fortifications on the river had men coming and going, though not thoroughly manned, and just now the upper one had no men stationed there, which accounted for the fact that Colonel McVeigh had to send farther for extra men. He could not spare his own orderlies, and Masterson's had not yet returned from following Pierson. Unless the raiders should meet with a detachment of bona-fide Confederates there was not one chance in fifty of them being suspected if they came by the back roads she had mapped out and suggested; *and* if they reached the Terrace before the Confederate guard, Monroe would be freed.

She had not known there was that hope when she wrote the note consenting to the marriage. She heard they had sent down to the fort for some men and supposed it was the first fort on the river—merely an hour's ride away. It was not until they were in the saddle that she learned it would

be an all day's journey to the fort and back, and that
the colored carrier had just started.

She knew that if it were a possible thing some message
would be sent to her by the Federals as to the hour she
might expect them, but if it were not possible—well—

She chafed under the uncertainty, and watched the storm
approaching over the far level lands of the east. Blue black
clouds rolled now where the sun had shot brief red glances
on rising. Somewhere there under those heavy shadows the
men she waited for were riding to her through the pine
woods and over the swamp lands; if she had been a praying
woman she would have prayed that they ride faster—no
music so longed for as the jingle of their accoutrements!

She avoided the rest and retired to her own room on the
plea of fatigue. Colonel McVeigh was engaged with his
mother and Judge Clarkson on some affairs of the plantation, so very much had to be crowded into his few hours
at home. Money had to be raised, property had to be sold,
and the salable properties were growing so few in those
days.

Masterson was waiting impatiently for the Colonel, whom
he had only seen for the most brief exchange of words that
morning. It was now noon. He had important news to communicate before that guard arrived for Monroe; it might en-
tail surprising disclosures, and the minutes seemed like
hours to him, while Judge Clarkson leisurely presented one
paper after another for Kenneth's perusal and signature,
and Mrs. McVeigh listened and asked advice.

Judithe descended the stairs, radiant in a gown of fluffy
yellow stuff, with girdle of old topaz and a fillet of the same
in quaint dull settings. The storm had grown terrific—the
heavy clouds trailing to the earth and the lightning flashes
lit up dusky corners. Evilena had proposed darkening the

windows entirely, lighting the lamps to dispel the gloom, and dressing in their prettiest to drive away forgetfulness of the tragedy of the elements; it was Kenneth's last day at home; they must be gay though the heavens fell.

Thus it was that the sitting room and dining room presented the unusual mid-day spectacle of jewels glittering in the lamplight, for Gertrude also humored Evilena's whim to the extent of a dainty dress of softest sky blue silk, half covered with the finest work of delicate lace; she wore a pretty brooch and bracelet of turquoise, and was a charming picture of blonde beauty, a veritable white lily of a woman. Dr. Delaven, noting the well-bred grace, the gentle, unassuming air so truly refined and patrician, figuratively took off his hat to the Colonel, who, between two such alluring examples of femininity, two women of such widely different types as the Parisian and the Carolinian, had even been able to make a choice. For he could see what every one but Kenneth could see plainly, that while Miss Loring was gracious and interested in her other men friends, he remained, as ever, her one hero, apart from, and above all others, and if Judithe de Caron had not appeared upon the scene—

Gertrude looked even lovelier than she had the night before at the party. Her cheeks had a color unusual, and her eyes were bright with hope, expectation, or some unspoken cause for happiness; it sounded in the tones of her voice and shone in the happy curves of her lips as she smiled.

"Look at yourself in the glass, Gertrude," said Evilena, dragging her to the long mirror in the sitting room, "you are always lovely, dear, but today you are entrancingly beautiful."

"Today I am entrancingly happy," returned Miss Loring, looking in the mirror, but seeing in it not herself, but Judithe, who was crossing the hall, and who looked like a Spanish picture in her gleam of yellow tissues and topazes.

"Wasn't it clever of me to think of lighting the lamps?" asked Evilena in frank self-laudation, "just listen how that rain beats; and did you see the hail? Well, it fell, lots of it, while we were dressing; that's what makes the air so cool. I hope it will storm all the rain down at once and then give us a clear day tomorrow, when Kenneth has to go away."

"It would be awful for any one to be out in a storm like this," remarked the other as the crash of thunder shook the house; "what about Captain Monroe having to go through it?"

"Caroline said the guard has just got here, so I suppose he will have to go no matter what the weather is. Well, I suppose he'd just as soon be killed by the storm as to be shot for a spy. Only think of it—a guest of ours to be taken away as a spy!"

"It is dreadful," assented Gertrude, and then looking at Judithe, she added, "I hope you were not made nervous by the shot and excitement last night; I assure you we do not usually have such finales to our parties."

"I am not naturally timid, thank you," returned Judithe, with a careless smile, all the more careless that she felt the blue eyes were regarding her with unusual watchfulness; "one must expect all those inconveniences in war times, especially when people are located on the border land, and I hear it is really but a short ride to the coast, where your enemies have their war vessels for blockade. Did I understand you to say the military men have come for your friend, the Federal Captain? What a pity! He danced so well!"

And with the careless smile still on her lips, she passed them and crossed the hall to the library.

Evilena shook her head and sighed. "*I* am just broken hearted over his arrest," she acknowledged, "but it is because—well, it is *not* merely because he was a good dancer! Gertrude, I—I did something horrid this morning, I just *could* not eat my breakfast without showing my sympathy in some way. You know those last cookies I baked? Well, I had some of those sent over with his breakfast."

"Poor fellow!" and Delaven shook his head sadly over the fate of Monroe. Evilena eyed him suspiciously; but his face was all innocence and sympathy.

"It is terrible," she assented; "poor mama just wept this morning when we heard of it; of course, if he really proves to be a spy, we should not care what happened to him; but mama thinks of his mother, and of his dead brother, and —well, we both prayed for him this morning; it was all we could do. Kenneth says no one must go near him, and of course Kenneth knows what is best; but we are both hoping with all our hearts that he had nothing to do with that spy; funny, isn't it, that we are praying and crying on account of a man who, after all, is a real Yankee?"

"Faith, I'd turn Yankee myself for the same sweet sympathy," declared Delaven, and received only a reproachful glance for his frivolity.

Judithe crossed the hall to the library, the indifferent smile still on her lips, her movements graceful and unhurried; under the curious eyes of Gertrude Loring she would show no special interest in the man under discussion, or the guard just arrived, but for all that the arrival of the guard determined her course. All her courage was needed to face the inevitable; the inevitable had arrived, and she was not a coward.

She looked at the wedding ring on her finger; it had been the wedding ring of the dowager long ago, and she had

given it to Kenneth McVeigh that morning for the ceremony.

"Maman would approve if she knew all," she assured herself, and now she touched the ring to remind her of many
things, and to blot out the rememberance of others, for in-
stance, the avowal of love under the arbor in the dusk of the
night before!

"But *that* was last night," she thought, grimly; "the
darkness made me impressionable, the situation made of me
a nervous fool, who said the thing she felt and had no right
to feel. It is no longer night, and I am no longer a fool!
Do not let me forget, little ring, why I allowed you to be
placed there. I am going to tell him now, and I shall need
you and—Maman."

So she passed into the library; there could be no further
delay, since the guard had arrived; Monroe should not be
sacrificed.

She closed the door after her and looked around. A man
was in the large arm chair by the table, but it was not Colonel McVeigh. It was Matthew Loring, whose man Ben
was closing a refractory banging shutter, and drawing curtains over the windows, while Pluto brought in a lighted
lamp for the table, and both of them listened stoically to
Loring's grumbling.

For a wonder he approved of the innovation of lamps
and closed shutters. He had, in fact, come from his own
room because of the fury of the storm. He growled that the
noise of it annoyed him, but would not have acknowledged
the truth, that the force of it appalled him, and that he
shrank from being alone while the lightning threw threats
in every direction, and the crashes of thunder shook the
house.

"No, Kenneth isn't here," he answered, grumpily. "They told me he was, but the nigger lied."

"Mahsa Kenneth jest gone up to his own room, Madame Caron," said Pluto, quietly. "Mist'ess, she went, too, an' Judge Clarkson."

"Humph! Clarkson has got him pinned down at last, has he?" and there was a note of satisfaction in his tone. "I was beginning to think that between this fracas with the spy, and his galloping around the country, he would have no time left for business. I should not think you'd consider it worth while to go pleasure-riding such a morning as this."

"Oh, yes; it was quite worth while," she answered, serenely; "the storm did not break until our return. You are waiting for Colonel McVeigh? So am I, and in the meantime I am at your service, willing to be entertained."

"I am too much upset to entertain any one today," he declared, fretfully; "that trouble last night spoiled my rest. I knew the woman Margeret lied when she came back and said it was only an accident. I'm nervous as a cat today. The doctors forbid me every form of excitement, yet they quarter a Yankee spy in the room over mine, and commence shooting affairs in the middle of the night. It's—it's outrageous!"

He fell back in the chair, exhausted by his indignation. Judithe took the fan from Pluto's hand and waved it gently above the dark, vindictive face. His eyes were closed and as she surveyed the cynical countenance a sudden determination came to her. If she *should* leave for Savannah in the morning, why not let Matthew Loring hear, first, of the plans for Loringwood's future? She knew how to hurt Kenneth McVeigh; she meant to see if there was any way of hurting this trafficker in humanity, this aristocratic panderer to horrid vices.

"You may go, Pluto," she said, kindly. I will ring if you are needed."

Both the colored men went out, closing the door after them, and she brought a hassock and placed it beside his chair, and seated herself, after taking a book from the shelf and opening it without glancing at the title or pages.

"Since you refuse to be entertainer, Monsieur Loring, you must submit to being entertained," she said, pleasantly; "shall I sing to you, read to you, or tell you a story?"

Her direct and persistent graciousness made him straighten up in his chair and regard her, inquiringly; there was a curious mocking tone in her voice as she spoke, but the voice itself was forgotten as he looked in her face.

The light from the lamp was shining full on her face, and the face was closer to him than it had ever been before. If she designed to dazzle him by thus arranging a living picture for his benefit she certainly succeeded. He had never really seen her until now, and he caught his breath sharply and was conscious that one of the most beautiful women he had ever seen in his life was looking at him with a strange smile touching her perfect mouth, and a strange haunting resemblance to some one once known, shining in her dark eyes.

"What sort of stories do you prefer—love stories?" she continued, as he did not speak—only stared at her; "or, since we have had a real adventure in the house last night, possibly you would be interested in the intrigue back of that—would you?"

"Do you mean," he asked, eagerly, "that you could give me some new facts concerning the spy—Monroe?"

"Yes, I really think I could," she said, amiably, "as there happen to be several things you have not been well informed upon."

"I know it!" he said, tapping the arm of the chair, impatiently, "they never tell me half what is going on, now!—as if I was a child! and when I ask the cursed niggars, they lie so. Well, well, go on; tell me the latest news about this Yankee—Monroe."

"The very latest?" and she smiled again in that strange mocking way. "Well, the latest is that he is entirely innocent; had nothing whatever to do with the taking of the papers."

"Madame Caron!"

"Yes, I am quite serious. I was just about to tell Colonel McVeigh, but we can chat about it until he comes;" and she pretended not to notice the wonder in his face, and went serenely on, "in fact, it was not a man who took the papers at all, but a woman; yes, a woman," she said, nodding her head, as a frown of quick suspicion touched his forehead and his eyes gleamed darkly on her, "in fact a confidential agent, whom Captain Masterson designated yesterday as most dangerous to the Confederate cause. I am about to inform Colonel McVeigh of her identity. But I do not fancy that will interest you nearly so much as another story I have for you personally."

She paused and drew back a little, to better observe every expression of his countenance. He was glaring at her and his breath was coming in broken gasps.

"There are really two of those secret Federal agents in this especial territory," she continued, "two women who have worked faithfully for the Union. I fancied you might be especially interested in the story of one of them, as she belongs to the Loring family."

"To our family? That is some cursed Yankee lie!" he burst out fiercely, "every Loring is loyal to the South! To

our family? Let them try to prove that statement! It can't
be done!"

"You are quite right, Monsieur Loring," she agreed,
quietly, "it *would* be difficult to prove, even if you wished
to do it." He fairly glared at the possibility that he should
want to prove it. "But it may have an interest to you for all
that, since the girl in question was your brother's daughter."

"My brother's—!" He seemed choking, and he gazed at
her with a horrible expression. The door opened and Mrs.
McVeigh entered rather hastily, looking for something in
the desk. Loring had sunk back in the chair, and she did
not see his face, but she could see Judithe's, and it was uplifted and slightly smiling.

"Have you found something mutually interesting?" she
asked, glancing at the book open on Judithe's knee.

"Yes; a child's story," returned her guest, and then the
door closed, and the two were again alone.

"There is a woman to be loved and honored, if one could
only forget the sort of son she has trained," remarked Judithe, thoughtfully, "with my heart I love her, but with my
reason I condemn her. Can you comprehend that, Monsieur Loring? I presume not, as you do not interest yourself
with hearts."

He was still staring at her like a man in a frightened
dream; she could see the perspiration standing on his forehead; his lips were twitching horribly.

"You understand, of course," she said, continuing her
former discussion, "that the daughter in the story is not the
lovely lady who is your heiress, and who is called Miss
Loring. It is a younger daughter I refer to; she had no
surname, because masters do not marry slaves, and her
mother was a half Greek octoroon from Florida; her name
was Retta Lacaris, and your brother promised her the free-

dom she never received until death granted her what you
could not keep from her; do you remember that mother and
child, Monsieur Loring?—the mother who went mad and
died, and the child whom you sold to Kenneth McVeigh?
—sold as a slave for his bachelor establishment; a slave who
would look like a white girl, whom you contracted should
have the accomplishments of a white girl, but without a
white girl's inconvenient independence, and the power of
disposing of herself."

"You—you dare to tell me!—you—" He was choking
with rage, but she raised her hand for silence, and continued
in the same quiet tone:

"I have discussed the same affair in the salons of Paris—
why not to you? It was in Paris your good friend, Monsieur
Larue, placed the girl for the education Kenneth McVeigh
paid for. It was also your friend who bribed her to in-
dustry by a suggestion that she might gain freedom if her
accomplishments warranted it. But you had forgotten,
Matthew Loring, that the child of your brother had generations of white blood—of intellectual ancestry back of
her. She had heard before leaving your shores the sort of
freedom she was intended for, and your school was not a
prison strong enough to hold her. She escaped, fled into
the country, hid like a criminal in the day, and walked alone
at night through an unknown county, a girl of seventeen!
She found a friend in an aged woman, to whom she told her
story, every word of it, Matthew Loring, and was received
into the home as a daughter. That home, all the wealth
which made it magnificent, and the title which had once belonged to her benefactress, became the property of your
brother's daughter before that daughter was twenty years
old. Now, do you comprehend why one woman has crossed
the seas to help, if possible, overthrow an institution cham-

24

pioned by you? Now do you comprehend my assurance
that Captain Monroe is innocent? Now, dare you contest
my statement that one of the Loring family is a Federal
agent?"

"By God! I know you at last!" and he half arose from
his chair as if to strike her with both upraised shaking
hands. "I—I'll have you tied up and whipped until you
shed blood for every word you've uttered here! You
wench! You black cattle! You—"

"Stop!" she said, stepping back and smiling at his im-
potent rage. "You are in the house of Colonel McVeigh,
and you are speaking to his wife!"

He uttered a low cry of horror, and fell back in the
chair, nerveless, speechless.

"I thought you would be interested, if not pleased," she
continued, "and I wanted, moreover, to tell you that your
sale of your brother's child was one reason why your estate
of Loringwood was selected in preference to any other as a
dowered home for free children—girl children, of color!
Your ancestral estate, Monsieur Loring, will be used as an
industrial home for such young girls. The story of your
human traffic shall be told, and the name of Matthew Loring
execrated in those walls long after the last of the Lorings
shall be under the sod. That is the monument I have designed for you, and the design will be carried out whether I
live or die."

He did not speak, only sat there with that horrible stare in
his eyes, and watched her.

"I shall probably not see you again," she continued, "as
I leave for Savannah in the morning, unless Colonel Mc-
Veigh holds his wife as a spy, but I could not part without
taking you into my confidence to a certain extent, though I
presume it is not necessary to tell you how useless it would

be for you to use this knowledge to my disadvantage unless I myself should avow it. You know I have told you the truth, but you could not prove it to any other, and—well, I think that is all." She was replacing the book in the case when Gertrude entered from the hall. Judithe only heard the rustle of a gown, and without turning her head to see who it was, added, "Yes, that is all, except to assure you our tete-a-tete has been exceedingly delightful to me; I had actually forgotten that a storm was raging!"

CHAPTER XXIX.

Miss Loring glanced about in surprise when she found no one in the room but her uncle and Madame Caron.

"Oh, I did not know you had left your room," she re-marked, going towards him; "do you think it quite wise? And the storm; isn't it dreadful?"

"I have endeavored to make him forget it," remarked Judithe, "and trust I have not been entirely a failure."

She was idly fingering the volumes in the book-case, and glanced over her shoulder as she spoke. Her hands trembled, but her teeth were set under the smiling lips—she was waiting for his accusation.

"I have no doubt my uncle appreciates your endeavors," returned Gertrude, with civil uncordiality, as she halted back of his chair, "but he is not equal to gayeties today; last night's excitement was quite a shock to him, as it was to all of us."

"Yes," agreed Judithe; "we were just speaking of it."

"Phil Masterson tells me the men will be here some time today for Captain Monroe," continued Gertrude, still speaking from the back of his chair, over which she was leaning. "Phil's orderly just returned from following the spy last night. Caroline made us think at first it was the guard already from the fort, but that was a mistake; she could not see clearly because of the storm. And, uncle, he came back without ever getting in sight of the man, though he rode until morning before he turned back; isn't it too bad for—"

Something in that strange silence of the man in the chair suddenly checked the speech on her lips, and with a quick movement she was in front of him, looking in his face, into the eyes which turned towards her with a strange, horrible expression in them, and the lips vainly trying to speak, to give her warning. But the blow of paralysis had fallen again. He was speechless, helpless. Her piercing scream brought the others from the sitting room; the stricken man was carried to his own apartment by order of Dr. Delaven, who could give them little hope of recovery; his speech might, of course, return as it had done a year before, after the other paralytic stroke, but—

Mrs. McVeigh put her arm protectingly around the weeping girl, comprehending that even though he might recover his speech, any improvement must now be but a temporary respite.

At the door Gertrude halted and turned to the still figure at the book case.

"Madame Caron, you—you were talking to him," she said, appealingly, "you did not suspect, either?"

"I did not suspect," answered Judithe, quietly, and then they went out, leaving her alone, staring after them and then at the chair, where but a few minutes ago he had been seated, full of a life as vindictive as her own, if not so strong;

and now—had she murdered him? She glanced at the mirror back of the writing desk, and saw that she was white and strange looking ; she rubbed her hands together because they were so suddenly cold. She heard some one halt at the door, and she turned again to the book-case lest whoever entered should be shocked at her face.

It was Evilena who peered in wistfully in search of some one not oppressed by woe.

"Kenneth's last day home," she lamented, "and such a celebration of it ; isn't it perfectly awful? Just as if Captain Monroe and the storm had not brought us distress enough! Of course," she added, contritely, "it's unfeeling of me to take that view of it, and I don't expect you to sympathize with me." There was a pause in which she felt herself condemned. "And the house all lit up as for a party ; oh, dear ; it will all be solemn as a grave now in spite of the lights, and our pretty dresses ; well, I think I'll take a book into the sitting room. I could not possibly read in here," and she cast a shrinking glance towards the big chair. "Is that not Romeo and Juliet under your hand? That will do, please."

Judithe took down the volume, turned the leaves rapidly, and smiled.

"You will find the balcony scene on the tenth page," she remarked.

And then they both laughed, and Evilena beat a retreat lest some of the others should enter and catch her laughing when the rest of the household were doleful, and she simply *could* not be doleful over Matthew Loring ; she was only sorry Kenneth's day was spoiled.

The little episode, slight as it was, broke in on the unpleasant fancies of Judithe, and substituted a new element. She closed the glass doors and turned towards the window, quite herself again.

She stepped between the curtains and looked out on the driving storm, trying to peer through the grey sheets of falling rain. The guard, then, according to Miss Loring, had not yet arrived, after all, and the others, the Federals, had a chance of being first on the field; oh, why—why did they not hurry?

The pelting of the rain on the window prevented her from hearing the entrance of Colonel McVeigh and the Judge, while the curtain hid her effectually; it was not until she turned to cross the room into the hall that she was aware of the two men beside the table, each with documents and papers of various sorts, which they were arranging. The Judge held one over which he hesitated; looking at the younger man thoughfully, and finally he said:

"The rest are all right, Kenneth; it was not for those I wanted to see you alone, but for this. I could not have it come under your mother's notice, and the settlement has already been delayed too long, but your absence, first abroad, then direct to the frontier, and then our own war, and Mr. Loring's illness—"

He was rambling along inconsequently; McVeigh glanced at him, questioningly; it was so rare a thing to see the Judge ill at ease over any legal transaction, but he plainly was, now; and when his client reached over and took the paper from his hand he surrendered it and broke off abruptly his rambling explanation.

McVeigh unfolded the paper and glanced at it with an incredulous frown.

"What is the meaning of this agreement to purchase a girl of color, aged twelve, named Rhoda Larue? We have bought no colored people from the Lorings, nor from any one else."

"The girl was contracted for without your knowledge,

my boy, before your majority, in fact; though she is mentioned there as a girl of color she was to all appearances perfectly white, the daughter of an octaroon, and also the daughter of Tom Loring."

The woman back of the curtain was listening now with every sense alert, never for one instant had it occurred to her that Kenneth McVeigh did not know! How she listened for his next words!

"And why should a white girl like that be bought for the McVeigh plantation?"

There was a pause; then Clarkson laid down the other papers, and faced him, frankly:

"Kenneth, my boy, she was never intended for the McVeigh plantation, but was contracted for, educated, given certain accomplishments that she might be a desirable personal property of yours when you were twenty."

McVeigh was on his feet in an instant, his blue eyes flaming.

"And who arranged this affair?—not—my father?"

"No."

"Thank God for that! Go on, who was accountable?"

"Your guardian, Matthew Loring. He explains that he made the arrangement, having in mind the social entanglement of boys within our own knowledge, who have rushed into unequal marriages, or—or associations equally deplorable with scheming women who are alert where moneyed youth is concerned. Mr. Loring, as your guardian, determined to forestall such complications in your case. From a business point of view he did not think it a bad investment, since, if you for any reason, objected to this arrangement, a girl so well educated, even accomplished, could be disposed of at a profit."

McVeigh was walking up and down the room.

"So!" he said, bitterly, "that was Matthew Loring's amiable little arrangement. That girl, then, belonged not to his estate, but to Gertrude's. He was her guardian as well as mine; he would have given me the elder sister as a wife, and the younger one as a slave. What a curse the man is! It is for such hellish deeds that every Southerner outside of his own lands is forced to defend slavery against heavy odds. The outsiders never stop to consider that there is not one man out of a thousand among us who would use his power as this man has used it in this case; the many are condemned for the sins of the few! Go on; what became of the girl?"

"She was, in accordance with this agreement, sent to a first-class school, from which she disappeared—escaped, and never was found again. The money advanced from your estate for her education is, therefore, to be repaid you, with the interest to date; you, of course, must not lose the money, since Loring has failed to keep his part of the contract."

"Good God!" muttered McVeigh, continuing his restless walk; "it seems incredible, damnable! Think of it!—a girl with the blood, the brain, the education of a white woman, and bought in my name! I will have nothing—nothing to do with such cursed traffic!"

Neither of them heard the smothered sobs of the woman kneeling there back of that curtain; all the world had been changed for her by his words.

She did not hear the finale of their conversation, only the confused murmer of their voices came to her; then, after a little, there was the closing of a door, and Colonel McVeigh was alone.

He was seated in the big chair where Matthew Loring had received the stroke which meant death. The hammock was still beside it, and she knelt there, touching his arm, timidly.

He had not heard her approach, but at her touch he turned from the papers.

"Well, my sweetheart, what is it?" he said, and with averted face she whispered:

"Only that—I love you!—no," as he bent towards her, "don't kiss me! I never knew—I never guessed."

"Never guessed that you loved me?" he asked, regarding her with a quizzical smile. "Now, I guessed it all the time, even though you did run away from me."

"No, no, it is not that!" and she moved away, out of the reach of his caressing hands. "But I was there, by the window; I heard all that story. I had heard it long ago, and I thought you were to blame. I judged you—condemned you! Now I see how wrong I was—wrong in every way—in every way. I have wronged you—*you*! Oh, how I have wronged you!" she whispered, under her breath, as she remembered the men she looked for, had sent for—the men who were to take him away a prisoner!

"Nonsense, dear!" and he clasped her hands and smiled at her reassuringly. "You are over-wrought by all the excitement here since yesterday; you are nervous and remorseful over a trifle; you could not wrong me in any way; if you did, I forgive you."

No," she said, shaking her head and gazing at him with eyes more sad than he had ever seen them; "no, you would not forgive me if you knew; you never will forgive me when you do know. And—I must tell you—tell you everything—tell you now—"

"No, not now, Judithe," he said, as he heard Masterson's voice in the hall. "We can't be alone now. Later you shall tell me all your sins against me." He was walking

with her to the door and looking down at her with all his
heart in his eyes; his tenderness made her sorrows all the
more terrible, and as he bent to kiss her she shrunk from
him.

"No, not until I tell you all," she said again, then as his
hands touched hers she suddenly pressed them to her lips,
her eyes, her cheek; "and whatever you think of me then,
when you do hear all, I want you to know that I love you,
I love you, I *love* you!"

Then the door closed behind her and he was standing
there with a puzzled frown between his eyes when Masterson entered. Her intense agitation, the passion in her words
and her eyes!—He felt inclined to follow and end the mystery of it at once, but Masterson's voice stopped him.

"I've been trying all morning to have a talk, Colonel," he
said, carefully closing the door and glancing about. "There
have been some new developments in Monroe's case, in fact
there have been so many that I have put in the time while
waiting for you, by writing down every particle of new
testimony in the affair." He took from his pocket some
written pages and laid them on the table, and beside them
a small oval frame. "They are for your inspection, Colonel.
I have no opinion I care to express on the matter. I have
only written down Miss Loring's statements, and the picture speaks for itself."

McVeigh stared at him.

"What do you mean by Miss Loring's statement?—and
what is this?"

He had lifted the little frame, and looked at Masterson,
who had resolutely closed his lips and shook his head. He
meant that McVeigh should see for himself.

The cover flew back as he touched the spring, and a girl's
face, dark, bright, looked out at him. It was delicately

tinted and the work was well done. He had a curious shock as the eye met his. There was something so familiar in the poise of the head and the faint smile lurking at the corner of the mouth.

There was no mistaking the likeness; it looked as Judithe might possibly have looked at seventeen. He had never seen her with that childish, care-free light of happiness in her eyes; she had always been thoughtful beyond her years, but in this picture—

"Where did you get this?" he asked, and his face grew stern for an instant, as Masterson replied:

"In Captain Monroe's pocket."

He opened his lips to speak, but Masterson pointed to the paper.

"It is all written there, Colonel; I really prefer you should read that report first, and then question me if you care to. I have written each thing as it occurred. You will see Miss Loring has also signed her name to it, preferring you would accept that rather than be called upon for a personal account. Your mother is, of course, ignorant of all this—"

McVeigh seemed scarcely to hear his words. *Her* voice was yet sounding in his ears; her remorseful repetition, "You will never forgive me when you do know!"—was this what she meant?

He laid down the picture and picked up the papers. Masterson seated himself at the other side of the room with his back to him, and waited.

There was the rustle of paper as McVeigh laid one page after another on the table. After a little the rustle ceased. Masterson looked around. The Colonel had finished with the report and was again studying the picture.

"Well?" said Masterson.

"I cannot think this evidence at all conclusive." There

was a pause and then he added, "but the situation is such that every unusual thing relating to this matter must, of course, be investigated. I should like to see Margeret and Captain Monroe here; later I may question Madame Caron."

His voice was very quiet and steady, but he scarcely lifted his eyes from the picture; something about it puzzled him; the longer he looked at it the less striking was the likeness—the character of Judithe's face, now, was so different.

He was still holding it at arm's length on the table when Margeret noiselessly entered the room. She came back of him and halted beside the table; her eyes were also on the picture, and a smothered exclamation made him aware of her presence. He closed the frame and picked up the report Masterson had given him.

"Margeret," he said, looking at her, curiously, "have you seen Madame Caron today?"

"Yes, Colonel McVeigh;" she showed no surprise at the question, only looked straight ahead of her, with those solemn, dark eyes. He remembered the story of her madness years ago, and supposed that was accountable for the strange, colorless, passive manner.

"Did she speak to you?"

"No, sir."

Judithe opened the door and looked in; seeing that McVeigh was apparently occupied, and not alone, she was about to retire when he begged her to remain for a few minutes. He avoided her questioning eyes, and offered her a chair, with that conventional courtesy reserved for strangers. She noted the papers in his hand, and the odd tones in which he spoke; she was, after all, debarred from confessing; she was to be accused!

"A slight mystery is abroad here, and you appear to be

the victim of it, Madame," he said, without looking at her. "Margeret, last night when Miss Loring sent you into the corridor just before the shot was fired, did you see any of the ladies or servants of the house?"

"No, sir."

There was not the slightest hesitation in the reply, but Judithe turned her eyes on the woman with unusual interest. Colonel McVeigh consulted his notes.

"Miss Loring distinctively heard the rustle of a woman's dress as her door opened; did you hear that?"

"No, sir."

"You saw no one and heard no one?"

"No one."

There was a pause, during which he regarded the woman very sharply.

Judithe arose.

"Only your sister or myself could have been in that corridor without passing Miss Loring's door; is Miss Loring suspicious of us?—Miss Loring!"—and her tone was beyond her control, indignant; of all others, Miss Loring! "Margeret, whatever you saw, whatever you heard in that corridor, you must tell Colonel McVeigh—tell him!"

Margeret turned a calm glance towards her for a moment, and quietly said, "I have told him, Madame Caron; there was no one in the corridor."

"Very well; that is all I wanted to know." His words were intended for dismissal, but she only bent her head and walked back to the window, as Masterson entered with Monroe. The latter bowed to Judithe with more than usual ceremony, but did not speak. Then he turned a nonchalant glance towards McVeigh, and waited. The Colonel looked steadily at Judithe as he said:

"Captain Monroe, did you know Madame Caron before

you met her in my house? You do not answer! Madame
Caron, may I ask you if you knew Captain Monroe previous
to yesterday?"

"Quite well," she replied, graciously; there was almost
an air of bravado in her glance. She had meant to tell him
all; had begged him to listen, but since he preferred to
question her before these men, and at the probable suggestion of Miss Loring—well!

Masterson drew a breath of relief as she spoke. His Colonel must now exonerate him of any unfounded suspicions;
but Monroe regarded her with somber, disapproving eyes.

"Then," and his tone chilled her; it has in it such a suggestion of what justice he would mete out to her when he
knew all; "then I am, under the circumstances, obliged to
ask why you acknowledged the introduction given by Miss
Loring?"

"Oh, for the blunder of that I was accountable, Monsieur," and she smiled at him, frankly, the combative spirit
fully awake, now, since he chose to question her—*her*!—before the others, "I should have explained, perhaps—I believe
I meant to, but there was conversation, and I probably forgot."

"I see! You forgot to explain, and Captain Monroe forgot you were acquainted when he was questioned, just
now."

"Captain Monroe could not possibly forget the honor of
such acquaintance," retorted Monroe; "he only refused to
answer."

The two men met each other's eyes for an instant—a
glance like the crossing of swords. Then McVeigh said:

"Where did you get the picture found on your person
last night?"

"Stole it," said Monroe, calmly, and McVeigh flushed in

quick anger at the evident lie and the insolence of it; he was lying then to shield this woman who stood between them—to shield her from her husband.

"Madame Caron," and she had never before heard him speak in that tone; "did you ever give Captain Monroe a picture of yourself?"

"Never!" she said, wonderingly. Margeret had taken a step forward and stood irresolutely as though about to speak; she was very pale, and Monroe knew in an instant who she was—not by the picture, but from Pluto's story last night. The terror in her eyes touched him, and as McVeigh lifted the picture from the table, he spoke.

"Colonel McVeigh, I will ask you to study that picture carefully before you take for granted that it is the face of any one you know," he said, quietly; "that picture was made probably twenty years ago."

"And the woman?"

"The woman is dead—died long ago." Margeret's eyes closed for an instant, but none of them noticed her. Judithe regarded Monroe, questioningly, and then turned to McVeigh:

"May I not see this picture you speak of, since—"

But Monroe in two strides was beside the table where it lay.

"Colonel McVeigh, even a prisoner of war should be granted some consideration, and all I ask of you is to show the article in question to no one without first granting me a private interview."

Again the eyes of the men met and the sincerity, the appeal of Monroe impressed McVeigh; something might be gained by conceding the request—something lost by refusing it, and he slipped the case into his pocket without even looking at Judithe, or noticing her question.

But Monroe looked at her, and noted the quick resentment at his speech.

"Pardon, Madame," he said, gently; "my only excuse is
that there is a lady in the question."

"A lady who is no longer living?" she asked, mockingly.
She was puzzled over the affair of the picture, puzzled at the
effect it had on McVeigh. In some way he was jealous concerning it—jealous, how absurd, when she adored him!

Monroe only looked at her, but did not reply to the scep-
tical query. Gertrude Loring came to the door just then
and spoke to McVeigh, who went to meet her. She wanted
him to go at once to her uncle. He was trying so hard to
speak; they thought he was endeavoring to say "Ken—
Ken!" It was the only tangible thing they could distinguish, and he watched the door continually as though for
someone's entrance.

McVeigh assured her he would go directly, but she
begged him to postpone all the other business—anything!
and to come with her at once; he might be dying, he looked
like it, and there certainly was *some* one whom he wanted;
therefore—

He turned with a semi-apologetic manner to the others in
the room.

"I shall return presently, and will then continue the investigation," he said, addressing Masterson; "pending such
action Captain Monroe can remain here."

Then he closed the door and followed Gertrude.

Judithe arose at that calm ignoring of herself and moved
to the table. She guessed what it was the dying man was
trying to tell Kenneth—well, she would tell him first!

Pen and paper were there and she commenced to write,
interrupting herself to turn to Masterson, who was looking
out at the storm.

"Is there any objection to Captain Monroe holding converse with other—guests in the house?" she asked, with a little ironical smile.

Masterson hesitated, and then said: "I do not think a private interview could be allowed, but—"

"A private interview is not necessary," she said, coolly. "You can remain where you are. Margeret, also, can remain." She wrote a line or two, and then spoke without looking up, "Will you be so kind, Captain Monroe, as to come over to the table?"

"At your service, my lady."

He did so, and remained standing there, with his hands clasped behind him, a curious light of expectancy in his eyes.

"You have endured everything but death for me since last night," she said, looking up at him. She spoke so low Masterson could not hear it above the beat of the rain on the window. But he could see the slight bend of Monroe's head and the smile with which he said:

"Well—since it was for you!"

"Oh, do not jest now, and do not think I shall allow it to go on," she said, appealingly. "I have been waiting for help, but I shall wait no longer;" she pointed to the paper on the table, "Colonel McVeigh will have a written statement of who did the work just as soon as I can write it, and you shall be freed."

"Take care!" he said, warningly; "an avowal now might only incriminate you—not free me. There are complications you can't be told—"

"But I must be told!" she interrupted. "What is there concerning me which you both conspire to hide? He shall free you, no matter what the result is to me; did you fancy I should let you go away under suspicion? But, that picture! You must make that clear to me. Listen, I will con-

25

fess to you, too! I have wronged him—Colonel McVeigh
—it has been all a mistake. I can never atone, but"—and
her voice sank lower, "it was something about that picture
made him angry just now, the thought I had given you some
picture. I—I can't have him think that—not that you are
my lover."

"Suppose it were so—would that add to the wrongs you
speak of?" His voice was almost tender in its gentleness,
and his face had a strange expression, as she said: "Yes, it
would, Captain Jack."

"You mean, then—to marry him?"

Something in the tenseness of his tones, the strange look
of anxiety in his eyes, decided her answer.

"I mean that I have married him."

She spoke so softly it was almost a whisper, but if it had
been trumpet-like he could not have looked more astonished. His face grew white, and he took a step backward
from her. Masterson, who noticed the movement, walked
down to the desk, where he could hear. Margeret was
nearer to them than he. All he heard was Madame Caron
asking if Captain Monroe would not now agree that she
should see the picture since it was necessary to defend herself.

But Monroe had gone back to his chair, where he sat
looking at her thoughtfully, and looking at Margeret, also,
who had remained near the door, and gave no sign of having heard their words—had she?

"No, Madame Caron," he said, quietly, "if there is any evidence in my favor you can communicate to Colonel Mc-
Veigh, I shall be your debtor, but the picture is altogether
a personal affair of my own. I will, if I can, prevent it from
being used in this case at all, out of consideration for the
lady whom I mentioned before."

CHAPTER XXX.

Kenneth McVeigh walked the floor of his own room, with the bitterest thoughts of his life for company. Loyal gentleman that he was, he was appalled at the turn affairs had taken. It had cost him a struggle to give up faith in the man he had known and liked—but all that was as nothing compared to the struggle in which his own love fought against him.

In that room where death apparently stood on the threshold, and the dying man had followed him about the room with most terrible, appealing eyes, he had heard but few of the words spoken—all his heart and brain were afire with the scene he had just left; that, and the others preceding it! Every word or glance he had noticed between Monroe and the woman he loved returned to him! Trifles light as air before, now overwhelmed him with horrible suggestions; and her pleading for him that morning—all the little artifices, the pretended lightness with which she asked a first favor on her wedding morning—their wedding morning! for whatever she was or was not, she was, at least, his wife!

That fact must be taken into conideration, he could not set it aside; her disgrace meant his disgrace—God! was that why she had consented to the hurried marriage?—to shield herself under his name, and to influence his favor for her lover?

The spirit of murder leaped in his heart as he thought of

it! He heard Gertrude send to the library for Margeret, and he sent word to Masterson he was detained and would continue the investigation later. When Pluto returned, after delivering the message, he inquired if Madame Caron was yet in the library, and Pluto informed him Madame Caron had gone to her room some time ago; no one was in the library now, the gentleman had gone back to the cottage.

He meant to see her alone before speaking again with Monroe, to know the worst, whatever it was, and then—

He used a magnifying glass to study the little picture; he took it from the frame and examined the frame itself. The statement of Monroe as to its age seemed verified. Certain things in the face were strange, but certain other things were wonderfully like Judithe as a happy, care-free girl—had she ever been such a girl?

The chance that, after all, the picture was not hers gave him a sudden hope that the other things, purely circumstantial, might also diminish on closer examination; the picture had, to him, been the strongest evidence against her; a jealous fury had taken possession of him at the sight of it; he was conscious that his personal feelings unfitted him for the judicial position forced upon him, and that he must somehow conquer them before continuing any examination.

An hour had passed; he had decided the picture was not that of his wife, but if Monroe were not her lover, why did he treasure so a likeness resembling her? And if she were not in love with him, why ignore their former acquaintance, and why intercede for him so persistently?

All those thoughts walked beside him as he strode up and down the room, and beyond them all was the glory of her eyes and the remembrance of her words: "*Whatever you think of me when you know all, I want you to know that I love you—I love you!*"

They were the words he had waited for through long days and nights; they had come to him at last, and after all—

A knock sounded on the door and Pluto entered with a large sealed envelope on which his name was written.

"From Madame Caron, sah; she done tole me to put it in yo' own han'," he said.

When alone again he opened the envelope. Several papers were in it. The first he unfolded was addressed to his wife and the signature was that of a statesman high in the confidence of the Northern people. It was a letter of gratitude to her for confidential work accomplished within the Confederate lines: it was most extreme in commendation, and left no doubt as to the consideration shown her by the most distinguished of the Federal leaders. It was dated six months before, showing that her friendship for his enemies was not a matter of days, but months.

There was one newly written page in her own writing. He put that aside to look at last of all, then locked the door and resumed the reading of the others.

And the woman to whom they were written moved restlessly from room to room, watching the storm and replying now and then to the disconsolate remarks of Evilena, who was doleful over the fact that everybody was too much occupied for conversation. Kenneth had shut himself up entirely, and all the others seemed to be in attendance on Mr. Loring. Captain Masterson was in and out, busy about his own affairs, and not minding the rain a particle, and she was full of questions concerning Captain Monroe, and why he had paid the brief visit to the library.

Judithe replied at random, scarcely hearing her chatter, and listening, listening each instant for his step or voice on the stair.

While she stood there, looking out at the low, dark

clouds, a step sounded in the hall and she turned quickly; it was only Pluto; ordinarily she would not have noticed him especially, but his eyes were directed to her in so peculiar a manner that she gave him a second glance, and perceived that he carried a book she had left on a table in her own room.

"Look like I can't noway find right shelf fo' this book," he said, with some hesitation. "I boun' to ax yo' to show me whah it b'longs."

She was about to do so, but when the door of the book-case opened, he handed her the book instead of placing it where she directed.

"Maybe yo' put it in thah fo' me," he suggested.

She looked at him, remembering she had told Pierson he could be trusted, and took the book without a word. Evilena was absorbed in Juliet's woes, and did not look up.

Pluto muttered a "thank yo'," and disappeared along the hall.

She took the book into the alcove before opening it, and found there what she had expected—a slip of paper with some pencilled marks. It was a cipher, from which she read, "*All is right; we follow close on this by another road. Be ready. Lincoln*"—she sank on her knees as she read the rest —"*Lincoln has issued the proclamation of emancipation!*"

It was Margeret who found her there a few minutes later. She was still kneeling by the window, her face covered by her hands.

"You likely to catch cold down there, Madame," said the soft voice. "I saw you come in here a good while ago, an' I thought I'd come see if I could serve you some way."

Judithe accepted the proffered hand and rose to her feet. For an instant Margeret's arms had half enfolded her, and the soft color swept into the woman's face. Judithe looked at her kindly and said:

"You have already tried to serve me today, Margeret; I've been thinking of it since, and I wonder why?"

"Any of the folks here would be proud to serve you, Madame Caron," said the woman, lapsing again into calm reticence.

Judithe looked at her and wondered what would become of her and the many like her, now that freedom was declared for the slaves. She could not understand why she had denied seeing her in the corridor, for they had met there, almost touched! Perhaps she was some special friend of Pluto's, and because of that purchase of the child—

"I leave tomorrow for Savannah," said Judithe, kindly. "Come to my room this evening, and if there is anything I can do for you—"

"Margeret's hands were clasped tightly at the question, and those strange, haunting eyes of hers seemed to reach the girl's soul.

"There is one thing," she half whispered, "not now, maybe, not right away! But you've bought Loringwood, and I—I lived there too many years to be satisfied to live away from it. They—Miss Gertrude—wouldn't ask much for me now, and—"

"I see," and Judithe wished she could tell her that there would never be buying or selling of her again—that the law of the land had declared her free! "I promise you, Loringwood shall be your home some day, if you wish."

"God forever bless you!" whispered Margeret, and then she pushed aside the curtains and went through the library and up the stairs, and Judithe watched her, thoughtfully wondering why any slave should cling to a home where Matthew Loring's will had been law. Was it true that cer-

tain slavish natures in women—whether of Caucasian or
African blood—loved best the men who were tyrants? Was
it a relic of inherited tendencies when all women of whatever
complexion were but slaves to their masters—called hus-
bands?

But something in the delicate, sad face of Margeret gave
silent negative to the question. Whatever the affection centered in Loringwood, she could not believe it in any way
low or unworthy.

As she passed along the upper hall Pluto was on the
landing.

"Any visitors today through all this storm?" she asked,
carelessly.

"No out an' out company," he said, glancing around. "A
boy from the Harris plantation did stop in out o' the rain,
jest now. He got the lend of a coat, an' left his wet one,
that how—"

He looked anxiously at the slip of paper yet in her
fingers. She smiled and entered her own room, where
everything was prepared for her journey the following day.
She glanced about grimly and wondered where that journey
would end—it depended so much on the temper of the man
who was now reading the evidence against her—the proof
absolute that she was the Federal agent sought for vainly
by the Confederate authorities. She had told him nothing
of the motive prompting her to the work—it had been
merely a plain statement of work accomplished.

Her door was left ajar and she listened nervously for his
step, his voice. It seemed hours since she had sent him the
message—the time had really not been long except in her
imagination. And the little slip of paper just received held a
threat directed towards him! In an hour, at most, the men
she had sent for would be there; she had laid the plan for his

ruin, and now was wild to think she could noways save him! If she had dared to go to him, plead with him to leave at once, persuade him through his love for her—but it seemed ages too late for that! And she could only await his summons, which she expected every moment; she could not even conjecture what he meant to do.

* * * * * * *

Neither could Captain Masterson, who stood in McVeigh's room, staring incredulously at his superior officer.

"Colonel, are you serious in this matter? You actually mean to let Captain Monroe go free?"

"Absolutely free," said McVeigh, who was writing an order, and continued writing without looking up. "I understand your surprise, but we arrested an innocent man."

"I don't mean to question your judgment, Colonel, but the evidence—"

"The evidence was circumstantial. That evidence has been refuted by facts not to be ignored." Masterson looked at him inquiringly, a look comprehended by McVeigh, who touched the bell for Pluto.

"I must have time to consider before I decide what to do with those facts," he continued. "I shall know tonight."

"And in the meantime what are we to do with the squad from down the river?" asked Masterson, grimly. "They have just arrived to take him for court martial; they are waiting your orders."

"I will have their instructions ready in an hour."

"They bring the report of some definite action on the slavery question by the Federal authorities," remarked Masterson, with a smile of derision. "Lincoln has proclaimed freedom for our slaves, the order is to go into effect the first of the year, unless we promise to be good, lay down our arms, and enter the Union."

"The first of the year is three months away, plenty of time to think it over;" he locked his desk and arose. "Excuse me now, Phil," he said, kindly, "I must go down and speak with Captain Monroe." He paused at the door, and Masterson noticed that his face was very pale and his lips had a strange, set expression. Whatever task he had before him was not easy to face! "You might help me in this," he added, "by telling my mother we must make what amends we can to him—if any amends are possible for such indignities."

He went slowly down the stairs and entered the library. Monroe was wiping the rain from his coat collar and holding a dripping hat at arm's length.

"Since you insist on my afternoon calls, Colonel McVeigh, I wish you would arrange them with some regard to the elements," he remarked. "I was at least dry, and safe, where I was."

But there was no answering light in McVeigh's eyes. He had been fighting a hard battle with himself, and the end was not yet.

"Captain Monroe, it is many hours too late for apologies to you," he said, gravely, "but I do apologize, and—you are at liberty."

"Going to turn me out in a storm like this?" inquired his late prisoner, but McVeigh held out his hand.

"Not so long as you will honor my house by remaining," and Monroe, after one searching glance, took the offered hand in silence.

McVeigh tried to speak, but turned and walked across to the window. After a moment he came back.

"I know, now, you could have cleared yourself by speaking," he said; "yes, I know all," as Monroe looked at him questioningly. "I know you have borne disgrace and risked death for a chivalrous instinct. May I"—he hesitated as he realized he was now asking a favor of the man he had insulted—"may I ask that you remain silent to all but me, and that you pardon the injustice done you? I did not know—"

"Oh, the silence is understood," said Monroe, "and as for the rest—we will forget it; the evidence was enough to hang a man these exciting times."

"And you ran the risk? Captain, you may wonder that I ask your silence, but you talked with her here; you probably know that to me she is—"

Monroe raised his hand in protest.

"I don't know anything, Colonel. I heard you were a benedict, but it may be only hearsay; I was not a witness; if I had been you would not have found me a silent one! But it is too late now, and we had better not talk about it," he said, anxious to get away from the strained, unhappy eyes of the man he has always known as the most care-free of cadets. "With your permission I will pay my respects to your sister, whom I noticed across the hall, but in the meantime, I don't know a thing!"

As he crossed the hall Gertrude Loring descended the stairs and paused, looking after him wonderingly, and then turned into the library. Colonel McVeigh was seated at the table again, his face buried in his hands.

"Kenneth!"

He raised his head, and she hesitated, staring at him. "Kenneth, you are ill; you—"

"No; it is really nothing," he said, as he rose, "I am a trifle tired, I believe; absurd, isn't it? and—and very busy just now, so—"

"Oh, I shan't detain you a moment," she said, hastily, "but I saw Captain Monroe in the hall, and I was so amazed when Phil told us you had released him."

"I knew you would be, but he is an innocent man, and his arrest was all a mistake. Pray, tell mother for me that I have apologized to Captain Monroe, and he is to be our guest until tomorrow. I am sure she will be pleased to hear it."

"Oh, yes, of course," agreed Gertrude, "but Kenneth, the guard has arrived, and who will they take in his place for court-martial?"

She spoke lightly, but there was a subtle meaning back of her words. He felt it, and met her gaze with a sombre smile.

"Perhaps myself," he answered, quietly.

"Oh, Kenneth!"

"There, there!" he said, reassuringly; "don't worry about the future, what is, is enough for today, little girl."

He had opened the door for her as though anxious to be alone; she understood, and was almost in the hall when the other door into the library opened, and glancing over her shoulder she saw Judithe standing there gazing after her, with a peculiar look.

She glanced up at Kenneth McVeigh, and saw his face suddenly grow white, and stern; then the door closed on her, and those two were left alone together. She stood outside the door for a full minute, amazed at the strange look in his eyes, and in hers, as they faced each other, and as she moved away she wondered at the silence there—neither of them had spoken.

They looked at each other as the door closed, a world of appeal in her eyes, but there was no response in his; a few hours ago she meant all of life to him—and now!—

With a quick sigh she turned and crossed to the window; drawing back the curtain she looked out, but all the heavens seemed weeping with some endless woe. The light of the lamp was better, and she drew the curtains close, and faced him again.

"You have read—all?"

He bent his head in assent.

"And Captain Monroe?"

"Captain Monroe is at liberty. I have accepted your confession, and acted upon it."

"You accept that part of my letter, but not my other request," she said, despairingly. "I begged that you make some excuse and leave for your command at once—today—do you refuse to heed that?"

"I do," he said, coldly.

"Is it on my account?" she demanded; "if so, put me under arrest; send me to one of the forts; do anything to assure yourself of my inability to work against your cause, though I promise you I never shall again. Oh, I know you do not trust me, and I shan't ask you to; I only ask you to send me anywhere you like, if you will only start for your command at once; for your own sake I beg you; for your own sake you must go!"

All of pleading was in her eyes and voice; her hands were clasped in the intensity of her anxiety. But he only shook his head as he looked down in the beautiful, beseeching face.

"For your sake I shall remain," he said, coldly.

"Kenneth!"

"Your anxiety that I leave shows that the plots you confessed are not the only ones you are aware of," he said, controlling his voice with an effort, and speaking quietly. "You are my wife; for the plots of the future I must take the responsibility, prevent them if if can; shield you if I cannot."

"No, no!" and she clasped his arm, pleadingly; "believe

me, Kenneth, there will be no more plots, not after today—"

"Ah!" and he drew back from her touch; "not after to-day! then there *is* some further use you have for my house as a rendezvous? Do you suppose I will go at once and leave my mother and sister to the danger of your intrigues?"

"No! there shall be no danger for any one if you will only go," she promised, wildly; "Kenneth, it is you I want to save; it is the last thing I shall ever ask of you. Go, go! no more harm shall come to your people, I promise you, I—"

"You promise!" and he turned on her with a fury from which she shrank. "The promise of a women who allowed a loyal friend to suffer disgrace for her fault!—the promise of one who has abused the affection and hospitality of the women you assure protection for! A spy! A traitor! *You*, the woman I worshipped! God! What cursed fancy led you to risk life, love, honor, everything worth having, for a fanatical fight against one of two political factions?"

He dropped into a chair and buried his face in his hands. As he did so a handkerchief in his pocket caught in the fastening of his cuff, as he let his hand fall the 'kerchief was dragged from the pocket, and with it the little oval frame over which he had been jealous for an hour, and concerning which he had not yet had an explanation.

It rolled towards her, and with a sudden movement she caught it, and the next instant the dark, girlish face lay uncovered in her hand.

She uttered a low cry, and then something of strength seemed to come to her as she looked at it. Her eyes dilated, and she drew a long breath, as she turned and faced him again with both hands clasped over her bosom, and the open picture pressed there. All the tears and pleading were gone from her face and voice, as she answered:

"Because to that political question there is a background, shadowed, shameful, awful! Through the shadows of it one can hear the clang of chains; can see the dumb misery of fettered women packed in the holds of your slave ships, carried in chains to the land of your free! From the day the first slave was burned at the stake on Manhattan Island by your Christian forefathers, until now, when they are meeting your men in battle, fighting you to the death, there is an unwritten record that is full of horror, generations of dumb servitude! Did you think they would keep silence forever?"

He arose from the chair, staring at her in amazement; those arguments were so foreign to all he had known of the dainty woman, patrician, apparently, to her finger tips. How had she ever been led to sympathize with those rabid, mistaken theories of the North?

"You have been misled by extravagant lies!" he said, sternly; "abuses such as you denounce no longer exist; if they ever did it was when the temper of the times was rude —half savage if you will—when men were rough and harsh with each other, therefore, with their belongings."

"Therefore, with their belongings!" she repeated, bitterly, "and in your own age all that is changed?"

"Certainly."

"Certainly!" she agreed. "Slaves are no longer burned for insubordination, because masters have grown too wise to burn money! But they have some laws they use now instead of the torch and the whip of those old crude days. From their book of laws they read the commandment: *'Go you out then, and of the heathen about you, buy bondmen and bondmaids that they be servants of your household;'* and again it is commanded: *'Servants be obedient unto your masters!'* The torch is no longer needed when those fettered souls are taught God has decreed their servitude. God has cursed them before they were born, and under that curse they must bend forever!"

"You doubt even the religion of my people?" he demanded.

"Yes!"

"You doubt the divinity of those laws?"

"Yes!"

"Judithe!"

"Yes!" she repeated, a certain dauntless courage in her voice and bearing. She was no longer the girl he had loved and married; she was a strange, wild, beautiful creature, whose tones he seemed to hear for the first time. "A thousand times—yes! I doubt any law and every law shackling liberty of thought and freedom of people! And the poison of that accursed system has crept into your own blood until, even to me, you pretend, and deny the infamy that exists today, and of which you are aware!"

"Infamy! How dare you use that word?" and his eyes flamed with anger at the accusation, but she raised her hand, and spoke more quietly.

"You remember the story you heard here today—the story of your guest and guardian, who sold the white child of his own brother? and the day when that was done is not so long past! It is so close that the child is now only a girl of twenty-three, the girl who was educated by her father's brother that she might prove a more desirable addition to your bondslaves!"

"God in heaven!" he muttered, as he drew back and stared at her. "Your knowledge of those things, of the girl's age, which *I* did not know! Where have you gained it all? When you heard so much you must know I was not aware of the purchase of the girl, but that does not matter now. Answer my questions! Your words, your manner; what do they mean? What has inspired this fury in you? Answer—I command you!"

"'Servants, be obedient unto your masters!'" she quoted, with a strange smile. "My words oppress you, possibly, because so many women are speaking through my lips, the women who for generations have thought and suffered and been doomed to silence, to bear the children of men they hated; to have the most sacred thing of life, mother-love, desecrated, according to the temper of their masters; to dread bringing into the world even the children of love, lest, whether white or black, they prove cattle for the slave market!"

"Judithe!"

He caught her hand as though to force silence on her by the strength of his own horror and protest. She closed her eyes for an instant as he touched her, and then drew away to leave a greater space between them, as she said:

"All those women are back of me! I have never lived one hour out of the shadow of their presence. Their cause is my cause, and when I forget them, may God forget me!"

"*Your* cause!—my wife!" he half whispered, as he dropped her hand, and the blue eyes swept her over with a glance of horror. "Who are you that their cause should be yours?"

"Until this morning I was Madame La Marquise de Caron," she said, making a half mocking inclination of her head; "in the bill of sale you read today I was named Rhoda Larue, the slave girl who—"

"No!" He caught her fiercely by the shoulder, and his face had a murderous look as he bent above her, "don't dare to say it! You are mad with the desire to hurt me because I resent your sympathy with the North! But, dear, your madness has made you something more terrible than you

26

realize! Judithe, for God's sake, never say that word again!"

"For God's sake, that is, for truth's sake, I am telling you the thing that is!"

He half staggered to the table, and stood there looking at her; her gaze met his own, and all the tragedy of love and death was in that regard.

"*You*!" he said, as though it was impossible to believe the thing he heard. "You—of all women! God!—it is too horrible! What right have you to tell me now? I was happy each moment I thought you loved me; even my anger against you was all jealousy! I was willing to forgive even the spy work, shield you, trust you, *love* you—but—now—"

He paused with his hand over his eyes as though to shut out the sight of her, she was so beautiful as she stood there —so appealing. The dark eyes were wells of sadness as she looked at him. She stood as one waiting judgment and hoping for no mercy.

"You have punished me for a thing that was not my fault," he continued. "I destroyed it—the accursed paper, and—"

"And by destroying it you gave me back to the Loring estate," she said, quietly. All the passion had burned itself out; she spoke wearily and without emotion. "That is, I have become again, the property of my half sister, my father's daughter! Are the brutal possibilities of your social institution so very far in the past?"

He could only stare at her; the horror of it was all too sickening, and that man who was dying in the other room had caused it all; he had moved them as puppets in the game of life, a malignant Fate, who had made all this possible.

"Now, will you go?" she asked, pleadingly. "You may trust me now; I have told you all."

But he did not seem to hear her; only that one horrible thought of what she was to him beat against his brain and dwarfed every other consideration.

"And you—married me, knowing this?"

"I married you because I knew it," she said, despairingly. "I thought you and Matthew Loring equally guilty—equally deserving of punishment. I fought against my own feelings—my own love for you—"

"Love!"

"Love—love always! I loved you in Paris, when I thought hate was all you deserved from me. I waited three years. I told myself it had been only a girlish fancy—not love! I pledged myself to work for the union of these states and against the cause championed by Kenneth Mc-Veigh and Matthew Loring; for days and nights, weeks and months, I have worked for my mother's people and against the two men whose names were always linked together in my remembrance. The thought became a monomania with me. Well, you know how it is ended! Every plan against you became hateful to me from the moment I heard your voice again. But the plans had to go on though they were built on my heart. As for the marriage, I meant to write you after I had left the country, and tell you who you had given your name to. Then"—and all of despair was in her voice—"then I learned the truth too late. I heard your words when that paper was given to you here, and I loved you. I realized that I had never ceased to love you; that I never should!"

"The woman who is my—wife!" he muttered. "Oh, God!—"

"No one need ever know that," she said earnestly. "I

will go away, unless you give me over to the authorities as the spy. For the wrong I have done you I will make any atonement—any expiation—"

"There is no atonement you could make." he answered, steadily. "There is no forgiveness possible."

"I know," she said, whisperingly, as if afraid to trust her voice aloud, "I know you could never forgive me. I—I do not ask it; only, Kenneth, a few hours ago we promised to love each other always," her voice broke for an instant and then she went on, "I shall keep that promise wherever I go, and—that is all—I think—"

She had paused beside the table, where he sat, with his head buried in his hands.

"I give you back the wedding ring," she continued, slipping it from her finger, but he did not speak or move. She kissed the little gold circlet and laid it beside him. "I am going now," she said, steadily as she could; "I ask for no remembrance, no forgiveness; but—have you no word of good-bye for me?—not one? It is forever, Kenneth— *Kenneth!*"

Her last word was almost a scream, for a shot had sounded just outside the window, and there was the rush of feet on the veranda and the crash of arms.

"Go! Go at once!" she said, grasping his arm. "They will take you prisoner—they will—"

"So!" he said, rising and reaching for the sword on the rack near him; "this is one of the plots you did *not* reveal to me; some of your Federal friends!"

"Oh, I warned you! I begged you to go," she said, pleadingly; again she caught his arm as he strode towards the veranda, but he flung himself loose with an angry exclamation:

"Let your friends look to themselves," he said, grimly.
"My own guard is here to receive them today."

As he tore aside the curtains and opened the glass door
she flung herself in front of him. On the steps and on the
lawn men were struggling, and shots were being fired. Men
were remounting their horses in hot haste and a few minutes
later were clattering down the road, leaving one dead
stranger at the foot of the steps. But for his presence it
would all have seemed but a tumultuous vision of grey-
garbed combatants.

It was, perhaps, ten minutes later when Kenneth Mc-
Veigh re-entered the library. All was vague and confused
in his mind as to what had occurred there in the curtained
alcove. She had flung herself in front of him with her arms
about him as the door opened; there had been two shots in
quick succession, one of them had shattered the glass, and
the other—

He remembered tearing himself from her embrace as she
clung to him, and he remembered she had sunk with a moan
to the floor; at the time he thought her attitude and cry
had meant only despair at her failure to stop him, but, perhaps—

He found her in the same place; the oval portrait was
open in her hand, as though her last look had been given to
the pretty mother, whose memory she had cherished, and
whose race she had fought for.

Margeret was crouched beside her, silent as ever, her
dark eyes strange, unutterable in expression, were fixed on
the beautiful face, but the stray bullet had done it work
quickly—she had been quite dead when Margeret reached
her.

*   *   *   *   *

Monroe told McVeigh the true story of the portrait that

night. The two men sat talking until the dawn broke. Delaven was admitted to the conference long enough to hear certain political reasons why the marriage of that morning should continue to remain a secret, and when the mistress of Loringwood was laid to rest under the century-old cedars, it was as Judithe, Marquise de Caron.

In settling up the estate of Matthew Loring, who died a few days later, speechless to the last, Judge Clarkson had the unpleasant task of informing Gertrude that for nearly twenty years one of the slaves supposed to belong to her had been legally free. Evidence was found establishing the fact that Tom Loring had given freedom to Margeret and her child a few days previous to that last, fatal ride of his. Matthew Loring had evidently disapproved and suppressed the knowledge.

Gertrude made slight comment on the affair, convinced as she was that the woman was much better off in their household than dependent on herself, and was frankly astonished that Margeret returned at once to Loringwood, and never left it again for the three remaining years of her life.

Gertrude was also surprised at the sudden interest of Kenneth in her former bondwoman, and when the silent octoroon was found dead beside the tomb of her master, it was Kenneth McVeigh who arranged that she be placed near the beautiful stranger who had dwelt among them for awhile.

A year after the war ended Gertrude, the last of the once dominant Lorings, married an Alabama man, and left Carolina, to the great regret of Mrs. Judge Clarkson and sweet Evilena Delaven. They felt a grievance against Kenneth for his indifference in the matter, and were disconsolate for years over his persistent bachelorhood.

When he finally did marry, his wife was a pretty little woman, who was a relative of Jack Monroe, and totally different from either Gertrude or Judithe Loring. Jack Monroe, who was Major Monroe at the close of the war, makes yearly hunting trips to the land of the Salkahatchie, and when twitted concerning his state of single blessedness, declares he is only postponing matrimony until Delaven's youngest daughter grows up, but the youngest has been superseded by a younger one several times since he first made the announcement.

The monument planned by Judithe has existed for many years; but only a few remember well the builder; she has become a misty memory—part of a romance the older people tell. She was a noted beauty of France and she died to save General McVeigh, who was young, handsome, and, it was said, her lover. He never after her death was heard to speak her name and did not marry until twenty years later—what more apt material for a romance? None of them ever heard of her work for the union of the states.

But when the local historians tell of the former grandeur of the Lorings, the gay, reckless, daring spirits among them, and end the list with handsome Tom, there are two veterans, one of the blue and the other of the grey, who know that the list did not end there, and that the most brilliant, most daring, most remarkable spirit of them all, was the one of their blood, who was born a slave.

THE END.

Standard and Popular
Books

FOR SALE BY BOOKSELLERS OR WILL BE
SENT POSTPAID ON RECEIPT OF PRICE.

RAND, McNALLY & CO., PUBLISHERS,
CHICAGO AND NEW YORK.

Standard and Popular Books.

A B C OF MINING AND PROSPECTORS' HANDBOOK.
By Charles A. Bramble, D. L. S. Baedecker style. $1.00.

ACCIDENTS, AND HOW TO SAVE LIFE WHEN THEY
OCCUR. 143 pages; profusely illustrated; leatheroid, 25
cents.

ALASKA; ITS HISTORY, CLIMATE, AND NATURAL
RESOURCES. By Hon. A. P. Swineford, Ex-Governor
of Alaska. Illustrated. 12mo, cloth. $1.00.

ALL ABOUT THE BABY. By Robert N. Tooker, M. D.,
author of "Diseases of Children," etc. Illustrated. 8vo,
cloth. $1.50.

ALONG THE BOSPHORUS. By Susan E. Wallace (Mrs.
Lew Wallace). Profusely illustrated; 12mo; cloth. $1.50.

AMBER GLINTS. By "Amber." Uniform with "Rosemary
and Rue." Cloth. $1.00.

AMERICAN BOOK OF THE DOG. Edited by G. O.
Shields ("Coquinta"). Illustrated; 8vo; 700 pages. Plain
edges, cloth, $3.50; half morocco, gilt top, $5.00; full morocco, gilt edges, $6.50.

AMERICAN GAME FISHES. Edited by G. O. Shields.
Large 8vo; 155 illustrations and two colored plates. Cloth,
$1.50; half morocco, $4.00; full morocco, gilt edged, $5.50.

AMERICAN NOBLEMAN, AN. By William Armstrong.
12mo, cloth, $1.00.

AMERICAN ROADSTERS AND TROTTING HORSES.
Illustrated with photo views of representative stallions. By
H. T. Helm. 8 vo; 600 pages; cloth, $5.00.

AMERICAN STREET RAILWAYS. By Augustine W.
Wright. Bound in flexible, seal-grained leather, with red
edges and round corners; gold side-stamps; 200 pages;
$5.00.

ARCTIC ALASKA AND SIBERIA; OR, EIGHT MONTHS
WITH THE ARCTIC WHALEMEN. By Herbert L.
Aldrich. Illustrated; 12mo. Cloth, gold and black $1.00.

AN ARKANSAS PLANTER. By Opie Read. 12mo. Cloth,
$1.00; paper, 25 cents.

ARMAGEDDON. By Stanley Waterloo, author of "Story of
Ab," "The Launching of a Man," etc. 12mo, cloth. $1.00.

ART AND HANDICRAFT—ILLUSTRATED DESIGNS
FOR THE NEEDLE, PEN, AND BRUSH. Edited by
Maud Howe Elliott. Cloth; 8vo. $1.50.

ART OF WING SHOOTING. By W. B. Leffingwell. Paper cover, 50 cents; cloth, $1.00.

AT THE BLUE BELL INN. By J. S. Fletcher, author of "When Charles I was King," etc. 16mo, cloth. 75 cents.

BALDOON. By Le Roy Hooker, author of "Enoch the Philistine." 12mo, cloth. $1.25.

BANKING SYSTEM OF THE UNITED STATES. By Charles G. Dawes. Cloth. $1.00.

BATTLE OF THE BIG HOLE. By G. O. Shields. Illustrated; 12mo; 150 pages. Cloth. $1.00.

BIG GAME OF NORTH AMERICA. Edited by G. O. Shields ("Coquina"). Illustrated; 8vo; 600 pages. Cloth, $3.50; half morocco, gilt top, $5.00; full morocco, all gilt edges, $6.50.

BILLIARDS, OLD AND NEW. By John A. Thatcher. Vest Pocket Manual. Cloth, 75 cents; leather, $1.00.

BONDWOMAN, THE. By Marah Ellis Ryan, author of "Squaw Elouise," "A Pagan of the Alleghanies," etc. 12mo. Cloth. $1.25.

BONNIE MACKIRBY. By Laura Dayton Fessenden. 16mo. Cloth. 75 cents.

CAMPING AND CAMP OUTFITS. By G. O. Shields ("Coquina"). Illustrated; 12mo; 200 pages. Cloth. $1.25.

CHECKED THROUGH. By Richard Henry Savage. Paper, 25 cents; cloth, $1.00.

CHRISTOPHER COLUMBUS AND HIS MONUMENT COLUMBIA. Compiled by J. M. Dickey. Illustrated. 396 pages. Vellum, $2.00; cloth cover, $1.00.

COLONIAL DAME, A. By Laura Dayton Fessenden. Cloth. $1.00.

CONSTITUTIONAL HISTORY OF FRANCE. By Henry C. Lockwood. Illustrated; 8vo; 424 pages; cloth, $2.50; half morocco, gilt top, $3.50.

CRUISE UNDER THE CRESCENT, A. By Charles Warren Stoddard. 100 illustrations by Denslow. 12mo. Cloth. $1.50.

CRUISINGS IN THE CASCADES AND OTHER HUNTING ADVENTURES. By G. O. Shields ("Coquina"). Illustrated. 12mo; 300 pages. Cloth, $2.00; half morocco, $3.00.

CRULL'S TIME AND SPEED CHART. By E. S. Crull. Limp cloth cover; edges of pages indexed by speed in miles per hour; 50 cents.

CURSED BY A FORTUNE. By George Manville Fenn. 12mo. Cloth. $1.00.

DAUGHTER OF CUBA, A. By Helen M. Bowen. 12mo. Cloth. $1.00.

DAUGHTER OF EARTH, A. By E. M. Davy. 12mo. Cloth. $1.00.

DEVIL'S DICE. By Wm. Le Queux, author of "Zoraida," etc. 12mo. Paper, 25 cents; cloth, $1.00.

DRAWING AND DESIGNING. By Charles G. Leland, A. M. 12 mo; 80 pages; flexible cloth; 65 cents.

DREAM CHILD, A. By Florence Huntley. Cloth. 75 cents.

ENOCH THE PHILISTINE. By Le Roy Hooker. 12mo. Cloth. $1.25.

EVOLUTION OF DODD. By Wm. Hawley Smith. In neat cloth binding, gilt top. 75 cents.

EVOLUTION OF DODD'S SISTER. By Charlotte W. Eastman. In neat cloth binding. 75 cents.

EYE OF THE SUN, THE. By Edw. S. Ellis. 12mo; Cloth. $1.00.

FASCINATION OF THE KING. By Guy Boothby, author of "Dr. Nikola." 12mo. Cloth. $1.00.

FIFTH OF NOVEMBER, THE. By Charles S. Bentley and F. Kimball Scribner. 12mo. Cloth. $1.00.

FONTENAY, THE SWORDSMAN. A military novel. By Fortune du Boisgobey. 12mo. Cloth. $1.00.

FOR HER LIFE. A story of St. Petersburg. By Richard Henry Savage. Paper, 50 cents; cloth, $1.00.

GEMMA. By Alexander McArthur. 16mo. Cloth. $1.00.

GENTLEMAN JUROR, A. By Charles L. Marsh, author of "Opening the Oyster," etc. 12mo. Cloth. $1.25.

GLIMPSES OF ALASKA AND THE KLONDIKE. 100 Photographic Views of the Interior, from originals, by Veazie Wilson, compiled by Esther Lyons. 25 cents.

GOLDEN NORTH, THE. By C. R. Tuttle. With maps and engravings. Paper, 50 cents; cloth, $1.00.

HERNANI, THE JEW. A story of Poland. By A. N. Homer. 12mo; cloth, gilt top. $1.00.

HONDURAS. By Cecil Charles. Cloth, with map and portraits, $1.50.

IN SATAN'S REALM. By Edgar C. Blum. 12mo. Cloth. $1.25.

IN THE DAYS OF DRAKE. By J. S. Fletcher, author of "When Charles I was King." 16mo; cloth. 75 cents.

INCENDIARY, THE. By W. A. Leahy. 12mo; cloth. $1.00.

IN THE SHADOW OF THE PYRAMIDS. By Richard Henry Savage. Paper, 50 cents; cloth, $1.00.

IN THE SWIM. A story of Gayest New York. By Richard Henry Savage. Paper, 50 cents; cloth, $1.00.

JUDGE, THE. By Ella W. Peattie. Large 16mo; cloth. 75 cents.

KING OF THE MOUNTAINS. By Edmond About. 12mo; cloth. $1.00.

KIPLING BOY STORIES. By Rudyard Kipling. Illustrated, 8vo, cloth. $1.00.

KITCHEN, THE; OR, EVERY-DAY COOKERY. 104 pages; illustrated: leatherette. 25 cents.

LABOR, CAPITAL, AND A PROTECTIVE TARIFF. By John Vernon. 72 pages. Paper cover, pocket size, 10 cents.

LADY CHARLOTTE. By Adeline Sergeant. 12mo; cloth. $1.00.

LAST DAYS OF POMPEII. By Bulwer Lytton. 58 full page monogravure illustrations from original photographs. Two vols., boxed. Library, $3.00; De luxe, $6.00.

LAUNCHING OF A MAN, THE. By Stanley Waterloo, author of "A Man and A Woman," "Story of Ab." 12mo; cloth. $1.25.

LOCUST, OR GRASSHOPPER. By Chas. V. Riley, M. A., Ph. D. Illustrated; 236 pages; cloth cover. $1.00.

LOST COUNTESS FALKA. By Richard Henry Savage. Paper, 50 cents; cloth, $1.00.

LORNA DOONE. By R. D. Blackmore. 40 illustrations. Two vols., boxed. Cloth, gilt top, $3.00; half-calf, $5.00.

MAID OF THE FRONTIER, A. By H. S. Canfield. Large 16mo; cloth. 75 cents.

MANUAL OF INSTRUCTION FOR THE ECONOMICAL MANAGEMENT OF LOCOMOTIVES. By George H. Baker. Limp cloth; gold side-stamp; pocket form; 125 pages. $1.00.

MARBEAU COUSINS. By Harry Stillwell Edwards, author of "Sons and Fatners." 12mo; cloth. $1.00.

MARGARET WYNNE. By Adeline Sergeant, author of "A Valuable Life," etc. 12mo; cloth. $1.00.

MARIPOSILLA. By Mrs. Charles Stewart Daggett. 12mo; cloth. $1.25.

MARRIED MAN, A. By Frances Aymar Matthews, author of "A Man's Will and A Woman's Way," "Joan D'Arc," etc. 12mo; cloth. $1.25.

MARSA. By Jules Clareti. Large 16mo; cloth. 75 cents.

MEMOIRS OF AN ARTIST. By Charles Gounod. Large 16mo; cloth. $1.25.

MILL OF SILENCE, THE. By B. E. J. Capes. Artistic cloth binding; gilt top. $1.00.

MISS NUME OF JAPAN. A Japanese-American romance. By Onoto Watanna, author of "Natsu-San," etc. 12mo; cloth. $1.25.

MODERN CORSAIR, A. By Richard Henry Savage. Paper, 50 cents; cloth, $1.00.

MY BROTHER. By Vincent Brown. Neat cloth binding; gilt top. 75 cents.

MY INVISIBLE PARTNER. By Thomas S. Denison. Cloth. $1.00.

ORATIONS, ADDRESSES, AND CLUB ESSAYS. By Hon. George A. Sanders, M. A. Cloth binding. Price $1.25.

PACIFIC COAST GUIDE-BOOK. 8vo; 282 pages; cloth, $1.00; paper, 50 cents.

PHOEBE TILSON. By Mrs. Frank Pope Humphrey. A New England Tale. 12mo; cloth. $1.00.

POLITICS AND PATRIOTISM. By F. W. Schultz. 12mo; cloth. $1.00.

POLYGLOT PRONOUNCING HANDBOOK. By David G. Hubbard. Flexible cloth; 77 pages. 50 cents.

PREMIER AND THE PAINTER, THE. By I. Zangwill. Cloth. $1.00.

PROCEEDINGS OF THE WORLD'S CONGRESS OF BANKERS AND FINANCIERS. 615 pages; bound in half morocco, with gilt top, price $5.00; bound in cloth, price, $3.00.

PURE SAXON ENGLISH; OR, AMERICANS TO THE FRONT. By Elias Molee. 12mo; 167 pages; cloth. $1.00.

QUESTIONABLE MARRIAGE, A. By A. Shackleford Sullivan. 12mo; cloth. $1.00.

RAND, M'NALLY & CO.'S POCKET CYCLOPEDIA. 288 pages; leatherette. 25 cents.

REED'S RULES. By the Hon. Thomas B. Reed. With portrait of the author. The latest acknowledged standard manual for everyone connected in any way with public life. Price, in cloth cover, 75 cents; full seal grain flexible leather, $1.25.

REMINISCENCES OF W. W. STORY. By Miss M. E. Phillips. 8vo; cloth. $1.75.

REPUBLIC OF COSTA RICA. By Joaquin Bernardo Calvo. With maps and numerous illustrations; 8vo; 292 pages. Price $2.00.

ROMANCE OF A CHILD. By Pierre Loti. In neat cloth binding. 75 cents.

ROMANCE OF GRAYLOCK MANOR. By Louise F. P. Hamilton. 16mo; cloth. $1.25.

ROMOLA. By George Eliot. 56 monogravure illustrations; two volumes, boxed; 8vo; cloth, gilt top. $3.00.

ROSEMARY AND RUE. By "Amber." With introductory by Opie Read. 12 mo; cloth. $1.00.

RULES OF ETIQUETTE AND HOME CULTURE; OR, WHAT TO DO AND HOW TO DO IT. By Prof. Walter R. Houghton. Illustrated; 430 pages; cloth. 50 cents.

SECRET OF SUCCESS; OR, HOW TO GET ON IN THE WORLD. By W. H. Davenport Adams. 338 pages; cloth cover. 50 cents.

SHIFTING SANDS. By Frederick R. Burton. 12mo, cloth. $1.00.

SHOOTING ON UPLAND, MARSH, AND STREAM. Edited by William Bruce Leffingwell, author of "Wild Fowl Shooting." Profusely illustrated; 8vo; 473 pages. Cloth, $3.50; half morocco, gilt edges, $4.50; full morocco, gilt edges, $6.50.

SIMPLICITY. By A. T. G. Price. Neat cloth binding. 75 cents.

SINNER, THE By Rita (Mrs. E. J. G. Humphreys). 12mo; cloth, gilt top. $1.00.

SONS AND FATHERS. By Harry Stillwell Edwards. Artistic cloth binding, gilt top. $1.00.

STRANGE STORY OF MY LIFE, THE. By John Strange Winter (Mrs. Stannard). 12mo, cloth. $1.50.

STRENGTH. A treatise on the development and use of muscle. By C. A. Sampson. A book specially suited for home use. Cloth, $1.00; paper, 50 cents,

SWEDEN AND THE SWEDES. By William Widgery Thomas, Jr. English edition: One volume, cloth, $3.75; two volumes, $5.00; one volume, half morocco, $5.00; two volumes, $7.00; one volume, full morocco, $7.50; two volumes, $10.00. Swedish edition: One volume, cloth, $3.75; one volume, half morocco, $5.00; one volume, full morocco, $7.50. Large 8vo; 750 pages; 328 illustrations.

THOSE GOOD NORMANS. By Gyp. Artistic cloth binding, designed by J. P. Archibald. $1.00.

TOLD IN THE ROCKIES. By A. M. Barbour. 12mo, cloth. $1.00.

UNDER THE BAN. By Teresa Hammond Strickland 12mo; cloth. $1.00.

UNDER THREE FLAGS. By B. L. Taylor and A. T. Thoits. Artistic cloth binding, gilt top. $1.00.

UNKNOWN LIFE OF JESUS CHRIST. By Nicolas Notovitch. 12mo; cloth. $1.00.

VALUABLE LIFE, A. By Adeline Sergeant. 12mo, cloth. $1.00.

VALUE. An essay, with a short account of American currency. By John Borden. Cloth. $1.00.

VANISHED EMPEROR, THE. By Percy Andreae. 12mo, cloth. $1.25.

WATERS OF CANEY FORK. By Opie Read. 12mo; cloth. $1.00.

WHOM TO TRUST. By P. R. Earling. 304 pages. Cloth. $2.00.

WHOSE SOUL HAVE I NOW? By Mary Clay Knapp. In neat cloth binding. 75 cents.

WHOSO FINDETH A WIFE. By William Le Queux. 12mo, cloth. $1.00.

WILD FOWL SHOOTING. By William Bruce Leffingwell. Handsomely illustrated; 8vo; 373 pages. Cloth cover, $2.50; half morocco, $3.50; full morocco, gilt edges, $5.50.

WOMAN AND THE SHADOW. By Arabella Kenealy. 12mo, cloth. $1.00.

WORLD'S RELIGIONS IN A NUTSHELL. By Rev. L. P. Mercer. Price, bound in cloth, $1.00; paper, 25 cents.

YANKEE FROM THE WEST, A. A new novel by Opie Read. 12mo, cloth. $1.00.

YOUNG GREER OF KENTUCKY. By Eleanor Talbot Kinkead. 12mo, cloth. $1.25.

www.ingramcontent.com/pod-product-compliance
Lightning Source LLC
Chambersburg PA
CBHW050901130726
47900CB00015B/1680